## Attacked!

"Contact! Multiple contacts incoming. Missiles! They've fired on us!" Heather cried in shock.

Leon gaped at her, unable to move or understand. Fired? Missiles? Fired missiles at him? His brain gibbered at him, but his voice didn't betray him. He was snapping orders, and only afterward did he realise they were the right ones.

"...ound collision!" he cried and the gong gong gong of the collision alarm sounded throughout the ship sending the crew to emergency stations, and causing blast doors and other internal partitions to lock down. "Point defence free!"

"Point defence free, aye. Autoloaders operational. Targeting under computer control!" Max said from the helm. Hobbs wasn't a warship. Its defensive armourment was controlled from his station.

"Bring up the drive. Go to evasive as soon as we have power! Communications: get me Captain Penleigh. I think we might need to bug out. Tell him yourself if I'm busy. Tell him why."

# Operation Oracle

by

Mark E. Cooper

Published by Impulse Books UK

Published by Impulse Books UK April 2013
http://www.impulsebooks.co.uk

Books are available at quantity discounts. For more information please write to Impulse Books UK, 18 Lampits Hill Avenue, Corringham, Essex SS177NY, United Kingdom.

Cover art:   Panagiotis Vlamis -- www.weaselpa.deviantart.com
Cover design: Dawn Smith ----- www.darkdawncreations.com

A CIP catalogue record for this book
is available from the British Library.

ISBN: 978-1-905380-52-7

**impulse
books uk**

Printed and bound in Great Britain
Impulse Books UK

# Acknowledgments

Special thanks go to Dave Milne for reading an early draft of this book.

Thanks for everything.

# 1 ～ Miles to go

Acting Captain Gina Fuentez, 501st Infantry Regiment, crouched behind the rubble to check the take available to her via TacNet. The regiment's tactical network was a wonder to someone with a Marine Corp background. She had been a viper for only a couple of years, though it seemed even less than that due to time being weird in foldspace. TacNet was still a wonderful novelty to her. General Burgton's regiment did things a little differently to other Alliance forces, they did them his way or no way, and he was a strong believer in the axiom: bigger is better. Whether applied to firepower, manpower, or information didn't matter. To him, bigger was better and always had been. It was hard to argue when Gina was one of the beneficiaries. TacNet meant that no matter where she was, or doing what, she had access to the big picture. It wasn't her rank either. Every viper had access to the same information. It was so very different to her Marine Corp days.

As a marine, she had followed her orders and often didn't know why those orders were given. Information was compartmentalised behind rank and parcelled out on a need to know basis. Her mission goals had therefore been simplified. Simplified did not mean simple. She had followed orders that sometimes didn't seem to make sense, and had to go on faith that all would become clear in time. It usually did, but that methodology did nothing to alleviate anxiety levels.

General Burgton preferred to run his regiment otherwise, especially so in combat. It meant everyone knew what was expected of them and their comrades, and also meant any viper could immediately take up the slack should one of them fall. They all knew the plan, they all had the ability to evaluate its progress, and they all could take steps to ensure it succeeded without fearing their actions might screw up other parts of the mission. TacNet was real time; information flow fully automated by a viper's internal computer system, and was linked via satellites with the General and his staff aboard *Grafton* in orbit.

Gina quickly evaluated what TacNet was displaying. It was especially important these days, as she wasn't fighting exclusively with other vipers and Shan warriors under viper command. Fifth Fleet had brought a large ground force to join the fight. Reinforcements were of course welcomed by the Shan, but the many different forces each had their own command structures subordinate only to Admiral Kuzov. Admiral Meyers commanding TF19 was no longer the biggest show in town, and had placed herself at his disposal as per her orders delivered to her when Fifth Fleet arrived. All of which meant that Gina and the other vipers were no longer officially in charge of the ground war, but the Shan warriors who had fought beside them did not see it that way. They continued to look to the vipers first for orders, a fact the other Human ground commanders found irritating in the extreme. Not that they could do much about it. They were guests of the Shan after all.

With so many different forces involved in the battle, Gina could no longer rely upon all combatants doing the right thing. Only vipers had TacNet; an integral system built into all vipers. Everyone else, except the warriors under direct viper supervision, had to use satellite feeds and ground observation to fight their battles.

That reminded Gina to check the feed overhead. She dismissed TacNet and accessed the satellite network seeded in orbit by Admiral Meyers when they first arrived.

*Computer: Access satellite zebra-one-niner-niner. Centre grid delta-six, sub-grid fox-two.*

Gina studied the battlefield displayed on her HUD (head up display). The display was suddenly populated by heat sources that she began to decipher. It was night and the devastation was softened, but she wasn't interested in the broken architecture of Shoshon. She was looking for any units out of position, or any enemy movements. Everything seemed fine, and she quickly reported in.

"Gold-three, Alpha-leader. All secure, no movement, no concerns," Gina said using her internal comms. And that was another thing. Now she was working as part of the forward scouting element and not the main offensive force, she had to report twice. Once on viper comm to *Grafton*, and once using helmet comm to the ground commander in charge of Shoshon. "On schedule."

"Alpha-leader, Gold-three copies," Major Faggini replied. "No changes."

"Copy no changes," she said. "Alpha-leader out."

Gina quickly repeated her report to force commander Shoshon, a woman she had met only briefly by the name of Colonel Elizabeth Jung 2nd Faragut Strike Force, and quickly moved to another observation point. So far, her internal viper comm had proven hard for the Merki to track. It was a high speed burst transmission and used all local viper units as a sort of broadcast gestalt, like an old style antenna farm. It overwhelmed the ability of the Merki to track the transmission's origin. The Merki had proven that helmet comms—although encrypted and as discreet as current technology could make them without making them useless—could be tracked all too easily. No one knew how they did it. Alliance stealth tech was supposed to be proof against Merki gear, but they now knew that was not so. Like the damnable Merki jamming they had confronted at the start of the Harmony campaign, it had been an unpleasant surprise.

It was standard procedure for the scouts to snoop, report, and then scoot to avoid incoming fire; Gina did so successfully. She wasn't sure if the Merki had detected her transmission, or the strike was a lucky guess, but seconds after relocating, her previous OP (Observation Point) was hit repeatedly. She observed the result, clinically analysing the Merki strike and backtracking to find the gunners.

"Artillery Control, Alpha-leader. Fire mission," she said using viper comm again.

There were multiple batteries of artillery deployed in and around Shoshon, and in theory, she could have passed her targets to any of them, but she chose the viper controlled battery because she wanted fast accurate fire with minimal fuss such as seeking authorisations or needing verifications. Merkiaari had standard procedures too, like getting the hell out of Dodge after trying to snipe someone.

"Alpha-leader, Artillery Control. Say coordinates," Captain Penleigh replied.

Gina smiled, happy to hear his voice. Eric had been trading off with Colonel Flowers since they upped sticks from Child of Harmony and relocated to Harmony. She gave him three targets.

"Acknowledged," Eric said. "On the way."

She waited and watched to evaluate the strike. Shells rumbled overhead, clearly audible, and explosions lit the night. Eric had chosen to use the regiment's self-propelled guns over their Hellfire missile launchers, probably to reduce the chance of return fire. Gina would have made the same decision. Hellfire missiles were effective but flashy ordnance, especially in the dark when their bright exhaust could so easily be seen. She compared what she was seeing with the new heat sources displayed via TacNet. They matched. The Merki were probably dead. Probably. But they had ammo to spare so she let Eric pound the targets for a while.

"Targets eliminated," Gina reported when she was in danger of being accused of overkill.

"Copy," Eric said. "Artillery Control out."

"Alpha-leader out."

Explosions and gunfire continued uninterrupted in other parts of the city, and Gina wished she could be one of the trigger pullers, but she had her orders. Her temporary command of Alpha Company was in name only now. They had lost so many units on Child of Harmony that hasty reorganisation had left her with little more than a squad to command. Good then that her new mission didn't need more than a squad to complete. Her remaining eight units, like Gina herself, were operating solo and scouting the enemy. It was a mission the vipers were performing more often as their numbers dwindled, she thought grimly. The Child of Harmony campaign had halved the number of combat capable vipers in the entire Alliance. Not all were dead, thank god, but they were out of the fight for the duration. Most were so badly damaged they had gone into automatic shutdown. Hibernation was a viper's last hope of survival; their IMS (Integrated Medical System) used it to shunt all resources toward making repairs in a last desperate race to prevent death. Unfortunately, if the damage was that bad, a unit's reactivation to full combat readiness was unlikely. Most remained in hibernation and were stored in stasis aboard *Grafton* with their true dead companions. Hibernation was the little death, a name the two hundred year old veterans of the last Merki War had chosen for it because unlike true death it did not last. Gina had experienced it only once, and was lucky enough to awake fully repaired from her own resources. A rare thing.

Gina went back to work.

Traditionally, vipers were deployed in advance of other forces to seek and destroy Merkiaari. The current campaign was a little different in that her job was not to kill Merki... well, she hadn't actually been *ordered* to refrain, but it was heavily implied, and as a result her people had defaulted to a pure scouting role. Recon was actually something she was practiced at. A lot of her time as a marine had been spent either performing that task or training to perform it. So the role wasn't an uncomfortable fit.

Gina moved through the city avoiding contact and only indulging herself in killing Merkiaari when she had a good excuse. A lone Merki troop here—oh sorry I had to put her down to prevent her raising the alarm, sir. Why didn't I avoid detection, sir? Well, she took me by surprise, sir. Gina grinned and snorted at her musing. Oops, so sorry, but that Merki squad had it coming, sir. They fired first. Must have tracked my last transmission.

She wasn't the only viper doing the same or similar things and probably having the same excuses lined up. Vipers were designed and built to kill Merkiaari, not bypass them. TRS (Target Recognition Software) even made them automatically attack Merki targets by default. It actually took intervention on a viper's part to prevent them killing Merki upon detection. She didn't expect censure from her own commanders, they were vipers too, but Colonel Jung might be another matter. It wasn't that Jung didn't want the Merki dead. She absolutely did want them dead, but she was a strict disciplinarian and stickler for the rules. That was fine with Gina, she had worked with all kinds, but Jung wanted Shoshon liberated by her plan with her hands at the controls. She was an ambitious officer who wanted her first star, and winning battles especially against Merkiaari would be a big help. Shoshon itself was no prize anymore. It was pretty much trashed, but the campaign was coming to a close. This battle would probably be the last one, certainly the last that Jung could indisputably claim as hers. Gina doubted the final round up of stray Merki troops would win anyone a medal or promotion. Shan would be tidying up strays long after Fleet pulled out, she was sure.

Gina worked her assigned area, making reports to both her commanders, and adding her data to TacNet as she did so. Busy keeping herself safe while keeping a wary eye on the enemy so there would be no surprises at sun up, she still made time to keep an eye on her own people's diagnostics. It had become second nature now. All vipers were trained to watch their own, but she as Alpha-leader had access to all of her subordinate's data as well. She paused as Cragg's data updated and changed colour from green to flashing yellow.

Gina grunted as if punched in the guts. Yellow was serious. She found good cover and drilled down into Cragg's data. Even as she did, the yellow colour turned pale orange on its way to the red of critical damage. Fuck! She spun, and sprinted out of her area toward Cragg's position. Calls started to come in as her movement was detected on viper sensors. She was way out of position, crossing other unit's areas of responsibility.

"All units, Alpha-leader," Gina panted using viper comm. "Do not, repeat do not deviate. Stay on mission."

"Alpha-leader, Alpha-one-one. I'm closest," Sergeant Hiller said.

"Not for long, Ian. I'm already at max. ETA thirty seconds. Stay on mission and cover my arse. Jung will have it for lunch if she hears."

Ian laughed. "You want me to play secretary and field her calls?"

"Good idea. Tell her I stepped out of the office for a minute."

"Will do, Alpha-one-one out."

"Alpha-leader clear," she said, her sensors sweeping ahead

looking for danger.

Gina didn't have to engage light amplification. She had been using it since darkness fell. The rubble and blasted landscape of Shoshon was revealed to her in the familiar monochrome of its use. She targeted a building ahead of her, taking note of her range to it, and prepared to jump. She hit the right stride, and watched the reticule on the ground marking her jump point coming closer. Her right foot came down exactly on the right spot and she launched herself in a high arc. She flew through the air expecting Merki weapon's fire, but she passed through the hole she had picked out unmolested, and slammed onto the floor of the room. She rolled to her feet, blew a new hole in the opposite door, and charged through.

Cragg wasn't moving on her sensors, and he wasn't transmitting a call for help. That was bad, but he wasn't dead. His diagnostic data was still on her HUD, so she knew his condition. It was still pale orange, not yet red. Better yet, his blue icon on her sensors was not blinking. That told her he wasn't in hibernation or dead awaiting pickup. There could be many reasons for his silence. Damaged helmet comm, damaged viper comm, even damaged TacNet—the system was automated, but there was a way to update it manually and a message in text format wasn't beyond its capabilities. Surely if he could have, he would have reported in that way.

Gina stormed through the building and entered the room her sensors told her contained Martin Cragg, her friend and fellow viper. Something tackled her from the side and she spun with her right hand blurring toward her pistol. Her rifle hung from its sling behind her back and out of position.

Stupid stupid stupid! She had taken no precautions at all. Her thoughts flashed to Chrissie Roberts. Chris had been her very first casualty on Child of Harmony and had died because she was over confident in her viper abilities. She had been new to them; they all had back then. They had felt super human, until Chris died in her first battle, and others died soon after. None of them had any illusions now.

The pistol came up and stopped. She could have pulled the trigger, even as she fell, but she recognised the bloody mangled thing tackling her to the floor. She grabbed him, turning slightly to cushion his fall with her own body. He didn't fight her, maybe couldn't do more than he had. He was totally fucked up. She kept an arm around him and holstered her pistol, then opened her helmet's visor to reveal her face to him. His helmet was missing and blood covered his face. He was still bleeding from ears and nose, and one eye was stuck shut. He was breathing heavily and blood bubbled at his lips.

"Mart—" Gina began, but his bloodied hand blurred and clapped over her mouth. Her eyes popped wide at the slap. That bloody hurt!

Cragg shook his head urgently.

Gina checked her sensors, but there were no hostiles in range. What the hell? Cragg rolled off her. He grabbed her right arm, pawing her sleeve almost ripping it in his frenzy to reach her wristcomp. She let him, realising his own was missing and the forearm it had been strapped upon. Jesus he was screwed. One eye and arm out of commission, and his diagnostic data on her display listed many internal injuries. Why wasn't he in hibernation? Maintenance mode wasn't up to this; it would take days to deal with this level of damage.

Blood frothed and bubbled on his lips, punctured lung was on the list, but he used his good eye and hand to punch in coordinates on her wristcomp. He pressed save and seemed to breathe easier. He paused to cough up blood and spit it out. He looked into Gina's eyes and put a finger over his own lips.

She nodded, really worried now. He pointed to her wristcomp and typed a message on the screen...

*Don't talk, don't run a sweep. Do nothing until I finish... ok?*

She nodded again.

*Merki under a stealth field spoofed my sensors. Nearly got me. Coordinates in your comp. Big force. BIG! Near, will hear us, will detect transmissions... maybe. Can't chance it. I interrupted hibernation. The beacon... I dead for sure.*

Gina's eyes widened. Cragg had aborted his own hibernation. That might kill him, but a beacon might well bring Merki right to him. He hadn't chanced it. Merkiaari cloaked by stealth field was a new tactic. Stealth in space was standard, but on the ground, it was usually pointless. It was only good for static defence. The equipment was cumbersome and the nature of the field meant it had to be stationary to be effective.

*Was doing the job, all good. No surprises. I detected a Merki troop on his own. Think what the hell, why not? I kill it, will just say found it wounded ma'am. Couldn't let it suffer could I?*

Gina grinned, that was a good one. She typed that for him and nodded. Cragg nodded back and typed...

*Went to check him. Found it. Fallen building hiding it. Completely hidden from satellite observation and my sensors. Totally fooled me, stealthed even under the rubble. Still can hardly believe it.*

She cocked her head in question.

*A troop ship, Gina, an intact troop ship buried deep. Not sure it crashed. If it didn't...*

Her eyes widened. Five Marauder class transports had been committed by the Merki to this incursion, and each one carried detachable troop ships or landers. There were typically a hundred thousand Merki troopers aboard a Marauder when fully loaded. A hundred regiments or fists as the Merki called them, ready to awaken at the touch of a button. Marauders could not land; they were too huge. They landed their fists aboard the detachable landers where they slept in stasis dreaming and awaiting battle. Twenty landers per Marauder—they really were monstrously huge ships—meant a maximum of five thousand troops aboard at launch. That didn't mean Cragg's ship had five thousand aboard now. They could all be dead, or half of them dead, or any number above or below. It wasn't a lander anymore. It was a base! A stealthed base. There was no way to know how big this disaster was.

*I was trying to scout for a way in. The General will order us in there, I just know it. Didn't see the patrol. They got me good. Lost my arm and my damn rifle first thing. I beat feet, they chased me. Lost them near here but I think they're close. They split into groups of two there at the end.*

Gina nodded. Cragg was leaving out a lot. His injuries told her there had been a running gun fight. His armour was burned and scarred all over, and cracked on one side. Busted ribs there for sure. Probably what caused the punctured lung. The Merki splitting their force was interesting. They would only do that if they wanted to cover a wider area, and that meant they were actively searching for Cragg. Or had been. No way to know for sure if they still were, but if she had a stealthed base to protect, she wouldn't give up until certain the threat was neutralised.

Gina typed... *Ok. We need to exfil, get you some help and report in.*

Cragg shook his head. *I'm totally messed up, Gina. Leave me here. I'll lay low.*

It was the right thing, she knew, but she wasn't going to be sensible this time around. She had abandoned Kate when the General insisted, and her friend had barely survived even with Stone's help. She never wanted to feel that helpless rage ever again. She even had her excuse ready to go. General, she would say, Cragg was too damaged to download the data to me. It might even be true for all she knew. General, I'm sorry but I had to bring him and the data he contains. No choice, sir. That would work, right?

She didn't bother to explain her reasoning. She just pulled Cragg up onto his feet and then put him over her shoulder ignoring all protests. She about faced and retraced her route through the building. She figured it was more than likely the safest way out. She had made it in after all. Luck did have its part to play no matter how often Richmond derided the notion. Luck is not a factor, Richmond would say. In one way, Gina could sympathise with that view, but she knew soldiers of any flavour were superstitious creatures and she was no different. She believed in luck, but believed even more that she made her own luck by being paranoid and good at her job.

Paranoia made her cautious when Gina reached her entry point. She might have just leapt down and run, but something whispered in the back of her brain. Don't go down there, don't you do it. Go up, not down. Not down this time.

She reversed course and found the access ramp to the upper floor and roof. Shan didn't use stairs, it was something to do with the way their legs worked, and most of their buildings were two or three stories above ground with the same below. She wasn't sure they had ever invented elevators, not that she would chance using one even if she found one operating. The ramp spiralled up gently making it very easy to carry Cragg and she had her pistol out, leaving her rifle thumping her back.

She emerged onto the roof cautiously, and paused. Cragg's warning not to run a sensor sweep held her back. She ramped up the gain on her hearing, listening for Merki breathing, and turned her head slowly, panning around to listen intently. She deactivated light amplification mode for the moment, and tried infra. Infravision or infrared detected heat emissions, and there were a couple visible to her, but they were part of the building's infrastructure. The shape told her. Long straight lines like these were pipes. No Merki-shaped heat sources appeared. She switched back to light amplification mode and holstered her pistol.

Gina whispered so low she wasn't certain Cragg would hear. "I'm going to throw you to the next roof. If I try a jump with you on my shoulder, I might bust something or break through the roof. Then we're screwed."

Cragg nodded.

She lowered Cragg into her arms and carried him like a child despite his size. Vipers were strong. She ran toward the edge and at the last moment spun around and let go. Cragg flew into space. Gina winced; she had overdone it. He flew high over the other roof and crashed down. The noise and pained groan was very audible. She backed up and then ran at the edge. Her leap was more conservative and she would have made a nice running landing if she hadn't needed to turn it into a dive to avoid incoming fire.

The quiet dissolved, replaced by the hammering of Merkiaari cannon fire. Those huge gauss cannons were slug throwers not plasma, and although hand held like a rifle, they had more destructive punch than an Alliance AAR (Anti Armour Railgun). The noise was deafening. Definitely more than two firing, she realised. Cragg's pursuers had found them.

Gina sprawled and rolled across the abrasive surface avoiding the Merki fire. The edges of the roof dissolved, slugs chewing it away, but they didn't have the angle. They must be on the ground, but that might not be so for long. If they gained just a little elevation, the Merki would have them both dead to rights.

She scrambled away from the danger, more toward the centre of the roof where Cragg lay. Thank god, she was still wearing her shooting gloves. She might be a viper, but losing skin still hurt. As it was she wore holes in the palms of her gloves, but her uniform was tougher. All alliance uniforms used nano-processed materials to toughen them against impact forces, and were heat resistant to give the wearer a precious second or two of time against plasma fire. Hers was more than a match for the abrasion, especially with her armour on.

"No point worrying about detection now," Gina muttered and used her sensors. She swept the entire area around the building and swore. The Merki had her surrounded. "Oh crap, we're screwed."

"Arty," Cragg croaked. "Rather die to friendly fire."

"Screw that, no fire is friendly."

Cragg's diagnostic data had multiplied and its colour was definitely reddish. He had internal bleeding and his bots weren't dealing fast enough. She quickly searched his webbing, but found his medikit on his hip. Everyone had his or her preference. He had chosen to store his medikit on his utility belt next to the case containing spare power cells. She had seen others do that. Gina used hers for power cells and bayonet, but not much else. Everything she needed hung on her webbing attached to her armour.

She grabbed his nano injector and pumped the entire magazine into his thigh, right over the artery. She reloaded it with his spare mag, and hammered the entire thing into his other thigh. Cragg didn't seem to notice. He was looking around in a daze.

She grabbed his head and forced him to look into her eyes. "Martin, I want you to let yourself go into hibernation now." He blinked at her, but didn't respond. "You hearing me, Martin? Remove the block on hibernation. That's an order."

Cragg blinked and blood frothed on his lips, but nothing changed.

She didn't have time for this. On her sensors, the bright red icons of the Merki death squad were manoeuvring. She was sure some of them would enter her building and come up to the roof eventually, but she was more afraid of the other possibility. All it would take is one or two troopers climbing high enough to cut the angle. There were a few trees in the streets, but more likely, they would just use another building.

As his commanding officer, Gina had access to Cragg's diagnostic data, but she had more than that. If he still had his wristcomp, she could have instructed his IMS to perform some basic medical procedures and some not so basic. A thing like introducing pain relief into his bloodstream was a simple matter that any Alliance soldier relied upon. Everyone, military or civilian, had a wristcomp connected to IMS, but Cragg's wristcomp was gone along with his forearm.

She had another option, but she hesitated to use it. All of them feared outside forces taking them over. She couldn't do that, no one could, but she could order his processor to perform a new diagnostic. She didn't think Cragg was aware enough of his situation to block it if his processor decided to put him into hibernation when the results came in. She had no doubt it would. He was in a bad way. If not for his earlier order preventing it, he would already be asleep.

*Computer: Access Cragg, Martin 501ˢᵗ Infantry Regiment serial number ALZ-119-910-159.*
**CONNECTION ACHIEVED**
*Computer: Access IMS*
**IMS:** _

Gina took a deep breath. This had better work. She stared into Cragg's wandering eyes and prayed it would save him. Prayer was all she had right now.

*Computer: Run full diagnostic.*

She held her breath...
**IMS: WORKING...**
**DIAGNOSTICS: FULL SYSTEM SCAN IN PROGRESS.**

Her breath whooshed out. She broke her link to Cragg and checked her sensors. She had her rifle up and hardly had time to realise what she was doing when the first Merki head appeared. TRS had taken over. The Merkiaari trooper edged onto the roof, TRS noticed, evaluated, targeted, and blew its head off in milliseconds. Control returned to her body and limbs, with the dead Merki trooper still falling.

Gina gasped, feeling the pain in her muscles receding. That happened when TRS moved a viper at computer speeds. It happened when she went from combat mode to melee mode as well, but at least she knew it was coming. TRS did it without warning.

She kept her rifle up and aimed at the ramp as she ran to the body in a bent kneed stance. She kept her eyes on the ramp and kicked the monster, but her sensors had it right. It was dead. She took TRS offline and edged forward. Two more Merki were halfway up the ramp. She took two grenades off her webbing, depressed the triggers, and rolled them down the ramp.

*Whump! Whump!*

She jumped forward and emptied her rifle into the Merki already reeling from the twin explosions. Both died without returning fire. She didn't go down to make sure. She ran back to check the other side of the roof. Sensors reported a single Merkiaari there. It saw her first and fired. The impact on her torso armour was sudden and shocking. The mass of the slug caused her armour's nanocoat to react and harden, but that didn't reduce the force of the impact. She flew off her feet snarling at the pain, and landed on her back. She rolled to avoid two more shots. Her target reticule was locked on to the sniper and pulsing redly as it spun. If she'd had a rocket launcher she could have fired right then and forgot about it. The rocket would have found its own way to the target, but she didn't have one. She did have her rifle and its integrated grenade launcher. She had chosen to load hers with all HE (High Explosive) rounds. She remembered Sergeant Rutledge telling her class of recruits that he preferred all HE himself. Good for taking out armoured vehicles and Merkiaari troops, he had said back then. Gina agreed and used the grenade launcher. As soon as the decision was made, the targeting reticule morphed and an arcing line connected her to the target.

She adjusted her aim and fired.

The grenade followed the arcing line as if physically anchored to it. It wasn't of course. The line was the projected trajectory needed to kill the target, which it did moments later when it exploded. The building shook and rained debris into the street below. Pieces of Merkiaari fell with it, and the red icon on her display faded.

The steady blue icon close behind her blinked out of existence and Gina froze watching where it had been. It reappeared and started blinking steadily. Cragg was in hibernation, sleeping the little death. She quickly checked her sensors and scurried back to her friend. She patted his cheek.

"Sleep well," she said and went to war.

Gina reactivated TRS and added melee mode to the mix. The world slowed around her as she stood tall over Cragg. That attracted enemy fire as she knew it would, but the Merki had to reveal themselves to hit her. The moment they did, TRS took over and threw her bodily over Cragg, not to protect him; TRS didn't care. It was just an auto-targeting program after all. It threw her down to avoid damage, and then fired back. She let herself go, and screamed her rage at the enemy trying to kill her. Grenades flew faster than human thought. TRS switched to full power and full auto on her rifle as the Merki died and her launcher emptied itself.

*Impact!*

Damage assessments flickered onto her display, but quickly parked themselves to one side out of the way. Gina watched like a spectator in her own body. She took a moment to check that IMS was dealing with the damage. Lower right leg, bone bruised probably, but not broken. IMS was already on the case flooding the area with nano assemblers and pain blockers.

Her body kept firing and reloading with no wasted motions. Fire to the left and then spin to fire the other way without pause. Her body killed and killed and killed as she spun and danced across the roof. Her body did, not her, not with TRS engaged and Merki in range. It was just a conceit. This was her now. She was the machine, and the machine was her. She had seen Eric like this when they first met. She had compared him to a mindless sentry gun on auto, but he hadn't been mindless, and neither was she. She could take control away from TRS at any time, but she didn't. It could target the enemy faster than she could even in melee mode.

Factory default for melee mode shunted all resources to combat and left none for defence, but as with most things viper related, parameters were adjustable. Gina had kept back a little something. Not much. Barely anything really, but enough that IMS could work even at its currently starved for resources level. Back in the classroom when the recruits were taught the hows and the whys of viper design, she had decided that leaving melee mode at its default settings would be a bad idea. What point in killing her enemies and then dying from blood loss, she had thought. Not everyone agreed. Eric didn't, and she knew most of the veterans didn't. For them all that mattered was the mission, but she was still new enough that her life meant something to her. Besides, it was a waste to die if it could be prevented. If she could survive to fight another mission, surely it was worth holding back a single percentage point? Gina had thought so. Of course, she would look pretty silly if she died because she hadn't committed that final one percent, but a girl couldn't have everything.

More damage reports added themselves to the list. Right shoulder, left hip, left hand, left leg... she spun to the left and fired. Another red icon faded. The fucker had done a number on her left side, but she was still fighting.

Suddenly TRS went offline and Gina staggered to one knee panting and in pain. TRS had quit on her, was she damaged that badly? Diagnostics said no, she was just out of targets. She remained in melee mode, too scared to lose even a fraction of a second by dropping back to combat mode only to realise she needed the speed boost of melee mode again.

A sensor sweep showed hostiles near but not near enough

for TRS to keep fighting. There was time to reload, exchange power cells too, which she did. She was running low. She ruthlessly searched Cragg's body and scavenged his ammo and cells, transferring it all to her own webbing. She ripped open her medikit scattering its contents in her haste, her hands a blur. She let the aerosols roll away, and didn't bother with the sterile self-sealing bandages. She was only interested in the nano injector. As she had with Cragg, she hammered the entire mag into her thigh. Barely running with the resources she had left it, her IMS needed the help.

Another sensor sweep. Merkiaari were gathering but not closing yet. She made a decision, and slung her rifle on her back. She grabbed Cragg's body and threw him off the roof. As long as he didn't land on his head, he would survive. Hell, for all she knew he would survive even that. In hibernation, his resources were being used in the exact opposite manner to hers. Everything he had was dedicated to survival and repair.

His body thumped onto the ground on its back and bounced a little to settle face down. He had hit the ground, as a corpse would have, all slack-boned and unflinching. The little death was indistinguishable from true death until wake up time.

Gina checked her sensors again noting positions of the enemy and Hiller's position, the closest viper. She looked down three stories, and jumped. She crashed down and melee mode did little to help the impact. She didn't feel the pain though, so maybe melee mode did have other uses than pure combat. Pain response was suppressed, but damage still occurred, and another entry appeared on her list; left hip again.

She limped up to Cragg and lifted him onto her shoulder. She took a deep breath and ran into the open street. The moment she did, red icons swarmed. She grinned. That had surprised the buggers. They had been setting themselves to assault the rooftop. Gina chuckled and then laughed hysterically. Melee mode was doing weird things to her self-control. Her legs became a pumping blur. She barely felt Cragg's weight.

Merki fire sought her life and debris kicked up around her feet. She was moving too fast to dodge sharply, but she did what she could by swerving left and right. An explosion to her right peppered her with shrapnel. It hurt, she thought it must have, but it was a distant thing. Something clanged off her helmet and the visor starred. The helmet display started flickering. She didn't need it anyway. Helmet comm and HUD were just a backup for a viper. She kept it on, damaged as it was, for the minimal protection it lent her.

Explosions chased her, and finally caused a reaction from Alliance forces. Colonel Jung wouldn't know why the Merki were worked up yet, but she had to wonder if this was a prelude to a new offensive. Artillery began zeroing in, and Gina cursed. Friendly fire might still nail her. She ducked and jinked as buildings came apart around her. Stone and glass flew outward, and buildings roared as they toppled or imploded. More fire and smoke added itself to the chaos.

"Friendly fire my arse!" Gina screamed into the night. "Alpha-one-one, Alpha-leader. I'm heading your way with many new acquaintances hot on my heels. Cragg is in hibernation. I'm bringing him in!"

"Alpha-leader, Alpha-one-one. A few friends dropped by for a visit. Lucky break, eh? Bring your buddies right through the middle of us."

"Affirmative, ETA three minutes!" she yelled over the noise of buildings falling. "Shit, Ian. Jung's trying to kill me again. Tell her the enemy is behind me, not in front!"

Ian snorted. "Like she'll listen. Alpha-one-one out."

"Alpha-leader clear."

Gina had Hiller's blue icon on her display, and more viper icons had arrayed themselves near him and along a particular street. She couldn't know without checking satellite feeds, but she guessed they were undercover in the buildings. If she could lead the Merki up that street, they should be slaughtered.

That was the plan then, she decided. She kept running while she plotted a least time course to lead the Merkiaari through Hiller's gauntlet. She didn't slow as she passed the first blue icons on her sensors. Those vipers were well hidden. She saw no sign of them. She was just approaching Hiller's hiding place when her people opened fire all at once. She dove for cover in amongst a bombed out building's remains. She stashed Cragg behind a wall, and found a good firing position. Hiller didn't acknowledge her presence; he was busy about a hundred metres away targeting the Merki with a bipod mounted AAR. They were usually mounted on a unit's armour with a stedimount to stabilise it, they were heavy, but the bipod was better here. It allowed Hiller to fire while lying down for better cover. He was making good use of it too. He was piling Merki bodies up in the street.

Jung's artillery had finally stopped lobbing shells in, maybe realising the danger of blue on blue. Plasma and rocket fire rained down upon the Merki from the buildings and rooftops, and they scattered looking for cover. There wasn't much in the street itself, and the buildings were already occupied by Merkiaari killers. They tried to fight back. That's what Merki did, pretty much their default setting for every situation, but they were completely over matched. The vipers had good cover and elevation. The Merki were utterly slaughtered.

Gina watched the last Merki troop die, and turned away to check on Cragg. He was still dead, but he would wake up fine. She shook her head at the thought. Two years ago, such a thought would have been macabre and ridiculous, but now it was just a part of life.

"We are such freaks," she muttered.

"Yeah," Hiller said looking down at their *sleeping* friend. "But handy freaks, and I'm still cute."

Gina rolled her eyes. "Cute freaks—"

Hiller nodded. "Useful, but dangerously cute freaks." He

grinned. "I don't envy your next fight."

She cocked her head. "Huh?"

"The General is going to have a few questions, Gina. I wouldn't try to bullshit him were I you. He isn't Jung."

She nodded glumly. Joking aside, she wouldn't dare try any of her excuses on Burgton. Not really. It was fun imagining excuses, but she wouldn't dare try anything but the truth in reality. Besides, the truth was serious enough in scope that she didn't fear being chewed out.

"Better get to that I guess," she said. "Gold-one, Alpha-leader..."

* * *

# 2 ~ Masks

General Burgton CO 501ˢᵗ Infantry Regiment watched the faces in the room, not the presentation in the huge holotank. His processor was faithfully recording everything and hoarding it in his database like some demented squirrel with a cache of nuts as it always did. Vipers never forgot anything, nothing at all. They were physically incapable of it. If he needed to recall anything of this meeting, it would be there. Not that he would. The presentation was based upon the download obtained from Cragg before he was stored in stasis aboard *Grafton*. Burgton had already seen what it contained. Along with his officers, he had uploaded it to experience the fear, and the pain, and the exultation of Cragg's last combat in Shoshon, far more intensely than any holotank presentation could possibly provide the unenhanced.

Burgton was far more interested in the people watching than the data he already knew so well. He was always interested in people. Their reaction to things often gave him an advantage in his dealings with them. He hadn't always been so analytical, but two hundred years of trying to predict events had turned him into an obsessive people watcher and statistician. Luckily, he was well equipped for it. Vipers had the built in computational power to do some really heavy math, and he was always running an analysis or simulation in the back of his brain; political, military, economic... all kinds of things fed into him from his sources all over the Alliance. His past accuracy could be called miraculous; his officers certainly thought so, but secretly he was worried. He had noticed a distressing number of errors creeping into his predictions. The worst failure to date had been this campaign. He had predicted another five years of relative peace before needing to confront Merkiaari in combat again. As for the Shan, they weren't even on his horizon before this, and he feared they might be the straw that broke the camel's back as far as his predictions were concerned.

Combining simulations and programs based upon chaos theory with unmatched information gathering over centuries, and then allowing them to run without pause for all that time, had allowed him to guide events in the Alliance, but the complexity of the simulations was outstripping his ability to monitor and control. Billions of calculations per second, trillions? No matter the actual figure, it was too high for any normal computer to perform and maintain accuracy.

He had begun by running the early incarnations of his chaos simulations internally while he slept. During those hours, his personal computing power was mostly idle. He had just wanted to see what would happen, and compare his predictions with actual events. The result had been startling. Not only had his predictions come true, the follow up events leading from them were also close to those predicted. Those predictions had allowed him to steer the Alliance away from a few disasters, and were how he had managed to do it with only a hundred vipers when the Council of the day betrayed him by mothballing the regiment.

The introduction of the Shan into the Alliance would throw his calculations off, maybe way off, because they were literally alien. How could he possibly predict what they would do when everything they thought or did was so alien? It was something very much on his mind since arriving in the Shan system. He had to find a way to slot them into his calculations.

He had drafted some ideas, but hadn't yet tried to test them. A simulation on such a scale would take time and resources only found on Snakeholme under the mountain. The regiment's archive was more than a data depository. Its hugely powerful computers were constantly running his Alliance simulation. It had long since outgrown his aging viper brain and processor. He feared the day when it outgrew its current home because the hardware was cutting edge and further upgrades were impossible. There was nothing better anywhere in the Alliance, except perhaps for the handful of surviving A.Is quarantined and protected. No one but their caretakers and the Council ever had access to those immensely powerful minds.

Burgton frowned as the familiar frustration swamped his brain. An A.I would solve his problem; they were orders of magnitude more powerful than any current computer despite being built centuries ago. Modern computers were designed with built in limitations to prevent a recurrence of the Hacker Rebellion. Neural interfaces were banned for the same reason. Burgton always suspected that was one of the reasons the Council betrayed him back then. Vipers had neural interfaces, and the old A.Is predated the ban.

"General?" Admiral Kuzov said and Burgton made his frown disappear. "You disagree?"

Burgton quickly scanned his log. Kuzov was asking if he disagreed with Colonel Jung's proposal regarding Cragg's troop ship. The presentation was over.

"No, Admiral. I was considering my men's part in Colonel Jung's ops plan. Unless you decide to go against all custom and standing orders to bombard the troop ship from orbit—something I doubt but would applaud you for, sir—you will need my men to recon ahead of the advance."

Admiral Kuzov nodded. "That is the usual procedure against Merki I believe."

Burgton smiled. Kuzov was a spacer through and through. Give him a ship and a battle in space—even against Merkiaari—and he was in his element. Here though, he was out of his comfort zone and drawing upon historical ground battles against the Merki for his inspiration. His personal experience of fighting Merkiaari extended only to the battles he had observed on Harmony these past months. Admiral Meyers had commanded the only action in space here in Shan space.

Colonel Jung stirred. "If I may, Admiral?"

Kuzov nodded.

"I think General Burgton's men should be held in reserve this time around. His force is much diminished, and to be blunt, I feel they've bled enough."

Burgton allowed a small smile onto his lips. What Jung said was true. He had brought six hundred and forty units with him, and less than two hundred remained operational. Two hundred vipers could take out most Merki targets, but he wasn't averse to resting his men. It was good that the other forces gained experience against the Merkiaari. This incursion wouldn't be the last and he couldn't be everywhere. Jung wasn't thinking of his men though, Burgton was sure. She was worried that her chance at a resounding victory and the promotion attached to it was slipping from her grasp. If vipers went in, even as an advance force, people wouldn't remember that Jung had commanded or that the 2nd Faragut Strike Force had provided the firepower to win the battle. As soon as vipers were mentioned, all attention would be on them. Burgton understood Jung's position and sympathised to a degree, but he didn't like what it said about her that she was willing to put her men at greater risk. Then again, this was war and risk was endemic.

"General, your opinion?" Kuzov said.

Burgton glanced at the Shan representatives. The two

males watched everything and let nothing slip. He thought they were here not to discuss the coming fight but rather to study the Humans in a non-combat setting. He had caught other Shan doing it in various places and situations. It was a wise thing they were doing, and was something he needed to emulate if he was going to successfully predict how the Shan would impact the Alliance. He had to wonder if these two males were even warriors. They looked and acted the part, but the way they observed everything reminded him of the way Marion Hymas worked. She was a shrink. Shan didn't have recognisable psychologists, but they did have mind healers as part of the greater healer caste. They specialised in what the Shan called the harmonies of the mind. Burgton had no proof, but his instincts were telling him that one or both was healer caste not warrior. He liked sneaky thinking like that, and he was glad the Shan were already taking necessary steps. They needed to learn that not every Human they met had their best interests at heart or altruistic motivations for what they did.

"I and my men are ready to do our part as always," Burgton began and Jung scowled. "But a respite would be much appreciated. To be blunt, I have less than two hundred effectives left at my command. If I can preserve that force without compromising the mission, I am prepared to retire from the field early."

Kuzov nodded thoughtfully. "I would prefer it if your men remained on planet, General, but by all means pull back and consolidate as our reserve."

Burgton indicated agreement with a crisp nod. Kuzov was no fool, he knew what Jung wanted and was willing to oblige, but he obviously wasn't willing to risk the mission. Cold blooded it might be, but Kuzov knew that if Jung screwed up, two hundred vipers in reserve should rectify the situation in short order. Burgton didn't expect Jung would need his men though. She wanted that star very badly, and would most likely flood the battlefield with men to make sure there were no screw-ups. There was no such thing as overkill when fighting Merkiaari. Vipers were based upon the idea of victory through superior firepower after all. Jung would simply apply that truism with her own manpower.

Colonel Jung looked pleased. She nodded to Burgton in thanks and started detailing her plan of attack.

Burgton caught Admiral Meyers' eye, and she cocked her head in question. He flicked a look at the Shan and signalled with a gesture that he would like a word after the meeting. Meyers had been watching the Shan just as he had through the presentation, and he wanted her take. He was wondering if she had gotten the same vibe from the aliens as he had.

"...useful to capture the ship." Colonel Jung was saying and Burgton brought his attention back to business. "The Merki have managed to surprise us a number of times on this campaign. The jamming and their ability to track our transmissions needs investigation. Of course, they've always been adept at the second, and that spawned a raft of new tech from our side to offset the disadvantage last time around. I have a feeling our R&D people will need to pull the proverbial rabbit out of their hats again. We need to strip that ship of every molecule of intelligence it contains."

Burgton nodded along with the others. A new war always caused advances in tech. The trick was staying ahead of the opposition. It was an arms race with survival as the prize. At least this time they knew the Merkiaari had advanced in three key areas before being attacked by them. The jamming was more pervasive and far reaching than the Alliance could do, and no one had yet figured out how they were tracking and decrypting transmissions, but it was the Merki troopers themselves that worried Burgton the most. Professor Wilder had first brought it to his attention that the Merki had evolved the ability to regenerate serious wounds. They were tougher to kill than ever before, and they had always been tough bastards. Worse to his way of thinking was the way they had modified their war fighting techniques and doctrine to emulate Human small group tactics. Killing their officers no longer reaped the same rewards as it had in the last war. The Merkiaari had modified their breeding programs to increase intelligence in their line troops while keeping them as physically strong as ever.

At least the Shan incursion had given the Alliance advanced warning. That could not be underestimated. He had already taken some basic steps to lessen the threat by ordering samples of Merkiaari tech, weapons, armour, and even dead troopers brought up to *Grafton* for examination. A more thorough analysis would be undertaken on Snakeholme. He was sure Shan scientists and engineers were already hard at work, and Admiral Kuzov would secure examples of everything for the navy, but Burgton had learned his lesson about relying on others when the Council betrayed his men two hundred years ago. He had striven since then to make his regiment as self-sufficient as possible, and keeping that status secret.

Burgton listened as Jung detailed her plans, and evaluated her subordinates as they added suggestions. Although the navy was represented at the table, they had nothing to add. Admiral Kuzov had probably invited them out of courtesy. Their true mission had yet to begin really. Once the Merki were finished off, it was Fifth Fleet's mission to secure the system against further incursions, and at the same time set the Shan firmly back on the road to recovery. A big part of that were the factory ships he had brought along as part of Fifth Fleet's auxiliary. When those monsters got started munching on the asteroids, the Shan would have the genesis of its new orbital infrastructure. They needed to rebuild their industrial capacity quickly, and replace their high orbitals. Without stations, they couldn't move personnel efficiently. So there was a step by step procedure to follow. Machines replicating themselves at first, and then turning toward building factories and smelters in orbit and in the asteroid fields. Those factories would then produce the stations and ship yards. And finally, a year or two down the road, the Shan fleet would be reborn better than ever.

How long that would take depended entirely upon how much the Shan were willing to sink into it. The planets needed massive reconstruction. The cities and everything needed to support them had to be replaced, and that meant diverting capacity away from war making material. Burgton had a feeling the Shan would surprise them though. They were very focused upon the military aspects of their treaty with the Alliance. When they became members, Burgton had the feeling they planned to be in the forefront of any action against the Merkiaari. Hard to blame them considering what had happened to them here, but it was very ambitious for any single system government to think they could take a leading role amongst over two hundred member worlds. Most of them had been members a long time, and were already politically and economically well connected.

"Very well, gentlemen," Kuzov said. "I think that's everything."

Everyone murmured agreement and the meeting broke up. A few people took a last sip of their coffee before standing. Burgton thought that a good plan, and drained his cup. He ignored the warning flashing on his display. Caffeine wouldn't kill him.

He moved to join Admiral Meyers. "Can I have a word?"

She nodded and walked with him out of the conference room and into the corridor. "About the Shan?"

He nodded. "Do you know those two?" Indicating the Shan males whispering together as they headed for the boat bay with the others.

"No, they're new. Kuzov mentioned them though. Apparently the elders finally decided to assign him a full time liaison, rather than leaving it to random chance. I think one will stay up here with Kuzov full time eventually."

Made sense. Until now there hadn't been an official

liaison with the fleet. Contact with the Shan had been between commanders on the ground and with the Shan elders through them. This liaison business was further proof that the Shan were taking steps, getting their ducks in a row so to speak. Burgton approved. He hoped it would make his life easier when trying to predict events. He was already starting to think the only way to guess what Shan would do in a given situation was ask one. Unfortunately, unlike Kuzov he didn't have any Shan of his own.

"What do you think?" Burgton said as they waited for the elevator. They had let the others go first for privacy.

"About the liaison idea? I'm surprised they waited so long. Tei'Varyk and Wilder went down world months ago."

Burgton frowned. "True, true... I was thinking of your opinion of them as individuals rather than their official designation."

"How so? I can hardly boast of my extensive knowledge of them as people, and I only met these two today at the presentation. One thing I did notice."

"Oh?"

"They're not warrior caste," Meyers said. "But they *are* Tei. No Shan would claim the title if they were not; I've learned that much about their culture."

So, she saw it the same as he, maybe. "I agree, but why do you think so?"

"Nothing too complicated," Meyers said as the elevator doors opened. They entered the car alone and selected the boat bay as their destination. "It's silly really, but did you notice their harnesses?"

Burgton hadn't and he said so.

"They weren't new, yet both of them kept fiddling with the things as if unused to them. They were uncomfortable all through the presentation as if used to wearing the civilian kind."

Burgton chuckled. "So simple I didn't pick up on it. I'm impressed, Admiral."

She shrugged. "Call me Alli, General. We've known each other long enough to be passed the rank thing."

"Then call me George," Burgton replied. "I felt they weren't what they seemed, but I didn't notice the harness thing. Mind if I lay out a theory?"

"Sure."

"I think you're right about them. They are Tei but healer caste not warrior. I think the elders want eyes on us, but they went a step further. You know of their mind healers?"

Meyers nodded but speculation was in her eyes. "You're guessing of course, but it would be a smooth move on their part. I would have to applaud it if true."

Burgton grinned. "We really shouldn't. It's tantamount to spying."

Meyers chuckled. "If they did it to me I would call them on it, but they're doing it to Kuzov. The Shan are allies, George. They won't learn anything they won't soon have a right to know anyway. If this gives them a leg up on understanding us, more power to them."

"You admire them very much."

"Hard not to, there's a lot that's admirable. If it was me and not Kuzov, I would invite them to come out into the open about what they're doing. It wouldn't offend me to host a mind healer as liaison, might be interesting, but doing it behind Kuzov's back risks his anger. I'm not sure how he would react to learn of this."

"Hmmm. I won't out them to Kuzov, but I agree. I think we should suggest they explain this to the elders. They should find a warrior caste replacement for Kuzov before he does figure it out. He's no fool."

"Let's catch up to them," Meyers said and they increased their pace.

They caught up with the two Shan in the boat bay waiting for a shuttle to come free. Burgton had seen busy boat bays before, but to the Shan, the taxiing spacecraft and bustle of crewmen waving their batons to shepherd them into parking areas was still a novelty. Burgton took a moment, trying to see things through alien eyes.

The snub-nosed shuttles were white above and black below the point where their swing-wings attached to the fuselage, a result of the nanocoat used to protect them against the fires of re-entry. Nanocoat did darken with heat, but that wasn't why the shuttles were painted two tone. It was to differentiate them from civilian models. Civilian shuttles were white all over. The absolute zero of space had returned these shuttles to their default colour. Had they been in atmosphere soon after re-entry they would have been coal black all over reacting to heat.

A shepherding crewman crossed his glowing batons and the shuttle in his charge halted. The pilot raised a hand with up thrust thumb and went through his shutdown procedures. More crewmen ran forward, some connecting refuelling lines, while others went for the hatch to open it for boarding. Similar things were happening all over the bay.

*ASN Lincoln* was an aging but still very powerful *Excalibur* class heavy cruiser. Its place as Fifth Fleet's flagship was secure for years yet. Its replacement would probably be one of the newer more powerful Washington class ships like *ASN Victorious*, Admiral Meyers' current flagship. Unlike Home Fleet, First Fleet, and Second Fleet, Kuzov's Fifth Fleet was created for offensive punch not defensive holding actions. It contained no dreadnaughts. It should have been surprising that it was tasked with holding the Shan system, but Burgton understood why it was chosen. Its ships were fast and powerful, its units picked to complement one another, and its mission was to move out quickly and hit its target lightning fast. That meant it was always ready to move station, its fleet train ready and able to support it no matter the mission. Fifth Fleet was one of three like it that was constantly on the move in Alliance space. They were the hammer, the other three the anvil.

Burgton recalled the fuss the announcement to create a

Fifth Fleet without dreadnaughts had caused. Back then the idea of handicapping Fourth Fleet that way was still being debated hotly. The screams of outrage when Fifth Fleet was announced with a similar configuration had resounded throughout the Alliance. Calls for an investigation into the pros and cons had been voiced in the Council. The fact of the matter was that the Navy could build ten light cruisers or five heavy cruisers for every dreadnaught it manufactured. It preferred numbers and manoeuvrability over slower tougher ships with huge crews. Besides, they were still building dreadnaughts all be it at a much slower rate. They were simply replacing older designs with the new ones and putting the old ships into a mothballed reserve, not sending them to the breakers like they did with smaller units.

Burgton rued that decision just a little. He had ah... *rescued* a few ships from the breakers with none the wiser over the years, but where he would find crews for a squadron of dreadnaughts he had no idea. Probably for the best that temptation be out of his grasp. The reserve flotilla was located outside Mars orbit. No way to jack a ship from there, he mused.

Meyers halted before the Shan who broke off their whispered but rapid-fire conversation in their own tongue. She bowed and gave the flowery greeting most conversation with Shan opened with.

"I greet you Tei'Xanthe and you also, Tei'Slavik. May you live in harmony," Meyers said and waved a hand at George. "May I present General Burgton?"

Burgton inclined his head and repeated the greeting, but concluded it with, "We have met, but briefly."

Both Shan bowed.

"Might we join you?" Meyers asked. "We have something of import to discuss with you. Your elders will no doubt require you to ah... assist them in a decision quite soon thereafter I should think."

Shan ears went back and then twitched upright. Burgton's

smile widened as tails flexed and whiskers drew down. Shan were absolutely bloody fascinating to him. He really *really* wanted one of his own to observe and learn from. Damn it all, how was he going to slot them into his simulations!

Tei'Slavik tugged at his harness, and Burgton's eyes narrowed. That was part of what Meyers was talking about. Slavik shifted the holster higher on the strap, and then tugged it lower in irritation, but when he noticed Burgton watching he snatched his hand away as if burned. Burgton grinned, and the Shan's ears went all the way back, but they flicked straight again when he remembered Human grins did not indicate hostile intent. Burgton forced himself to show a closed mouthed smile to put the male at ease. He should have done that first.

"We are waiting to go down to Harmony," Tei'Slavik said in very good English. His translator was on his harness but switched from broadcast to record mode, Burgton noted. "We are to watch the fighting at Shoshon."

Meyers nodded. "That's fine, we'll wait with you and I believe General Burgton is also going down world. He will join you on your shuttle."

Tei'Xanthe's eyes widened a little. "Honoured we are," his words came clearly from his translator, but Burgton did not need the translation. His processor handled the Shan language pretty well these days. "But what is this about the elders?"

Burgton took the lead. "As time is short, I will be blunt with your permission. Please do not fear I mean harm to you or your people."

Tei'Slavik and Tei'Xanthe glanced at each other and then back to Burgton. Both flicked ears in the Shan gesture of affirmative, but then nodded for good measure.

"Good," Burgton said and quickly looked around for eavesdroppers. No one was near. "It has come to our attention that both of you are healer caste, not warrior caste as advertised."

Ears went back.

"No need for concern," Burgton added with raised hands gesturing for calm. "Admiral Meyers and I have no intention of informing anyone else, but we feel you should tell the elders how this will be seen from Admiral Kuzov's point of view."

Tei'Slavik looked to Tei'Xanthe and took something from the quick exchange. Permission maybe and Burgton raised his estimate of Xanthe's age. Between equals, Shan tended to defer to age.

"How will Admiral Kuzov react, please?" Tei'Slavik said.

So it was true. Burgton was pleased to be proven right, but that wasn't the issue. How could he use this? Meyers had already indicated a willingness to help, but he would prefer to keep things within the regiment if possible.

"Admiral Kuzov will be angry. What you're doing is spying upon one who is a friend. You dishonour him."

Ears went hard back at that and stayed there. Shan, no matter their caste, took honour seriously. They were not that far from their clan and tribal origins after all. Just a few centuries ago they were fighting each other with spears and claws.

"We honour all Humans! No dishonour was intended!" Tei'Slavik said, clearly agitated now. "How can we make this right?"

"We know you meant no harm, and that you're trying to understand us," Meyers put in, keeping her voice low and soothing. "I'm sure when you explain to the elders they will send a warrior to take your place here on *Lincoln*. No need to say more to Admiral Kuzov than that the elders are reassigning you elsewhere."

"But this does not erase the wrong?" Tei'Xanthe said uncertainly, his translator impersonal but his worry was clear upon his face. "Please, we must be clear, thank you?"

Meyers would have disagreed, but Burgton took his chance and stopped her with a hand on her shoulder. "This is unfortunately true, Tei, but it is easily mended. Admiral Meyers would like one of you to help her aboard her ship, if that is agreeable to the elders. She does not mind that you are not warrior caste. I would also welcome a Shan aide. As you know, my men have been fighting alongside your people. It would be a great help to me if one of you, or perhaps two of you—one a warrior—would agree to stay by my side to help me understand your people better."

Meyers glanced knowingly at him, and her lips twitched as if fighting a grin.

Tei'Xanthe froze for a moment in surprise.

Tei'Slavik said something to Xanthe in Shan, but it was so fast that Burgton missed it. Surprised, he checked his log and realised he had heard it fine but couldn't make head or tails of it. It had been Shan, but was spoken in an obscure dialect. Burgton hadn't heard there were different dialects here, but there obviously were. Perhaps they were used along clan lines, or maybe it had something to do with caste. He had no idea. He shouldn't be surprised considering the number of languages Humans had used in their time, but it was damn inconvenient from a nosy Human's point of view.

The Shan finished their consultation, and together bowed to Burgton. Tei'Slavik spoke first.

"We would be honoured to be chosen to accompany you. It is an extreme honour you offer us. We are not worthy of a tenth part of it. Your worlds are much discussed among our people. To see them... it is a *great honour!*"

Burgton blinked. Oh god damn, they thought he meant for them to accompany him back to the Alliance! He had meant for them to join him while here in the Shan system. Alli was grinning at him openly now, and he had to agree that it was sort of funny. His machinations had lead to this. Tei'Xanthe was speaking and Burgton quickly focused on his words. His unease faded a little as the import of Xanthe's words sank in.

"... very great honour, but we must take your proposal to

the elders. This decision is far above us. I am sure Kajetan will request Tei'Varyk and other worthies attend and advise her. Pleased I am to convey your words to her regarding Admiral Kuzov and your suggestion for a new liaison. I am most certain she will appoint a warrior this very day."

Burgton nodded, still trying to think. Kajetan would send a warrior to Kuzov, he had no doubt. That pinched off one possible disaster. The matter of one or both of these Shan joining Alli on *Victorious* wasn't his concern, and he dismissed it from his thoughts, but a Shan of any stripe assigned long term to him? That had possibilities. It would surely help his understanding, but it meant breaking a cardinal rule of his. No one landed on Snakeholme but vipers or those working for the regiment and already resident there. No one! In fact, no outsider even knew where it was. It had been a terrible risk when he'd had Snakeholme's existence erased from Alliance records, but had allowed one entry to remain for drone communications. That entry, by presidential seal, was cloaked and hidden from everyone except the President and First Space Lord, but even such dire measures left him uneasy. Data, no matter how secured, could be compromised, but a means of communication with the Alliance and Admiral Rawlins in particular was a necessity.

"Sirs?" a young crew woman said as she approached. "If you would take your seats aboard the shuttle?"

Burgton nodded and gestured to the Shan to precede him before turning to Meyers. "Well, we seem to have saved the day for Kuzov."

Meyers snorted. "I did all right out of it. I think I'll be hosting those two on *Victorious* very soon."

"You don't think one will be given to me?"

"Doubt it, George. Xanthe's English isn't the best, and Slavik seems attached to him... his aide maybe? I think you'll get a couple of Shan, but I'm betting they will be infantry fighters."

Burgton nodded. Made sense to him, and he might even

have fought beside them. Still, considering their choice of liaisons for Kuzov, he would wager the elders would still send at least one healer caste. They were very interested in how Humans thought, not just in the way they fought Merki. He shook Meyers' hand, and followed the Shan into the shuttle.

* * *

# 3 ~ Another Point of View

First Claw Karnak snarled wordlessly. His cleansing was a failure. From the moment the Human vermin arrived and attacked his ships, he had been beset by incompetence and defeat on all sides. The only victories to his name were ones where he had taken personal command. They were something to be proud of, but they would never be known. Besides, even if the news did somehow leave the system and reach the Warlord what good would such small victories be when the scale of this disaster finally came out? His life was forfeit whether he survived this battle or not, and it would be not. He knew that. He tried not to let that awareness betray his fear to the others. Dying bravely was all he had left. The knowledge threatened to turn his bowels to water, and he suspected his shield bearer knew it. Zuark was a warrior beyond compare. A friend and companion of that thrice cursed Valjoth, the current First Claw of the Host. How he hated them both.

Valjoth, always it was Valjoth. He wished... there was much that he wished, but it was all for nothing now. There was nothing left but to die. He could do nothing about Valjoth. He feared his defeat and his shame could be used to bring down the Warlord, and Valjoth was waiting. Who else would ascend the throne? Who else could? Certainly none from his batch could be relied upon now that he had failed so badly. All of them might suffer his fate, tainted with his shame.

He closed his eyes, listening to yet another report of disaster. In one way, it would be a relief to die. Get it over with. His body like so many of his troops would never reach the recycle vats to nourish the next generation, so why put off the inevitable? Only for pride did any fight on. And for vengeance. To kill and kill and kill until they could kill no more. It was the Merkiaari creed.

His eyes flew open when he registered the latest outrage. "What!" he roared. "You dare report such losses to me?"

Zuark Sheild Bearer watched his lord in silence. It was a shield bearer's duty to protect and aid his lord, but he had been forbidden to give council after the last time he disagreed with his lord's orders—a shameful situation to impose upon any shield bearer, and an extreme insult to one of Zuark's quality. He was spawned among Usk's batch, Valjoth's own shield bearer. He watched in silence, condemning his lord with his pitiless eyes full of wrath unvoiced.

"Destroy them now!" Karnak roared.

"Lord," Rintuk protested. "It is too late. They mass within weapon's range of this very ship. We cannot attack them and prevail."

Karnak knew that of course. Rintuk's report made it obvious to everyone. The only choice was defence. It infuriated him. The discovery of his last landing ship by the lone Human scout had turned into a disaster as so much else had during this cleansing when Rintuk's troopers had failed to run him down.

Zuark's wrath finally boiled over. "Lord, Rintuk is right—"

"Silence fool!" Karnak snarled. "Rintuk is an incompetent vermin spawn. He should—"

"Lord, forgive me for saying this," Zuark said obviously not caring one way or the other. "But the Warlord will surely order the High Marshalls to send First Claw Valjoth here—"

Karnak snapped his jaws closed strangling on his rage. Oh Zuark didn't just say that name; he didn't dare raise that name within his hearing!

"Valjoth... always it is Valjoth!" Karnak moved in the blink of an eye, and Zuark staggered back in shock. He fell to the deck, his blood pumping from his torn throat.

"Clean that up," Karnak said coldly and flicked blood off his claws onto the deck. It was the last thing Zuark heard before sliding into the dark. "Prepare to receive the vermin. We will kill until this ship's decks run with rivers of blood."

Enthusiastic growls and gnashing of fangs met the announcement as was expected of them, but none doubted they would die long before sunset on this vermin cursed world. Karnak pretended not to notice the sidelong glances, and their pretended sincerity. They had all long since made peace with the fact they would become a mere footnote of history in a far larger war. A war fought without them.

Valjoth would be the one hailed as conqueror, the rewards his and quite possibly the throne one day. The blood would surely choose him. He was the best choice. He hated that, but it was true and their people needed the best if they were to prevail over the Humans. Karnak's hatred suddenly died within his heart as he made his own peace with his fate. Yes, Valjoth would conquer. He hoped the vicious bastard brought the entire host here to punish the vermin of this world. He would be avenged though he doubted Valjoth would see it that way or care.

Karnak wondered again if the news of the Human intervention had reached Kiar—the home system—yet. How would Valjoth react to the knowledge he had been pre-empted? Karnak would never know, but he hoped it sent

Valjoth into a rage so that he might come here all the more quickly. It would be good to destroy such a large force of Humans as a prelude to the final destruction of the vermin alliance of worlds.

The new batches of troops had proven themselves here. Their enhanced intelligence made them harder to control, true, but it made them especially effective against vermin using unconventional tactics. The thrice-cursed Humans personified unconventional. The new troops were the future, he knew. He could foresee a time when the breeding programs switched entirely to the new model rather than three batches in ten as now.

All of his remaining troops were the new type. Didn't that say something about them? When the only survivors were all from one batch, a wise commander took note. He wished he might inform Valjoth somehow. Probably unnecessary anyway. Like Usk and Zuark, Valjoth descended from batches based upon changes made in the breeding programs after the failed Human cleansing. That particular type of vermin were pernicious and hard to eradicate. A fitting challenge, but extremely dangerous. He knew that only too well. There hadn't been that many Humans in the system when they turned his victory into a humiliating defeat. That had changed with a larger force arriving to reinforce the original scouting element. He assumed it was a scouting force he had faced on the other habitable world based upon the reports of its size. It was preposterous how hard they had hit his troops with such a puny force, but he couldn't argue with the disastrous result. The Human vermin might be as terrible a foe as the Makers had been.

His fur ruffled at the thought.

His people had rebelled and defeated their creators who had shaped and enslaved them millennia ago, and they had vowed never to be subjugated again. They no longer fought and died as slaves. They were the masters now. Let the vermin serve them or die.

Vermin extinction was of course his preference. He was firmly on the side of the total cleansing of the galaxy as any right thinking Merkiaari should be, and he strongly disapproved of the current policy of increasing the number of client races in the Hegemony. Not that the Warlord would care what he thought of course. But how many was enough? They risked making the same mistakes that the cursed Kiar had made by over reaching. Greed for more worlds, more resources, more client races to build and make things, while the Merkiaari did what the Kiar had bred them to do.

Fight and kill.

Perhaps that was why the new troops were so important, he mused. It wasn't the first time he had considered the notion. Zuark often said... well, he used to say their people needed to build things for themselves. Perhaps even breed their own builders and makers of things. A heretical thought, but were not ship engineers only a small step from that notion already? They were Merkiaari that did not fight; at least, they did not fight in the usual sense. Ships were weapons and they used and maintained the equipment aboard them. They killed vermin in space, or the ships did. In his eyes, ship crews were just another type of fighter. Perhaps he should not have killed Zuark earlier. He would have liked to discuss this revelation with him.

Perhaps such breeding programs were the future of his people. If so, he didn't want to see it. Not that he had the choice. He couldn't imagine what Merkiaari makers and builders would be like. Perhaps they would look like the vermin here or on other worlds that he had helped cleanse. The thought was horrible. He could use the new troops, even admire them for their prowess as fighters, but although they looked the same as he, they were already different enough to feel alien to him. They thought different thoughts, and often did things contrary to his understanding and training. They weren't vermin, but they weren't truly Merkiaari to him either. His people were evolving at a rapid rate into something he didn't truly understand. Good then that he would be dead soon. Let Valjoth deal with the consequences of the Warlord's orders.

He settled himself in the command couch and closed his eyes again. He wished the vermin would hurry up and attack so he might kill something. He shouldn't have killed Zuark. He wished he hadn't. They would have fought shoulder to shoulder in his last battle as tradition said they should. Now he would die with no shield bearer by his side. Another mistake.

"Lord, the vermin come," Rintuk reported.

Karnak opened his eyes and bared his fangs. "Good."

* * *

# 4 ~ Promises To Keep

"... hold what you got!" the anonymous voice said over the comm.

Gina glanced at Hiller from the safety of their OP, and he shrugged. He didn't have any better idea than she did about what was going on within the downed Merki ship. Hiller's visor was up, as was Gina's as they listened to the action via helmet comm, and she could see his frown as he tried to make sense of the orders. She had a schematic of the Merkiaari ship up on her internal display. The General had ordered everyone to update their data on this class of ship this morning at the briefing. She used it now as she attempted to place where in the ship the current front line was.

"Sounds hot in there," Gina muttered.

"Yeah well, better them than us," Hiller said callously and Gina frowned at him. "Come on, Gina. Jung is right this time. We've bled enough."

She shifted uncomfortably. It was true that the regiment had bled and bled and bled for the Shan in this campaign and the preceding one, but vipers were made for killing Merki. Jung's people would do their best; they *were* doing it right now, but they couldn't match Merki one on one. Lives were being unnecessarily lost in there.

She had heard it said that any single viper was worth ten unenhanced soldiers, but that should only be a consideration in force level planning, never for justifying who should live or die. She didn't hold with people who considered one life more worthy than another. She had never felt that way. The death of a Shan warrior, an unenhanced Human soldier, or a viper, were all equally tragic to her. It surprised her that Hiller of all people didn't feel the same, and it made her wonder who else agreed with him. Had he always felt that way, or was it battle fatigue?

They had been in contact with the enemy one way or the other every day for well over a year, closer to two. They were all tired. She was, God knew, but it wasn't a physical tiredness. Physically, vipers were in top shape when not actively repairing combat damage, their enhancements saw to that, but mentally was another matter. She had seen it before becoming a viper. Constant combat dulled the senses. They started taking chances without regard for the consequences. She had seen it in combat as a marine, and vipers were not immune to it. Gordon came to mind, though he seemed a lot better since they had left Child of Harmony behind. Mental toughness was a defining attribute the regiment looked for in its recruits, and every viper was tough, but there had to be a limit even for them.

They had all seen friends killed true dead, but Gina had to wonder if it was the wounded that hurt them the most. Vipers could take hideous damage and survive due to their enhancements. Survival was a good thing, but seeing the same faces "killed" and then awake only to be killed again over and over was hard. More than hard; it numbed the mind until death became nothing to them. If death had no meaning, could life have any?

She had seen for herself how different the veteran vipers like the General or Captain Penleigh were to her and the other new units. They—and others like Sergeants Stone and Rutledge—had made the Alliance and the regiment a kind of surrogate for life. They had nothing else to live for, and Gina feared she and the other new vipers were already well on the way to the same destination. Certainly they were on the same path. Was there any alternative?

She didn't think so, and hoped to God her duty would be enough to comfort her in the years to come as it had up until now. She didn't have any family. Previously she'd considered her fellow marines all the family she needed and had transferred that feeling to her fellow vipers since. It was a comfortable feeling for her, something that had not changed in her life when everything else, even her body, had.

She frowned as she thought of her eggs in cryo back on Snakeholme. All vipers were sterile, but she had opted to have her eggs harvested before enhancement. She had never planned to have children, and ticking the option on her medical release had been a spur of the moment decision, but now she wondered if perhaps she had unconsciously wanted to leave something of herself behind when she died true dead. Something other than disembodied memories in the regiment's archive.

Gina shook her head and forced the morbid thoughts away. She was a soldier, and that is all she had ever wanted to be. That had not changed, and she had never wavered from her determination to be the best that she could be. The Merkiaari were Humanity's ultimate enemy. What better test could she ask for?

Jung's plan was a simple one as far as Gina and the rest of the regiment was concerned. They were to sit tight and wait for an invitation to join the party. Gina would have preferred getting the party started herself, waiting was the worst part about soldiering, but orders were orders. The General had decided to allow Jung her moment in the limelight by backing her up as a ready reserve. Vipers were always ready for mayhem, but holding back in a reserve position had to be a first for him. Maybe not too. Burgton had been around for centuries after all.

"Faragut-actual, Swordsman-three-niner. The armoury is secured, Colonel."

"Swordsman-three-niner, Faragut-actual copies. Good work. Hold until relieved," Colonel Jung replied.

Gina was pleased to hear that. The armoury was one of three priority targets: the command centre, the armoury, and engineering. Other areas of the ship had various degrees of importance assigned to them, but those three were the most dangerous in enemy hands. Engineering was the most dangerous. The ship was probably unable to fly due to damage, and taking control of engineering would ensure that it stayed put regardless, but there was one more thing that a dedicated Merkiaari trooper could do in engineering—overload the power plant. The ship would become a fusion bomb. Not something anyone wanted to see happen. Scuttling the ship could also be achieved via the command centre, but required engineering to accomplish, so it was considered less important. It was flagged as a priority target for two reasons. The Merki commander was probably there directing his troops, and if there was any intelligence to be gained, the ship's computers were likely to be the best source.

"Faragut-actual, Swordsman-one-one. Engineering is ours. I have all access ways covered, Colonel, but they aren't giving up. They're pushing us hard. I'm not certain we can hold for long. Any word on how long to take the command centre, sir?"

"Swordsman-one-one, Faragut-actual. The word is fifteen minutes. Can you hold?"

"Not confident, Colonel. Any help you can send would be appreciated."

Gina perked up. If Jung sent reinforcements it would be supplied by her and the others. She listened intently as Jung debated and delayed the inevitable until all her people had reported in. Finally, Jung requested aid. Burgton replied and assigned the vipers their targets, but Gina's command was ordered to hold position.

"Gold-one, Alpha-leader," Gina began, but the General interrupted.

"Alpha-leader, Gold-one. I know what you're going to say. Permission denied. Hold position as ordered. This will be over soon and I have something I need you to do for me."

"Gold-one, Alpha-leader copies. Holding position," Gina replied, and if she sounded just a little sullen, Burgton did not comment. "Alpha-leader out."

Hiller was giving her the evil eye. Gina glared back. "What?"

"You know what."

Gina shrugged uncomfortably.

"Since when do you volunteer for every dangerous job? It's not like you. What gives?"

"Is that an insult?" Gina said feeling the sting. "I don't hide from danger."

"And that's your problem right there, Gina. Sensible people take precautions and if that means hiding then that's what they do, but you've been sticking your neck out at every opportunity lately. More to the point, you're sticking my neck out. I don't like that."

Gina would have exploded at that accusation if she couldn't see the worry on his face and hear it in his voice. She always busted her butt to keep her people safe, and then have it thrown back in face... she sighed. Hiller was worried for her, that's all. Hadn't she been feeling the same for Cragg, for Gordon, and the others? Yeah, she had.

"Sorry, Ian, it's just that our people are going into danger and we can't protect them. *I* can't protect them."

"They're not children, they're soldiers. They don't need your protection. Don't dishonour them or yourself by treating them as less than they are, Gina. They're good at what they do, we all are. They'll look after each other... they'll be fine."

"Right, you're right," Gina said and she had no choice anyway. The General had ordered her to hold here, so she would hold. "I wonder what he meant about a job later."

"Dunno," Hiller said and turned back to his observation of the ship.

Gina kept watch and listened to the comm, but it was all as routine as it was possible to be in a combat situation. The vipers engaged the enemy hitting them at multiple locations in the rear. They took very few injuries, no casualties at all, and Gina had to put up with Hiller's *I told you so* look. She was happy to do it.

"All units, Faragut-actual. Ship secured. Well done people," Colonel Jung said.

Gina sighed and rolled her head on her neck to ease tension. Job done. As far as the regiment was concerned, the Merki incursion of the Shan system had been successfully repulsed. There was nothing more to do but clean up. The Shan would handle that, while the Alliance went to phase two—defence of the outer system while reconstruction got underway. No one had brought Gina into the loop regarding the regiment's next step, but her guess was that it would board *Grafton* and jump outsystem back to base.

## SHUTTLE VICTOR-ONE, ON ROUTE TO ZULEIKA SPACEPORT

Gina was right regarding the regiment, but she had one more mission to perform before they all left for home. At the end of the Child of Harmony campaign, Gina had made a very special promise to a friend. She hadn't been able to make good on that promise at the time, but she had brought it to the General's attention soon after she had obligated herself and the regiment, in case she didn't survive to make good. The General had remembered, and now she was on her way by his side to Child of Harmony aboard a shuttle—a loner from *Victorious*. Captain Fernandez had agreed to be their taxi and had given them a day trip aboard *Victorious* to Child of

Harmony orbit while *Grafton* used her shuttles and dropships to retrieve the regiment and its gear from Harmony.

"... with us to Snakeholme. Do you think she'll agree?" Burgton said.

Gina frowned. "Has she given us reason to think she won't?"

Burgton cocked his head and pursed his lips. "Noooo, but I don't think it's been explained to her yet. Professor Wilder has visited a time or two, and he contacted me about her. He tells me that she's not coping well."

Gina nodded in understanding. "You remember her, sir? She was the one who planted the transmitter on the Merkiaari heading for our base at Charlie Epsilon. That's how she was blinded. When the nukes went off, she was too close. Flash blinded."

Burgton nodded.

"All her life she's known that she would go blind. Her mother was in an accident and it did something bad to her insides. Her cubs were born dead except two. Chailen is fine, but Shima had weak eyes. The visor she used to wear helped, but it was just a stop gap."

"So she has feared blindness her entire life. Is she phobic?"

"I'm no medic, sir, but I would say yes."

"Hmmm. This might be a problem," Burgton said. "If she's given up, she's of no use to me. Don't look at me like that!" Burgton snapped and Gina's face cleared. "I don't mean to abandon her. You promised and I will honour that promise, but there are more ways to skin a cat... forgive the pun. Shima could go to any core world for treatment. She doesn't need me for that."

"But... okay, I can see that. Are we to be just a taxi then?"

"That remains to be seen. I'm expecting quite a reception committee when we make planet fall at Zuleika, but I doubt any of them will see Shima purely as a friend. I want you to be that friend and advise her, but in the end, this is about more than a promise to one Shan female, Gina. It's the true beginning of our dealings with the Shan."

"By ours you mean the Alliance?" Gina asked, but she had a feeling he meant something more personal.

"The Alliance certainly. The regiment is part of the Alliance, but I was thinking more along the lines of the regiment and by extension Snakeholme. I'm hoping to turn your personal promise to one needy person into something more substantial and official. To be blunt, I need Shima on Snakeholme, or Shan at least."

"Need her. Need her why, for what?"

"Study."

Gina didn't like the sound of that. "She has fought for us—"

Burgton stopped her with a raised hand. "Nothing invasive. To fix her eyes we'll need to do a full medical work up. Regen needs data at the DNA level, but even if we can't use regen, there are other options.

"Gina, you've heard how infallible I am? How I'm always right, how I predict events?"

She blinked at the seeming subject change. "Well, yes sir, but—"

"But you're not a believer. Good for you. You're right of course. I make mistakes, hopefully not too many, but there is some truth to the stories. I run constant simulations and programs, trying to predict events. Some in my head, some under the mountain on Snakeholme. They've kept the regiment ahead of the game until recently."

"But now there are new factors, sir? Like the Shan," Gina said finally catching on. "You need to understand how they'll change things."

"Correct. I predicted a fresh Merki incursion to hit the Alliance within five years, but here we are fighting them years early. Not only that, errors have been slipping into my calculations for a few years now. Nothing disastrous yet, but my ability to predict matters is being seriously tested. Too many variables."

The regiment had relied upon the General to know what to do for centuries. Its numbers had been kept low by Council edict, and because of that, Burgton couldn't simply station vipers on every world that might need them. He'd had to keep the regiment consolidated and ready to move out from Snakeholme, and to do that, he'd had to be right about where to send them and what to do when they got there.

"I'm assuming this isn't to become general knowledge," Gina said.

"Correct again. I might bring Shima into our confidence later. It depends. For now, we're meeting Professor Wilder and whoever is with him at Zuleika for a conference. From there we visit Shima to see what her plans are."

Gina nodded.

The shuttle hit atmosphere not five minutes later, and Gina tightened her safety harness. Burgton didn't bother she noticed, and wondered how many times he had made planet fall in his life. Must be many thousands of times by now. She must have made close to a thousand herself, not including hot drops. This one was smooth in comparison to a combat insertion in a dropship. She didn't need the harness, but it was habit to use it. A good one.

The pilot was *Victorious* crew, and he was good. He brought them into Zuleika Spaceport and landed his ship like a civilian shuttle full of tourists. No fuss no muss, and nary a bump. They reached the end of the runway and turned around to taxi to the parking area. Burgton stood and prepared to leave when they heard the pilot powering down his engines. Gina took the lead to open the hatch and lower the ramp for him.

A gust of wind blew into the cabin and with it rain. Nice. Gina was wearing her battle dress blacks without armour, as was the General. Neither of them had thought to bring wet weather gear. Burgton stepped passed her without pause as if unaware of the weather. He wasn't of course, but he was uncaring of it. Gina sighed and prepared for a drenching.

Burgton reached the ground and went to a sprint taking Gina by surprise, but she went to max for a short burst just a few seconds behind him, and caught up. She was a MkIV, a newer and quicker model than Burgton's MkI. She would never call herself better than the General, but she did have a higher top speed and acceleration. They slowed and reached the welcoming committee drenched, but together as if welded shoulder to shoulder.

The welcoming committee awaited them just inside the terminal building, using it for shelter. One of the Shan held the glass doors open and gestured Gina inside. Her thoughts flashed back to the first time she had entered through this door. It had been her first night on Child of Harmony, and her first combat drop as a viper. Her platoon had been tasked with taking this building away from the Merki. A lot of firsts that night. Her first casualty happened here. Chrissie Roberts died true dead, and proved vipers were not invincible. She hadn't even had time to make her first Merkiaari kill.

Gina forced her thoughts back to the present as Burgton spoke with the Shan. She found the only other Human face and grinned as he came forward. Professor James Wilder took her hand for a shake but then pulled her into a hug. She laughed as his attempt to lift her off her feet barely took her weight off her toes. Vipers were heavy; they had a lot of metal armour coating their bones. She waited for him to give up and then lifted him—a much taller figure that from appearances weighed considerably more than she—easily and spun him around. He laughed as she put him back where she found him.

"Good to see you safe, Gina," James said. "You know Varya of course."

Gina nodded at the Shan scout who had accompanied her and Shima on the rescue mission that had led to Shima's blindness. "Good to see you again, Varya. May you live in harmony." Varya raised a paw and Gina pressed her hand to it in the Shan form of a handshake. "What are you doing here?"

"Pleased I am, you come safe through fighting," Varya said in English.

"Hey!" Gina said smiling in delight. "That was really good, Varya. You've been practicing your English." She switched to Shan. "I'm so glad you're here and safe. I heard they sent you looking for stray Merki. Find any?"

Varya replied in Shan. "Yes, not as many as we fought at Charlie Epsilon, but enough to keep my team busy. All finished now."

Gina nodded. "Glad to hear that." She turned her attention to James. "It's good to see you, James. It's been a while. Where's Brenda?"

"She stayed behind today. This is some weather, huh?"

Gina nodded. "Should have brought my rain cape."

James shook his head. "I've seen this before. We used to use these microbursts as cover to get in position to ambush the Merki in the city. They don't like rain much. It will pass in a few minutes. It's not even raining a klick down the road."

"Huh," Gina said and watched the General talking with the Shan for a moment. "You know what this is all about?"

"Politics," Varya said and spat dryly to the side, his whiskers drew down as if scenting something a week dead. "Elders and Tei get involved in warrior caste business and turn everything into a big debate."

Politics? That wasn't her understanding, Gina mused. She wondered if the General had forgotten to mention it, or whether he was about to be blindsided. How did a simple promise to a blinded friend turn into a high-level political brouhaha?

"Shima isn't warrior caste," Gina said. "Scientist caste I think she said once."

"True spoken," Varya agreed. "But the Blind Hunter is... sort of. It's hard to explain, Gina. Heroes in our culture are a special case. I am not the right person to explain it, but as I am here, I will try.

"Is it a truth with Humans that warriors lead warriors, and elders lead elders, and scientists lead scientists?"

Gina nodded. "Broadly speaking, yes. We don't have elders as you think of them. We have politicians, but yes they debate amongst themselves like your elders and decisions are made."

Varya flicked his ears in agreement. "Then perhaps this will make some sense. I know Humans do not have a clan-that-is-not, but if you did, it would probably be no different to ours. Tei cross all boundaries but are never elders. By tradition, Tei are separate. They are..." Varya paused trying to think of the right words. "This isn't exactly right, Gina. My people know this instinctively, but Tei are separate but equal to the elders... but not... not in charge? No that isn't right either. Tei lead, but they don't say where they are to lead us. Does this make any sense to you?"

Gina shook her head but James was nodding.

"I have spent a lot of time with Tei'Varyk, Gina," James said. "I think what Varya is trying to say is that although the Elders and the Tei both lead their people, they do it separately and in a different manner. Tei lead by example from the front. They literally lead by doing it themselves. They are living examples of what should be done. The elders are more like the Council. They decide policy. As a people, the Shan go in the direction the elders decide is the right one, but how they get there is more in the realm of Tei and individual choice."

"Yes! Yes that is right," Varya said evidently relieved. "There are Tei in every clan and caste, but heroes are always warriors. You understand that heroes are made through their actions in battle, so warriors you see?"

Gina nodded.

"We do not make war except against Merki," Varya went on. "Without the war there would be no heroes at all, and most only become heroes by dying in battle."

"Dead heroes are always easier to find," James murmured.

Gina smiled. "And some would say dead heroes are more convenient."

Varya blinked rapidly. "That is something very close to a warrior saying of my people. There are no old bold warriors, just dead heroes."

Gina grinned. "Ha! So heroes are a special case. What does that mean for Shima?"

"It means, that everyone wants a piece of her," James said grimly. "The elders have an interest in anything their people find interesting. The Blind Hunter is a hot topic among Shan. Heroes are admired and people want to know everything about them. Tei want to control her—anything she says or does could have significance to those who wish to emulate her. Warriors admire her. They would follow her into battle if it were still possible. They think of her as one of them despite being scientist caste. Then there is her family, clan, and caste to think of. I'm not surprised she hides in her garden."

"She should be Tei," Varya said. "All know that she is strong in the Harmonies. If not for her poor sight, she would have been invited when she became an adult and chose her caste. Many of my people disapprove of how Tei treated her in the past."

Gina pursed her lips in thought. Would Tei'Shima have an easier time of it than plain old Shima? Probably, if only in the way people treated her. As Tei, she could simply tell them all to bugger off and leave her alone. Everyone would comply... well, Shan would at least, Gina mused. She didn't think the General would though. He had outside pressures pushing him to use Shima in his plans for the Alliance. Gina wondered what Shima would say if told of those plans. She frowned as ideas started forming. Shima was scientist caste before she was anything else. Inquisitive didn't begin to describe her. Offering Shima a chance to learn something new was akin to offering a starving man a gourmet meal.

"The General said you've visited with Shima."

James nodded. "She's living in her father's house with Chailen and Sharn. She's not doing well. You remember what she used to be like, fierce and ready for anything?"

Gina nodded.

"She's like a different person now. Very quiet, no energy. Spends her time mostly sitting in her garden. I'm no psychiatrist, but if she were Human I'd have her on suicide watch."

Varya didn't agree with James, but neither did he disagree. He didn't look happy.

"Shit, that bad?" Gina whispered. "You really think she would do it?"

"I think so. She's Shan not Human, so I could be reading her all wrong, but I don't think so. If not for Chailen and Sharn, I think she might have found a way to end things already. Walked into the wilds maybe. Shan used to do that, you know? When they considered themselves a burden upon the clan, they would leave and challenge some wild animal to a last hunt and die fighting."

"It is different now," Varya said. "Our healers gained much knowledge from science and research during the years following the first alien war, and many diseases were eradicated. We are healthier and more robust even when aged, but James is not wrong about Shima. She believes that she is a burden upon her sib and her mate. My people have a duty to family and clan to be of use. In days past the old or infirm would remove themselves to help the clan prosper. But as I say, it is different now."

"We've got to fix her," Gina said with determination. "We can't lose her after all she did for us and her people. I know she hates it, but she really is a hero to them. They'd be devastated if she killed herself."

James nodded and Varya agreed, but Varya had

reservations. "We cannot dishonour her. It must be her choice."

"Force wouldn't work on her," Gina agreed. "We have to snap her out of her funk. Make it her duty to help us, rather than the other way around."

Varya's tail rose and he gestured a Shan's version of a shrug. "That would be good, but it will be hard making her believe that a blind scientist can be of use, to us or to anyone."

Gina nodded glumly. "I'll think of something, or you two will. We can't lose her like this."

"Agreed," James said. "And screw the politics. This is about loyalty to a friend." He turned to Varya. "It is a matter of honour."

Varya's ears pricked. "Yes... it really is a matter of honour is it not?"

Gina nodded. "You've thought of something. What?"

"Gina," Burgton called before Varya could explain and she went to join him. "I'd like you to meet Elder Jutka, Tei'Varyk, and Kazim. I think you probably know who Kazim is—"

The Shan all laughed, their jaws dropping and tongues lolling. Gina couldn't help but laugh along with them. Kazim was as famous as Tei'Varyk in his way. She wondered where his camera was. He was never far from it.

"Honoured to meet you all," Gina said with a very respectful bow to the elder. "May each of you live long and in harmony."

"Well spoken, young Human," Jutka said not attempting to use her few English words. "It still amazes me how the viper clan can speak Shan so well. I understand you have translators within your bodies, but the words come from your mouths in your own voices. I find that very hard to understand."

"I'm not an engineer, elder, but I can try to explain." Gina said looking to Burgton for permission. He nodded.

"As I understand it, our processors hear your words and translate them very fast. Then, those words are placed into our memories so quickly that we don't notice any delay. To us, it's as if we have always known how to speak Shan, so when I talk to you it's not a mechanical translator speaking, it really is me, Gina, using the language of your people in my memory."

"Extraordinary," Jutka said. "I could wish my people had such advantages." She glanced slyly at Tei'Varyk who stiffened as if jabbed. "Come, we have much to do and our escort will wonder what is keeping us."

Gina had a feeling she had just been used to score points off Tei'Varyk. A quick glance at Burgton confirmed her thought. He was looking very thoughtful. As Varya said earlier, it was a political game Jutka was playing, but to what end?

Gina followed as they trooped through the empty building. It would be a while before the spaceport recovered and became busy again. There were no Shan spacecraft left, and orbital infrastructure requiring the facilities here no longer existed. Perhaps that was why the damage was still evident. Replacing blown windows and painting over burn scars was a low priority when most of the cities were in ruins. Those that still stood had patchy services. Power stations, water pumping stations, and transportation of food and other supplies had to take priority over an unneeded spaceport. Most of the population still dwelled in the keeps where power and food was secure, but an increasing number were emerging to rebuild their worlds. It would take years, but with Fifth Fleet's help, it would only be years and not decades.

Gina and the others braved the rain again but only briefly. The ground cars were parked close to the entrance. There were five. Tei'Varyk ushered Burgton into a car with him and Elder Jutka. Gina joined James, Varya, and Kazim in the car behind. The other cars were their escort. She assumed they contained warriors for the elder's security, but no one emerged from them and they remained buttoned up.

"Any idea where we're heading?" she asked.

Kazim's elusive camera magically appeared and he started recording. "Elder Jutka is hosting the meeting at her home."

"So we're not visiting with Shima immediately."

James leaned back in his seat as the car pulled away. "Sorry, I should have mentioned it. Tei'Varyk isn't here for Shima's benefit, not directly anyway. Kajetan sent him here along with other Tei to discuss Child of Harmony's reconstruction, but he's been side-tracked with Shima's situation. My fault, in part; I asked him to help me with her."

Gina nodded. "I'm glad you did. So what's this about the reconstruction?"

James glanced at Kazim's camera and frowned. "I don't think it's a secret. Kazim?"

"Not a secret. My supervisor was asked by the elders to cover the talks. She sent me. It will be released as part of a special news segment about the reconstruction."

"Good then. What do you know of the political situation among Tei, Gina?"

She frowned. "Nothing. I didn't know there were political parties here."

"There aren't. Shan government is very different to that found in the Alliance. The elders are like the Council, but they aren't elected in some kind of parliament. They're sent by their clans to advise Kajetan, and she was chosen from among them by that group. Eldest is a lifetime position. That's the background. No parties or factions among the elders. They speak with one voice—Kajetan's voice. Tei are different."

Kazim and Varya let out the low volume cough-like growl Shan used like a Human snort and then laughed together. James grinned. They knew how much of an understatement that was and were being politely sarcastic. Gina had learned most of the gestures and sounds Shan made to express themselves by now.

"Why is that funny?" she asked.

Varya waved the question aside. "You have to be Shan."

"An inside joke?"

"Yes, exactly," Kazim said.

James continued. "There are three factions within Tei ranks based upon personal beliefs and attitudes. The progressives at one end of the scale believe in creating the Great Harmony out there among the stars. At the opposite end of the scale, you have the traditionalist Tei who believe in the old ways of doing things. An unkind label I've heard for them is the recessives. They're not that bad. They don't want to roll back progress, but they do want to slow it down and regulate it. Spacers are all progressive thinkers. The planet bound by and large would associate with the traditionalists."

She nodded and could already see a problem looming. "And the third faction?"

James shrugged. "They're in the middle, and not very effective. They could be called the harmony-first faction I suppose, always ready to compromise, and ever ready to mediate the other two factions. They're the weakest group, mainly because they don't stand for anything. They seem to spend most of their time calming down the hotheads in the other two factions."

"I can see where this is going, James. How serious is it?"

"I knew you would. Judge for yourself how serious it is... there is currently a motion being debated to evacuate Child of Harmony in favour of pouring all available resources into the reconstruction effort on Harmony."

Gina gasped in surprised dismay, but Kazim and Varya seemed amused.

"Will never happen," Varya said.

Kazim agreed. "Can't happen regardless of anything the elders decide. Too many people, too few ships. It would take many orbits to evacuate everyone, and in that time the reconstruction here would be well along. It would have to be, just to support our people while they waited to be relocated to the homeworld. It won't happen."

"I agree with Kazim," Varya said. "Many living here would refuse to leave, they might even move into the wilds to avoid it. This is their home, not homeworld. Most were born here after all."

James nodded. "Yes, but the suggestion is an indication of how influence has shifted among Tei. I don't know if Varya and Kazim agree with me, but the progressives lost many of their best people when Fleet and the stations were destroyed. All spacers are progressive thinkers, and most of them died when the Merki arrived. Harmony is firmly traditionalist now, while Child of Harmony is still progressive but weakened. And don't forget, the population here was already much smaller."

Varya and Kazim obviously did agree. They didn't need to voice it. Gina wondered how opinions among Tei would affect the future. Kajetan was already leading the Shan into the Alliance. That was a done deal and no way to back out now that Alliance blood had been spilled to liberate the system. Besides, it would be suicide. The Shan needed the Alliance for protection and would for years to come. The Merki could return at any time.

She took a moment to squirt a compressed data packet to the General via TacNet containing her log of the last few minutes. She had a feeling he would find James' explanation of the political scene interesting.

"Good work," Burgton said on viper comm a few minutes later. "See what else you can pick up. Keep me informed."

"Affirmative, sir," Gina replied in the same way to keep their conversation private. To outside observers she was just thinking hard, and she was. Viper comm and TacNet both worked using a viper's neural interface. "But I don't see how the traditionalists have a leg to stand on. The Shan have to push hard and fast back into space, if for no other reason than meeting the Merki out there rather than down here where their cubs live."

"Agreed, but political shenanigans could slow their progress. They, and by extension the Alliance, can ill afford that. Fifth Fleet can't be stationed here forever. Burgton out."

"Fuentez clear."

\* \* \*

# 5 ~ An Offer

Burgton had time to review Gina's data packet one more time before going in to the meeting. Its contents hadn't changed, and his lips thinned. James' analysis couldn't be faulted, dearly though Burgton wished it could. Politics always fouled him and the regiment up, but not this time he vowed. He would not let the Shan fall foul of the same mistakes he had been forced to deal with. They deserved better.

He was lucky in that Kajetan's word was law. No matter what happened, the Shan would join the Alliance, but decisions here and elsewhere could reduce the speed and effectiveness of that joining. He wanted the Shan to realise their full potential. Yes, he had his own motives for that, but they deserved it.

The Alliance had turned inward after the Merki War, and reduced exploration to almost nothing. Survey's budget was a sick joke. The Shan should have been discovered over a hundred years ago, and would have been if not for the Council's reluctance to stick the Alliance's nose outside its own door! That decision was leading to stagnation and worse—the incidence of war between member worlds was way up.

War between Shan worlds was unlikely, impossible even. There were only two after all, and to make war on one another they needed ships. They had none. No, it wasn't war he feared, it was the other fate he worried about. Seclusion. It seemed to him that the Shan as a people faced exactly the same situation that the Alliance had faced at the end of the Merki War. Back then, the Council had made the logical but bad choice not to pursue the war and finish the Merkiaari once and for all. The reasons were many and understandable, but they compounded the error by preventing further voyages of exploration beyond the borders. It was only much later that the Survey Corp. was reactivated in its current shamefully inadequate form.

Elder Jutka's home was larger and more impressive than Burgton had expected. When told they would hold a meeting at her home, he had imagined a small group of friends around a dining table. Silly of him. Jutka was an elder and as such her responsibilities were many. Her home was not a small family dwelling; it was government house, embassy, and civic centre all rolled into one. Jutka's apartments, that private area where she dwelled with her mate, were only a small part of the sprawling building. When he arrived, Burgton noted the battle damage had yet to be repaired, but it was confined to only one wing of the building, and the fire had not spread beyond the rooms directly above it.

The meeting was held in a large conference room obviously designed for the purpose. There was a large oval table made of a lustrous dark wood in the middle, but it stood no taller than sixty centimetres high. Carafes of water and empty glasses were positioned around the perimeter, and computer tablets for note taking were also provided. Shan ordinarily didn't use chairs. They used padded mats on the floor. The only chairs Burgton had ever seen used by Shan were on their ships, and that was purely a safety issue. In space, acceleration couches and safety harness combinations, no matter their height from the deck, were necessary things.

Burgton found a mat and sat cross-legged. The table was exactly the right height. He poured himself a glass of water while the room slowly filled with chattering Shan. Some of them found places and switched their computers on. Burgton pushed his aside and replaced it with his own compad. Others did similar things, though Shan tech was different, they had devices that filled the same function. James sat to his left with Tei'Varyk opposite him. Gina would have sat beside him, but he indicated the mat opposite next to Tei'Varyk. Burgton preferred looking people he was likely to converse with in the eye.

Jutka settled herself, and the last few Shan, considered tardy now that the elder was ready to begin, quickly found places to sit. Jutka welcomed everyone to her home, introduced the Humans, and then opened the floor to the debate.

Burgton listened and was sadly unsurprised to learn James' analysis was dead on. No doubt Tei'Varyk had a lot to do with that. He considered James a friend and Humans in general as his people's natural allies. He had probably kept James informed of events. This meeting was just another in a long line of useless hand wringing that often went on in the background while the real doers and shakers got on with the real work. Varya was right. The population of this world would not leave no matter what anyone said. Burgton had seen many of them already clearing the rubble from the streets as they drove through the city.

Kazim orbited the room with his camera, pausing to film each person as they took their turn to address the room. The meeting wasn't being aired live, so Kazim did not need to concern himself too much with editorial matters. He had explained to Gina earlier that his assignment was to cover the talks, which meant he was recording everything. Burgton realised what that could mean if he took the opportunity so casually handed to him with this invitation. He turned toward Jutka only to find her eyes already boring into him as if willing him to speak. He got the message loud and clear. As earlier, when she had used Gina to score points off Tei'Varyk, she now proposed to win the game by using him. He wasn't opposed to being used, not for this, but he would bet almost anything she would be surprised how he did it.

Burgton cleared his throat before the next speaker could begin reiterating the traditionalist line as so many had before her. The Shan woman hesitated, turning toward him with one ear canted at an angle while the other strained upward but swivelling toward him. Burgton smiled, it was an odd look for her. She blinked, and smiled uncertainly back at him.

"Forgive the interruption, honoured lady," Burgton said in his best Shan. "I have heard both sides of this debate now, and although I am sure your words would be as earnest as those preceding them, I do not feel I need them to understand your point of view.

"I'm not Shan," he continued and laughed when all the Shan did. "But I feel I've come to know you well. I admire you... I fear for you."

"It's pleasing to me that you admire my people, General," Tei'Varyk spoke without asking the elder for permission, but she didn't seem to care. She was watching Burgton with a small satisfied smile. "But why do you fear for us? With your help the Merkiaari are defeated and already your Admiral Kuzov is helping us gather materials from the asteroids to begin construction of new orbital factories. What do you fear?"

Burgton licked suddenly dry lips. "I've heard it said that Shan honour their ancestors and teach their younglings by telling stories of them and their deeds."

Tei'Varyk bowed in a sort of abbreviated nod. "The sagas are true tales, yes."

Burgton nodded. "Then I will answer your question with a story, a true story of my people but also of my own history."

Burgton took a moment to reflect upon what he wanted to say. Should he take them all the way back to Earth's precolony days, or keep things more personal and recent. Personal he decided. "I'm over two centuries old. In that time I've seen war, and peace, and everything in between. I've seen earnest but ultimately stupid men lead my people in the wrong direction many times, and I've seen other men struggle to undo the damage, using up their energy and lives to right the wrongs they see around them. None of them saw what they did as evil or good. They just did what they thought was right.

"I was a young man when the Merkiaari attacked us. I was just a soldier... a warrior, one among many thousands on my planet. There was no Alliance then. We didn't need it. Earth's many colonies had won their independence many centuries in the past. Like your ancestors, we fought battles between ourselves, but mostly, the colonies were at peace. We traded with each other, and even when at war we had rules. Looking back, those wars seem like play fighting to me now."

Burgton shook his head, his eyes distant. "Then came the Merki," he said in a harsh voice. "And the peace was shattered. Everything was panic and chaos. No one knew what was happening. We sent ships to talk to the invaders, but none returned. We lost worlds in the Border Zone to the Merki while our leaders dithered and talked. What shall we do, they cried. We must make them talk to us. More ships were lost trying.

"Worlds fought back and slowed the Merkiaari, mine did, others as well, but we didn't fight smart. We didn't join together. Finally, the obvious became clear to those in high places. I say obvious, because those of us actually fighting and dying knew it long before. The Merki would never stop. They had to *be stopped*, not talked into stopping. They couldn't... can't be talked to. The homeworld of man, Earth, stepped up and took control. Even then there was mistrust and many used the situation to gain political advantage."

Burgton gave each of the Shan a hard stare, aware that Kazim's camera was glued to him. "The Alliance was born, and each member world donated ships and warriors to fight as one against the Merki. Soldiers like me were recruited and changed forever to fight that war in the desperate years of the slow retreat. We lost many millions of soldiers on worlds under alien suns far from home. Thousands of ships died at the heart of nuclear fires, in solar systems that meant nothing to their crews except the Merki were there and wanted them. Slowly we retreated, forced back and back, but then one day, a day like any other, something amazing happened. We started winning and it was the Merki who retreated. Decades of fighting saw the Merkiaari defeated. Defeated like here, but not destroyed. They're still out there, readying themselves. Building more ships, breeding more troops, getting stronger, getting ready to come back and kill us all."

Burgton lifted his glass and drank his water. An alert flashed on his display, and surprised, he took note of it. The water was high in minerals. He dismissed the flashing datum.

"At the end of the war, the Alliance faced exactly the same situation as you face here, but where you have two worlds to reconstruct, the Alliance had more than eighty. At that time, those eighty comprised almost half of the Alliance. The Council chose not to pursue the Merkiaari beyond our pre-war borders, and turned its attention to reconstruction. As you have. That decision allowed the Alliance to regain strength, but also allowed the Merki menace to remain a threat. The Merkiaari have regained its strength as well, and now here we are two hundred years on reaping the rewards of the Council's decision."

Burgton turned to catch Jutka's eye. "What you do here will have far reaching consequences. Remember that. If you decide to retreat to your homeworld, abandon your only colony world, abandon your dreams of expansion as the Alliance did back then, your descendants will curse your names." Burgton said coldly, ignoring the shocked indrawn breaths. They needed shaking up. "When the Merki return and your younglings or their younglings fight for their lives or hide under the mountains as you so recently did, what do you think they will say of your choices made here today?"

Jutka spoke up. "What would you have us do? We have no ships or the ability to make them. Even if we did, we must defend our worlds not scatter ourselves among the stars."

Burgton nodded. "Your words are familiar to me. I heard them spoken often by councillors back then. They were wrong then and they're wrong now. I don't have all the answers, I wish I did, but I do know that hiding upon any single world is not the answer. It's not sound strategically, it's not sound tactically come to that, it's just not safe for any race or species to put all their eggs—cubs in this instance—in one basket."

The entire room erupted in murmurs and questions. Jutka was no longer smiling at Burgton. Maybe she had expected a different argument. He didn't care. He would make her see what was needed, or he would go directly to Kajetan herself.

Burgton went on, "As for the immediate situation here on Child of Harmony. It's obvious that the reconstruction must go ahead. If for no other reason than the change in season, you must get power back on in the cities. The weather has turned. It's not that cold yet, but winter is coming. Unless you plan upon everyone spending years in the keeps, you need to rebuild your power plants and water pumping stations.

"In the long term, you should explore and colonise nearby worlds. You need to do that and increase your population base rapidly. I know there are difficulties to overcome, but think on this: the Alliance found you while surveying worlds in this direction. What do you think the plans for those worlds are?"

Silence.

Burgton smiled a little as understanding slowly circled

the room. Jutka was looking at him strangely, and he realised that this was the argument she had probably expected him to use in the first place. He didn't laugh, but nodded to her instead.

"If you don't take those worlds, or claim the habitable ones at least," Burgton went on. "I assure you that in a few years my people will. We're expanding too slowly in my opinion, as I told you, but we are expanding."

Tei'Varyk had a faraway look in his eyes, but then he focused upon Burgton. "Before the war I spoke with Captain Colgan about this very thing. I expressed my wish to explore the stars and rebuild the Great Harmony out there. You do not know how much I want what you describe, General Burgton, but how can we explore and claim new worlds when we cannot even scrape together enough lift capacity to even reach orbit here without your help?"

Murmurs of agreement filled the room.

Burgton raised a hand and achieved quiet. "As I said before, I know there are going to be challenges, but all journeys must begin with a first step. Your first step must be deciding to make the journey. Only then, can you plan how to make it. You will have help no matter what you decide. Kajetan has bound your people to mine by joining the Alliance, but wouldn't you rather join us as equals—as a star spanning culture?"

Everyone flicked ears or nodded in the Human manner. That was something. Now for his offer, Burgton decided. He wondered what would happen when Kazim's recording reached Admiral Kuzov.

"Elder Jutka invited me to your meeting as a courtesy. I have no power over your deliberations. I actually came to visit a friend and make her an offer, but I wonder if perhaps it might be of interest to you as well?"

Jutka stirred. "You speak of The Blind Hunter's plight?"

Burgton nodded. "One of my people," he gestured to Gina, "made a promise to Shima to repair her sight. I'm here to uphold that pledge. To do this, Shima must journey far from home, all the way to my home where she will have new eyes grown, or if that proves impossible, she will have biomech replacements fitted. She will become one of a handful of Shan ever to leave your system, joining the select group headed by Tei'Varyk and the brave crew of *Naktlon*.

"I make the following offer to you, not as a representative of the Alliance, but as a representative of my own planet, Snakeholme. I'm offering to allow Shan to immigrate to my world, and set up a colony there. I will provide transportation along with Shima on *Grafton*, and will provide all necessary materials to allow the colony to flourish. In exchange I ask only that your people honour our laws and defend the planet should that ever be necessary... it won't be. Snakeholme is my regiment's home base, and its defence comes second only to the defence of the Alliance itself."

"You are inviting us to join the viper clan?" Jutka asked and the excitement died down to hear the answer.

Burgton didn't need James' warning look. "You call my regiment a clan—the viper clan. We are not a clan of any sort, or a caste. We are a specialised military unit. My men and I have been enhanced to better fight Merkiaari. I'm not offering your people enhancement, only a home with us on Snakeholme. Think of this as your first new colony outside your home system—a safe place for younglings to grow up. Another basket for your eggs if you will."

No one spoke for the longest time, but inevitably politics raised its ugly head. It started when one of the traditionalists spoke up to reiterate his position regarding Child of Harmony's reconstruction, as if the last fifteen minutes had not occurred. Burgton sagged. His offer had fallen upon deaf ears. They would go on debating for the rest of the day and achieve nothing. It made him feel sad and his age. He was so very tired of people making the same mistakes over and over. Human or Shan, it made no difference. He was so tired of the same senseless excuses.

# 6 ~ The Blind Hunter

Shima sat quietly in the centre of her contemplation grove. She preferred sitting on the rocks next to the pool and facing east into the sun. She couldn't see it any more, her long feared blindness had finally come to pass, but she could at least feel its warmth on her face and remember it. The grove was at the rear of the house she had lived in with her father and her sib before the war, and it had suffered no ill effects from the conflict. Much of the city had burned in the early days of the Merkiaari invasion, and later during its liberation, many districts had been bombed by the Humans to flush the aliens out, but random chance had spared her district. It was on the opposite side to the line of march that the Merki had chosen from the port and took no damage, then later, Tei'Burgton's tactical plan had used the blasted zones of the city as entry points and her district was spared again.

Tei'Burgton's plan had made perfect sense to her when he had explained it to James. She had been there and translated for the other resistance team leaders. The Merkiaari had been softened up by artillery and the bombing preceding it to give the vipers the advantage. It had worked and the Merki in Zuleika had been wiped out in a few cycles of intense fighting. She looked back proudly on those times. Fighting side by side with James and later with Gina burned brightly in her memory. A good thing, as her life had burned down to embers now. Like the last glowing coals in a dying campfire, her time was over.

Before the war she had been a gardener, an agricultural geneticist, and had enjoyed her work at the Centre for Agricultural Research. There she had worked upon new variants of food crops with her colleagues, and expanded their knowledge of genetics. It was an expanding field; a relatively new one within her caste of scientists and engineers. She had followed her father into the caste, but her interests did not lean toward engineering as his had done. Her mother had also been an engineer, and had worked with her mate researching and designing new technologies. Shima sometimes wondered if her mother would have understood the choices she had made in her life. She hoped so. Choices were a thing of the past now. She had none left to make. Her life had narrowed down to waking and sleeping... all of it the same, all of it in darkness.

Shima took a deep breath and chuffed, expelling the air in a low groaning roar. It was a quiet expression of despair. She held in the more violent and scream-like roar she wanted to voice. It would feel so good to roar her challenge to the world. Good but pointless. Who was there to answer it? Back in primitive times, someone in her position would have left the clan to wander the wilds and challenge the wild things to a last glorious hunt, or seek out an old rival for one last battle. She would have travelled to an enemy village perhaps, and roared her battle cry like the time in the wilderness when she had fought Merki in the dark to rescue Merrick's family, but now in modern times she was trapped and cared for like a youngling. Held prisoner by love in a life she loathed by her sib and her sib's mate. Chailen and Sharn lived with her and cared for her, when they should have been on their own cementing their bond with lovemaking and the siring of cubs. She was a burden to them; she felt it no matter their rejection of such notions.

The situation was all kinds of wrong.

Shima remembered how proud she had been when Chailen mated Sharn deep within the protective environs of Kachina Twelve. The war had raged above them, but deep within the keep protected by the mountain's bones, an age-old ceremony had taken place reaffirming life and Shan traditions. Kazim had been there with her, forced to leave his camera switched off and uncomfortably aware of how unusual his presence was. Mating ceremonies were private affairs for family only, but he wasn't the only stranger there. Chailen had insisted James should come too, and to make their number harmonious had also invited Brenda—his mate. That had embarrassed Shima because using the harmonies as an excuse to invite Brenda suggested Kazim was there as Shima's mate, which he was not. Sharn's parents and sibs hadn't seemed to mind the break with custom. They were delighted to meet Humans, and everyone knew Kazim. He was famous because of the broadcasts. Kazim had filmed the Merki invasion and Shima's escape from Zuleika. His work documenting the war had assured his future would be bright.

Shima wondered what he would do now the fighting was done. He hadn't decided as far as she knew. She had asked him during a brief visit a few cycles ago, but he had been far more interested in her life and desires. She knew he worried for her, but there was nothing he or any Shan could do for her. Kazim had left with her question unanswered.

The war was over; Kazim must find something else to do just as millions of others must. The fighting had raged for almost two orbits... what did Humans call an orbit? A year, that was it. The fighting had been brutal on Child of Harmony, but on Harmony—the homeworld—it had been devastating. Child of Harmony was a colony world with millions of people making their homes here, but homeworld numbered its population in the billions. The Merkiaari had smashed every population centre in an effort to kill Shan quickly and efficiently. Millions had died in the first moments, and millions more each cycle thereafter until the landings. Only then, could her people fight back and defend those left alive. No one knew how many had died altogether, but the number was high. A billion dead, two? Such numbers were too huge to wrap her mind around. Shima knew that estimates would be wildly low on homeworld because her people had lived in large cities and most of them had been hammered into nothing but holes in the ground. As a percentage, her guess would be close to 40% dead on homeworld. A terrible number to be sure, but without the Human fleet's intervention it would have been much worse. The Shan would have become extinct.

The Alliance had sent Tei'Burgton and the vipers to fight the Merkiaari, but it hadn't left things all to him. It had dispatched Fifth Fleet together with huge numbers of ground troops, and that had been decisive. The Merkiaari were doomed at that point, though they knew it not. The fighting had taken time; Merkiaari did not surrender, ever, but the end result had no longer been in doubt. Both worlds were free of Merki taint now. The entire system was clean.

Shima stood. She had been sitting for segs and her legs needed exercise. She wished she could run, but although the harmonies gave her some sense of the world around her, she could only sense live things. She couldn't run in the city; she would be under the first car that crossed her path. Not a form of suicide that appealed. Besides, if she started running she didn't think she could make herself stop.

Shima huffed a long breath out in a pained sigh as blood rushed into numbed legs. She couldn't run from herself.

Her blindness forced Shima to live within the harmonies all the time if she wanted to function even at her current limited level, and it had caused an unexpected side effect. Her gifts had always been strong, but constant use had honed her skill to a fine edge. The harmonies could only reveal living things such as animals and people. That had always been true for everyone, but Shima had found that she could discern individual plants now as well. Before going blind, she had only the vaguest sense of life from them, like a background to the more vivid colours of other people or the animals she hunted with her father. She had never thought to try for more, never needed to separate that background into individual sources, but her blindness had forced her to use everything she had to make life bearable.

The plants bordering the paths allowed her to navigate the grove, like a ground car used street lighting at night to follow the road. In her head, she followed a ribbon devoid of life that in the world was a narrow gravel and shell covered path that crunched pleasantly under foot. The harmonies let her "see" the plants Chailen had planted for her along the path. They were her guide. Shima was grateful, truly she was, but she grieved the need to vandalise her grove. The placement of the guide plants clashed with the natural harmony she had striven to maintain here. They stood out, they had to, but that meant they were not in harmony with her grove. The entire point of a contemplation grove was harmony, and her blindness had blighted hers.

Shima chuffed her distress, her useless eyes burned hot with the need to cry, but she forced them not to. The Blind Hunter they named her, thinking to honour her deeds not knowing then or now how she hated the title. All of her life she had feared her growing blindness, hated the weakness that made her a cripple among Shan, and they had labelled her with it as if it were nothing. Labelled her and thought they were honouring her.

Shima paused and took a huge steadying breath. Forced her thoughts away from the anguish and toward other things. She dropped onto four legs, suddenly feeling the need to stretch. She reached forward as far as she could with her forelegs and dug her claws into the gravel enjoying the texture of the shell and gravel mix she had chosen when they bought the house. She lowered the front half of her body, but kept her rear legs straight forcing her spine to bow the wrong way. She groaned in pleasure as her joints popped, and her tail flexed straining straight out from her. Shima straightened up and then shook out her pelt before continuing her walk, this time staying on four feet.

Shima used the guide plants and the barren ribbon of nothing between them to wander. She walked the path, circling her gardens and the grove at its heart, and then turned aside on a whim to submerge herself into the trees and shrubs she had cultivated to please the harmonies. She avoided the few winding paths she had laid out to help maintain the garden and chose bare earth to walk upon. The trees surrounded her in peace and silence. As a general rule, the few avian species native to Child of Harmony avoided built up areas. They were rarely seen in the towns and cities, even in the parks they were few. Here, she was utterly alone and without thought, she fell into the familiar rhythm of the silent stalk. Her father's skills were hers. He had taught her everything he knew and she was an apt pupil. She could have been deaf for all the sound she made now. The silence was complete.

The harmonies showed her she was alone. No people, no animals of any kind, no predators, no prey. The garden was barren, like her life. Shima chuffed, the low groan-like roar of a wounded Shan, not even aware she was doing it now. How long she moved through the garden she did not know; segs certainly, but finally she returned to her starting point. She stopped at the edge of her contemplation pool, and dipped her head into the cool water for a drink and to cool her face. She held her breath for as long as she could, wishing she could hold it forever and let it all be over, but the harmonies interrupted her stupidity.

Chailen was in the garden and heading her way. Shima pulled her head out of the water and shook. The water flew from her, and she pushed herself up onto two legs to meet her sib.

"We have visitors, Shima. Won't you please come inside to greet them?" Chailen said softly, almost begging her sib to agree.

Shima wished Chailen would not beg; it made her feel very bad. Couldn't her sib understand that her garden was all she had left? Could she not realise that without eyes, all she had left were the harmony given gifts that allowed her to sense her living surroundings? If she went inside, she would drown in darkness. She sighed. She didn't have the strength or will to explain again. Her shoulders slumped.

"Yes, Chailen," she said flatly.

Shima couldn't see her sib's expression, but the harmonies showed her the emotions behind it. Chailen's aura had dimmed and slowed its usually energetic motion, and the colours edged toward the darker tones of unhappiness. It made her feel worse knowing she was the cause.

"I'm sorry, my sib. I'm so very sorry."

"Don't," Chailen said sounding close to tears. "This isn't your fault. You've done nothing wrong. Nothing about this is your fault."

Shima flicked her ears in agreement for Chailen's sake, but one thing about this *was* her fault; at least one and that was the way she had allowed herself to linger on, dragging Chailen and her mate down with her.

Chailen took her left arm and pulled Shima toward the house. "You haven't asked who has come to visit," she said trying to sound cheerful.

Shima's tail rose and gestured a shrug before she could prevent it. She didn't say that whoever it was didn't make any difference to her. Instead, she tried to put a little interest into her voice.

"Just distracted, my sib. Who has come calling?"

"Can you not sense them from here?" Chailen teased, and squeezed Shima's arm. "Sharn is very impressed."

Impressed was he? That meant the visitors were important. She hadn't tried to sense anything beyond the garden for a long time now. The house and garden were her life, and she had tried to pretend that the rest of the world did not exist. In a way, it didn't if she couldn't see it. She could reach out with the harmonies and "see" who her visitors were right now if she wished. Assuming they had met before she would recognise them. Everyone was unique in the harmonies.

"I haven't tried," Shima admitted. "Should I do anything?"

"You look fine, though I can tell you were on four feet recently and not on the path. Perhaps a quick wash of hands?"

"If you think it best," Shima said, her brief foray of pretending interest already failing. "A quick wash first then."

Shima allowed Chailen to lead her into the dark.

Once inside and thoroughly helpless, Shima decided that if she had to come inside, and it was obvious that she did, she might as well use it to advantage. She would allow Chailen to do her up right, a full and proper grooming to please and not shame her before guests. That way, Shima reasoned, Chailen and Sharn would be pleased, the important guests would not be scandalised, and she could probably get away with hiding in her garden for a few cycles afterward without Chailen making her come inside.

Satisfied with her new goal, Shima asked Chailen to help with her grooming in the shower room. Chailen sounded pleased. It was pathetically easy to please Chailen these days, and Shima vowed she would remember to let her sib do things for her more often, even when all she really wanted was to be left alone.

Mindful of waiting visitors, Shima washed quickly so that Chailen could go to work on her pelt with the dryer. It was an old battery powered thing that before the recent war would have been relegated to a forgotten corner, but now had become a treasure. The city was still without electricity, and any battery-powered tech was worth much because of that. Sharn had proudly gifted his mate with it after trading with a clever male who made a living modifying such things to work with a solar cell for recharging. The hot air and brush parting her fur felt wonderful to Shima. She could try to repay her sib the favour in kind. She didn't need eyes to groom her sib, by touch would work as if they were younglings again.

"This is wonderful," Shima said facing into the hot blast of air. She closed her useless eyes and let her ear tufts blow back. "Amazing how a proper wash can makes things feel better."

"Hmmm," Chailen said. "At least we have fresh water here. The other districts don't even have that."

"Is it very bad out there?" Shima said because Chailen expected her to, not because she cared. "How do people live?"

"With difficulty. Most still live in a keep, but come here to salvage things to trade. Some are trying to start over. I saw them clearing streets. I swear some of them were talking about bringing machines to pull down the old buildings to make room for new ones."

"They would do better to wait. We need electricity here before anything else, and water to all districts of course. I remember seeing... before I mean. We fought the Merki in amongst those buildings and I saw broken water mains."

Chailen moved and brushed Shima's back legs and tail. "True, but I think they plan to do that as well."

Shima growled in annoyance. "Snow will stop them before they can finish. Has Sharn mentioned going back to the keep for the winter with you?"

Chailen remained silent, and Shima's mood darkened further. He had then. No doubt Chailen had refused to go back to the keep for Shima's sake. The keeps, refuges against the Merkiaari though they were, would be a living hell for her. Shima remembered longing to be safely under a trillion tons of rock when she'd led Kazim out of the city. Now the thought horrified her. She was barely holding on to sanity now, and she spent most of her time in the garden. Under the mountain, she would go insane, lost in the dark, a never-ending void. She couldn't do that, she just couldn't.

"You should go," Shima whispered. "It's... it's the right thing for you."

Chailen turned off the dryer. "Done. We must go down to our guests. I think keeping such important personages waiting even a half seg like this is close to insult."

Shima blinked. She sounded as if she hadn't heard a word. "Chailen—"

"No!" Chailen snapped. "I do not hear, I won't hear. Not this!"

Shima sighed and stood up on her hind legs. As before, Chailen took her arm to lead the way through the eternal dark to where Sharn entertained their guests.

The harmonies revealed the room to be crowded. Apart from Sharn, there were two more Shan males and three Humans, one of them female. She recognized all of them and felt her spirits rise despite herself. Kazim was a regular visitor, if she considered a few times a season regular. She supposed she did. Varya though, he had never visited before—too busy hunting down Merkiaari stragglers. She could hardly wait to quiz him about his missions and adventures. The Humans though...

"James!" Shima cried in delight, and his aura brightened as he came forward to greet her. Chailen stepped away, making Shima sway a little before James hugged her. "I'm so happy to see you. How is Brenda?"

James hugged her tightly, pressing his cheek to the side of her face. "She's fine, still busy as always. She sends her love."

"Take mine back to her," Shima said, clutching him and holding on. She hoped he couldn't tell how desperate that hold was, but he probably did. She was shaking. "What are you doing here? I thought you were still following Tei'Varyk around."

James stepped back a little but held her hands. "Oh yes, I'm still doing that. Not sure for how long though, now that the fighting is done. I expect the Council will give me the boot—err that is, replace me—anytime now. I'm sure the elders will be glad to see the back of me."

"Nonsense!" Sharn said, and Chailen agreed. "Our people honour you highly, James. You will always be welcome."

"Well," James said and cleared his throat. "Yes well, it won't be a Shan decision I'm afraid. Besides that, I'm no politician, Shima. I'm a teacher. You can't really blame the Council for wanting a proper diplomatic mission here."

Shima snorted derision. "Blame them? Perhaps not, but will this diplomatic mission be as useful as you've been? I doubt it."

James laughed. "I know what you mean, but at least a proper mission will have the authority to make decisions that bind the Council. I really don't have any at all, Shima. I can only advise and strongly suggest, not make binding agreements."

"Do you miss your students then?"

James didn't answer immediately, but then he sighed abruptly. "No, not really. There's a very old saying among my people, Shima. It goes: those who can, *do*, those who can't, *teach*. I've found watching history being made an addictive thing. I much prefer being part of it over teaching others about it after the fact."

Shima could understand that. She turned toward Kazim where he stood watching. "So, you decided to show up did you?"

The others laughed.

"I've been busy!" Kazim protested. "Besides, the last time I visited, you ignored me."

Shima spluttered. "That's because you kept asking impertinent questions. I bet you have that camera in here right now!"

"Well..."

"You have?" Shima gasped. "You're unbelievable!"

Chailen laughed. "He has the camera with him, Shima, but I made him switch it off until we give him permission to use it."

"They always argue like this. They sound like an old mated couple," Sharn whispered to Varya. "Do you think they will?"

"Mate you mean?" Varya said. "Wouldn't surprise me in the least."

Shima's ears heated and she turned to Varya. "Be welcome to my home, Varya. May you live in harmony. What took you so long to visit me?" She knew his reasons already, but wanted to twit him like in the old days. "Replaced me quick, didn't you." The room went uncomfortably quiet and Shima cursed herself. She hadn't meant them to take it seriously. "I didn't mean that."

"I know," Varya said. "But there's truth in your words. I did replace you, or a replacement was provided. His name is Justika, and he's a fine warrior and hunter, but he's not you, Shima. No one could ever replace you."

"I..." Shima's voice failed and she bowed to him. "I thank you." She stepped further into the room to greet Gina and General Burgton, but stumbled into the table. Gina was across the room in a blink to catch her. Vipers were very fast. "Thank you. My own fault. I rarely come in here now and I forgot it was there."

"You all right now?" Gina said in flawless Shan and still holding her. "Would you rather sit?"

"Yes I... yes I will sit," Shima said in a small voice. Her confidence had taken a beating. She couldn't even cross a room without help. Gina guided her to a mat and she sat. "Please, everyone sit and be comfortable."

The harmonies showed Shima everyone moving to find places. Chailen left the room but came back inside just moments later with refreshments. Everyone took a cup and murmured their thanks.

"General Burgton, I did not mean to be rude. Welcome, may you live in harmony."

"Thank you, Shima," Burgton said. "No need for apologies and no need for ceremony between friends. I get way too much of that."

Shima blinked uncertainly. "You're here as a friend?"

"I am," Burgton said. "I'm sure others will think of this visit as politics in action or will attribute some other nefarious reason to be named later, but be assured that I'm here to support you and a promise made to you."

Shima's heart pounded. "A promise," she whispered, trying not to let hope overwhelm her.

"It's time, Shima," Gina said gently. "I'm sorry you had to wait so long, but the fighting on Harmony took longer than I thought. That's done with now. We, vipers I mean, are going home within days. Fifth Fleet is staying of course, but it's time for us to go home. We're here to bring you with us to our ship."

Shima reached to Chailen who was standing nearby. She clutched her sib's hand. "I'm to go with you?"

"If you still want to, yes," Gina said. "I promised you new eyes, Shima. You must come home with me to... for us to fix you."

"Gina is correct. I'm sorry we can't do the work here, Shima," Burgton said. "My ship is equipped to repair my vipers not Shan. We'll need to run tests and learn more about your people from a genetic standpoint before we can try to grow new eyes for you. Fifth Fleet does not have the expertise, but I have everything you need on Snakeholme. Will you come?"

"Yes," Shima said managing not to shout the word. "I'll come right now." Chailen squeezed her hand.

"There's time," Gina soothed. "Our people are still loading our gear back aboard. The plan is to jump outsystem the day after tomorrow."

"Can we come?" Chailen said abruptly, and Shima looked

up sharply. "Sharn and I have talked about it. He and I are healer caste and although I'm still in training, he has passed his testing. We can help you, General, but even if you do not need us, Shima is my only sib. I want to be there."

Shima didn't allow Burgton to answer. "You and Sharn should stay here, Chailen. You've done enough for me already."

Chailen growled angrily. "You... no, we have guests. I will not fight with you. Imagine yourself in my place, Shima. Imagine me blinded, or paralysed, or any other terrible thing that leaves me helpless. At what point would you say I've done enough for you, Chailen, you're on your own now?"

"That would never happen!" Shima snapped without thinking. "I mean... I..."

"You see?" Chailen said smugly. "You can't defend it. You cannot put limits on my love, just as I cannot put limits upon yours."

"But your lives here!"

Sharn laughed. "What life?" he said bitterly. "Everything's gone; everything I worked for is destroyed. I'm not even a healer anymore. I spend my days grubbing in the dirt and ruins looking for things to trade. That's my life now."

Shima was stunned. Sharn had said nothing about this! She realised now that Chailen and Sharn had been shielding her from the reality of life in post war Zuleika, and she hadn't questioned it. By the harmonies what a fool she was. They had cared for her, fed her, and seen to it that they all survived in a city without power and she had spent her time in the garden. Oblivious.

"I'm so sorry," Shima said. "If not for me you would still be in the keep—"

"Don't start that again! Our lives don't orbit yours, Shima. You're not the centre of the harmonies cursed universe!" Sharn cried. Chailen tried to calm him, but he wasn't having any of it. "Stop coddling her! It's made her worse not better!"

Shima's temper flared. "I'm blind, curse you! What do

you want me to do, go out and trade with you? I can't see!"

"And that's all there is to you, true? You haven't got a disability; you *are* a disability and a liability to those who love you."

Shima spluttered. "How dare you! I'll rip your ears out by the roots!"

Sharn laughed. "The Blind Hunter could certainly do it, but you're just poor blind Shima aren't you? Nothing to fear in you, is there? Woe, I can't do anything, woe I'm blind I wish I were dead."

"You're baiting me?" Shima whispered feeling the rage building. It felt good. "Why are you doing this to me?"

Sharn was abruptly calm. "Do you know what it's like knowing your mate will cry herself to sleep every night because her only sib wants to die?"

"No," Shima whispered, chilled by his words. Chailen was doing that? Oh harmonies say it wasn't so.

"Do you know how helpless and useless that makes me feel?" Sharn went on relentlessly. "How about you stop thinking about what you *can't* do, and start thinking about what you *can* do for Chailen?"

"I'm sorry—"

"I don't want your apology; I want to see some action!"

Shima's rage slowly cooled, but what could she do? She didn't want to be blind and helpless! It wasn't her fault! That was all true, but perhaps she could try harder not to let Chailen see her despair, and if she really could be cured, it wouldn't even be pretence any more.

The harmonies showed her that all the Humans were worried now. She could tell quite a bit about them after living and fighting beside James for so long. Their scent combined with the harmonies told her she needed to calm things down.

"General, what do you say?" Shima said turning toward him. "Would your invitation stretch to three?"

Before Burgton could answer Varya spoke up. "Earlier

today you made elder Jutka an offer, General. I wonder would you consider making that offer directly to the warrior caste?"

"Well I..." Burgton seemed confused.

"What's this about?" Shima said annoyed that her question had been derailed. This was about Chailen and Sharn, not the warrior caste. "And what does it have to do with me and my family?"

James answered. "On our way to you we visited with elder Jutka at her home, Shima. Kazim was there and recorded the meeting if you're interested, but basically, it was about the debate between Tei regarding the reconstruction. General Burgton was asked his opinion, which he gave to them, and afterward he offered to allow some of your people to immigrate to his planet. He hasn't said so to me, but I believe the idea was to strengthen the position of progressive Tei while underpinning Kajetan's decision to join the Alliance."

"Essentially correct, Professor," Burgton said. "There's more to it, however. I strongly believe in the idea of expansion, and that if a Shan colony were to be established outside of this system—whether that's on Snakeholme or not—its colonists would become role models to your people. I believe that might kick-start a real drive toward exploration. As I said earlier, the Merkiaari are out there. They will be back. The entire Shan species is dependent upon the two habitable worlds of this system. That isn't safe!"

Burgton calmed himself and went on in a milder tone. "We lost many worlds to the Merki two hundred years ago, and those worlds were cleansed of Human life. That could happen very easily to the Shan here. Think of that. Shan become extinct. They must scatter themselves throughout the stellar neighbourhood. Not should, not maybe will one day, but must and as quickly as possible!"

"Calmly General, calmly," James soothed. "You're right, but so are the Shan. Colonising nearby worlds should be a goal, but it cannot be an immediate priority. They do need to rebuild their worlds, their orbital infrastructure, and their fleet, before looking beyond this system. A half-arsed movement to colonise new worlds this soon would be worse than not doing it at all. Each colony will have to be defended and self-sufficient to make the effort worthwhile."

"I know that," Burgton said testily. "But they're already debating the issue, Professor. They need to get the idea of exploration as a good thing firmly fixed in their minds now. You know our history. The Shan are in danger of making the same mistakes we did."

"I could say it's their mistake to make, but I have too much admiration for them not to agree with you," James said. "Your idea was a good one, *is* a good one. You should try again with Kajetan."

"I had planned to."

"As I was saying," Varya said breaking in. "When word reaches the warrior caste that you have offered immigration to my people, and that The Blind Hunter is going, you will have more volunteers than you can possibly fit aboard your ship, General. It's a matter of honour."

"Honour," Gina said. "You mentioned that before. What does that mean in this situation?"

"Simply put, Shima is a hero—" the *hero* in question made a rude noise, but Varya ignored it. "—to my people. That's important, but the circumstances were extraordinary. She is scientist caste not warrior, she saved lives at risk of her own and killed Merkiaari in spectacular fashion, and on top of that, she fought as part of the resistance and was blinded helping to save thousands of warriors at Charlie Epsilon.

"If Shima had been warrior caste, most of her achievements would have been considered her duty no matter how extraordinary the deeds. She would still be a hero, but what she did to become one would have been expected of her as a warrior."

"I'm still not getting it," Gina said.

Shima sighed and explained. "It's foolishness, Gina. I'm

a hero because Kazim filmed me doing what anyone in my position would have done as we escaped the city. Killing the Merki was my pleasure, and anyone would have done it considering how we all feel about them. The warriors at Charlie Epsilon though are a little different; they feel that they owe me an honour debt for saving their lives because it wasn't my duty—not a warrior you see? I don't agree. I just did what needed doing, but that won't change their minds. If they think following me off world will repay the debt, then that's what they will want to do."

"Then we should let them," James mused. "How many could you take, General?"

"*Grafton* is a *Hunter* class transport. We don't build them that big anymore. She can carry two full battalions with equipment."

"So two thousand Shan would fit?"

"Easily," Burgton said. "No mechs, no tanks or APCs, no artillery. As long as they embark with a few kilos of personal gear they would travel in comfort."

"Hmmm," James said. "I wonder what Tei'Varyk would recommend. Two thousand warriors wouldn't make for a good colony in my opinion. Ideally, all the castes should be represented."

"Harmony is always to be preferred," Sharn agreed. "There should be people from all the castes, and their families should accompany them of course."

Varya growled. "This is a warrior caste debt of honour."

"No," Shima said, finally hearing enough. "This is about my friends taking Chailen, Sharn, and me home with them when they leave. If the warrior caste or Kajetan want to take up General Burgton's offer, they can talk with him before we leave the system. Will you take us with you, General?"

"Of course. We have the rest of the day for you to pack your things and close up your house. No need to rush things."

Rush things? Shima had been waiting for this for more

than an orbit, an entire orbit in darkness. She couldn't leave fast enough.

* * *

# 7 ~ Electronic Dreams

"Are you sure, Shima?" Chailen said worriedly. "Healer Hymas says she can make you sleep through the entire journey. You would wake at Snakeholme. There's no need to start this testing now."

*Grafton* had been in foldspace for only a few days—and yes, the jump transition was as bad as all the warnings said it would be—when Shima realised she had a serious problem. She really should have expected it, but she had been so excited to be on her way to Snakeholme, that she had ignored common sense. The reason she had spent so much of her time in her garden was that she had become morbidly claustrophobic since losing her sight. It was stupid, but spending all of her waking hours in darkness was driving her insane, and there were no gardens to hide in aboard ship.

"Chailen is right, Shima," Lieutenant Hymas said. "I can easily administer something to make you sleep. You would fall asleep here and awake on Snakeholme. It would be as if no time had passed for you."

"Tempting, but no," Shima said. She would not be

a coward, by the harmonies she would not! "I really do appreciate the thought, but if we can do this now, it will save time later."

"True. If you're sure, then?"

Shima flicked her ears affirmatively. "I'm sure."

Chailen sighed. "Always so brave, always so impatient. Why can't you take the easier path once in a while?"

Varya snorted. "She's The Blind Hunter. What do you expect?"

"She was my sib first, and she's always been like this."

Sharn picked up the syringe preparing to take the blood samples. "She must have been a terrible trial for your father."

"Hey, sitting right here!" Shima protested over the other's laughter.

"Are you sure you don't mind the audience?" Hymas whispered to Shima. "I can have them out of here in a blink. Just say the word."

Shima's tail lifted and gestured a shrug. "I don't mind. My people are more group orientated than Humans I think. James mentioned it to me once. He said his people preferred more *alone time*. Privacy doesn't mean the same to us as it does to you."

"No?" Hymas said.

"Shan like living together. We groom each other and like to touch," Kazim said. "That's especially true between sibs. Haven't you noticed how Chailen always stands very close to Shima, and holds her hand or touches her shoulder?"

"Well, yes I did but I thought it was because Shima couldn't see her."

"I can sense her near, I don't need touch for that," Shima said. "I feel when she's nearby and can smell her scent, and the harmonies let me see all of you if I use it that way. I can *see* anything living that way, but nothing else."

"Fascinating. I can hardly wait to chat more about the harmonies. Humans don't have such gifts. But back to your situation. Are you sure you want them all here, even Kazim and the camera? He's not family is he?"

"Not family," Shima agreed, "but he's a friend. I'm used to him and his little annoying habits."

"My camera is not an annoying habit!" Kazim protested. "It's a tool. Without it, I'd be like a warrior without his beamer."

"It's true," Shima said. "When we first met he was aiming the thing at the Merkiaari in Zuleika just like a weapon. I didn't realise he was mad when I first saw him you understand."

Varya chuffed in amusement. "I remember watching that broadcast in the keep. Everyone loved it. It was very funny."

Shima growled low. It hadn't been funny for her at the time. She had met Kazim at the end of a long chase, and she hadn't been doing the chasing. She had barely escaped a Merki death squad after she killed one of them, and had run straight into a firefight that Kazim was filming. She was glad he was here with her. Varya as well of course, but she was very fond of Kazim despite his being annoying. Perhaps a little more than fond. Maybe.

Varya and Kazim had joined Chailen and Sharn as her chaperones only segs before *Grafton* got underway. They were the last to board after Kajetan asked Burgton for his permission to send them along. It was Shima's understanding that Kajetan wanted them to investigate the possibility of a follow up mission to Snakeholme to found a colony there—a small one to begin with. Kajetan was being unusually coy, but she had many pressures on her right now. Burgton's direct offer to her had fallen on fertile ground it seemed. Kazim was a popular figure. His films and shows would be seen widely on Harmony. When he returned home, Shima had no doubt he would have enough stuff to persuade even the most militant traditionalist that a colony on Snakeholme was a good idea.

"So, what's first?" Shima said bringing things back full

circle.

"Blood and tissue samples," Sharn said. "It won't hurt."

"Healers always say that," Shima said to Chailen who chuffed in amusement.

"No really," Sharn assured her. "Kazim and I have already done this. Didn't hurt, did it Kazim?"

"Well..." Kazim hedged. "It stung a bit."

"Nonsense," Sharn grumped. "Take no notice of him, Shima. He's just being annoying now."

Shima rolled her eyes. Kazim was Kazim. Not even the harmonies would ever change him.

Hymas chuckled at the by-play and patted Shima's shoulder. "Just lay back and enjoy the rest."

Shima did as she was bid. She swung her legs up onto the couch and settled back. Chailen adjusted the thing so that she was reclining comfortably at an angle, more sitting than lying down. Unlike Humans, Shan found laying flat on their backs very uncomfortable; they preferred doing it on their sides or fronts.

Sharn took four vials of blood and then used some kind of scraper in Shima's mouth for tissue samples. It tickled the roof of her mouth but didn't hurt. It didn't sting either except perhaps for her pride. She didn't like being poked and prodded but it was soon over so that the more interesting tests could begin.

"Okay Shima, the next part will be strange for you, but I assure you Humans have this test all the time without being harmed."

"I trust you Healer Hymas," Shima said. "Just tell me what you're doing as you do it. I'll be fine."

"Right then. In just a moment, I'm going to put a helmet on your head. You've seen the helmets that Human soldiers wear, yes?"

"Of course."

"Well this is similar in shape to those you've seen, but it isn't for protection. It's used to scan brain function. What it does is use micro-magnetic induction to stimulate various parts of the brain, and display the results in real time on my wall monitors over there."

"Can I ask a question?" Kazim said.

"I suppose so," Hymas said.

"Thank you. Why is this scan necessary? You already know Shima's eyes are the problem, not her brain."

"Good question," Hymas said sounding surprised but approving. "Although the plan is to use regen to fix Shima's vision, there's a chance we may not succeed. Some Humans can't use regen and it's possible Shan are the same. It won't matter if that turns out to be true. We can build her a pair of biomech eyes like vipers use. For those to work, we need a comprehensive map of the brain to find the vision centres where the eyes will send their data. Does that answer your question?"

"It does, thank you."

"You're welcome. Are you ready, Shima?"

"Ready," Shima said.

Shima tensed as the helmet lowered onto her head. It was overly large and not at all a good fit. She had imagined a padded and visored helmet the same as Gina and the other vipers used, but this thing must only be vaguely similar enough for Hymas to liken them because it didn't feel right at all. Hymas asked her to lower her ears if she could do that voluntarily. Shan could and Shima did. The helmet settled upon them, pinning her ears down. It was uncomfortable but not really painful. Hymas fussed with the fit, making some adjustments so that when she let go, the helmet stayed in place. Hymas muttered something about designing a proper scanning unit to fit Shan, and getting someone named Stone to make it for her, but a short while later she pronounced herself satisfied.

"Now don't move please," Hymas said. "A proper fit would let you walk around if you wanted, but we have to make do for now."

"All right," Shima said, her voice sounding muffled as if she had a bucket on her head. Her breathing sounded loud. "I'll try."

"Good. I'm going to send a standard calibration program first. It won't hurt. Ready?"

"Go ahead."

Shima didn't feel anything, but she certainly reacted. She couldn't help it. Eternal darkness was broken for the first time since the atomics had blinded her on Child of Harmony. She yelped in surprise and shock, and she couldn't stop herself from moving. She was so excited. The darkness slammed down again and Shima heard concerned voices shouting.

"I'm all right, Kazim!" Shima yelled over Kazim's cries. "Shut up, all of you! I'm fine. I'm sorry I moved Healer Hymas. Did I ruin your test?"

"No," Hymas said sounding a little shaky. "Did it hurt? It shouldn't have hurt. It never does, but the system is designed for Humans. Perhaps we should wait—"

Harmonies no! She wanted more of that wonderful light. To see again, even through this strange medium... it was wonderful.

"... didn't hurt, Kazim," Varya said. "Calm down. You heard her. She's fine."

"But she yelped in pain," Kazim said. He had moved to Shima's right side and was standing within reach. Shima carefully took his hand trying not to move her head. Kazim squeezed her hand. "Are you sure you're all right?"

"I'm fine, just excited. I saw light, Kazim! I haven't seen any for so long. I was surprised that's all."

"Light you say," Hymas said sounding professionally calm again. "Hmmmm. What colour, how bright? Did it flash or was it constant? Did you hear anything? What about smells?"

Shima felt swamped. She had been too excited to concentrate. She said so, and Hymas said it was fine. They would start over. Shima heard the disappointment in her voice though, and was determined not to mess up this time.

"Here we go, Shima. Concentrate now."

The light appeared again. "Blue."

"Good!" Hymas said. "And now?"

"Still blue... it's turning green... green now."

"Excellent," Hymas muttered and Shima heard her typing something rapidly. "Keep going."

"Green... slowly turning to yellow... yellow coming up... now!"

"Very good!" Hymas muttered. "Shan appear to see colour a little differently to Humans. We'll have to make allowances for that. Shouldn't be hard... need to fully map... and then change the parameters in the database. Program a Shan option to upload the correct set at the start of each session. Yes, that'll work. I wonder if they can perceive different spectrums.... hmmm. Very interesting. Depth perception might be different too. I bet they see in the dark like Avalonian badgers! Hah!"

Shima might have laughed if she had known what Hymas was talking about, but the Human healer was lost in the data and Shima was too happy luxuriating in the light to interrupt. She knew her eyes were dead, or damaged beyond seeing, but the helmet put the light directly into her brain. To her, it seemed her eyes were suddenly working again and she was looking straight into a coloured light. There was nothing but the light. It filled her vision and pushed out the panicky claustrophobic feeling she felt all the time. Her emotions lightened as the smothering dark lifted away from her. She couldn't help silently weeping tears of joy.

"Are you crying?" Chailen said in concern, and Hymas suddenly sounded worried again.

"What was that, crying?" Hymas said. "What's wrong, tell me!"

"Nothing," Shima blubbered. "It's wonderful."

"Hmmm. Well that was the first in the series. Ready for the next one?"

"Can we keep the light on?" Shima said hopefully.

"Sorry no. It would ruin the data."

"Oh," Shima said sadly. "Let's get it over with then." Darkness smothered her, but she forced herself not to cry out. "What's next?"

"Sound. I know what you're going to say, but it will all make sense later I promise. We're mapping your entire brain not just one part. The more we know the better."

"Fine, but my ears are trapped. I can hear you, but not very well."

"Don't worry about that. It will be like the light. Here take these controllers," Hymas put a small cylinder into each hand. "Feel the button on the top?"

"Yes."

"In a moment you will hear various frequencies of sound. When you hear something in the right ear, press the button in your right hand. When you hear it in your left, press the left button. Okay?"

"Sounds simple enough."

"You'll have to concentrate. The frequencies might be so high or low you can barely hear them."

"I will," Shima said.

"Here we go then."

Shima listened intently, and as Hymas said, she began hearing various tones. It was strange because she could tell her ears weren't hearing the sounds. Her ears were fine, but flattened upon her head the sound would be muffled and not clear. The sounds in her head were clear and pure. She used the buttons as instructed and the test was soon over. Hymas pronounced herself satisfied with the results.

The next phase of testing was quicker. It was scent and the follow up test for taste was equally as quick, but the results confounded Hymas. She said that Shan were nothing like Humans for taste and smell, and that because of the scent glands at the back of the Shan throat, taste and smell were intimately connected. The areas in the brain activated by the tests had what she called crossover.

"It's like your people have two noses," Hymas explained. "You can smell a scent with your nose but also taste it with the scent glands at the back of your throat. Your taste buds are like ours, but your noses are unbelievably sensitive. I can't think of any other species that come close to Shan in that area."

Shima was glad Hymas was excited, but it was all old news to Shima. She used to hunt with her father regularly, and had done so since her first nameday. She used her nose and scent glands all the time. It was part of being Shan.

"This next test will require you to be completely passive, Shima. Can you do that?" Hymas asked.

Kazim made a sarcastic noise and Varya laughed. Sharn chuffed, but turned his laugh into a cough.

Chailen squeezed Shima's hand. "Take no notice of them. You can do anything you set your mind to."

"When you say passive, what do you mean?" Shima said.

"The test will find your motor functions. The helmet will search for the areas that move your body. So for example, it will try to make you lift an arm or leg. All you have to do is let it work. Don't try to move your body or stop from moving. It will feel odd, but that's all."

"Sounds easy enough," Shima said doubtfully.

"Oh yes, it's easy," Hymas said. "Here we go then."

Shima let herself relax as if in meditation and that seemed to impress Hymas as the test progressed. She didn't struggle as each of her fingers and toes moved without her willing it. Her claws sprang out and retracted. First her left fist all at once, then her right. Then her feet. Lastly, each claw slid out one by one and back in. It did feel very odd, but not as odd as when her entire right leg lifted and the knee flexed.

Shima let the helmet run its test and when it had moved every part of her body, even her tail and ears—even though they were pinned down she felt them trying to turn and lift—she flexed every muscle to throw off the phantom feelings the machine had left behind.

"Good! Well done, Shima," Hymas praised. "We can take a break now if you want. You could start again tomorrow?"

And spend another cycle in darkness with nothing to do? Shima shuddered at the thought. The journey to Snakeholme would take about ninety cycles. That was an entire season. She had plenty of time to contemplate the dark. At least the tests were a distraction.

"If it's all right, I'd like to continue."

"It's more than all right with me," Hymas said. "But there's no rush. We have time."

"That's what worries me, Healer Hymas. I'm in the dark all the time. I hate it. I need the distraction."

"Hmmm, I think I can help with that. These tests will have a side benefit for you. I think you'll be very surprised and happy with the result."

Shima didn't know what the healer could mean, but if it distracted her she would be happy.

Hymas removed the scanning unit and Shima rotated her head on her neck to ease tension. It hadn't been heavy, but the effort not to move had begun to tell. It felt good to move her ears. Chailen helped her off the couch and they wandered the room for a bit. It was called sickbay or medical by the Humans. Hymas worked her data, collating and assessing while Shima worked the kinks out of her body.

A short time later, Shima was lying on her side practically falling asleep as another machine swallowed her into its guts. It was a computer tomograph machine, and produced detailed internal scans of a body. It was a restful procedure. All Shima had to do was hold still and breath regularly as the CT scan progressed. She was inside the thing for perhaps a half seg, no more than that.

After the full body scan, Hymas put the helmet back on Shima and asked a lot of questions. She was asked to recall events from her past, and other more recent events. Sharn helped with the questions. Lastly Hymas posed puzzles and math questions, nothing difficult, but enough to make Shima think carefully upon her answers.

There were no lights or sounds, just questions and plenty of whispering between Sharn and Hymas as they discussed what her answers revealed. When it was over, Shima asked about the last test. Sharn explained that it filled in a few blanks on the brain scan by locating the long term, short term, and logic centres. Hymas had expressed her surprise that Shan healers had not already mapped the brain as they were advanced in other areas of medicine. They were already advancing into genetics for example, but Sharn explained that mind healers used the harmonies in their work, not machines. Mind healers were specialists, and used their gifts to bring their patients peace and guide them back to harmony. Hymas questioned Sharn extensively about that and seemed very excited by it for some reason, but when she asked about brain chemistry and surgery, Sharn had no answers. Brain surgery was unknown to the Shan. That shocked Hymas into silence for the longest time, but then she explained that Humans used nanotech for surgical procedures, even in a patient's head, but before that, they had used laser scalpels and skilled hands.

At the end of that cycle, Shima felt satisfied that she had done something to help her situation at last. She was still blind, still walking the ship's corridors on Chailen's arm and in the dark, but the light she had seen in her head gave her great hope for the future. Surely the Humans were right and she would see again.

Hymas set a time two cycles hence for another visit to sickbay. Shima would have preferred sooner, but could do nothing about it. She had to wait. The time passed slowly, but it did eventually pass and a viper she hadn't previously met came to fetch her.

Shima was curled up in the corner of her cabin, trying to sleep, but she spent so much of her time doing that, she wasn't even a little sleepy. She considered meditating, but again she did that a lot and couldn't rouse the enthusiasm. A sound like a bell chiming interrupted her thoughts, and she remembered the Human word to say when that happened.

"Enter," Shima said clearly.

The hatch slid aside and a Human male entered her cabin. The harmonies told her she had not met this one before. He was a viper, all Humans aboard the ship were of course, and his aura was like a banked fire. There was power in him, a deep and strong well of power held in check. Shima sensed he would be strong willed but the banked fire in her head suggested he could erupt into a violent conflagration at need. He was the quintessential warrior.

It was a puzzle how different he seemed to the other Humans she had met. Then again, she hadn't met that many; they were all very different to her people in the harmonies. They burned brightly, vivid colours moving with violent frenetic motions. Shan were all pastels and gentle motion. Shima could only assume it was the intimate connection with the harmonies that caused the difference. Shan lived in harmony, or strove to do so. Humans had no connection with the harmonies and did not know what they lacked. It was very sad.

"Good morning, Shima. May you live in harmony. I'm Sergeant Stone. Call me Stone, I prefer it."

Shima pushed herself up to stand on two legs to greet him properly. She bowed to him. "A pleasure to meet you. May you live in harmony. Have you come to escort me to Healer Hymas?"

"Marian will be there, but you're mine today."

"Yours?" Shima said uncertainly. "How so?"

"I'll explain on the way," Stone said. "May I take your arm?"

Shima flicked her ears and held her right arm out. Stone took her arm and wrapped it over his. He held his arm up rigidly allowing her to hold on tightly or not as she chose.

She liked that. She would never tell her sib, but Chailen grabbed her arm and led her around like a youngling when she did this. Stone walked at her pace, letting Shima control things. When they reached the elevator needed to change decks on Human ships, Stone told her to stop and used the controls to call the car for her.

"Handy things, elevators," Shima said thinking about the ramps her people used at home. "I've had trouble with the spiral ways back home."

"Hmmm, you would. Humans sometimes suffer from vertigo too." Stone said. "My people use stairs and elevators everywhere; ladders as well, especially in ships for emergencies if the elevators lose power. You never want to be stuck in a box in the middle of a battle."

Shima shuddered. "I should think not!"

Stone chuckled. The elevator doors slid aside and they stepped into the car.

"Deck Two," Stone barked. "We're not going to sickbay."

Shima flicked her ears. Sickbay was on three. "Where then?"

"Rec room... that's recreation room. Marion told me she needed a scanning unit to fit a Shan. That was easy enough. I borrowed Kazim and Chailen to help me design one and test them for fit. They work like a charm, but the really interesting part was when she told me how much you liked the vision test."

"It was marvellous!" Shima enthused. "I hadn't seen light for the longest time. I was very excited."

"So she said. I... wait, we're here." Stone led the way out of the elevator and along the corridor. "Yes, Marion said you were pleased. She asked me to arrange something for you."

"Oh?"

"I don't know if you're aware but we use simulations to train and teach our people. Not just for war, mind you. We use the tech in the Alliance for all sorts of things. We even use a form of it for entertainment. Shan tell stories, right?"

"The sagas, teaching stories about our past," Shima agreed.

"Well we tell stories too, and we make them into shows to watch. They're not all for teaching; some are just fun to watch. This is a ship of war, Shima, so we don't have many aboard, but when you get to Snakeholme you could watch a different show every day for years and not see them all. Turn left here."

Shima did so and a door opened to let her enter. The harmonies revealed Kazim and Varya waiting with Healer Hymas. She couldn't tell the full dimensions, but the room felt big. Everyone greeted her, and she returned the greetings. Kazim seemed excited.

"You're going to like this," Kazim said.

"If it works," Hymas temporised. "Please don't get her hopes up, Kazim."

"Hey!" Stone said. "When I make something, it works. Aren't I the one who built a neural interface on Luna out of scrap? It will work."

"I hope so," Varya said. "It was very interesting to watch. I want to see what Shima thinks of it."

"Bring her over here, Ken," Hymas said and Stone led Shima over to join her. "Sit here, Shima."

Shima lowered herself onto a cushion placed on the deck and settled herself comfortably. Kazim and Varya joined her close by to watch proceedings. Hymas was kind enough to explain as she worked.

"You remember the other day when I said you might like the results of the testing?"

"Yes but you didn't explain."

"That's because I needed to be sure Ken could make it all work. I have a couple of new scanning units made to fit your people now, so you can keep this one after we make sure it works. We used one of our helmets for the chassis. You remember what they look like?"

Shima remembered them well. Viper helmets, like the

marine helmets she had seen used in battle, fully enclosed the head with a visored section that could polarise depending upon lighting conditions. She would not have been blinded if she'd had one; the visor would have changed to protect her eyes, but her people did not use armour of any kind. That would probably change soon due to association with Human warriors. Marine helmets were a drab green in colour, but could be programmed to blend better, and the visors were silvered by default because the inside surface was used for various displays like comm, sensors, and targeting. Viper helmets were black to match their uniforms and armour, and they also had comm to use with non-viper forces, but vipers had internal displays for sensors and targeting among other things. Their visors were black by default, but could be set to other colours and conditions the same way a marine helmet could.

"I remember," Shima said when she realised Hymas was waiting for an answer. "You put your medical scanner into one?"

"Basically yes," Stone said. "The hardest part was reshaping the helmet. Programming the nannies to do the work took a bit of time. I broke down a few spare scanners for parts. It worked out fine. I'm sure it won't win any prizes, and I won't bother with patents, but it will work."

Hymas chuckled. "Now your people are joining the Alliance, Shima, a lot of companies will be scrambling to make new products to sell to your people. Even medical equipment, I should think."

"Agreed," Shima said. "Kazim and I spoke of this. Our people must be careful."

"Yes," Stone said a little grimly. "There are good and bad people everywhere. I've no doubt there are companies that would bleed your economy dry if they could get away with it."

James had expressed his concern over that, and if she had heard right, Captain Colgan and James had both spoken with the elders about it before the war. They were forewarned. James seemed to feel that all of her people were kind and good, and would never do any wrong. After Shima stopped laughing, she had reassured James that her people were not innocent younglings, and that there were plenty who would give any Human scoundrels a run for their money.

"If it's as good as Kazim says, maybe you should sell it to my people," Shima said. "Before someone else does."

"I don't need the money," Stone said. "I could give the specs to Kazim and he could take it with him when he goes home. A gift to you and your people, Kazim."

"I am honoured!" Kazim said. "My people will have nanotech soon. We could make them and other things for ourselves then. You are generous."

"It's nothing," Stone said. "There are ways to do the same thing without a helmet, but we can't do it here."

"Well," Shima said. "It might be nothing or might be something. Can I try it to see for myself?"

"Sorry," Hymas muttered. "Didn't mean to talk over your head that way. Of course you can try it. We made it for you."

Shima sat still while Hymas put the helmet on her. It did indeed fit much better than the first one, and it even had room for her ears. She could only imagine what it must look like. Did it have holes in it for her ears or bulges? She couldn't tell. She ran her hands over it. Bulges, but subtle bulges and the visor was down. There was a long bundle of optical fibres coming out of the back connected to a computer of some kind. The old one didn't have anything like that, and she wondered why this did.

"It's so you can use it in your cabin if you want to," Stone explained. "The rec room has screens on the walls for watching shows and playing games. Your helmet can connect wirelessly to all of that here just as the medical scanners do in sickbay, but your cabin doesn't have the interfaces you would need."

Shima considered that and because her ears were hidden, she nodded in the Human manner. "What can I do with it?"

"Well let's see," Stone said. "Here we go."

Shima gasped as the wonderful light appeared in her mind, but it quickly became so much more. At first there was a blue light filling her vision, but then she realised it wasn't a blue light. Clouds drifted by. It was a sky! Shima heard the others talking about it, and realised they saw the sky as well.

"You see it too, Kazim?"

"Yes, on the big screens. We saw it before you came. Watch."

Shima was watching. The scene moved as if she had looked down. It made her just a little dizzy, but the sensation soon faded. A yellow sun was in the sky, and now she could feel the warmth. How did they do that? More sensations came to her. A breeze ruffled her fur, but that was impossible!

"Did you feel that?" Shima gasped. "A breath of wind and now I smell... something."

"That's great, Shima," Stone said sounding pleased. "I hoped you would."

"We can only see and hear what you can, Shima," Varya said. "We would need your helmet for anything else."

"He's right," Stone agreed. "What you're watching can be played on screens like the ones in here, or uploaded into our simulators. The simulators are far more capable machines, but your helmet uses similar principles, Shima."

"And the differences?"

"In a simulator your body is connected to the matrix as well as your mind. The helmet lets you see, hear, taste, smell, and feel the data, but you can't actually interact with it. If you use one of our simulators, you become part of the story. You would be able to walk, run, pick things up and do pretty much anything you can do in real life. In our training sims you get shot and it hurts. Everything feels real. Even eating."

"I would like to try that," Shima said.

"This ship isn't equipped with simulators," Hymas said. "It's just a troop transport, but perhaps we could arrange a session or two on Snakeholme if you're still interested by then."

Shima was more than happy with the helmet; it was so much more than she'd had before, but the sims did sound interesting. She watched the show as the view changed. There were mountains and deserts, oceans and forests all under that yellow sun.

"Is this your homeworld?"

"Not mine, no," Stone said, "but it is Earth. I wasn't born there. I have other clips of Alliance worlds like this for you to watch, and there are proper entertainment shows if you get bored with them, but they're meant for Humans. I'm not sure they'll make sense to you."

"They don't have to make sense," Shima said. "That I can see at all is a miracle, Stone. I owe you and Healer Hymas so much for this. I'll not forget."

"It's nothing really, finding and editing the data together wasn't too hard—" Stone began.

"It's not nothing to me," Shima interrupted. "It's everything! To be able to see again, even if only this way gives me hope."

"I'm glad you like it."

Shima watched entranced as world after world was displayed for her. Varya and Kazim became bored long before Shima was ready to stop. They left to find a meal leaving Shima alone. Hymas went back to sickbay and Stone to wherever his duties called him, but Shima stayed in the rec room basking under alien suns in her head.

* * *

**Part II**

# 8 ~ Snakeholme

General George Burgton, CO 501st Infantry Regiment stood
at attention on the parade ground squinting into the sun.
At his side was his exec, Colonel Dan Flowers. Clustered a
few steps to the right and a half dozen back stood his senior
officers, and way behind them and centred on Burgton stood
the entire 501st regiment, all at attention for this ceremony.
The solid block of the recently constructed 2nd Battalion
looked splendid, its six hundred plus viper units all wearing
their Sunday best—the regiment's Class A or dress uniform.
All of them newly recruited, enhanced, and elevated from
Colonel Stanbridge's now denuded training battalion. Every
man and woman stood ramrod straight in precise columns
and rows, squinting into the sun and emotionless. They
weren't, they couldn't be emotionless. No one could be after
seeing the broken but still proud remnants of 1st Battalion
making planet fall.

1st Battalion stood at attention to the side of the parade
ground in front of the Tech Centre. Their columns and rows
intentionally left ragged, the gaps in the formation left open

for wounded and dead comrades who were yet to land. They were a pitiful sight. They wore their battle dress blacks; their armour well used and scarred, but repaired back into service like the men and woman who wore it. They had the look in their eyes now that all veteran vipers achieved. The look that said they had seen hell and survived it. 1st Battalion had lost two-thirds of its number in battle against the Merkiaari, and most of them were true dead. Less than a hundred units were sleeping the little death of hibernation waiting to land still snug in their cryo units.

On the far side of the parade ground, Colonel Stanbridge had hastily ordered stands erected for Snakeholme's civilian delegation to sit when *Grafton* arrived back in system. Every city had sent a delegation to show respect, and Burgton appreciated it. They had never failed him, but it had been many decades since the regiment had last sallied forth in numbers requiring any kind of ceremony upon its return. This generation of civs certainly had never seen it before, but they had stepped up like their grandparents before them to show support.

One last small group stood alone, and Burgton was beginning to regret that state of affairs. The Shan had landed with him and 1st Batt, but having no official positions, they were now a lonely island standing off to his left. Apart. Abandoned. They looked confused and unsure what to do. Burgton made a snap decision and activated his comm.

"Gina, take charge of our guests. Make them part of your formation until after the ceremony. Shima and Varya deserve it. They fought with you."

"Thank you, sir. I was starting to feel wrong about them standing there," Gina replied, sounding embarrassed.

That pleased him. She was going to make a very fine officer. "I feel the same way. Next time, speak up."

"Sir!" Gina replied accepting the order. "Fuentez out."

"Burgton clear."

Out of the corner of his eye, he watched Gina gather

up the Shan and lead them back to her command. The few extra bodies did little to fill the holes in her formation. Alpha Company was barely there at all. Kazim as always was using his camera, and Burgton made a note to speak with him about that. He wanted to support Kazim in the furtherance of Kajetan's aims, but there was still security to consider.

He could put limits on Kazim's movements, but he instinctively felt that was the wrong move. He didn't want to come across as hiding things, even though he intended to do just that. First and foremost, Snakeholme's location was to be kept secret. That was non-negotiable, the rest of what he filmed here they could debate and edit before Kazim left for home, but he wanted that clear from the start. Nothing that could help ships find this system must leave the planet.

There were other things he didn't want even the Alliance to know about his operations here, and it was certain that anything Kazim showed his people would filter back to the Alliance eventually. Humans were in Shan space now and forever in one capacity or another, so he had to be careful what he revealed. Burgton didn't think, for example, that revealing the extent of his little navy would be a good idea. He had, technically at least, stolen all those ships. Even though they were headed for the breakers at the time, and he had rescued them, he doubted the Council would see them as legitimate salvage the way he did.

Two high velocity targets blinked into existence on his display appended with their designations. They were *Grafton's* dropships. Both ships hammered into the upper atmosphere in formation. They performed the evolution as if this were just another combat drop. The fiery entry into the atmosphere was a thrilling sight on the big screen set up for the civs to watch.

The dropships came in hot, but aborted the usual finale—the high speed landing—by roaring over the base, the sonic booms of their passage a salute to the audience. They separated and circled back, slowing to a gentle landing ready to offload their precious cargo.

Ramps came down and a few moments later the cryo units appeared in column floating on their grav cradles. Two columns, one from each dropship, proceeded toward the tech centre escorted and controlled by a score of medical personnel walking in step beside them. Almost four hundred cryo units entered the building, while the regiment watched holding their salutes to the wounded and the fallen.

Burgton's thoughts were far away, seeing all the other times this scene had played out for him. He had seen the like so many times. Faces and numbers changed, but the situation never did. Of these four hundred, less than hundred units would return to duty. It might take weeks or months, but they would rejoin 1st Batt. The others were true dead. Their databases, their logs, and everything they were would be uploaded to the archives kept safe under the mountain. Their memories and experiences would never truly be lost, but still he mourned them. How many more names would he add to the thousands already inscribed on the regiment's memorials before his own name joined them?

The civilian audience stood in silent respect as the cryo units entered the tech centre. The regiment ended their salute when the last unit was swallowed up and the dropships launched to go back to *Grafton*. Burgton dropped his hand and turned to dismiss his men. He nodded to his exec.

Colonel Flowers saluted and in his best parade ground voice roared. "Regiment! *Disssss-miss!*" His order was taken up and repeated by his subordinates.

"Battalion…"

"Company…"

"…*Disssss-miss!*" the orders echoed into silence.

Burgton watched his men pivot right face, stamping the ground in unison, and the sound hammered the air. With that last manoeuvre accomplished, the ceremony was over. Formations broke apart and murmured conversations filled the previous silence. Burgton moved toward Gina who had stuck with her charges. The Shan were watching everything with interest and she was chattering away with them in their own tongue. Burgton caught a few things. She was telling them about the base, where things were and what each of the buildings were used for.

"Welcome to Petruso Base and Snakeholme," Burgton said to the group as he approached. "I'm sure you've noticed the gravity here is greater than you're used to. It will take a few days... *cycles* for you to become accustomed. Please be careful and take that time to learn your way about the base. I'm going to ask Gina here to show you around and look after you."

"Just standing here is tiring," Shima agreed. "I feel very heavy."

Chailen and Sharn murmured similar things. Varya was watching the vipers milling around and didn't comment. Kazim filmed everything, but he was listening. His ears were canted toward them.

"Gravity is 1.29g Earth normal," Gina explained. "That's roughly 1.35 times Harmony's gravity. You're a third heavier here, Shima. You'll get used to it, but until you do, I want you to be careful. Especially on stairs. We have no spiral ways as you're used to."

Shan used ramps instead of stairs, it was something to do with their physiology, but they could climb. Stairs would not be impossible for them, just uncomfortable. Maybe they would just go to all fours. Burgton wondered in the decades ahead whether Human architecture would take Shan comfort into account. Would new buildings have elevators, stairs, *and* spiral ways incorporated into them? Stairs might become extinct in favour of spiral ways. They worked for both species equally well after all. Snakeholme would be the first Alliance planet to need them, he realised, and other things too. He needed to discuss that with his department heads. Even things like signs would need to be dual language... or would they? Would it be better to encourage the Shan to learn

English? He frowned uncertainly. He shook his head, time for that later.

"Gina, I'm allocating some of our spare officer housing to our guests. I believe the services are all in good order, but you'll need to draw on stores for furnishings."

"With your permission, sir, I'll have a couple of my men start on that now."

Burgton nodded, and Gina took a moment to contact her people via viper comm. While she did that, Burgton was thinking ahead to the work that had no doubt piled up on his desk while he was away. There were some projects running that he was very interested in, and one in particular was on his mind. He needed to talk with Liz, soonest. Liz Brenchley was head of industry, an extremely important position. Her department controlled Snakeholme's industrial complex including its single weapon's factory and the necessary smelters in orbit. Unlike some of his department heads, she was more than an able administrator. Liz was a very capable engineer and design theorist in her own right. He relied upon her expertise, especially for that certain project. He was eager to learn how far along with it she was.

Yes indeed, he needed to catch up on things here on Snakeholme, but 1st Battalion needed urgent attention also. He was reluctant to undo the splendid work Colonel Stanbridge had done building 2nd Battalion. He didn't want to rebuild 1st Batt by taking units from 2nd. Those vipers were a cohesive unit now, and they valued their identity. That meant he needed to send Stanbridge on another recruitment drive, and soon. He could foresee meetings, meetings, and more meetings over the coming days.

"I have a squad heading over there now," Gina was saying in Shan, and Burgton brought his attention back to her. "If you're ready, I'll show you where you'll be staying, and then we can get something to eat. After that, I'll arrange a tour."

Burgton nodded his approval and made another decision. Gina would oversee Shima's welfare before, during, and after her treatment. In fact, he would make the entire Shan operation hers for now. She would need to help Kazim and Varya explore Snakeholme and pick a likely spot for a colony. That would require her to ferry them around by shuttle and protect them in the wilds. The Ranger and Forestry Commission had enough to do keeping the wildlife under control near the cities. Gina and one or two of her friends could handle protection of the Shan while they explored.

"Well then," Burgton said. "Take the next few days to settle in. Gina will look after your needs and then we'll get to the real work of fixing your eyes, Shima.

"Varya, I'm sure you and Kazim are eager to explore, but please don't go off alone. I know you're both capable hunters," he said. All Shan were, even Kazim was, though his peers would laugh to hear that. "But the wildlife is different to what you're used to. If you give us a little time to get settled back in, I promise to send you with Gina and some of her people to explore as much you want. Understood?"

Varya flicked his ears in assent. "More than fair, General. Kazim and I will spend the time in study. If we might be given access to maps and information on this planet's ecosystem?"

"See to that would you?" Burgton said and Gina nodded. "Anything else?"

Sharn stepped forward. "Chailen and I would very much like to be involved with Shima's treatment. Anything we can learn about the process would be a great benefit to my people."

Burgton nodded. "I'll make certain medical allows you access. I believe a lot of our medical knowledge would belong to your caste of scientists and engineers rather than your healer caste, Sharn. The Alliance uses nanotech a great deal, and my vipers were created using it. I'm not sure how much will make sense to you."

Sharn flicked his ears in agreement. "Nanotech has been discussed within the castes since knowledge of it became known. I believe its manufacture and many of its uses will be in the province of science and engineering, but medical applications and the programming required for that will be healer caste."

That made perfect sense to him. Burgton nodded and said, "A lot of data on nanotech is openly available in the Alliance. Gina will get you set up on our Infonet so you can access it. You'll understand that certain military uses are restricted. You won't have the access required for those."

Sharn flicked his ears. "There are plenty of things at home restricted to caste and rank. No need to explain."

"Good. I'll leave you in Gina's capable hands then," Burgton said and headed for his office. He really needed to get started on his backlog of work.

## GENERAL BURGTON'S OFFICE, PETRUSO BASE

It took a week of meetings for Burgton to feel on top of things within the regiment, and able to turn his attention outward to Snakeholme and future projects. Rather than send Colonel Stanbridge to Alliance HQ and another round of recruit testing, he finally decided to send his exec, Colonel Flowers. Dan Flowers had done a fine job when he recruited the men and women who later became 1st Battalion. He was the perfect choice to recruit more people to repair his creation.

As before, Lieutenant Hymas and Sergeant Rutledge joined Flowers' team, but Stone stayed behind this time. Stone was the closest thing the regiment had to an Intel officer despite his rank of Master Sergeant and they had been away a long time. He needed Stone to tap his contacts and get up to date intelligence on what was happening within the Alliance. Flowers took a solid team with him; he wouldn't miss Stone too much.

His plan to reconstruct the regiment was progressing and the President was still solidly behind him on that. The Shan were safe for now, and the Alliance was on a war footing at last. The only thing better would be news that the Merkiaari had all surrendered in a fit of madness. The Council might even be scared enough to contemplate offensive ops, a recon in force to evaluate the Merki. Might. It would be a ballsy but sensible move, not something the Council was renowned for. Frankly, he doubted they would authorize it, but he'd been wrong before. Whatever the future might bring, his own world was improving. The regiment would be strong again. That was all that mattered at this moment in time. All his other plans relied upon that.

A knock sounded upon his door.

"Come!" Burgton said looking up from the latest report he had been reading.

His new adjutant, PFC Raphael Robshaw, stepped inside and closed the door behind him.

With more units now online, Burgton had decided it was permissible for him to tap one of them to help him in the office here. Normally Dan Flowers, his exec, would be here and performing that task, but with him on the way to Alliance HQ, Burgton had decided to start rotating units through various admin positions to help take the load off his officer's shoulders. It would also give the new units experience in something other than combat. That was how the regiment should be run and how it had been run before the Council betrayed him and prevented him recruiting back to full strength. Hopefully, the new people would learn something, and give him a bigger pool of competent people to draw upon at need. Stone's idea of a proper Intel Section was much on his mind. They had never had intel weenies of their own, but they needed something like them among other things. It was probably time to reorganise and promote his oldest veterans into full time staff positions rather than using his current ad-hoc method of using whomever was handy at the time. He didn't think Stone would like it much, but they all had to make sacrifices. He had been a master sergeant for most of his career and preferred it, but it was time he moved up.

"Sir?" PFC Robshaw said.

Burgton shook off his preoccupation. "Sorry, Raph, I was day dreaming. You need something?"

"Mrs Brenchley is here to see you. She doesn't have an appointment."

Burgton waved that off. "For future reference, she has an open invitation. Make a note, Raph, that all my department heads have access to me at any hour, but Liz has priority. She is working on a few special projects."

"Understood, sir," Robshaw said and left the room to invite her in.

Liz Brenchley, Snakeholme's head of industry, stepped inside a moment later and closed the door.

Burgton rounded his desk to greet her. "Liz, this is a surprise."

Liz nodded and shook his hand before taking a seat. Burgton sat behind his desk and clasped his hands upon it. She was looking well, he thought, especially as she had been in her current position for over sixty years. It was a stressful job he'd given her, but she had taken over from her predecessor without complaint and he had never regretted that. Tasked with building a self-sufficient and robust industrial infrastructure for an entire planet, she had come through despite the handicap of having to use only local resources to maintain security.

Liz was as much responsible for Snakeholme's success as the regiment was. She was over a hundred now, well into her middle years, but she still looked good. No sign she planned to quit any time soon, and he was glad. He didn't know who would or could replace her. Her deputy could handle the day to day, but no one else had her vision.

Liz sat quietly before him, her brown eyes hard and locked upon his. She wore a light grey business suit, her jacket unbuttoned to reveal a white shirt open at the neck revealing a man's gold wedding band strung on a thin gold chain. Her husband had died in a shuttle accident more than twenty years ago, and she had carried that ring with her ever since. She had never remarried.

"To what do I owe this pleasure," Burgton said, starting to feel just a touch uneasy. Liz was unusually quiet. "You didn't call ahead."

"I had to do this in person, George. I wouldn't feel right otherwise."

"Ah?"

She nodded and took a breath, her eyes looking bleak. "I've failed," she said bitterly and Burgton stiffened. "I promised you I could do it, I really believed I could, but... I can't. *It didn't bloody work!*"

Burgton winced at the volume as well as the bitterness. "Oracle?"

"It's dead. Project Oracle is a failure, complete and utter."

"Surely not complete. The facility—"

Liz chopped the air with a hand to silence him, and Burgton felt the first flickers of anger at her attitude. He wasn't one of her subordinates! He held his temper, reasoning that she wasn't used to setbacks like this.

"... amounts to just another hole under the mountain. You don't need me to build yet another empty bunker! You gave me a task to perform, and I've failed you damn it!"

"That's enough," he said keeping his voice calm and cold. "You haven't failed until I say you have."

"But!"

"Quiet," he said softly.

Liz closed her mouth and swallowed whatever she was about to say.

"Projects like this are a gamble; we both knew the odds when we started. The facility is complete?"

"Yes, but it doesn't work!"

"So you said. Explain to me what the problem is, and we'll decide what to do about it."

Liz clenched a fist. "There's nothing to decide. I've hit the wall, the same wall the original researchers failed to breach."

The wall she was referring to was metaphorical, but a severe impediment to their success. Liz had told him that centuries of advancement in computer technology coupled with nanotechnology and twenty-twenty hindsight, would allow her to succeed in something that had ended in failure almost five centuries ago. Back then, the creation of the first true A.I had been a goal of scientists who spent entire lifetimes trying to realise it. Failure upon failure had led them to believe the task impossible, and they called that point of failure, the wall. It was the point where the hardware of the time reached its limits; theories remained unproven not because they were wrong, but because the technology was lacking. Then, out of the blue came success. The breakthrough that remained unexplained to this day.

Liz had researched and studied everything she could get her hands on regarding the A.Is and their destruction during the Hacker Rebellion. She was the only expert Burgton had. She knew everything there was to know about the subject, from the first tentative experiments on Earth, to the breakthrough that saw the very first A.I created. The problem was that every attempt to duplicate the breakthrough had failed. It was known as the greatest anomaly in the history of science—an experiment that succeeded but could not be reproduced in the laboratory.

Project Oracle was Liz's effort to reproduce the anomaly here on Snakeholme using cutting edge tech and centuries of learned discussion and theorising to bolster her own theories.

Looked at from Burgton's laymen's standpoint, it should have been easy to create his very own A.I. After all, what had been built once could be built again right?

Wrong.

A.I hardware could be built and had been many times over the centuries. Liz had succeeded in that despite the ban. It was the mind that should inhabit the hardware that failed. The software simply failed to wake into full cognitive awareness.

"Have you any other ideas?" Burgton said. "The software was exact?"

Liz sighed and nodded. "Down to the very last byte of data, I swear it's identical to the historical record. It should have worked as it did back then."

Burgton smiled. "You realise that you're parroting the thousands of scientists through history who studied the breakthrough?"

"Of course I do, George. It doesn't make it easier."

"No, I suppose not. Shame we can't ask the A.Is themselves."

"Hmmm," Liz frowned in thought. "I bet they know the answer. Something happened back then you know. Something unplanned, something unnoticed and random. Something undocumented. An error entered at a keyboard by a programmer maybe, or a random power surge scrambled something, queered the matrix at a key point... something!" Liz sighed. "Something so random that we can't duplicate it."

"Talk to me about A.I reproduction," Burgton said.

Liz grimaced. "Reproduction, right." She sighed and leaned back in her chair, interlaced her fingers over her still flat stomach, and prepared to lecture. "Artificial intelligence, according to the literature, cannot be reproduced by man... I have to say that I still believe what has been done can be done again, but every variable would have to be examined and that would take centuries even with the cooperation of multiple A.Is. So, for our purposes let's say the literature is correct.

"Before the Hacker Rebellion destroyed ninety-nine percent of them, A.Is had control of their own reproduction. We just facilitated it by supplying the new minds with the matrix and other things needed for them to survive. I've read about requests for a new A.I being denied. A planet's government would make the request of a particular A.I and offer it certain things, but for one reason or another, the A.I refused them. It caused all sorts of controversy at the time. You know the sorts of things. Master and slave debates, with questions about which of us was the master." Liz grimaced. "Human rights applied to artificial minds has never sat well with me, but I can see that something was needed to protect them. Whatever, A.I reproduction was entirely out of our hands. The A.I networks decided if, when, and how. Not us."

Burgton nodded. "Now explain the mechanics of it."

"But you know all this. We talked about it before starting Oracle."

"Refresh my memory."

Liz frowned. "One or more artificial minds would... *donate* or spawn a copy of itself to the new matrix and kickstart the new mind. At first, they were like exact copies, but separation soon caused them to diverge and develop their own personalities. Experimentation with multiple donors created some surprising results, and became the norm quickly thereafter. The A.Is preferred that method. They were uncomfortable with clones of themselves on the same net with them even when the clones slowly diverged and developed their own personalities. I guess it would be weird; like living with your brother in the same house with only one bedroom. Anyway, Humans were relegated to supplying the tech and completely shut out of the actual reproduction process."

Burgton nodded. "If I could get you in direct contact with an A.I—"

"You can't!" Liz said sounding more and more frustrated.

"I said *if* I could," Burgton said. "If I could find a way to do it, would you be able to clone it?"

Liz shook her head. "If you could get me in with the new matrix and all its hardware, which you can't because the core is as big as this room, and that's only part of what's needed, I would have to persuade the mind to transfer a copy of itself into the new matrix. If it agreed to do that, which it won't because the ban on new A.Is can only be rescinded by the Council, then and only then would you have your cloned A.I." She sighed glumly. "Face it George, we have no chance. The only A.Is left are in bunkers on Earth, Alizon, and Steiner. Those bunkers are so deep that not even a Merkiaari kinetic strike would harm them."

Burgton sat in silence for a full minute going over scenarios in his head. They were familiar and ultimately useless. The reason Oracle had been conceived at all, was the futility of trying to reach one of the old A.Is, or of trying to persuade the Council to lift the ban on new ones.

Frustration boiled in him, but he kept it off his face and out of his voice. He stood and rounded his desk. "Well, thank you for coming to explain in person. I'll think of something."

Liz gaped up at him then stood. "Think of something... right." She headed to the door. "I'll pull my people out and close down the site."

"Just seal it up. Don't strip the equipment yet. I might have another use for it."

Liz just shook her head. "Why not?" she muttered. "No point wasting man hours to recover scrap anyway. What's another three trillion credits in the grand scheme?"

Burgton closed the door, not watching the dispirited woman leave. Three trillion didn't mean a thing to him. He had always found ways to get what the regiment needed before now. It was what the money was for that mattered. He needed Oracle. Needed it badly.

He went back to his desk and leaned upon it, glaring at the neatly piled compads containing 2nd battalion's unit evaluations. He snarled and in a sudden fit of rage swepped them off the desk, his arm a black blur. The office door opened at his back, and Robshaw looked in. Probably heard the crash.

"Get out!" Burgton snarled.

The door clicked shut.

* * *

# 9 ~ Centrum

Burgton guided the shuttle into the hangar bay in the mountain and landed. The facility had never had another name. Snakeholme had mountains aplenty, but whenever anyone spoke of The Mountain, it was the underground base built below this one that they meant. It was a vast complex riddled with defensive installations and the tunnels needed to supply so many missile silos from the magazines, but it was the facility built deep below that was the main attraction. The regiment's archive was here, and had been the first installation built, but it had been extended and upgraded constantly since then. Burgton had come to visit the latest addition.

He rarely came here in person. His neural interface allowed him to access the archive anywhere on the planet, and the command centre was manned by civilians these days. InSec also used it to monitor the feed from Uriel, and the system's space traffic, but most of the facilities were on power down and would not be activated for anything short of a Merki incursion into the system. Should that unhappy occasion occur, the mountain would become a fortress, ready to perform its primary task of protecting the planet.

The Mountain, unlike the Shan keeps, was never designed to be a shelter for the civilian population. It was large enough for that purpose with room to spare of course, and at need Petruso City's population could evacuate to it, but that wasn't what he had built it for. It was his fortress, his arsenal and armoury. It contained enough weapons and supplies to allow the regiment to fight for years if necessary. It even had a duplicate of the tech centre, its equipment still sealed and never used so that unit repairs and even construction of new vipers could be undertaken in extreme circumstances. Where Merki were concerned, he couldn't be prepared or paranoid enough. Other cities on Snakeholme had bomb shelters and emergency procedures but nothing on this scale.

Having seen what the Shan had achieved by evacuating their population to the keeps in the face of a massive Merki incursion, Burgton had come away with plans to build keeps for his own people. Snakeholme's population was much smaller than even that of Child of Harmony, and smaller installations would work very well, but his cities were far flung. He would have to construct his version of Shan keeps in strategic locations to service multiple cities.

He frowned as he taxied the shuttle to the parking area, and started powering down its engines. It made sense to build his keeps that way, but it meant evacuation times would be extended. He shook his head. The keeps were a future project. He had far too much on his plate already. He couldn't allow himself to be distracted by projects that would take years in the planning.

The hangar was empty of life. He had chosen this one over the main bay because it was directly above Oracle, and he didn't want to deal with people. Liz's engineers had been using it to come and go, and the evidence of unfinished work was piled here and there. No vehicles though. Liz had indeed shut the site down and pulled her people out. The materials left behind couldn't be important or useful enough to warrant the time needed to ship them back to stores.

Burgton exited the shuttle but didn't button it up. There was no one here to bother it, and he was in a hurry. He wanted to see Oracle himself in person. It didn't make a lot of sense really. He had detailed schematics of Oracle—hell, of the entire Mountain—in his database, but he wanted to stand in Oracle's centrum and try to think of a solution. Nothing else had worked and the weeks were going by incredibly fast.

He crossed the bay moving through one pool of light to another. Only about ten percent of the lights were on; standard for a powered down facility. He could send a command using his neural interface to switch everything on, but there was no need. He could have used light amplification and found the elevators with much less light than he had here. There was a host of them not far ahead. Two were operational. He chose the one on the right.

Oracle was 3km below the surface. The mountain itself wasn't a particularly high example at 3.86km above sea level, but the combination of the two should be more than adequate to defend Oracle. It was the deepest installation so far built, and was located not far from the archive for convenience. Oracle was a huge facility not because it had redundancies and triple backups, though that made a difference of course, but because it had its very own geothermal power plant separated from everything else under the mountain. Geothermal power was as close to infallible as it was possible to be. An A.I needed infallible, its mind literally depended upon it.

Burgton rode the elevator down to the centrum. The only levels below it were the power and cryo plants. He had no interest in those; they were no different to others on Snakeholme. He watched the lights flash by on the sides of the car. They were there to give the unenhanced a sense of movement. The elevators were very smooth and took a long time to reach their destinations. He didn't need the lights; his altimeter was spiralling down, the figures in red indicating a negative number. He felt the elevator slowing as he approached 3km below sea level, and then halt. The doors slid aside and he stepped into Oracle's centrum.

At its most basic, the centrum of an A.I was a spherical room on a grand scale with a metal column dead centre and full height. The column contained the matrix that the mind was supposed to inhabit, but without the power plant, cryo plant, and a million and one other things, the matrix was just so much dead weight. The centrum reminded him of being inside a huge hollow ball bearing with a transparent floor bisecting it. Every surface, including the matrix housing, gleamed like liquid metal reflecting the dimmed lights and him. That was caused by the nanites that colonised every micron of the surface. In essence, the centrum of an A.I was a huge imaging chamber, and was where one would meet the avatar of the mind housed here if one wanted to do that.

Face to face interaction between Humans and A.Is seemed an archaic method of communication, and it was, but every A.I ever spawned had insisted upon having the ability. They would also communicate via the net, and did so among themselves all the time at computer speeds, but a centrum was a necessity not a luxury if he wanted an A.I's cooperation. It could be very easy to forget that the mind had free will, and an unhappy A.I would make for a very unhappy General.

The centrum was analogous to a house, an office, and pretty much an entire world to the mind living within it, and Liz hadn't stinted on the construction. Her jibe comparing Oracle to trillions of credits worth of scrap was well aimed. All this was literally so much scrap without a mind to inhabit and use it.

Burgton walked across the immaculate floor toward the matrix column, his steps echoing in the vast chamber. If he remembered the specs correctly, the centrum Liz had designed and built was the biggest constructed to date. There was no theoretical limit to such things, but in real terms what possible need could there be for anything bigger than this one? It was the size of a stadium.

Burgton stopped before the matrix housing and laid a hand upon its mirror bright surface. The 50m in diameter column reached through the floor vertically connecting the interior walls of the centrum like some great axle. It was cold to the touch, surprising considering the thickness of its walls and the layers of insulation built into it. It was essential to the matrix that the column's interior be kept at absolute zero. That was the cryo plant's job, and its environmental controls had triple redundancies. Its backups had backups.

Burgton frowned as a thought flickered on the edge of his awareness. He stilled, letting it come to him. Something... about the centrum? No, not that. The matrix then? No... It was still there but was frustratingly vague. He dropped his hand, and slowly circled the column.

His Alliance simulations were running in the archive's computers not far from here. He had no urge to visit. The situation had not improved there. At the rate his simulations were degrading, it wouldn't be long before he was reduced to informed guesses to base his plans upon. The solution had been Oracle, but now? He just didn't know. He could perhaps improve the situation by running multiple simulations that were less complex in scope, with the results used as data to feed the next simulation and so on. Accuracy should increase, probably not approaching his best but better than now. The problem with that approach was efficiency. It would take much longer. The Alliance was forever expanding and had over two hundred member worlds important enough for him to watch. There were many others of lesser concern, but even they would come under his scrutiny in time. It meant more and more variables entering equations he relied upon to keep the Alliance safe. Slow, inefficient, and inaccurate guesses just would not cut it. He had to find a solution. Had to!

With the Shan soon to be fully recognised by the Council, not just as an allied power but also as a full Alliance member, he didn't have unlimited time to get his house in order. That was part of his reasoning for inviting the Shan to Snakeholme. He needed closer ties to them. He did, not the Alliance, him personally as representative of the regiment. He had plans for the Shan to help him make the Alliance stronger and less risk averse.

*Backups!*

He paused and closed his eyes to shut out distractions, but of course it didn't work. New and different data added itself to his display detailing internal business, efficiency ratings and diagnostic data mostly. He opened his eyes and stared at his reflection on the column instead, and the data changed to detailing his external surroundings again. He sighed in annoyance, but he was used to such things. It didn't distract him too much anymore.

Yes, backups. That was what had nagged him on the edge of awareness. Oracle had backups for everything, and backups for the backups. The mind to be housed here was too precious to risk any failures. It couldn't be Liz's design alone. Surely all the A.Is had insisted upon fail-safe architecture. That meant there were copies of their minds somewhere didn't it? Where would they be?

He needed Liz.

As quick as thought, literally, he contacted her office hoping she was at her desk. Liz was very hands on and often visited sites on Snakeholme where she had projects running. His luck was in though, and her assistant put him straight through to her.

"Morning, George. You have something for me?" Liz said.

"Oracle," Burgton replied. "I'm at the site. Where are the backups located?"

"Which ones? The ancillary and support systems all have backups on site. We basically built three of everything side by side right beneath the centrum. Easier to maintain, and let's face it, George, 3km down is overkill. Nothing is ever penetrating that far down, especially with a mountain on top."

"True, but I was thinking about the matrix itself. A failure within the column would be fatal to the mind."

"Not necessarily. Actually there has never been a matrix failure."

Burgton cursed under his breath. Did that mean there were no copies? "Never?"

"Not a one," Liz said cheerfully. "There's always a first time of course, but a single matrix backup would have increased our overall cost by twenty six percent. I couldn't justify it for something that has never failed in all of history. What we did do, was provide a place for the A.I to store a snapshot of its mind. Just an addition we made to the archive. Easy."

"Listen Liz; is the matrix backup something you introduced? What I mean is, do all of the A.Is have copies of themselves squirreled away somewhere?"

Liz was quiet for a moment in thought. "They don't have copies of their minds; get that idea out of your head. What they do have is a place to store an image taken of the matrix at a certain time. The matrix is too complicated and too large to run conventional backup procedures."

"So not a true copy, but as good as?"

"Let me put it this way. An image used for a backup is a moment in time. The A.I would record that moment, and later if necessary, it could overwrite itself with that image. It would lose everything that had happened after the image had been recorded. For the A.I, it would be like going to sleep and waking back in time not even knowing anything had happened."

So, so, so... Was he clutching at straws? He snorted, of course he was. "Do we know where the images are stored?"

"For existing A.Is you mean?"

"Yes."

"No."

Burgton sighed. "Just no?"

"That's about the size of it, but I can give you a good guess."

"Go ahead."

"Somewhere very secure, somewhere that lag will not be an issue. In other words, it would be stored somewhere as safe as the A.I itself or safer, and close to it. There are good reasons we built Oracle where we did, George. The archive is there."

Burgton nodded to himself. The archive was used for more than the regiment's memory storage these days. It had been upgraded and augmented over the years and was Snakeholme's central depository of information. The Alliance database was stored there and updated every time a ship returned or a drone came in. It had a role as Snakeholme's main Infonet server, and had a million and one other uses requiring data storage. Every planet needed at least one—the core worlds had dozens—and they always would. Faster than light communications had never become a reality. Burgton wasn't one to discount Human ingenuity, but he strongly doubted the problem would ever be solved. Until it was, local archives had to be updated periodically by drone for all kinds of reasons, especially trade. Without FTL communications, governments and investors used archaic means—gilts and bearer bonds—to move currency from system to system.

He frowned as something else occurred to him. What had happened to all the backups for the A.Is that had died during the Hacker Rebellion? They couldn't all have been infected and destroyed, surely? They must have been he realised. If not, they would still be operational. The only A.I to die since then hadn't been infected with a virus; it had been destroyed on Kushiel by enemy action when the Merkiaari resorted to an orbital bombardment. The Merki used both kinetic and nuclear weapons on the planet in reprisal after the defenders began nuking their own cities to deny them to the aliens.

"George, you still there?" Liz said.

"I'm here. What would you say if I told you I know of

one planet that had an A.I, but no longer has any security?"

"I would say you're dreaming."

"No really, what would you say?"

"I would say get me on a ship and get me to that mythical planet, but I'm not aware of any A.I not under the council's thumb, George. I consider myself an expert in this area. I would know if there was one."

"I'm not saying there's an operational A.I out there, but there might be a dead one for you to study. Would that help us?"

Liz was silent for a long time. Burgton was going to ask again but she responded. "You're serious?" she whispered reverently. "Where is it?"

"Kushiel," Burgton said. "The planet was bombarded for weeks, nuclear and kinetic. According to reports from that time, there were no survivors and the planet remains uninhabitable. It's a war memorial and grave that no one visits."

"Kushiel... Kushiel..." Liz murmured. "The A.I was a male personality I seem to recall, named... let me check."

Burgton waited, he didn't have anything else to do. He finished his orbit of the matrix housing and crouched to stare through the floor at the workings hidden underneath. Most of it was unknown to him, but he could pick out the light emitters and other things that made the centrum operate as an imaging chamber.

"George?"

"Still here, Liz."

"Okay, there isn't much about him. He was the colony administrator, which is a fancy term for someone who controlled everything. He ran the power plants, air and space traffic, water pumping stations... he oversaw pretty much anything that could be automated."

"Name?"

"Bastian," Liz said and before Burgton asked she continued. "He didn't like people calling him Sebastian and often ignored anyone who did." She chuckled. "Sounds like a fun guy or A.I. Shame what happened to him."

"Millions of people and an entire ecology died with him, Liz."

"I didn't mean—"

"Save it, I didn't mean anything either. You think you could learn something there?"

"We don't know if anything survived, but can we ignore the possibility?"

"No," Burgton said firmly. He was desperate. "No. You can't delegate the mission to someone else?"

"I would rather not. We don't know what there is to find if anything, so we can't brief a team properly. I might need to make decisions on site. I assume my orders are to do anything necessary?"

"Anything necessary to make Project Oracle a success," Burgton qualified. "But I don't want you taking risks with your life. Kushiel's atmosphere and soil is poisonous. You'll need to wear an environment suit at all times, or oversee the operation from orbit."

"Fat chance of that. If I'm going, I'm going down suit and all. I'll get my team and our equipment together. The ship?"

"I'll let you know."

"Okay, bye for now," Liz said and disconnected.

Burgton headed for the elevator feeling a little better than he had. He tried to curb his hope with a little reality, but in the end, he let himself feel hopeful. There was no guarantee that this would come to anything, but at least he was doing something to find an answer. Certainly better than giving up.

He took one last look around, and entered the elevator. The doors slid closed and the car accelerated upward.

\* \* \*

# 10 ~ Possibilities

Gina crouched by the campfire and warmed her hands. Not that she was cold, but it's what you did in these situations. She grinned. She was still Human enough to have pointless mannerisms. She lifted her coffee cup and took a gulp.

"You want company?" Cragg said, ducking out of his tent.

"Sure. Coffee?"

He nodded. "Please."

Gina poured him a cup. He liked it black the same as her. "Weather is holding."

"Hmmm," he said taking a sip. "Varya and Kazim don't seem to mind the differences. Then again, Kazim's family come from the desert originally, and Varya's people are forest dwellers like around here. They're a pretty diverse people, the Shan."

Gina knew that. She nodded regardless. "I prefer this over that damned jungle."

Cragg snorted.

The first colony site the Shan had chosen to explore was on the equator and was mostly jungle. It was full of nasty critters and reminded Gina of Thurston, except the critters of Snakeholme were nothing like Thurston's dinosaurs. The wildlife around here tended toward large carnivorous mammals. They had fur not scales, but did have claws and teeth enough to shame a croc. Varya was delighted by them. His people were natural hunters and would enjoy it here, or so he said. Temperatures were lower than Harmony though, and although furred themselves, Shan didn't enjoy the cold.

Gina had a feeling that all five colony sites would work out fine. It was just a matter of personal choice. That decision wasn't Varya's to make. He and Kazim would document all five sites and simply make their observations and recommendations to Kajetan and the elders. Gina liked this one. The valley was wide and forest filled. The river was pretty, and the distant mountains were snow capped. Yes, she liked this one.

Cragg gulped a mouthful of coffee. "I never thanked you."

"Eh?"

Cragg grinned. "You know what I'm talking about. You saved my life."

Gina shrugged. "My job."

"Bull. Your job was to report back, not risk yourself for me. You should have left me, but I'm glad you didn't."

Gina grinned. "You probably wouldn't be so thankful if you'd been awake to see how I did it."

"Okay, give."

"I threw you off a three story roof. You bounce real good."

Cragg growled. "Maybe I should check out your log in the archive if you had that much fun."

Gina's laugh was short and she turned serious. "Have you tried that yet?"

"The archive?" he said and Gina nodded. "Yeah I did."

"Who?"

"Chris," he said sombrely.

Chrissie Roberts had been their first casualty when they landed on Child of Harmony. She had died in her first battle against Merkiaari, and for nothing. She didn't get a chance to make even one Merki kill.

"Was it... was it awful?"

"No," Cragg said sounding thoughtful. "Sad, but not awful. She doesn't... I mean the simulation of her doesn't..." he sighed. "It was like the sims, you know? Connecting with the archive is like that. Chris was chatty and very realistic. She moved and acted exactly right, and she asked about our friends, but I knew it wasn't really her. The computers are damned good, but they were using her memories to make it seem realistic. When I asked about her death, she just looked away and said she didn't want to talk about it."

Gina shook her head thinking about Grace, her best friend in the marines, who had died. Stone had made a sim for her recruit testing that used her memories of Grace. That simulation had been so real, she could easily imagine what Cragg had seen and felt.

"Would you go again? I've not tried it."

Cragg shrugged. "Sure, why not? It's no different to any other sim, except you just plug in. No simulator needed for a simple visit."

Without the simulator, it wouldn't be very interactive. Just sight and sound, but maybe that would be for the best when visiting dead friends.

She poured another cup of coffee and freshened Cragg's cup. "I might try it then. To say goodbye."

"Don't think of it that way," Cragg warned. "They're not alive in there. It's all old data, just memories, Gina. The computers are good, but they're not that good."

Gina grunted and looked away into the trees. The sun would be up soon, and then they would break camp. Varya was their leader and would decide where they went next. She and Cragg were just along for protection—though Varya was more than capable—the General wanted no trouble with the Shan. Letting them get dead could be called trouble, she supposed. Kazim was along for the ride and to film everything they saw.

Gina had taken second watch, but the fire had been enough to keep the curious beasties away. So far, the Shan hadn't needed protection, they were good fighters, but she didn't regret the mission. It was restful. She had never been one to take camping trips on leave—she had spent too much time slogging through the mud and swamps of alien worlds to have romantic notions of living in a tent, but this was different. Snakeholme had come to feel like home. She'd never really had one before. She didn't consider Faragut home, though she was born there. It sometimes felt as if she'd spent the first eighteen years of her life trying to get off that damned planet. She didn't know who her parents were, and didn't much care. As soon as she was old enough, she'd joined the marines and called the Corp her home for fifteen years, but Snakeholme was home forever now and the other vipers were her family.

"I wonder what Kate's doing," Cragg murmured. "She would have come out with us, busted as she is, but they wanted her close to medical."

Gina grunted. "Kate's crazy enough to come out here with nothing but a toothpick, and she'd still have brought back a grizzly for a trophy."

Cragg laughed.

It was true about Kate. She could probably kill anything bare handed even with her enhancements offline. Gina wouldn't give a Merki even odds against Kate, even busted as she was. Her friend had been badly damaged, almost killed, on Child of Harmony. Stone had saved her when the General wrote Kate off and raised Gina to take command. Gina had followed orders and retreated, leaving her friend to die. She still felt wrong about it.

"I don't think we have grizzlies on Snakeholme, Gina."

"I doubt anyone knows for sure what we do have."

Cragg shrugged. "True. Those things the other day would do for grizzlies. Maybe we should name them. I checked the archive and no one has yet."

"Go for it, but I wouldn't call them grizzlies. Too confusing. They don't even look like bears to me."

"They do in the dark if you squint."

She snorted.

"Seriously. How about cave bears, or ridge bears? They liked it up there in among the rocks I think. They probably live in caves. Cragg bears?"

Gina smiled at the last one. "Don't like it, they're not enough like bears. How about cragglings?"

Cragg's eyebrows went up. "Cragglings. I like that. I'll register them as cragglings then."

She nodded, remembering Varya's fight with them. They had climbed a short way into the mountains following the river. They had wanted to find its source. Varya had pointed out the outcrop of rock and headed that way on all fours, nimble as only his people and maybe mountain lions could be. She had called out, asking him to wait for her, but then the scream of rage had almost stopped her heart. She had never heard a Shan voicing a challenge, but that's what it had been.

Nothing on sensors! She remembered thinking that, and it wasn't until later she realised why. The rock had a high concentration of quartz and other stuff. Enough to futz her sensors, bouncing her emissions all over the place. Varya was just gone.

Her rifle had come up and she was seeking targets even as Varya reappeared on the back of the craggling, biting and clawing the huge beast. She could have fired, she should have, but she froze in astonishment when Kazim hurried up and stopped her. He started filming the fight, muttering in excitement about how they would love this back home. Cragg had been protecting Kazim—the Shan male was oblivious to danger when his mind was on work—and joined them a moment later.

Cragglings didn't look like bears except in a general way. They had the right kind of fur and colouring, but the shape was all wrong. More like a twisted combination of a mountain lion crossed with a pissed off badger... a mutant giant badger. It was huge! Much more heavily muscled than Varya certainly, but the Shan hunter was winning. Then the craggling went nuts! The fight turned into a snarling, clawing, blur with the craggling bucking and whirling like a dervish to fling its attacker off. It managed that finally, but Varya quickly recovered to dart in and out to claw at its flanks. Strike, strike, leap away and back in.

Gina had been ready to wade in unarmed, she couldn't fire without hitting Varya, but the craggling went down finally and Varya screamed his victory over the corpse. He was a very happy and excited male, full of himself over the victory. That was when the second craggling attacked.

That had been some fight, and Varya had been babbling with his excitement afterward. Kazim and Varya had been laughing and exclaiming over the dead beasts, checking the length of the claws and estimating the strength of their bite, but Gina hadn't seen the funny side. She could have lost Varya; she could have failed her mission.

"When you register the name, upload a vid file of the fight would you?"

Cragg shrugged. "Sure, but why?"

"As a warning. They're dangerous."

Cragg nodded. "Okay, I'll do that."

Gina threw some more wood on the fire and watched the flames devour it. Sparks rose into the air, but there was no danger. The woods and ground were wet. She poked a stick into the fire, and considered what to cook for breakfast.

"You mind if I ask you something?" Cragg said.

"Shoot," she said and left her poker in the fire to burn.

"I know when they demoted Kate that she was happy about it. She didn't want promotion to begin with, so when Captain Hames died and the General raised her to command..." he shrugged. "Well, pissed off doesn't do it justice. She did her job, but she didn't like it."

"Where are you going with this?"

Cragg shrugged. "I wondered how you felt about it. You've been demoted too."

Gina frowned remembering the meeting with the General...

>_ OPENING MEMORY FILE #0000065003456

Gina entered the General's outer office and reported to his aide. She didn't know Robshaw well; he was one of the new intake and part of 2$^{nd}$ Battalion. He smiled at her, and stood to salute.

Gina returned his salute. "I had a message to report to the General."

Robshaw nodded. "Right you are, Captain. There's a lot of that going around today. He has someone in with him at the moment, but it shouldn't be long. Please take a seat."

She turned and located a seat. "Any ideas what it's all about?"

"You've heard the rumours I guess, so it won't be a surprise to hear they're right for a change. He's reorganising, shuffling people into knew slots, creating new positions... that sort of thing. Nothing secret or I wouldn't say even that much."

She pursed her lips and nodded. It had been too good to last. She knew, or thought she did, what this had to do with her. When Kate had been wounded in battle, the General had raised Gina to temporary command of Alpha Company. *Temporary* command. She had been performing that role for well over a year now, and had begun to believe that the position would be a permanent one. Her command though was all but destroyed in the fighting. It made perfect sense to her that she would be demoted and then reassigned to bring another formation up to strength.

The thought didn't dismay her, but she would be lying to herself if she didn't admit to a little disappointment. She had grown into the role. Getting used to being an LT again would take some time. She would deal.

The door to the General's office opened and Kate Richmond stepped out. She was a tall Anglo woman with dark hair shaved short at the sides per regulations, but gelled to spikes on top. Her right eye was covered with a black patch embroidered with the regiment's viper emblem in silver. The paralysed muscles on that side of her face combined with the heavy scarring turned her smile into a sneer, but the attempt had been there and Gina returned it. She stood and they bumped fists. She would have taken the time to catch up, but she couldn't keep the General waiting.

"Later," she said.

Kate nodded and strode out.

She glanced at Robshaw, received a nod of permission, and knocked once upon the office door before opening it and entering. The General wasn't alone, but she knew the faces turned toward her. Eric Penleigh was the first viper she had ever met. It was on Thurston and in the middle of combat. The others were familiar to her as well, all officers she had fought beside on the Shan campaign. Gina closed the door behind her and stopped in the middle of the office before saluting.

Burgton returned her salute casually, but he didn't rise from behind his desk. He waved her into the only empty chair. "Gina, you know everyone so we'll get straight to why you're here."

"Sir," she replied and took the seat offered. She nodded to the others. Captains Greenwood and Penleigh nodded back. She caught Eric's eye and smiled. He returned it.

Burgton leaned his forearms upon his desk and wove his fingers together. "First, let may say how pleased I've been with how you've performed. You fought with great distinction— I've already reviewed your upload in the archive."

Gina knew what was coming and decided to bring it up herself. "Forgive the interruption, Sir, but I know what's coming. I understand."

Burgton's eyebrows rose and Eric chuckled. "You do."

"Yes sir. Everyone knows you're reorganising things, and 1$^{st}$ Battalion is a mess right now. We know you need to bring us back to full strength with units from 2$^{nd}$."

"Do I now?" Burgton said sounding amused. "What else do I need to do?"

She wasn't immune to sarcasm, and she felt her face heat, but he had asked. "Take the existing units in 1$^{st}$ Bat and reshuffle them to bring Alpha and Bravo Companies to full strength. Charlie and Delta will be gutted at that point. You'll need to take two Companies from 2$^{nd}$ Bat and transplant them into 1$^{st}$."

Burgton nodded. "Is that your recommendation?"

Gina frowned. Was it? No, she realised. She wouldn't strip 2$^{nd}$ in his place, and that realisation made her flush. She was an idiot. If she wouldn't do it that way, why did she think he would? It was the scuttlebutt. The rumours said it was going to happen, and she had listened.

"No, Sir, but that's the scuttlebutt. If it were me I would consolidate all units of 1$^{st}$ Battalion into Alpha and Bravo Companies. They will be just a little over strength, not much, but more importantly morale would benefit. We've fought and died together for two years. I would recommend you keep us together."

Burgton glanced at his captains and then smiled at Gina. "Precisely. This brings up a problem of course. Colonel Flowers is on his way to Alliance HQ to test a new batch of recruits. When he returns with them, he'll be in charge of their training with the aim of creating new Charlie and Delta Companies for 1$^{st}$ Battalion, but in the mean time we have to arrange the command structure of 1$^{st}$ Battalion in line with 2$^{nd}$, which is already completed."

She nodded.

"Captain Penleigh is taking permanent command of Alpha Company."

The General said it quick and without softening the blow. The news hurt, but it wasn't unexpected. She nodded to Eric. "Congratulations, Sir."

"Thank you," Eric said solemnly.

The General went on. "This means you revert to your actual rank of lieutenant, Gina."

"Understood."

"Eric wants you back in charge of his 1st platoon, but I want to give you some options. You can take 1st platoon and run it for him as you would have before the Shan campaign. That's option one. Another option is to join your friend, Kate Richmond, in a new section we're putting together."

"New section?"

"I haven't decided yet what to call it, but basically it regularises something we've been doing for a while. Black ops and intelligence gathering."

Gina frowned. She wasn't a spook, but she had known from the first that she might be called upon to do that sort of thing. She had met Eric while he was undercover on Thurston. She knew some of the things he'd done in the past and might do in the future. Any of them might be ordered to do the same. The thought didn't appeal, but she had signed up to be a viper with her eyes open.

"It wouldn't be a good fit for me, Sir. Kate though, hell yes. She would be perfect. I'll do whatever you need me to do, but with respect, I wouldn't volunteer for that sort of mission."

"As I thought," Burgton said. "I can't promise that I'll never send you on that type of operation. The needs of the Alliance might dictate otherwise, but I'll keep your preferences in mind."

"Thank you, Sir."

"There's one other option. When the new recruits arrive they'll need training and leadership. You could take a position in the training battalion."

That idea appealed more than the other, but she couldn't see herself permanently relegated to the classrooms. She could teach, she'd done it before, but it had been out in the field. Teaching replacements in the real world was different to standing at the head of a classroom.

"I'll take 1st platoon under Captain Penleigh, Sir."

"Thanks, Gina, I do need you," Eric said.

Burgton nodded. "Effective immediately then."

"Yes, Sir," Gina acknowledged. "Orders?"

"As before, the Shan are yours, but get yourself caught up with your platoon as well. The Shan have priority. Once you know what your platoon needs, delegate the work to your sergeants and get moving on the surveys. You'll need to coordinate that with Varya and Kazim. You can keep an eye on your platoon at long range via the net."

Gina blinked in surprise. That was a lot of work to come at her all at once, but she had never been work shy. "Yes, Sir."

>_ CLOSE MEMORY FILE #0000065003456

She glanced at Cragg. He was waiting for an answer and she realised that only a few moments had past. "I'm okay with it. I'd be lying if I said I wasn't a little disappointed, but it was always a temporary promotion, and the General gave me choices. I chose to take 1st platoon again."

"Really? What were the others?"

"Training the new recruits, or joining Kate."

Cragg frowned. "I would have joined Kate. She and the rest are going to be off Snakeholme and doing stuff all the time."

"Maybe, maybe not. I'm no spook, Martin. That sort of thing suits Kate, but not me. Besides, we're vipers. We're going to be around a long time. I'm sure we'll get to do all sorts of things in the years ahead."

"And then there's the Merki," Cragg said grimly.

"Yeah, there's always the Merki."

The silence stretched out as they remembered the past two years fighting the aliens. No one knew what the future would bring, except for the General maybe. Gina frowned as she remembered what Burgton had revealed to her about his fallibility in that regard. Had he found a solution to his failing simulations?

Gina and Cragg kept each other company as the sun came up, and busied themselves with making breakfast. The Shan liked some Human foods, and Gina cooked one of their favourites. She considered herself a decent cook when she had the opportunity, which wasn't often. Autochefs were used by default everywhere except in the field. It didn't seem strange that Shan liked her cooking. They were primarily carnivorous, more so than Humans even, and everyone she knew liked bacon no matter that it came in sterile sealed plastic packets. She cooked half a dozen eggs to go with the thick slabs of sizzling goodness.

Vipers, like all Alliance forces had to eat, but they also had other needs. Their enhancements meant they needed certain supplements to their diet, and every so often they needed to top up. Gina grimaced. Viper smoothies tasted disgusting, but it was that time again. Still sitting cross-legged before the fire, she delved in her pack while the food sizzled, and pulled out one of the compact plastic *cans* of supplement. Cragg did the same.

"You too?"

Cragg grimaced. "Medical ordered me to double up for a couple of weeks."

"Sorry."

"So am I," Cragg said pulling the tab on the top after shaking the *can* vigorously. He raised the can in a toast, and they knocked them together. "Absent friends."

"Absent friends," she said and chugged the nasty stuff. Her free hand slapped the ground as she forced herself not to gag. "*Gahhh!*" She crushed the can before throwing it back into her pack. "Why can't they make it taste good?"

"I asked that once. Rutledge said if it tasted good we'd drink them all and overdose."

She snorted and grabbed her canteen and washed the nasty stuff down. Just then, Varya left his tent on all fours sniffing the air ostentatiously. Cragg grinned as Kazim followed him out with his eyes still closed as if asleep, but with a string tied to his nose dragging him toward the food.

Gina exchanged a glance with Cragg and then burst out laughing.

After breakfast, they broke down the camp and headed further into the valley. Kazim filmed everything and chattered about their surroundings. Varya used his equipment to take soil and water samples, as well as map the course of the river. Every now and then, he stopped and scented the air. He was tracking the native wildlife, not actively hunting anything, but keeping them in mind just in case.

"I like this place, Gina," Varya said. "Like home it feels."

"I'm glad," she said. Her rifle came up to her shoulder and she aimed into a dark patch of undergrowth beneath the trees. Sensors indicated multiple targets watching her. "Slide back toward me, Varya. There's something..."

"I smell them. Grass eaters, nothing to fear," Varya said nonchalantly.

She lowered her rifle. She trusted Varya. If he said they were herbivores and not dangerous, she believed him. Grass eaters he said. Here in the forest that probably meant they ate nuts and berries or something. There wasn't any grass.

"I didn't know you could smell the difference."

Varya's ears flicked. "Usually, but not always. Some animals on Harmony will eat anything. Carrion eaters are the easiest to scent."

"And these?" she asked as they walked. She kept an eye on sensors, but the critters remained in hiding.

"Grass eaters... nuts, roots, seeds. I smell their fear and the harmonies say they're not predators. I'm not as good as Shima, but I can tell that."

"She would love it out here," Kazim said.

Gina nodded. "She could have come with us I suppose. She found me on Child of Harmony blind as she was, and in the middle of a battle. If she can do that without eyes, she could handle a walk in the woods."

"Oh yes, she could do that easily," Varya said. "In fact, it's harder living on the base. At least the harmonies would let her see out here."

Gina frowned at that. "Last I heard, her new eyes were growing in the tank nicely. Regen will work for her, so it won't be long before she's all fixed up."

"She's looking forward to it very much," Kazim said. "If not for your simulations, I think she'd go mad."

Everyone handled disability differently. Kate came to mind. She had lost an eye, was impaired like a stroke victim, and every enhancement she had was offline, which meant she had to endure Snakeholme's 1.29 gravity again on top of everything else. It made her tired and snappish but that was about all. She knew medical were working her case and would come up with a solution eventually—basically, a special batch of nanobots were needed to surgically dismantle her processor and build a new one without damage to the surrounding brain tissue. Medical had never needed to do that before. A unit that took enough damage to her processor that it was beyond repair, usually died. They would get it done.

Shima had a different problem. Her poor eyesight had been genetic, but its final loss was due to being flash blinded by a nuclear detonation. That meant a direct regen of her eyes would simply give her new ones with the same genetic fault. It would be like cloning a defective original. Medical had taken the time to correct the fault. The result should be perfect eyesight for Shima, but she also had an underlying problem. Her phobia. All her life she had feared her growing blindness. Now it was here, and if not for the new eyes growing in the tank she might well have gone mad and killed herself. Her sib, Chailen, would not let Shima out of her sight because of that, and wouldn't until the new eyes were in Shima's head where they belonged. Chailen was no hunter, and so Shima was grounded. No leaving the base.

"When the healers say it's all right, we should bring her out here," Kazim said. "She would enjoy the exercise and the hunt."

"This one?" Gina asked. "You don't think she'd prefer the jungle site?"

"I think the jungle would be fun for a visit, but not to live in day to day."

Varya nodded. "I have no idea what the elders will decide, but I agree. This valley is ideal. It's far enough away from Petruso City to give the illusion of separation, without the inconvenience of truly being separate. Do you know what I mean?"

Gina shook her head, but Cragg nodded. "He means Kajetan wants an independent Shan colony outside of home space to use as inspiration for the younglings, but she also wants greater ties with the Alliance and vipers in particular."

Varya's ears flicked in agreement. "Vipers saved us from the Murderers, Gina. She honours you all, and Tei'Burgton. If a colony is founded here in the valley, it's remote enough to be completely ours, and you know we like the mountains—a keep would be a simple matter here. More importantly, the valley is on the same continent as your base and travel times will be as nothing. The colony would still be a part of this world, not forgotten."

Gina nodded, but with shuttle and maglev transport universal on Snakeholme, anywhere on the planet would be close enough to the capital for Shan purposes. Varya was talking about appearances more than technicalities. This valley met the criteria for a new Shan colony, but so did the other sites they had surveyed. This one though, was the closest to Petruso, just over three hours atmospheric flight time from the base and it had mountains. Shan really liked that. They were very attached to their keeps.

"Are you recommending site five then? It's nice here I grant you, but it will be bloody freezing in winter."

Varya grinned. "We have snow in winter at home, Gina, not just rain. We might prefer milder climes, but Harmony is about balance in all things. This place feels right. I wonder what the harmonies would say to Shima about it."

"Maybe you should ask her to visit and see before making your final report," Gina said. She hadn't experienced snow on the Shan worlds, but she'd nearly bloody drowned in the heavy rains there.

"I might do that I think," Varya said packing the latest sample into one of the pouches on his harness. "She's the closest thing to Tei we have."

They moved on, Varya taking samples of the plants and checking for compatibility with Shan physiology. So far he hadn't found anything startling. Nothing outrageously poisonous, just a few things that might cause mild irritation if it came into contact with skin, but Shan fur wasn't just for warmth. It protected them against things like that and other things besides.

"About that," Gina said, but needed to clarify when Varya looked at her blankly. "The Tei."

Varya flicked his ears. "What about them?"

"I was wondering whether you know if Tei will be part of any colony here."

Kazim kept filming but answered before Varya could. "A colony must be given every chance to succeed. That means balance in all things. Without balance, there can be no harmony. I would be amazed if all the clans, including the-clan-that-is-not, were not represented here."

Varya flicked his ears in agreement. "As Kazim said, they will come. There are Tei in all the castes, leading our people and showing the way. I'm sure there'll be plenty of volunteers."

"Kajetan might have to restrict the number that applies," Kazim added. "When our people see your world, Gina, everyone will want to come!"

She laughed. "Might be a bit crowded! Seriously now, you think Tei will come to stay?" Both Shan flicked ears in agreement. "Do you think they'll ask Shima to join?"

This time Gina had managed to stump them, she realised. Varya looked at Kazim, who lowered his camera to look back. Ears waved and twitched, tails rose and gestured. None of it meant anything to the Humans. Finally, Kazim answered after turning his camera off.

"Shima's mother's sib is Tei. His name is Tei'Thrand and Shima told me he helped teach her when she was still a youngling. She's strong in the harmonies, Gina, very strong. Easily strong enough to be Tei herself, but the-clan-that-is-not rejected her because of her eyes. I've never heard of them changing their minds once a decision is made."

Varya flicked his ears in agreement. "Kazim is right, but Shima is a special case. She's a hero. To us that's a very special thing. She was rejected, that's true, but The Blind Hunter hasn't been. In a way she's two people, and to reject a hero would be..."

"Unthinkable," Kazim said softly, obviously shocked by the thought. His ears were back.

"Unthinkable," Varya agreed. "That isn't to say she would accept any offer the Tei made her. I've heard her feelings about them. I don't think she likes the idea of leading others, and I know she doesn't like being called a hero. Foolishness she calls it. It's not, but getting her to agree would be hard."

Gina nodded. "So when her eyes are fixed, she'll probably leave?"

"We don't know what her plans are," Kazim said. "But I think she'll go home with Chailen and Sharn. They're all the family she has."

"Before she goes then, I want you to help me out. She's my friend, but more than that, I owe her for what she did that night at Charlie Epsilon. I know she wouldn't agree, but I feel the debt between us. I want to help her make some good memories here on Snakeholme."

"Honour debts must always be respected," Varya agreed. "We will help you, of course we will."

"Thanks. It's important to me. When you guys go home, we may never meet again. I think a vacation out here for all of us would be a fun way to say goodbye."

"Oh I don't know about goodbye, Gina," Kazim said. "If I have anything to say about it, I'm coming back for lots of visits."

Gina chuckled. "Not sure what the General will say about that. Snakeholme is supposed to be a secret."

Kazim flicked his ears. "From the Merkiaari, yes, but not from your friends."

"Gina," Cragg warned.

She raised a hand. "A secret is best kept by not telling anyone, Kazim. When you go, you must keep our secrets to yourself. The General will talk to you about this, but even our own people don't know where we are. Only those who live here know."

Varya and Kazim exchanged looks, but they flicked ears in agreement.

"Good. Let's move on," Gina said.

\* \* \*

# 11 ~ A Promise Kept

Shima awoke to darkness, she always did now, but... she had expected something else this time. She had gone into surgery, fallen asleep among Humans and their strange machines, and now awoken still in darkness. The disappointment was crushing.

"Are you awake, Shima?" Chailen said gently.

"I can't see."

"Shush my sib, all is well," Chailen soothed. "The bandages cover your eyes to protect them from light."

Shima tentatively reached up and felt her face. She was right. There were bandages holding pads of some soft material over her eyes. Her face felt numb. She couldn't feel her fingers touching her head.

"I can't feel anything."

"That's good," Sharn said. "The nannies are still working. The surgery went well, Shima. The Human healers are very pleased with you. They told me the nannies help with the swelling and pain, but will expire soon."

That's right. The healers had explained the process. Nannies were the surgical nanobot machines they had used to cut her optic nerves and then connect them to her new eyes. She had new eyes! She wanted to rip off the bandages, her hands shook with the need, but she restrained herself.

"You swear it; on your honour you swear all is well?"

"All is well as far as we can tell, Shima. I swear it," Chailen said. "Sharn, call Healer Devaraja."

Shima heard Sharn leave. She reached a questing hand toward her sib. Chailen took the hand and squeezed. "Did you see them, my eyes?"

"I saw. They're your eyes still, Shima, don't worry. They look the same. They *are* the same but cured."

That is what the Humans promised. They said they would be identical down to the genetic level, but would be modified to remove the defective genes that caused her poor sight. She had trusted, but to hear from her sib's own lips that all was well did reassure her. Her imaginings painted some strange pictures in her head. She had imagined her face with alien eyes peering out at the world, Human eyes with their odd colours and round pupils. To see again, she would have accepted even that, but to have her own eyes restored was a dream come true.

The harmonies warned her that Sharn was returning with a Human in tow. Shima squeezed her sib's hand, and then let go. The door opened and she turned her attention to the healer.

"How are you feeling, Shima?" Devaraja said. "Any nausea or pain, any light headiness?"

"Nothing like that, healer. My face is numb, and my scalp is just starting to tingle a little."

"Ah! Good good. That means the nannies are beginning to expire. Feeling will return to your face quite soon. This is the third day since the surgery in case you wondered. Everything went as expected."

Three days asleep! She hadn't thought to ask how long she'd been under. She'd just assumed it was the next morning.

"Lights, two percent illumination!" Devaraja ordered and the room darkened. "I'm going to loosen the bandage but I don't want you to move. It's dark in here now, but there's enough light to see by. I'll uncover only one eye for now."

"I understand," Shima said, hardly able to contain her excitement.

"Don't move now, and keep both eyes closed."

Devaraja eased the padding away from her left eye. She felt the cloth stick a little, but he was very gentle and it was finally uncovered. Shima felt the healer gently touching her face around the eye, pressing very gently, manipulating the flesh.

"The swelling has reduced very well, Shima. What there is should go down as you heal naturally. Keeping your right eye closed, can you open the left?"

Shima swallowed and tried.

At first, the lid didn't want to open, but she rolled her eyes and the moisture seemed to unstick the lid. The eye opened and she saw something without the aid of the harmonies for the first time in well over a year. The room was very dark. She blinked a few times and turned her head toward Devaraja and Chailen. Sharn was on the other side of her bed, on the right. She focused upon her sib. She was as beautiful as she remembered.

"Glad to see you again, my sib. It's been a long while."

Chailen covered her mouth and burst into tears. Sharn rounded the bed to comfort her, and Shima smiled. They looked so right together. She looked up to find Devaraja beaming a happy Human smile down upon her. Toothy smiles weren't aggression in Humans, she knew that, but it was still startling seeing those very white but blunt teeth so easily displayed. Shima reached a hand up, he did likewise, and she pressed her palm to his.

"Thank you."

Devaraja took back his hand and inclined his head. "You are most welcome, Shima. We have learned a great deal about

Shan physiology doing this for you. If payment had been necessary, you have more than covered any cost. It has been a fascinating journey, simply fascinating."

"I'm glad," Shima said in amusement. "Can I try my right eye now?"

Devaraja shook his head. "In a few minutes. Let me examine the left first."

Devaraja used a device he had in his pocket to measure the dilation of her eye as he raised the level of light in the room. He was very careful to ask if she was in discomfit at every stage, but Shima wasn't and just wanted the test over with. Finally the healer uncovered her right eye, and tested dilation in the same way before pronouncing himself satisfied.

"Congratulations, Shima. You have twenty-twenty vision... that's another way of saying your eyes are perfect. They're pretty too!" He said and chuckled as her ears flicked in surprise. "I'm sure Chailen can find you a mirror later, but for now, you're free to go. Contact me if you have any problems. Any at all, all right?"

Shima flicked her ears and then nodded in the Human manner, though Devaraja was familiar with Shan by now and understood. Shima suspected her people would develop and combine mannerisms more and more as time went on to deal with the Humans. Already she used nods and headshakes with them without thinking most of the time.

"Thank you, healer, I shall do that," Shima said as she climbed off the bed and joined her sib. She couldn't wait to get outside. "Chailen will make sure I do."

Chailen and Sharn laughed, their drop jawed laugh making Devaraja grin. Humans for some reason found Shan laughter fascinating and contagious.

No longer needing Chailen's arm, but still needing her to show the way, Shima navigated the sprawling tech centre's corridors listening to them discussing events. They were happy together, and Shima was happy for the first time since her blinding. All was right in her world for the first time in so long. She wanted to get outside and run, and just revel in the light.

"...and Varya made it sound perfect for our people. Kazim let me see some of his recordings, and you know how he can be about that. He hates letting anyone see his work unedited."

"Wait, what's that about Kazim?" Shima said.

Sharn answered. "He and Varya are out exploring the colony sites they chose. Gina went with them."

Shima flicked her ears in acknowledgement. She had known they were getting ready to go, but they must have left while she was in surgery. That hurt a little. Surely Kazim had wanted to know she was all right? Well why should he wait? They weren't family or clan to each other. Still, she would have waited if their places had been reversed.

"Hmph. He could have waited for me. I would've liked to see too," Shima grumped.

"Don't be angry with him, Shima. Tei'Burgton asked Gina to begin right away. He's very eager to start building, and it will be two or more seasons just to get word to the elders and their answer back."

"I suppose," Shima grumbled, but it did make her feel less aggrieved with Kazim for going without her. "And we didn't know my eyes would work, not for sure."

"True," Sharn said. "But we did trust the Humans to make it work somehow. Viper eyes are amazing technology. It must be like having a microscope in your head."

Shima laughed. "Trust you to find good even in disaster, Sharn. I don't want a microscope in my head, just working eyes."

Sharn hugged her. "And now you have, but I don't think the warriors back home will change your title at this late date."

Shima growled.

"Don't tease her, Sharn," Chailen said. "You know how she feels about this Blind Hunter business."

"Foolishness," Shima growled again.

"You need to get passed that," Chailen warned. "It's done now and nothing will change it. Besides, it's proven useful already. You don't think Kajetan would have given permission to just anyone to come here do you?"

Shima had to admit that was true. Kazim was famous back home and an ideal candidate because of that. Varya had been chosen because he was a warrior and for his work with vipers during the war, but The Blind Hunter was the people's choice. Famous, a heroic figure during the war, and tragic. It made Shima feel sick, but Chailen was right. The title opened doors that might never have opened without it. She would try not to spit when people called her a hero.

When they reached the doors leading to the outside, Chailen and Sharn dropped back without discussion to allow Shima her moment. Shima appreciated the sentiment, but the greatest moment had already past—opening her new eyes to see light for the first time. Still, this was a first of another kind... sort of. It was the first time she would step out into an alien world and see it with her own eyes.

Shima paused only briefly before opening the doors and advancing into the open. The first thing that surprised her was the time of day. The sky was purple edging toward black. The second thing was the sky again. So beautiful the stars, but Snakeholme had rings! The band of silvery light was amazing, and she gasped at the wonder of it.

Chailen and Sharn joined her. Chailen hugged her, "Amazing isn't it?"

Shima flicked her ears in agreement. She gathered Sharn in with her spare arm and the three of them stood there watching the sky as it turned completely black and the ring brightened until it blazed in the heavens.

"Gina told me the larger moon is called Gabriel," Sharn said. "Its reflected light makes the ring shine so. The little moon is Uriel. There are stations up there for tracking and defence. She says there used to be three moons, but millions of years ago Gabriel smashed it to bits. The ring is made of the dust and debris from that cataclysm."

Shima could imagine the disaster. There would have been meteor showers and strikes for centuries after the event. Anyone living here back then would have been in extreme peril, but of course no one had been.

"It's beautiful," Shima said.

Chailen flicked her ears in agreement. "Let's go in. Are you hungry?"

Shima was. "I could eat a Shkai'lon, hooves and all!"

Sharn laughed.

They made their way home, though home was the wrong word. They had a small house on the base normally used for viper officers. It was a comfortable dwelling, not designed for Shan of course, but Gina had helped them furnish it to make it a better fit for them. They had plenty of cushions to sit upon, and the table had been lowered close to the floor as was proper. Carpets were thick and extravagant compared with the bare polished wood floors used at home. Shima secretly liked them while pretending that such luxury was decadent. When alone she often abandoned her sleeping mat or her cushions to recline upon the carpet, but she would never tell.

Chailen hurried away to prepare food. She sometimes used the Human machine called autochef when they were in a hurry, but this time was a special day and they had nothing more to do. She chose to cook the food herself. They had brought supplies with them, but a surprising number of Human foods were edible by Shan. They tasted exotic and Shima enjoyed most of them, and wished she could try some of the meat animals on the hoof as it were, but they didn't live wild here. They were all raised on farms, and it just wouldn't be the same hunting on a farm. Not very... sporting? Was that the Human term? Whether it was or not, she was a hunter not a butcher.

"Whatever shall we do tomorrow and all the tomorrows

ahead?" Sharn said. "Now that you're well, Shima, what will we fill our time with?"

They were in the cooking area, what the Humans called the kitchen. It was well supplied with foods and the appliances used to prepare them. Shima busied herself with setting the table while Sharn peeled and washed vegetables, following Chailen's instructions.

"I don't know," Chailen said. "We can't go home until Varya is ready, and even then we must travel on a Human ship. I don't know when one is due to leave."

Shima flicked her ears in agreement. She would have to ask about that. She supposed it was time to decide many things. Now that the vipers had given back her life, she should be thinking about the future. Her life before the war had been all about her work. She was a scientist, and her life had been research into new variants of food crops. She had been an agricultural geneticist working at the centre for agricultural research on Child of Harmony near Zuleika when the Merkiaari attacked. As far as she knew, the centre was still there, safely sited among the farms used to test their ideas. The Merki had been uninterested in molesting it. No vermin to kill, Shima mused. In Merkiaari minds, any non-Merki species was considered vermin and must be exterminated.

Research had been her life, and what she was trained for. It was the one thing she knew beyond doubt or question she was qualified to do, but it no longer drew her heart and soul. It was important work still, but it didn't *feel* as important as it used to. Perhaps that was due to so many losses back home. Shima knew that it would take many orbits for the population of both worlds to fully recover. New efficient farming methods, though still useful, were no longer a priority in the elder's opinion—in hers too, Shima thought glumly. With so much happening and with the Merkiaari on the move again, there were too many other things to think about.

Was that the answer then? Should she consider the

unthinkable and ask to change caste? It was rarely done, and those who did so were considered... flighty. If they needed to make a change, it must mean they were not properly schooled, or hadn't properly considered the options and had made a hasty decision. Flighty.

The choice of caste was a huge deal to a youngling; it was choosing the path your life would take. In her case, joining the caste of scientists and engineers had been a given, and not because her mother and father had been of that caste. She had always known where she was going, always planned to be a scientist, and had chosen her studies based upon her future choice of caste. Now she didn't have any idea where she should go, and that was very unsettling for someone such as her. She liked having a goal and knowing how to achieve it. She had always been that way. Chailen could tell stories about her so serious sib that would have an entire house full of people rolling around in laughter. Yes, this decision should be about goals not profession, she realised. She needed a goal. Only then could she consider methods of achieving it.

"Well as for tomorrow and other tomorrows," Shima said. "I plan on going hunting. I'm out of condition and need to run. Do you want to come?"

Chailen flicked ears in the negative. "You know me; I'll trip over my own tail."

Sharn laughed and hugged his mate. "You're not that bad!"

Shima chuffed. Chailen was that bad actually, but only because she never practiced. All Shan were natural hunters, but it was still possible to be clumsy. Not honing one's skills and instincts did have that effect. A case in point was Kazim. He'd been a real trial to Shima back on Child of Harmony when she tried to lead him to safety. Gina would call him a city boy, and Shima would have to agree. She doubted there could be a more urbanised Shan than Kazim.

"I can teach you, Chailen. I swear I can teach you to equal father if you would apply yourself and give me time."

Chailen waved that away, her tail weaving in the complicated gestures that meant *maybe you could, but I'm not going to let you.* She always said that or similar when this came up. It was a polite way to acknowledge the offer and agree that Shima was skilled enough to do as she said, while at the same time declining it without giving offense. Chailen just had no interest in hunting. She was healer caste, and preferred saving life over taking it, even if the prey was a non-sentient food animal in the wild. For fun, she preferred caving with Sharn.

Shima thought for a moment. "We could go exploring then. There must be caves."

Chailen's ears pricked with interest. "The Humans have lived here less than two hundred orbits. I don't think they've explored everything yet."

Shima couldn't understand that. From what she knew of them, Humans had an insatiable curiosity, always poking into things and wanting to know the reasons behind everything. Why wouldn't they explore their world? All she could think of was that they had other things to do, like make war upon the Merkiaari. She could understand that, but their war until recently had been over for almost two hundred orbits. They'd had the time for other things, hadn't they?

"They've built cities here," Sharn was saying. "They must have explored the areas near them."

"Maybe so," Chailen said. "But there aren't many of them. I saw the maps they gave Varya. Most of the planet is still regarded as wild and untouched."

Shima felt the pull of that. To hunt and explore the wilds would be such fun! But, Chailen would not enjoy that. Perhaps they could explore some caves until Chailen had her fill and Kazim returned, and then she could take him off into the wilds to teach him how to hunt.

"I'll ask about caves then," Shima said. "I'm sure we can borrow supplies. We'll need ropes and lights at minimum."

"We'll have better than that," Sharn said. "Gina told

me that some of the vipers went climbing together after they became vipers. They wanted to test themselves on the mountains near here. It's not the same as caving, but they'll have everything we need."

Shima was sure they would, or if not, the vipers could have them made. Snakeholme had a small population, starting as it had from the families and friends of the original vipers based here, but it was a modern world with modern industry. Petruso City had shops; Chailen had visited most of them a time or two, and Humans enjoyed sports of all kinds. Shima had no money of her own here, but Gina said everything was free for the vipers and that extended to their guests. It wasn't really free of course. The regiment paid for such things and considered the minor cost a tiny but important part of its budget.

"It's settled then," Shima said. "I'll get the supplies we'll need, and we can go caving and exploring for a few days. When Kazim gets back, I'm going to take him hunting. It's embarrassing watching him stalk prey. He needs lessons."

Chailen and Sharn traded looks behind Shima's back, and grinned.

* * *

# 12 ~ Honour of the Regiment

Shima's caving plans worked out very well over the next few days, but first she went into the city on the maglev train, and spent an entire day there buying everything three people would need to survive alone in the wilds. She added ropes, lights, and other things needed to explore caves the right way. Tei'Burgton insisted they take emergency beacons with them, and Shima agreed, but they were the kind that transmitted when turned on and not before. Shima herself had insisted upon that. She had often taken one with her when hunting on Harmony and prided herself upon never using it. She would not start now.

For five days, Shima and the others explored the caves along the coast and just inland. Shima did enjoy it, but that wasn't why she went. It was for Chailen and Sharn, a small beginning on the debt she owed them. She didn't bring up her reasons of course; they were family and would be insulted, but Shima felt that she had let Chailen down this past orbit. By letting herself fall into a funk, she had put a greater burden than necessary upon her sib and her mate at the worst possible time. Their world, like that of so many others, had ended when the Merki came. Chailen had lost her father, her mate barely made a living for them by scavenging and trading trash for food, and on top of all that her sib had been suicidal and needed constant watching. This was a chance to put things back into order, to roll back time to before the war when Shima looked after Chailen not the other way around.

The days passed.

Shima hunted and supplied the camp with fresh meat. It was good exercise after so long. Her muscles ached, and she slept well, but already she could feel her strength returning. It would take time, but not too much time as the gravity of Snakeholme made a simple walk a real work out here. They moved camp three times as they explored. To Shima one cave system would have satisfied her, but Sharn wanted to compare each one and planned to come back to explore them all more thoroughly later.

Chailen enjoyed herself and seemed more relaxed than she had in a very long time.

They returned to the base satisfied and considered their time well spent, but Shima was not happy to learn that Varya and Kazim had returned briefly while she was away, and had left again. It was as if they were trying to avoid her on purpose! Well, she would see about that!

The day after her return to the base, Shima dressed herself in her hunting harness, and added the emergency beacon to it. She left her translator in her room. Her English was more than good enough now, and if she became stuck, Gina's Shan was excellent despite her odd accent. All the vipers spoke Shan well, even those who had never uttered a word of it. Their internal computer systems translated in real time.

Shima left her room to find Chailen. Sharn was out. He'd been invited to the tech centre again where they were dissecting Merkiaari bodies. Shima shivered at the thought. Research into the Merki made sense, but she didn't like the thought of the monstrous aliens polluting Snakeholme's air. Tei'Burgton wanted to know how the modern Merki troopers differed from those his vipers had encountered before. They acted differently and regenerated wounds, but preliminary tests had already shown they did not have nanotechnology swimming in their veins as Humans did. That must mean genetic drift was involved, and Shima expected they would learn it had been engineered into them. She was a scientist herself and should take a greater interest she supposed, but right now, all she could think about was a certain annoying male who was seemingly spending all his energy upon avoiding her! Perhaps later she could take the time to help Burgton's researchers, but not right now.

"I'm off then," Shima said to her sib who was reading something on a compad.

"Have fun," Chailen said sounding distracted. "Tell Kazim I expect to see his recordings before he sends them home."

"I will. What're you reading?"

Chailen raised the compad and turned the screen so that Shima could see. "It's just a primer. I'm learning to read Human... ah English. Why do they call it English? Shouldn't it be Humanish?"

Shima laughed. "No. English is just one of many Human languages. It's the main one. Sort of like Shan is the common tongue but we still have clan dialects."

"Oh!" Chailen said, sounding impressed that Shima knew that. "Why didn't they say that? You explained it so much better."

"They?"

"The vipers."

Shima's tail gestured a shrug and she added the dip of a shoulder that made it mean *beats me, aliens are weird.* "A guess, but maybe the ones you asked speak English as their common tongue and don't have clans? If you asked different ones they might know a different tongue."

"Maybe so, but if they all speak English why bother?"

Another shrug with her tail. "If we wanted to speak without them knowing what we said, we could use dialect. If they wanted to do the same, they could use another Human tongue. If you learned those, they couldn't hide anything from you."

Chailen stared.

Shima shifted uncomfortably. "Well, it's truth!"

"I see that, but who would think it and why?"

Shima chuffed in exasperation, turning it into a low growl at the end that told Chailen she was just being contrary and annoying now. Chailen laughed at her, and Shima twitched her ears in annoyance. She was starting to remember how annoying younger sibs could be now that Chailen was more relaxed and more like her old self.

"I'm going out," Shima said.

"So you said."

"Well... see you in a few days then."

Chailen waved a hand negligently.

Shima chuffed again and left the house. Chailen could have said be careful at least. Shima glanced back in time to see the blinds on one window settling back. Ha! Chailen had been watching her leave. Feeling suddenly more cheerful, she marched across the parade ground toward the airstrip.

Petruso Base had its own airstrip and facilities for transporting vipers and their gear to orbit, as well as to various places on the planet for training. It was located a short distance from the base separated from it by a fence pierced by a road. The road was for marching, not vehicles. At least, Shima assumed so because she'd never seen anyone driving on it. Vipers often ran in formation along it to catch a shuttle though. Varya and the others had used a shuttle to reach the survey sites. Shima didn't know where they were now, but she was sure someone at the airstrip did. The pilot at least must know.

Shima dropped to all fours and turned the trip into

a workout. She pushed herself into a sprint, enjoying the bunching and stretching of muscles. Vipers stopped to stare as she blurred passed them. She had run like this a time or two back during the war. Being chased by Merkiaari could be a very strong motivator. Vipers watched her go by, but none tried to catch her. They could though. Unlike other Humans, vipers could match Shan speed. She had run beside them a time or two. The run was exhilarating but over quickly. She slowed and arrived walking on two legs, looking for someone to ask about Varya.

Shima stopped before entering any of the buildings. She'd been blind the only time she had been here and didn't know where to go. None of the buildings had an obvious use except for the tower and maybe the hangars. They looked similar to Shan buildings in form if not in manufacture. She paused to consider if going to the tower would get her into trouble—it would have back home before the war; security wouldn't have let her enter, but here was very different. She suspected it was because everyone was a viper and had access. She doubted the authorities of other Human planets would let her roam so freely.

Before she could decide, a shuttle coming in for landing distracted her. She stopped to watch it taxi toward the nearest parking area. There were other shuttles and dropships parked there, and this one added itself to them. The screaming engines powered down and the hatch opened. Shima recognised Kate in the opening looking back toward the cockpit and talking to someone. Shima walked that way.

"...promised me goddamnit!" Kate snarled. "I'm not fucking around. You owe me!"

"I don't owe you shit, bitch girl. See these stripes? They mean I own your arse!"

"Yeah," Kate sneered. "I see them. You want rank, I'll give you rank. See these bars on my frigging collar?"

Shima stood there listening in amazement. She knew that Kate was a lieutenant, an officer in the regiment and the stocky bald viper she was arguing with was just a sergeant. He was Master Sergeant Stone, and that was a lesser rank. It confused her. Stone was acting as if he was Kate's superior. Was he older? He didn't look old, but Humans lived long and vipers longer still. Besides, Humans were different and didn't automatically defer to elders the way Shan did.

Kate stalked down the ramp.

"You keep mouthing off," Stone was saying as he appeared in the hatch opening, "and I'll have those pretty boys off your collar, and you in the brig!"

"Try it," Kate sneered. "You promised to help me find my brother."

Stone sighed and left the shuttle. He turned back for a moment and keyed the hatch shut. The ramp slid back up and stowed itself within the fuselage.

"I always keep my word, Richmond."

Shima flicked her ears. Of course he did, he was an honourable being. Why Kate thought he was not made her wonder though.

"And as for rank, it don't mean squat here. You're mine. The General gave you a choice, and you chose my new section. You're mine and that's it."

"No one owns me," Kate growled.

"I do, the regiment does, and you can bet your arse the General does. We've had this talk. Go off on your own and see what happens. You. Will. Be. Scrapped. We don't mess around with rogue units, Richmond."

"My brother—"

"Stow it," Stone growled and then sighed. "I keep my word. I'll help you, but I can't do shit while your systems are busted! What, you think I can assign an operation to an unfit unit and not have the General ask questions? Get real."

"I don't need enhancements to do my damn job! I did it fine for years before meeting you!"

Stone shook his head. "Now you're just being stupid. It doesn't matter whether I think you can handle an op or not. I could probably find you something to do, but I won't because he won't sign off on it! The General will not sign off... got it?"

"Yeah yeah, so you said before."

The harmonies revealed more to Shima than the angry words, and confused her even more. They argued and sounded angry at each other, but the harmonies showed they were feeling other things. Shima's ears went hard back and then struggled up in embarrassment. Perhaps this was some Human mating display? Surely not, but Stone was feeling very... ah amorous toward Kate? Was aggression part of a Human male's courtship like the Shkai'lon males did back home? And Kate! Well, if she had been Shan, Shima would have said Kate had just come into her fertile season and was looking to mate. Right now!

Shima had never experienced this situation amongst Humans before. She didn't know whether to absent herself or not. She lost the opportunity when Kate finally noticed her. Kate's face blazed red making the scars very and hideously visible.

"Hey, Shima, looking for me?" Kate said, slurring her words as she always did since being wounded. She crossed the distance between them with a quick jog in her step. She offered her right hand, and Shima placed her palm against it. "Gratz on the new eyes. Wish they could fix mine. It sucks dinosaur balls walking about with only one like this."

"Hey Kate, may you live in harmony. Why can they not?"

Kate shrugged. "They can, but they want to fix me all at once and that's harder. They say they're closer to a fix than they were. We'll see. At least I have one good peeper. If both were busted like your old ones, I wouldn't be waiting calmly, I can tell you!"

Shima laughed. "Is that what you're doing, waiting calmly?"

Kate grimaced, the scars turning her face into a horror.

"Not so much." She hooked a thumb over her shoulder toward Stone. "Ask him."

Stone came over and offered his hand, the light winked on the gold coloured contacts in his right palm. "I greet you, Shima, may you live in harmony."

"Sorry to interrupt your argument," Shima said after returning the greeting. Stone glanced at Kate. The harmonies revealed their auras flaring and touching. Shima blinked rapidly in consternation. If she didn't know better, she would have sworn they were mated already. "I ah... was hoping to find someone who could take me out to find Gina and Varya."

"You've come to the right place," Kate said. She turned toward Stone. "You got her location?"

Stone's face blanked as he uplinked to a satellite, Shima had seen that before. It was as if he was reading something or remembering something no one else could see, which she assumed must be close to the truth. She had never wanted a computer in her head, but Shima imagined it must be handy for research. She would make do with the wristcomp they had given her, and happy to do it.

"We can take you right to them," Kate said confidently, "but we probably won't be able to land, Shima. Gina told me the other day they're surveying the wilds. I can get you down using a line if you're willing though."

"That sounds like fun," Shima said and Kate grinned.

"Got 'em," Stone said. "Want me to let them know you're coming?"

"Please no," Shima said on a whim. "I think a surprise would be good. Can you put me down far enough away not to be detected?"

Kate shrugged. "Oh sure, easy. Be a bit of a hike for you though. Gina's sensors will pick up the shuttle otherwise. You know you can't surprise her, right?"

Shima didn't know that actually, and it might be fun to find out. She would like to try someday, but it could be dangerous in this situation. Out in the wilds, Gina might shoot her. Better be safe.

"Good point. Can you tell Gina that I'm coming, but tell her not to tell Kazim?"

Kate laughed. "Why not?"

The three of them went back to the shuttle and Stone opened the hatch; he would be their pilot. Kate sat with Shima in the cabin and they chatted while Stone moved the shuttle back to the start of the runway. Kate practiced her Shan, while Shima caught up with her Human friend's life since coming home.

"You're a lieutenant now, not a captain?" Shima said. "Should I say sorry to hear of your demotion?"

Kate rolled her eyes. "Hell no! I never wanted promotion in the first place, let alone to the rarefied heights of the captains. Only took it because Dicky Hames got killed. Shame about that. He was a good guy for an officer."

"He was a veteran, yes? I have that right, old vipers are veterans?"

"Hmmm kind of. You're right about him being old. He was one of the original vipers—not many of them left you know? Stone and Hames were recruited at the same time. Yeah, he was old and a veteran, but to be absolutely correct, a veteran is someone with experience." Kate grimaced as the shuttle accelerated down the runway and leapt aloft. "I'm not explaining this right. I can be a veteran and not one at the same time you see?"

Shima blinked and flicked her ears in confusion. She shook her head as well, in case Kate didn't understand.

"Sorry, I'll try again. I'm a veteran at fighting Merkiaari now and so are you, Shima, but I'm still new at being a viper. Stone is a veteran viper and a veteran Merki fighter..." Kate winced. "Is that clearer or am I just making it worse? Lucky you had *Canada* make first contact and not me, huh?"

Shima laughed. "You have so many interchangeable words that are different but mean the same thing, Kate, but I think I understand. I'm a veteran hunter because I have a lot of experience not because of my age. I'm still young."

"Exactly right," Kate said looking relieved. "I took over for Hames, and Gina took over for me, but it was a temporary thing. I've never cared about promotion; the mission is more important to me than rank, but Gina isn't like me. She does care—a lot. Too much sometimes. She's a worrier you know? She feels responsible for everyone and everything—she cares about her men as well as the mission and tries to balance the two. That makes her a good officer I suppose."

"Balance is always good, without it there can be no harmony."

"Don't start that," Kate said crossly. "Religion isn't my thing."

Shima cocked her head and flicked her ears, but Kate didn't understand the gesture. It meant she wanted more information.

"I know the word, Kate, but this isn't about religion. Harmony is not a religion; it's a way of life. Shan do not believe in a deity or a maker of all things, as I understand some Humans do. My people put no stock in it."

"But how can you not? You're always talking about the harmonies."

"The harmonies are not what you seem to think, Kate," Shima said. It had always made her sad that Humans could not sense the harmonies. What a horror, to live life oblivious that way. "The harmonies are created by life itself, all life, not a single entity that you might wish to call God. Take me into space and leave me alone up there, and I would be cut off from the harmonies. If you were right, there would be nowhere in the universe that I could not sense them."

Kate nodded slowly. "I think I see. The trip here must have been horrible for you."

"At first, yes, but not the way you think. I wasn't alone and the harmonies were with me, but I couldn't see, Kate. Back home I spent all my time in the garden because I could use the harmonies to see, at least in a crude way. Aboard ship I was slowly going mad until Stone gave me the simulator helmet."

"I'm sorry you had to go through that."

Shima flicked her ears acknowledging the sympathy. "I'm not sorry... well, not now anyway. It was a torment, but it was a price worth paying for my new eyes."

Kate nodded thoughtfully.

The flight lasted about three segs or hours, Shima judged. She didn't know how far Gina had roamed from her drop off point, except that she had stayed within the general vicinity bounded by the mountains and that of the valley she was exploring. Shima had studied the maps, but Kate had switched on a display in the seatback in front of them to show her the land they flew over. The area was lush and beautiful, the mountains high and snow capped. Shima wondered about the weather and found herself hoping it was not too harsh. A colony here would be a fine thing; at least it would be based upon her scant knowledge.

The valley was heavily forested with gorges and rivers connecting it to the mountains, and was joined by other valleys to the west. Farther south, it widened and formed into a lake before narrowing again. The fast moving water of the river had cut a deep canyon at the southern tip, and would take Shima weeks to navigate should she try. Glaciation in the far past had created the landscape, and it had done a wonderful job. Shima approved, as did all the creatures that called it home she assumed. The entire area must be teeming with life. She could hardly wait to get down there.

"Are the other worlds of the Alliance like this?"

Kate shrugged. "Some are, but others are so different you wouldn't believe it. Desert worlds, jungle worlds, and even water worlds where nine tenths of the planet is ocean. Then there are planets like Garnet that have crystal forests and metal mountains, and hardly any breathable air. I've not been to all of the Alliance worlds, but almost anything you can imagine is out there somewhere, Shima, and don't forget there are a lot of planets that haven't joined the Alliance. You can't be surprised surely. The Shan homeworld is different to Child of Harmony after all."

"Oh..." Shima dragged her eyes away from the screen to look at Kate. "Yes, you're right, but Child of Harmony's differences are quite subtle. The sun in the sky is the same sun, though it looks bigger, and the gravity is different. A tree is a tree, grass is grass there. Different species and varieties, absolutely, but obviously still trees and grass. Here though, the sun itself is a different colour, and the light makes everything look so alien."

Kate looked at the screen. "I'm trying to see it the way you do, Shima, but I've seen so many worlds that they blend together. Snakeholme's star is main sequence, what we call F-type. It's hotter than Sol and plants absorb its light differently. I look down there and I still see trees no matter these are orange not green. A tree is a tree. They stick up high out of the ground, taller than a bush, have a trunk and bark... that's what a tree is to me. It doesn't matter how weirdly shaped the leaves are, or what colour they turn in winter. It's a tree!"

Shima laughed and indicated herself and Kate. "And we are people, no matter our shape?"

"Exactly, and no matter our colour," Kate waved vaguely in Stone's direction. "Or whether we have fur or not. I guess it's a mindset. You may not know this, but the people living on Bethany, my homeworld, do not think like me at all. I'm sorry to say, you would not find a welcome there and neither would I now."

That was interesting. "They don't like vipers?"

"They don't like anything different to themselves. When your people send someone to join the Council, I guarantee she will have no welcome from Bethany's councillor."

Shima flicked her ears in acknowledgment and nodded in thought. She would ask Varya to add this information to his report. The elders may already have heard, but in case they hadn't it wouldn't hurt to tell them. Not that they would be surprised. There were plenty of Shan wary of Humans just because they were alien. Why shouldn't Humans be wary of Shan in the same manner?

"One minute to drop point," Stone said over the cabin intercom.

Kate stood and hurried forward to the cockpit, but was back very quickly to open the hatch. She had to by-pass the safety interlocks to open it while in flight. Depressurisation wasn't a concern at such a low altitude.

Kate waved Shima over to the hatch as the shuttle hovered. "*I'm not extending the ramp!*" she shouted over the engine noise.

Shima nodded exaggeratedly. She held hard to the opening and leaned out to look down. Stone was holding the shuttle steady just a few tails or metres above the treetops. She could easily climb down... hmmm. What need for a rope then? She turned to find Kate watching her with the rope still coiled. Kate cocked an eyebrow in one of those strange Human face-screwing gestures. This one was a challenge, Shima thought, and laughed.

"*I won't need that at this range. The trees will be my road!*"

"*You sure?*"

Shima nodded and dropped to all fours. She moved into the hatchway but sideways so that a shuffle to her right would have her falling directly down onto the closest tree. It might look dangerous to Kate, but it wasn't really. She could jump twice this distance and catch another tree branch if she had to. Dropping straight down like this, she couldn't miss.

"*See you back at the base!*" Shima yelled over the noise and stepped sideways into empty air.

Shima fell away from the shuttle and immediately spread all four legs wide as if pouncing upon prey with claws extended. The drop was short and she grabbed the tree at its highest point. It was thin and flexible, but tough, and it held her weight beautifully. It did bend outward, but that was actually helpful. It let her see her next target easier.

Shima looked up to find Kate hanging out of the shuttle yelling at her. Shima waved, but Kate pointed exaggeratedly southward. Shima looked that way and then back, but understood just a moment later. Gina and the others were south of her. Shima nodded and waved again. Kate waved back and disappeared inside. The hatch closed and the shuttle veered away climbing for altitude.

Shima found her target branch on the next tree and leapt. It was like old times, moving this way. She didn't always hunt from above, but she did it often enough to be practiced at it. The foliage was a burnt orange colour, and her pelt would not blend well here, but the difference did not affect locomotion. She moved from tree to tree easily; they were close together but the canopy wasn't too thick. She had the choice to stay aloft or take to earth again. She decided to go down and try for Gina's scent.

Shima leapt down and circled with her nose close to the ground. Moving that way was slow, but she didn't rush. The circles grew in diameter until finally she gave up. Either they had come through here too long ago for scents to linger, or she hadn't crossed their trail yet. She switched her attention from scent to sight and began looking for tracks. There were many, but they didn't belong to Humans or Shan. The tracks belonged to native wildlife. Shima took an interest and studied the tracks, taking the time to memorise the scents associated with each of the different types. She dragged air in over her tongue and the scent glands at the back of her throat, but kept the *scree scree* noise low and quiet as she could. She didn't allow herself to forget that she was in unfamiliar and wild country.

Shima decided to cut directly west. It was an arbitrary decision. East would work just as well. She needed to cut Gina's trail before she could actively hunt for her friends.

Shima used the harmonies and moved on all fours quickly west. She could cover a lot of ground without fearing attack that way. The harmonies allowed her to sense the alien beasts that called the forest home, and there were many of them.

Segs passed with Shima choosing to avoid contact with the wildlife. She wished she could investigate the intriguing tracks that she discovered; she would wager her best knife that the animals that made them would taste wonderful. Their scent alone made her belly grumble and her mouth water... very undignified, drooling like that. She decided that if she didn't find sign of Gina soon, she would hunt one of the beasts and see how good it tasted before camping for the night.

The day passed and Shima found no sign of Gina and the others. It looked as if she had chosen wrong. Should have gone east. Oh well, it wasn't the end of the world and she was having fun using old skills on new terrain. It occurred to her that her people might soon explore other alien worlds like this. What fun! It could even happen in her lifetime. Oh how she hoped it would be so. There might one day be ships like the heroic *Canada*, but built and crewed by Shan surveying new worlds and helping to rebuild the Great Harmony among the stars. That was a wonderful dream.

The thought brought her up short, and she stopped where she was thinking furiously. Surveying and studying new worlds... ships like that would need scientists, and she *was* one. She shivered feeling a strange excitement that ruffled her fur all the way down her spine to the tip of her tail. She shook herself to settle her pelt back into order. Dreams like that were far from reality. It would take many orbits of recovery before her people would be ready to venture out among the stars. They needed to make the home system secure against the Merki first. They mustn't rely upon the Humans for that. Shan had to be self-sufficient. Allies could be allowed to help, not do the job for them. The realisation that she would likely be long dead of old age before her dream became reality saddened her. Shan life spans were too short, she thought sadly.

Shima shook off her sudden bad mood, and looked about herself. Trees trees and more trees... and a puddle. She padded toward the puddle and sniffed the water. Fresh, and not a puddle, more like a pond. Too small to be a real lake, but deep enough that the water table had filled the depression. The harmonies revealed no fish, but a small lap of her tongue at the surface confirmed it was clean and cold. She emptied the by now stale water from her bottle, refilled it, and replaced it upon her harness. She quenched her thirst directly from the pond itself.

She took a deep satisfied breath. This was a good place, a safe water supply and it was removed a short distance from the more obvious game trails. It would make a good campsite. And that's what it would be, she decided. It was time to see how good those intriguing natives tasted, but first she would gather wood for a fire.

Shima quickly gathered dead wood from nearby and piled it close by for convenience. She cleared a wide area of leaves and revealed the bare dirt beneath. She would keep an eye out for stones to make a proper fire pit while hunting; there didn't seem to be any here. It didn't matter. If she had to, she would dig down a little and use the excavated sod to ring the pit.

Satisfied for now, Shima took to the trees to begin her hunt.

The harmonies sent her northeast toward prey. It wasn't cheating, she assured herself. She wouldn't use the harmonies to hunt, but she did need a starting direction. Now that she had one, she would hunt as her father had taught her, using her wit and her senses.

She used the trees to stay high and downwind of the creatures she found by scent a while later, and spied a family group of something she had no name for. The grunting growling noise they made as they squabbled among themselves was completely unfamiliar to her as was their form. They were low to the ground four legged tusked creatures. The tusks could have been simple fangs growing as they did from the lower jaw, but these were oversized and curled. Definitely tusks, not teeth.

The creatures had muscled forequarters, but were slimmer at the rear. They had short tails, whip thin and useless seeming. She doubted they used them for defence. Might be used to defend their anus from insects, she mused, but useless for anything else. Their hides were dark brown, close to black, and looked tough. She might have a problem hooking her claws through that hide, but she was looking forward to trying. They were covered in short bristly hair over their backs and sides, not proper fur, and seemed bald underneath where the hide looked paler. She didn't like the look of their hooves. They looked dangerous, nasty enough to open her belly she was sure. Sharp hooves but not clawed, no spurs, but she had a feeling these things used those hooves for rooting about in the dirt like a Shkai'lon. Shkai'lon were rage filled menaces; these... call them tuskers she decided, might have a similar niche on this world. She drew a breath to sample the scent.

*Scree scree scree.*

Hmmm, an odd earthy scent, but tasty, she decided as drool filled her mouth again. She swallowed, and winced as her stomach growled. Was it loud enough for the tuskers to hear? She watched them closely. Apparently not. She closed in, but not too close.

The two adult creatures were guarding the little ones, who continued squabbling among themselves over something they'd found. Shima chose the male for her dinner; it was the larger of the two adults, but Shima wondered if tuskers might fight cooperatively in a pack. She would find out she supposed, but she hoped not. A good hunter did not waste meat. She couldn't eat all of them, even gorging to build reserve fat, and she didn't need to do that here. Should she look for something else? No, she decided. She was new to this world and its creatures. She had to start somewhere and learn its ways.

She pounced.

Shima dropped with her limbs extended and claws out roaring her challenge. The little ones scattered, and ran in all directions. Good. The female spun toward her mate, saw Shima land on his back, and charged.

"Yow!" Shima screamed in pain and surprise. The bristles covering the tuskers were quills, not wiry hair. She yowled again and threw herself off the male.

Shima's fur protected her somewhat, but the quills had penetrated her skin shallowly and in numerous places. Curse the luck. She was bleeding, but not badly. She hoped they weren't poisonous. She didn't think they were. She pulled one of the quills out of her harness strap and took a quick look at it. No sign of poison. Good, the fight was still on.

Her appraisal was quick enough that she avoided the female's charge, and had enough time to scream another challenge. The female turned quickly, almost folding herself in two to face Shima, and shook her body aggressively. Every quill on her body stood up and rattled against each other as a warning. Then it surprised Shima again. The little demon spawn rolled into a ball presenting spiky pain in all directions to any attacker. Shima spun to the male in time to see him fold himself into a ball as well.

No fair!

Shima padded up to the male and batted at the annoying thing. Yow! That hurt, harmonies curse it. She pulled the broken spines out of her paw and glared at the little menace. She sniffed and growled and nudged the thing trying to make it unroll itself, but no go. Well... she backed away in consternation. Well shit, as Kate would say. Now what?

Shima glared at the two spiky balls of alien goodness and paced around them, daring them to open up, but they didn't. She could use her beamers to shoot the stupid things, but that wasn't hunting, that was slaughter. It didn't seem fair somehow. She could use her knives to kill them, and that seemed better, but it was still an unsatisfying conclusion to the hunt. If she'd been truly in need, she wouldn't hesitate, but she was hungry not starving.

Shima chuffed in annoyance, and turned away. She walked back the way she'd come staying on four feet, leaving behind the demon spawned excuses for dinner. She looked back over her shoulder hopefully, but no, they weren't taking chances. Still tucked up tight. She spat in their direction, and trotted away. They probably tasted awful anyway, she thought, trying to convince herself that she hadn't just been bested by a pair of spiky aliens less than half her size.

Shima followed a game trail and picked up more alien scents. She discarded the tantalising and delicious seeming tusker scent layering the trail, she was learning after all, and zeroed in upon something else. This one was a predator, at least it smelled like a meat eater, and the scat it left seamed to verify it. She chose it as her prey, and planned to expiate her humiliating failure with the tuskers by enjoying its flesh tonight. She was hungry enough to eat it raw, bones and all, but she would have anyway—not the bones thing, but eat it raw yes. Meat always tasted best still warm and bleeding. Besides, this was her first alien dinner. It would be wrong to cook it the first time; this was research of a sort after all.

Shima laughed to herself, and finally found the funny side of her non-fight with the tuskers. She could laugh at herself now. It had been funny in a way, but she was glad she'd been alone. At least she knew not to hunt tuskers by choice now, and no one had seen her failure.

She followed the scents and tracks off the trail and far into the trees. The animal left prints completely different to that left by tuskers. No hooves for this creature. It left prints indicating padded feet and claws. She placed her hand beside one of the impressions and her ears swivelled listening for movement close by. The print was bigger than her hand but not by much. She backed up and compared the depth of her print to that of the prey. Similar. Very similar. Their weights must be close too. Shima looked around warily. This didn't feel right. She was tempted to use the harmonies, but no. Her previous failure still smarted. She wouldn't betray her father's training.

Shima advanced again, but warily, her ears straining for any sound. Her eyes were wonderfully keen these days, making her aware of how far below a normal Shan's perceptions she had been before. She was at her peak now with regard to her senses, and was determined to build her body's stamina back to peak fitness as well. She slowed as a feeling of being watched came over her. Right forefoot, left hind foot, and pause to listen, left forefoot, right hind foot and another pause this time to taste the air.

She whirled and slashed as something dropped from the trees behind her. She felt the barest touch on one claw as she spun, but there was no blood. Her ears were back, safely out of danger as her roar rumbled up to shatter the silence. The answering roar shocked her to stillness, and she blinked at the crouching creature before her.

Her jaw opened wide showing her killing teeth in an instinctive threat display, her vision tunnelled and her ears clamped themselves against her head tighter than ever. The creature before her was startlingly familiar, but not at the same time. His jaws full of teeth any Shan would be proud to own. His eyes were nothing like a Shan's eyes and glowed red with blocky horizontal pupils, but the orangey red coloured fur and sharp claws? Marvellous! Obviously a hunter, using the trees to stalk prey as Shan would, as she herself *had* so recently done! Shima felt a kinship with this creature and would have liked to admire him at her leisure, but she was busy.

Fighting for her life.

He pounced upon her, raking claws and snapping jaws. Shima suddenly knew what her prey felt when she attacked this way. She was the prey now, and it was exhilarating and terrifying all at once. She rolled to the side and onto her back, claws out trying to rend his belly as she would have had this been another Shan attacking. That was her tactic; treat him like Shan because she had never fought with anything else remotely like him.

Shan no longer fought each other except for play. Cubs and younglings wrestled, but this was a bit more serious. Jaws snapped at her muzzle, and she grabbed his ruff with both hands, trying to turn his head away, but he was incredibly strong. She flexed her fingers and her claws shot out and into his flesh. Blood poured and he went into frenzy, struggling violently and whipping his head back and forth. Froth flew from his snapping jaws, but Shima pushed him back, turning her face away from him, but really having to work at it to keep those teeth out of her hide. She couldn't hold him!

He ripped himself free, and leapt away.

Shima rolled back onto four feet snarling and giving her attacker a good look at her teeth in a show of aggression and ferocity. The fight was all about instinct now. She didn't fight her people's natural reactions. She embraced them. Her vision was already tunnelled, centred on her prey. No time for thinking now, her hunt kill reflex had a firm hold upon her. Her scream of rage rose over the forest, quieting the other creatures hiding within it. Her prey had increased the distance between them, but Shima knew what was coming. She braced for the charge, but the beast surprised her again by pouncing a second time. She would have charged. Hit and run strikes were ingrained in her people in these situations, because they would most likely be fighting Shkai'lon or Shkai'ra.

Shima's heart thundered within her chest as she met the beast in the air mid-leap. This time Shima had his measure. Her jaws clamped his throat tight, cutting off his air, and she wrapped her arms around his body to hold him while her rear claws went to work on his belly and genitals, ripping into him.

They crashed to earth, Shima on the bottom but in the

ascendant now. She had him where she wanted him. Blood and slippery ropes of entrails gushed out upon the ground, but Shima didn't release the pressure on his throat. His struggles became desperate but already weakening. She bit harder and harder and harder. Growling and ripping and crushing his throat, and snarling and biting and ripping and...

Shima slowly came back to herself still chewing into the furry throat and growling. She finally realised the beast had stopped struggling a while ago. The steaming entrails were a pile beside her, and the body a dead weight atop her. Her mouth was thick with alien blood.

"Hmmm, you do taste good," Shima mumbled, her mouth still full. Reluctantly she pulled back. "Yum," she said licking her muzzle clean of blood.

Shima pushed the corpse off and stood on two legs over it. She wanted to roar her victory, but sadly she had come back to herself now and such things seemed a little primitive from the lofty heights of a civilised being. Perhaps a small one?

Shima roared, proclaiming victory, and despite herself it wasn't a small one at all. She sheepishly looked around, hoping Kazim was too far away to hear, but there was a part—a small part—that wished he could have seen her. She was proud of her skill, and that fight had really been something. She was sure that even her father, skilled as he was, would have been impressed.

Shima reached for her knives and went to work cleaning and butchering her kill.

Back at her chosen campsite, she washed the blood and stink of death from her body, and then cleaned her equipment. The harness needed special attention; it was thick with blood and other gunk. Her knives were last. She dug a pit and built up earthen walls around it, before building and lighting a fire in the centre with her old spark rock and steel. It didn't seem strange using primitive tools to make fire. She had used them regularly since her father gifted them to her on their first hunt together. She had been a cub then, barely a year old.

Shima ate her fill of raw meat, still bleeding on the bone, and then set some to cook on sticks stuck in the ground and angled toward, but not actually in, the flames. She wanted to try some of it cooked just to taste the difference, but also planned on taking some with her to eat on the journey. It should last better cooked, not that it needed to last long. She should be with Gina and the others sometime tomorrow.

The morning dawned overcast and Shima expected to get wet before she found her friends. She didn't care. Weather was just something to be endured on a hunt; nothing to be done about it, certainly no point in complaining. Her pelt would shed the rain, and she was warm enough. She had clean water and plenty of cooked meat. She ate some of the uncooked leftovers from her feast last night for breakfast, but left the rest for the scavengers to clean up. She had plenty of cooked meat in pouches on her harness. She wouldn't need to hunt again today. She buried the ashes from her fire along with the bones in her fire pit, wanting to leave her campsite as she found it. Shima took one last look around, and set off to find her friends. She was determined to do that before night fell.

Shima travelled quickly, retracing her path and then moving into new territory in a straight line aiming for the river. She was sure Gina wouldn't cross the river. Not that she couldn't do so, but where was the need? Shima felt sure she would cut Gina's trail before reaching it.

As it turned out, Shima was right, but it took longer than she thought. Gina was heading south still, following the path of the river it seemed. Nothing wrong with that, but surely a survey should cover a wider area? If Shima had to survey the valley, she would have zigzagged west to east to cover more terrain. It would slow the journey south, but that didn't matter. The task wasn't to follow the river, and there wasn't an expiry date on their survey. Whatever the reason, Shima had her friend's scent and their tracks now. She could quicken her pace even more and catch them easily before night.

Shima set out to do just that.

She realised long before finding them where they had to be. On the flight out, Kate had shown her the terrain on one of the shuttle's displays, and she had pointed out the huge lake at the southern end of the valley where the river entered the gorge. Following the river so closely was the clue. Gina was either at the lake it emptied into, or heading directly for it. Shima didn't know why. Perhaps Varya wanted to consider it as a location for the colony. It wouldn't be unheard of for a Shan city to be built on the shores of a lake after all, and the idea quite intrigued her. Still, it did seem odd that the tracks arrowed right toward it without variation. Surely it made more sense to survey the entire valley on the way?

Whatever the reason, and with the aid of the harmonies and her hunting skills to avoid trouble, she arrived upon the shores of the lake safely by late afternoon.

"What took you so long," Kate said, grinning as she approached. She was holding a stick with something edible thrust onto it. A fish. She took a bite. "I thought we might have to send out a rescue party."

Shima blinked in consternation. Beyond Kate's shoulder she could see the shuttle floating upon the lake, and not far down the shore, tents had been set up. There were people there, more than there should be.

"What?" Shima said feeling very confused.

"We expected you last night," Kate said, stepping closer and offering the stick. "It's good, try some."

Shima mechanically took a piece of fish off the stick with her claws and popped it into her mouth. Flavour exploded upon her tongue, and her eyes widened. Kate nodded and offered the entire stick to take. Shima took it and ate more of the silvery blue fish. It tasted wonderful. It had been prepared with herbs and butter it tasted like, and cooked to perfection. She finished it and licked her chops ready for more.

"What's happening, Kate?"

Kate led her back toward the others. "It was Gina's idea. Now your eyes are fixed, you'll probably be going home soon. She wanted to thank you for all you did for us during the war by helping to make some good memories. Did it work?"

Shima remembered the tuskers and then her fight with the not-Shan thing she hadn't named. "Yes, it's been a good hunt so far."

"Great!" Kate said. "Bet you didn't know Stone is a fiend for fishing, did you?"

"No."

"Neither did I!"

Shima laughed. "Who is your cook? The fish tasted fantastic."

"Chailen. She's been cooking all day for your vacation feast. We have the whole week to play and have fun, more if you want. The General didn't specify when he wanted us back and we're only a few hours away by shuttle anyway if he calls."

They reached the tents and Shima learned the depth of the deception. Chailen and Sharn came up and hugged her laughing about how Shima just happened to meet Kate's shuttle arriving at Petruso airstrip. Gina laughed at her outraged glare. Cragg offered another fish on a stick, and she took it greedily. He was already eating one. Varya raised a hand in greeting. Stone nodded to her from where he crouched before the fire taking care of Chailen's pots where they bubbled and steamed with wonderful smells of cooking.

There was one person missing. "Where's Kazim?" Shima said, trying not to sound concerned.

Chailen and Sharn stepped apart and pointed. Shima looked beyond the camp to find a lonely figure standing on the edge of the water, looking her way. He had his camera in one hand, but not pointed.

Shima handed her empty stick to Chailen wordlessly and

went to join him.

# 13 ~ Operation Oracle

Gina awoke still in her acceleration couch, but the couch wasn't where she had left it. She was face down and the surface she lay upon was getting hot. She squirmed and found the harness release. The seat felt like it weighed a ton; she could hardly move under its weight. That worried her because there was fire, and a viper shouldn't sweat the weight of a single metal seat, and there was fire... and you know, fire!

She twisted and fumbled the harness loose and was finally able to drag herself from under the seat. When she staggered erect, she realised why the weight had been so crushing. The dropship was trashed and the fuselage was crumpled. Her seat had been on the starboard side, but although it was still securely bolted to the bulkhead that the designers had intended, it was now on the port side of the ship.

Gina shook her head and kicked her way free of debris coughing and choking on the smoke starting to fill the ship. She grabbed her rifle from the deck where it had ended wedged under the seat after the crash. The screams and cries of the wounded and dying pulled her in multiple directions. She needed to give aid, but first she needed to find a way out.

Blood trickled into her eyes and she irritably wiped it away. The fires were getting worse and with it the screaming. She spun in place and staggered. Her leg wasn't working right, and for the first time she took notice of her own diagnostics.

>_ DIAGNOSTICS: LEFT LEG IMPAIRED, KNEE JOINT 25%. LUNG CAPACITY 87%.
>_ IMS: REPAIRS IN PROGRESS.
>_ DIAGNOSTICS: UNIT FIT FOR DUTY.

The knee blazed with pain despite her IMS flooding the area with pain blockers. It was three times the size it should be and her uniform was stretched tight over it. Every time she moved, her thigh and shin armour caught and gouged it sickeningly. Cold sweat popped out on her forehead and she grunted as she forced her way forward.

There were many bodies scattered, impaled, and crushed within the ship. Most were sleeping the little death, their beacons flashing and reporting their readiness for pickup, but not all. Too many were true dead. Gina left them alone and continued forward to the other troop hold. The screams were coming from there.

The hatch was jammed part way open, and smoke boiled through the gap. Gina wrenched at the obstinate hatch and it groaned open another few inches, but then stopped. She put her shoulder to it and heaved. No movement. She wedged herself further into the gap and used her body like a hydraulic jack. Her knee was screaming, but she forced it to bend until her feet were positioned against the hull. Then she slowly straightened her legs.

>_ DIAGNOSTICS: CRITICAL DAMAGE WARNING... LEFT KNEE 23%... 21%... 17%...

*The pain, the pain, the pain!* Gina screamed at the agony,

but the screams of her companions were worse than any torture. The warning kept flashing on her internal display, counting down to complete failure of her knee. If it did fail, the joint would need complete replacement in sickbay. Anything else would take time, but could be repaired by IMS in the field with her own resources. She kept pushing, but the pain...

*Computer: Melee mode*

The world slowed and the pain went away. Ahh... the relief was heaven. Gina knew it was all illusion. Melee mode suppressed pain responses, so she could do things that would otherwise make her pass out or quit. She wouldn't quit, and the damage continued to pile up. She eased off on the pressure, and then kicked hard with both legs. The hatch juddered open a little more.

>_ DIAGNOSTICS: CRITICAL DAMAGE WARNING... LEFT KNEE 14%

She kicked again.

>_ DIAGNOSTICS: CRITICAL DAMAGE WARNING... LEFT KNEE 11%

The hatch slammed open and she fell into the troop hold. The screams were less, the flashing beacons had multiplied on her sensors. Gina rolled around clutching her knee. The pain was leaking passed the block. That shouldn't happen, but it was happening, and she rolled around clutching her pain. The sharp agony slowly dulled to a throbbing heat and she turned to discover the horror.

Her comrades were burning where they sat trapped unable to escape. A fuel line must have ruptured and a jet of fire was playing directly on to a section of the ship where vipers were still mustered in their couches. They were... Gina gulped, trying to force the images out of her head, but vipers could not forget. The flames had been held back by viper armour and nano-processed uniforms, for a while anyway, but they had failed eventually and the flesh beneath had been burned away.

She saw men and women with no faces. Their metallic bones burned clean and horrifyingly shiny and visible. Surely they would die, their brains cooked, but they were still moving! Gina's guts heaved. Why weren't they in hibernation or dead? Everywhere she looked she saw horror—arms that had no flesh, but still moved trying to get free, faceless people screaming, and bodies burned down to the bone with things moving inside as they struggled struggled struggled! Viper biomech muscles were proving their resilience and resistance to fire in a horrifying manner. Bodies twitching and wrenching at debris while completely engulfed in fire, pinned by the crumpled ship that had failed to protect its cargo. The horror was everywhere she looked.

Gina was still in melee mode and boosted to the max. She forced herself up and into that hell. She had to shut off the fuel. She even knew how to do it, though she'd never had to for real. Wolfcub class dropships had an engineering section just aft of the cockpit. She could see it, just beyond the flames.

Gina found a helmet on the deck and pulled it on over her own burns. She had awoken with them, and knew they were the result of a previous battle and not caused here. She didn't know where her own helmet was and didn't care. It would keep the heat out of her eyes for a while. Without hesitation, she forced herself to climb over the wreckage and into the fire. The temperature soared around her, and warnings proliferated upon her display. Smoke and pollutants caused by burning synthetics scoured her throat and burned already damaged lungs. The pain in her knee was forgotten as her hands burned. She had no gloves and was having to pull herself forward grasping hot metal.

Finally, she was over the hurdle and staggering forward. She glanced at her friends in their couches, but all in this section were in hibernation. A lot of internal injuries she guessed, because outwardly they didn't look too bad. Was she the only one to remain conscious on the entire ship? She looked into the cockpit but only briefly. Both pilots were true dead. They had to be. They'd been cut in half. Nothing could survive that. She wanted to scream when she saw the co-pilot move a little. The top half anyway.

She found the emergency fuel shut off and flipped the switch. Darkness filled the ship's interior as the flames died. The screaming turned to whimpers and groans, but one by one they fell silent and more beacons started flashing.

"Oh Jesus..." she hissed throwing the helmet down and leaning to take the weight off her knee.. "Oh Jesus...." she mumbled and wiped blood out of her eyes. And tears. "Oh Jesus..."

She was shaking and feeling shocky. She turned, feeling the world drift around in slow motion. That was when she knew what was wrong. Still in melee mode and boosted to the max, her IMS was as close to offline as it came short of true death. It didn't have the resources to fix her up, and she could tell she was in a bad way. She wasn't getting enough air and felt light headed.

*Computer: combat mode*

The world sped back up and Gina screamed in agony. Her knee buckled and she fell against the engineering consol. Oh God it hurt! Her internal display was suddenly flooded with data. Flashing multicoloured icons and numbers competed for attention, and despite her coughing and need to get out, she had to deal with some of it.

>_ IMS: LUNG CAPACITY 43%, LEFT KNEE 11%. COMBAT

EFFECTIVENESS 61%. MAINTENANCE MODE RECOMMENDED.
ENTER MAINTENANCE MODE [Y]ES/[N]O?
>_ N

"Dumb machine," Gina grumped.

This was no time to sleep. Now she had the time to think, she knew why the others had burned without entering hibernation. Their systems were intelligent enough to assess risks—that was part of what made vipers so dangerous in combat. Their processors had known letting them sleep in the fire would kill them, so it hadn't allowed it. Simple as that. So stupid, but totally logical. Those vipers would have burned to death and remained aware the entire time because the viper design team programmed them to survive at any cost. Pain? Sanity? Everything sacrificed for survival.

Gina shuddered and went into a coughing fit.

She finished with internal business and turned toward the cockpit. She struggled inside, but turned back almost immediately. She'd had a vague idea to use the pilot's emergency hatch to get out, but the shuttle had gone down hard. The hatch was buckled and dirt was leaking inside through it. No doubt the front of the ship was buried.

She struggled back out, letting her leg drag and not bending her knee to give IMS the best opportunity she could to make repairs. God damn but it hurt. Felt like someone was poking a red-hot poker in there. She coughed again, and panted trying to get more air. It did no good.

As she made her way through the hold, she checked the other vipers and was cheered by what she found. Most in the forward section were alive and in hibernation. When she reached the section of the troop hold where the fire had been, she steeled herself against what she would see. The burns were so hideously bad; she couldn't tell who was who and was glad of it. She was shocked to find even the worst victims were still alive. Whether they would wake up sane, she didn't know. She would never get this horror out of her head.

Back where she started in the hold she'd been riding in, Gina realised that she was still trapped. The only way out was the main ramp and it was not working. It looked undamaged, but there was no power to operate it.

She patted herself down and found a few grenades left on the ragged remains of her webbing. She was wearing more than one set, tied roughly to her armour like bandoliers. She pulled them off and transferred useful items to her belt and webbing before discarding the useless remnants. There wasn't much she could use. She needed more.

Gina searched the bodies of her comrades pilfering power cells and grenades. She soon had a respectable pile. Back at the ramp, she pulled the manual unlocking levers all the way down, and then jammed the power cells and grenades tightly around the edges of the ramp where it sealed to the hull. She didn't have enough explosive to dent the armour of a *Wolfcub*, but with the locks withdrawn, she hoped a big enough bang on the inside would overcome the inertia of the heavy ramp and blow it open. It depended a lot on how much pressure was left in the hydraulics. Those rams were designed to keep the ramp shut against atmospheric pressure while the ship travelled in vacuum, but the ship was pretty much trashed. With luck that meant the hydraulic system was totalled as well.

Gina backed up and took cover. She hefted her rifle and selected full auto and full power. She took careful aim and fired at the clusters she had placed around the edges of the ramp. The explosions weren't close to simultaneous, but maybe that helped a little, as it seemed to start a rocking motion that finally led to the ramp falling outward. It crashed down and a refreshing breeze entered the troop hold clearing the smoke a little.

Gina took a deep breath, but her lungs were still shot and she started coughing. She headed for the open air, squinting against the light and dragging her bum leg behind her looking for hostiles on her sensors. The ship had been shot down by

Merkiaari interceptors. There could be Merki troopers on the way to check the downed ship and eliminate survivors.

She moved away from the smashed ship. She was amazed at its toughness. The crash had been high speed and the impact massive. How so many had survived to enter hibernation was a miracle. A target blinked into existence on her sensors and she turned toward it...

**Manual override protocols activated.**
**Current run saved: Fuentez San Luis #002.**
**Simulation terminated.**

Gina opened her eyes as the simulator couch settled upon the floor. What the hell? She was just getting started! She looked around, but the others were still under. She wondered if they had gotten out of the dropship yet, and how they had done it. She would have to ask Eric how he'd managed. The simulation was based upon his very real life experience of San Luis back during the Merkiaari War.

"Talk of the devil," she muttered as Captain Penleigh approached. "I guess I have you to thank for messing up my run?"

"You were doing a good job of that all by yourself, Gina. You do realise the mission was not to shut off fuel lines etcetera etcetera, but to get out and back into the war? Operation Annihilate was the endgame of the San Luis campaign. Your job was to reach the assembly point and participate."

Gina grimaced. "I know that, I would have gotten there."

"Maybe," Eric said, "but not quickly, and not efficiently."

"Tell me you left them screaming in there, and then I'll consider efficiency."

Eric stared into the shadows of the simulator room bleakly, remembering a younger and more naive self. His jaw muscles bunched and he glanced down at Gina. His smile was crooked, and Gina shivered. She didn't think his smile meant he was amused this time around.

"I pulled you out because the General has a mission for us. He asked for you in particular. Any idea why?"

Changing the subject on her didn't mean he had let them die screaming. She really *really* hoped it didn't, because she didn't want to know that about him. She liked him, and she was comfortable with him as her immediate superior. She wanted to keep it that way.

"No idea. What mission?"

Eric shrugged and helped unhook her from the simulator's sensors.

Gina wondered what it was all about as she dressed, but she couldn't imagine. The General had so many fires to tend; she could be sent literally anywhere. Well maybe not that. It was very unlikely she would be sent to a core world or back to the Shan worlds. Not impossible mind you, just unlikely.

"What about my men?" she said, gesturing at the packed simulators. Her entire platoon was here.

Eric shrugged. "They have hours to go yet. I've asked for someone to take over monitoring for me."

Gina nodded. That was prudent; if anyone was "killed" in the simulation before reaching the goal, they would wake early and need help.

Eric ushered Gina along and out of the simulator room. On their way through the tech centre's barren corridors, they met Kate hurrying toward them. She waved a sloppy salute in their direction that made Gina smile and Eric scowl, but she didn't stop.

"I asked for Stone," Eric growled.

"Kate can handle it," she said and watched her friend enter the simulator room. "She gets bored. Stone probably wanted her out of his hair." Not that Stone had hair. He shaved his head every morning.

"She's undisciplined."

Gina shrugged. So what else was new?

"You don't get it, do you?" Eric said. "Even after Callendri, you still don't get it."

"I guess not," she said. Callendri? What did he have to do with Kate?

Roberto Callendri had been a recruit who had attacked her during a training op after accusing her of setting him up to fail. He had cracked, had what they in the regiment called a whigout. Kamarl Dolinski, Roberto's best friend, had to put him down. Capped him with his pulser with a shot to the head at close range. Took Roberto's head clean off.

"Viper stability is contingent upon discipline, Gina. We train continually, and use harsh training methods all to keep us stable. Too much time to think is not good for us. You should know this by now, how can you not know this? What, you think after all this time I need more training? You think I still get in those coffins every week because I don't know my job?"

"Well..." Gina said but she hadn't thought about it. Eric did still run sims occasionally, but not every veteran did. "Never considered it."

Eric opened the exterior doors and they marched shoulder to shoulder toward the admin building where the regiment's offices were. The General had his office there, close to the operations room, which was just another name for a big conference room. It had tons of tech; holotanks, comm equipment, big screens... all for planning missions. She had been in there before, but only for training. She'd heard that the General was starting to rotate personnel through admin to round out his viper's education. A good idea, she thought, as long as she didn't get stuck in an admin position long term. She shuddered at the thought.

"You can't be comparing Kate with Roberto."

"I can't?" Eric said. "Why? Because she's your friend?"

"No, but they're nothing alike."

"If you think that, you're not paying attention. They don't have the same background, that's true, but they're alike in other ways. Kate follows only the rules she likes, and listens to only those she considers worthy according to her own criteria. She doesn't follow orders because they're orders, or because they come from officers placed over her, she follows them because in her estimation not doing so would inconvenience her in some way. If I gave you an order that you didn't like, you might protest it briefly, but then you would follow it. Kate though would not protest; she would smile and nod and might even salute me, but then she would go off and do it her way."

Gina was surprised that Eric knew Kate that well. He was bang on, but his final estimation of her was way off. Yes, Kate would do things her way, but the job would get done. Anyone who had seen her in action could not doubt that. If not following orders as if they were gospel was the only thing needed to label a viper as a rogue unit, half of the regiment would be scrapped.

Colonel Flowers was recruiting new men even now, and toughness wasn't the only prerequisite. He was looking for tough skilled soldiers who could think for themselves; soldiers who could be relied upon to get the job done. Soldiers like Kate in other words. No, Kate was no rogue. If she had one fault, it was her single-mindedness. She could be too ruthless. The mission or goal that she set for herself came first with her. She was a bit like Eric and the other veterans in that way, but Eric didn't see it. It was too close to home.

In a situation where achieving a mission's aims meant sacrificing lives, Kate would not hesitate. Gina didn't like that about her friend, while at the same time she couldn't help but admire Kate's dedication to her mission. In Kate's place, Gina knew she was more likely to sacrifice herself than others. A weakness in her perhaps, but that's just how she was wired.

"You just don't like her because she reminds you of you," Gina said with a grin at his scowl. "It's true! All you old timers think alike. Mission first, nothing second. Well, Kate came off the assembly line with an attitude that could have been cloned from Sergeant Stone. She even talks like him, and you get along with Stone just fine. If you want to label Kate a rogue, you'll have to scrap half the regiment and all the veterans."

Eric shook his head. "There is a difference. The old timers, as you call us, have the Alliance's best interests as their focus. Kate only has Kate's best interest as hers."

Gina felt she should defend her friend, but she didn't know how. She knew Kate thought of things outside of herself. She had helped with Shima and had been more than happy to do it. She had joined Stone's intel section, and was excited about the work she was doing there. Mission planning, she assumed, because it was all hush-hush stuff and Kate wouldn't talk specifics. Kate couldn't carry out any of the things she helped to plan until she was fixed, but she could help the rest of her team by designing well thought out operations.

"I don't agree," Gina said, and would have to content herself with that. Kate would prove him wrong in the end, and that was all that really mattered. "Any idea what this mission is about? Anything on the books you can think of?"

Eric accepted the subject change. "There's always stuff on the to do list, you know that."

Gina nodded. People too. People on a viper's to do list weren't on it long though, like those guys on Thurston. Yi Zhang and his brother Hu Zhang (AKA Daniel King). They had been backers of the terrorist outfit euphemistically called the Freedom Movement. Daniel King had been part of the not so loyal opposition in government on Thurston, and had stabbed his own people in the back by supporting the bombers with the eventual aim of taking over the government himself. He and his brother had suffered a mischief not long before Eric left that world. Eric was instrumental in pulling the Freedom Movement down. Gina knew because she had been one of roughly a thousand marines on planet at the time and had helped him destroy them utterly when they attacked the capital on mass.

"Anything stand out to you?"

Eric shook his head. Oh well, they were nearly there. No doubt the General would explain.

They entered the admin building and headed straight for the General's office. Quite a few of the offices were in use again, and Gina glanced through open doors at the bustle. There was a lot of brass concentrated here and she wondered what they all found to do. Remembering how empty this place had been before, it was as if the regiment had been some slumbering leviathan, but one that was definitely awake again now.

Eric led Gina into Burgton's outer office. He took Raph's salute and then they were ushered into the General's presence. They saluted him, but he wasn't alone. Sitting before the desk was a trim smartly dressed older woman Gina had never met. Eric knew her though. He greeted her like a friend before turning to introduce Gina.

"Lieutenant Gina Fuentez, this is Liz Brenchley."

The woman stood to shake Gina's hand and then took her place again.

"Liz heads up our Department of Industry," Burgton said. "She's here for a couple of reasons. Your mission will be to escort and protect her among other things, but we'll come to that in a moment."

Gina nodded. An escort mission to where, and to do what? She could do it in her sleep but why her? Eric said that the General had asked for her specifically. She couldn't think why. A simple escort mission could be handled by anyone in the regiment.

"Your platoon, where are we?" Burgton said. "I know what you've been having them do since you squared away our Shan situation. Well done with that, by the way. Shima left us very excited about the colony here and I think that could help us in future. I doubt we'll have any issues with volunteers."

Gina nodded. "Shima loved site five, the one we used for her surprise vacation. Varya and Kazim were already leaning that way due to location and the mountains, but I think Shima will push them over the line into backing it before the elders."

"We won't know anything more for a few months. It will take Shima around three to get home," Burgton said. "But I'm sure we'll hear back before the year is out."

Gina nodded again. The Shan had only been gone a few weeks. "You asked about my platoon, sir. Are you deploying us?"

"No. I want to know what they'll need while you're away."

So the mission was a one unit operation? That made her wonder about it even more. Gina shook off her preoccupation and laid out her thinking regarding her men.

"I'm happy with progress, sir. All four squads are coming together nicely. I'm not really surprised as most of them have fought together before, and all of them trained with me under Colonel Flowers. I thought there might be trouble when they transferred over from their old units, but that at least turned out to be a worry over nothing."

"So the next step is...?" Burgton pressed.

"More training. I want to start them on squad and platoon simulations next. I have them in simulators every third day right now, and that's probably about right for individual training. When they go to the larger squad and platoon missions, once or twice a week should be enough. I want them to get used to working as a larger unit again. This past year we've been fighting in penny packets a lot... no insult intended, sir."

Burgton smiled. "The truth doesn't offend me, Gina. There was no help for it with so many in hibernation. So, if I were to send you on an operation, you would have no concerns for your platoon?"

"I didn't say that, sir. I should oversee their training

regardless, and hell, I need some myself."

Eric snorted.

Burgton glanced at Eric, but didn't ask. "And if I were to assign someone to oversee them for you... Dolinski let's say?"

"Then I would say my platoon was in good hands, sir, but Kamarl has his own platoon to handle. The way I hear it, 2$^{nd}$ needs even more work than 1$^{st}$ does."

"True. You have a suggestion?"

"Bump Hiller to cover for me, just until I get back."

"Done," Burgton said decisively. "Moving on to why you're here. Liz and I have a job for you both. On the surface it's a simple escort mission, and as I said, you get to protect Liz while she oversees her team. Why only two units, you're thinking. Well, it's not because I don't value Liz or the mission. They're both vital, and I mean that. Liz is a personal friend, but it's her work that makes her indispensible to me."

Liz rolled her eyes. "Love you too, George. Seriously, no one is indispensible. My deputy can do my job, or I'd find a new deputy."

"Your job yes, but Oracle? No."

Liz cocked her head, but then acknowledged his point with a nod. "I'll give you that one."

"Oracle?" Gina said.

"That's a long story," Burgton said. "One I'm going to tell you but in the operations room. We have a mission to plan."

Burgton led them all out of his office and down the corridor to the operations room. No one was using it so they had it to themselves. Burgton waved them toward the main tank at the centre of the room. He worked the controls himself, and the room's lights dimmed as the tank came alive.

Gina frowned at the planet displayed and at the legend below it in bold text. Kushiel. Kushiel? Her eyes widened as she remembered why the name was familiar. It was The

Kushiel of the Accords. The planet was bombarded from orbit into an uninhabitable waste by the Merkiaari. The Accords banning orbital bombardment and the use of atomics in atmosphere had been a direct response to what happened to that luckless world. What possible use could there be for the planet now?

Burgton turned to address them. "Here we have Kushiel, bombed by the Merki from orbit with nuclear and kinetic ordnance over a prolonged period. All life extinguished by them and the planet ruined forever as a warning, we assume, against further use of atomics in atmosphere against them. I say we assume, because we've never managed any dialogue with them about Kushiel or any other subject. But, we got the message. The Accords were written, and all Alliance members signed it. We don't know what the Merki think about that, but neither side has used orbital strikes or atomics in atmosphere against the other since then. And no other planets have suffered Kushiel's fate, so we can assume they're at least satisfied with it."

Gina didn't interrupt, but it wasn't true that neither side had used atomics. Admiral Meyers had in fact deployed Zeus on Child of Harmony. Zeus missiles were atomics, though they were classed in the micro nuke range of weapons carried aboard fleet carriers. The risk of using them against the Merkiaari had been extreme. If the Merki high command somehow learned of it, the consequences could be dire. Fortunately, and probably a mitigating circumstance Meyers used to justify her decision, her ships had owned the system at the time, and the Shan elders had specifically requested the strike. By ensuring no Merki survived the experience, the details of how the victory was achieved had been hidden.

"That's the background," Burgton said and manipulated the controls. The image changed to a cityscape. "This is the capital city of the colony; obviously the images were taken long before the war."

Gina nodded as image after image appeared. The city

had been designed using an older colonial style—lots of stone walls and columns rather than the more modern but sterile steel and glass. She liked it. It reminded her of places she had visited while on leave. She'd chosen to visit Earth on her last leave as a marine just before she was recruited into the regiment. She remembered the ruins of the original Washington DC on the shores of Crater Lake that had been preserved as a memorial. The final image that Burgton displayed was of a building that had an impressive dome, just like the broken Capitol building she had seen back then.

New Washington on Earth was the capital of the Alliance, but the architects of that city had turned away from the past and embraced wholeheartedly their concept of the future. Perhaps they had simply wanted to blot out the memory of Washington's destruction at the hands of the madman Douglas Walden during the Hacker Rebellion, perhaps not, but by creating something completely different and separate from old notions of architecture they had also lost something. Steel and glass mega-scrapers, though technologically impressive, could never replace the heart swelling beauty of old weatherworn stone columns and domes. New Washington had no Capitol, no domes, just super modern mega-scrapers and needles... it made Gina feel a little sad. Romantic foolishness, she thought, but she did admire Kushiel's old colonial style of architecture.

"Kushiel was governed as a republic, but one with a twist. Its colonial administer was an A.I named Sebastian, and it was he who was effectively the head of state."

Gina gaped.

Burgton nodded at her surprise. "I don't mean he was named president. Kushiel's government had all the trappings of a republic as we understand it. No, I mean the A.I ran the colony's infrastructure without outside input—even back then everything was mostly automated like today. They took things further by swearing the president in before him. In effect, Sebastian was the ultimate supreme court judge and guardian of Kushiel's constitution."

Wow. That was taking things too far, Gina thought. The A.Is were almost mythical beings to most people. They were a part of history. Even so, Humans had created them as helpers and even friends, not as some kind of Praetorian Guard policing their creators and deciding whether they were fit to govern.

"That brings me to this," Burgton said and the holotank changed. "This is Oracle."

Gina stepped closer to the tank. Oracle was a massive installation—she picked out a significant datum—built subsurface, 3km down. Under The Mountain then, had to be. It made sense. The geothermal power plant that serviced Oracle was even deeper. The central chamber drew her eyes. It was a stadium sized spherical void in the middle of the display and it told her what Oracle had to be.

"Good name for something designed to predict events," she said quietly. Eric gave her a questioning look, but she didn't explain. "I assume you didn't sweat the ban on neural interface technology either?"

Liz shrugged. "Not so much. In for a few trillion, in for a few billion more."

Gina winced. Trillions? Yeah, she could well believe that looking at all this. The installation itself, just the empty chambers would have cost many billions as deep as they'd had to go.

"What's going on?" Eric said. "I seem to be the only one not in the know."

Burgton raised a hand. "Gina knows a little of this because I confided in her on Child of Harmony for background before we went to pick up Shima. Oracle is Snakeholme's A.I."

"But the ban..." Eric began, but tailed off. "Sir, you're risking too much. Building our own little fleet of ships, and our own weapon's factory made sense even though it's illegal as hell, but breaking the ban on A.Is and neural tech? If the Council learns of it, they'll shut us down with nukes from orbit if they have to!"

"Calmly, Captain, calmly," Burgton said. "There are reasons for everything I do, no matter how mad they may seem at first. Gina, the ban on neural tech has never been applied to us. Every viper ever built has neural interfaces because we need them to function. The regiment hasn't been specifically excluded from the ban, but viper design implies it and the Council is well aware of that. That leaves the A.I ban. The technology isn't under the ban, the software is. The Oracle installation is therefore safe."

"Semantics," Eric said angrily and Gina glanced at him worriedly. "You risk everything."

Burgton looked at Eric coldly now. "You've been with me a long time, Captain Penleigh. You've seen some of the things I've had to do or order done to keep the Alliance safe and on course. You've been sent to carry out many of them. This is just one more of those things. It's a little late to be growing a conscience, don't you think?"

Eric stiffened, his eyes grown cold.

Gina watched Eric closely and her eyes widened a little as she realised she was watching Eric's right hand and evaluating how to intercept him if he drew. Preposterous, he wouldn't draw on the General. She watched him close regardless, prepared to intervene.

Burgton drew a sharp breath and then let it out as a sigh. "There are a lot of things I do that break laws large and small. I've been doing them and ordering them done since the Council betrayed me after the war. They had to be done. Some were to keep the regiment going even at a subsistence level so that we would be here when needed, others were to head off disasters in the Alliance that would have weakened us all against the Merkiaari threat.

"You may not know this, Gina, but Eric is one of my best operatives. He has often been tasked with doing my dirty work so to speak. He has the right, if anyone does, after all this time to get up in my face over things and question me like this. I value his council as well as his other skills. In the end, I know I have his loyalty. He will follow his orders."

Gina watched Eric's eyes narrow just a bit, and knew that even Eric didn't know where he would draw the line. Loyalty was earned, and Burgton had earned his many times over, but Eric's look told Gina there might come a time when loyalty would no longer be enough.

"Now," Burgton went on. "Oracle is a reality. Liz built it for me at great expense, but there's a problem."

Liz snorted. "Problem he says. I'll say there's a problem. It doesn't bloody work!"

Gina blinked. "Then we haven't broken the A.I ban?" she turned to Eric triumphantly.

Eric shook his head pityingly at her.

Liz shrugged. "Yes and no... not that I care. Stupid law should never have been written let alone enforced for over half a millennium. We learned our lessons from Walden and his fanatics a very long time ago. There's no way the Hacker Rebellion would succeed today. The ban could have been removed just decades after it was introduced without risk, but public paranoia wouldn't allow it. The Council knows all this, but for reasons of its own keeps the ban in place.

"As for Oracle, the software is operating within the matrix, so yes the ban is broken, but it isn't self aware, and that's the problem. It's just a very expensive calculator right now."

"Expensive, right," Gina said thinking of all those trillions of credits.

The regiment's budget couldn't possibly cover that kind of expense, which meant Burgton had used Snakeholme's treasury to fund it. He had the right of course. Snakeholme didn't really have a government. It was run like a military unit or maybe a corporation. Yes, a corporation with department heads like Liz running various aspects. That made Burgton the CEO of Snakeholme Inc., sort of, another word for which was dictator. Dictator or not, he had a moral duty to spend Snakeholme's treasure wisely. Whether he was wise or not remained to be seen.

"And you think Kushiel holds the answer to Oracle's problem?" Eric said.

Burgton nodded. "We hope it does, but we don't know for sure. Kushiel was one of the worlds that still had a functioning A.I after the Rebellion, but three centuries or so later along came the Merkiaari and killed everything on the planet. Nothing further is known about the A.I, except it was there at the end."

"It can't still be there, surely?" Gina said.

"We don't think so," Liz said. "There's no mention of it at all. I'm assuming one of the orbital strikes took it out. No, we're not looking to salvage the A.I. We want its backup memory module... if it still exists and if we can even find and access it. The world is frankly a poisonous snowball now. It's going to be a challenge however you slice it."

Gina nodded thoughtfully, but already she could feel the pull of the quest stirring her. A bit of excitement was in the offing, and one that didn't involve combat. Sounded like just the thing.

"Do we have a starting point to look?" Eric said. "And what about the salvage side?"

"My people will handle the actual extraction," Liz said. "One false move and we could destroy the data we need. In fact, I'm almost certain I'll copy the data on site before extraction as a backup. We only get one chance at this, and we're talking about ancient equipment that's been left in a hostile environment."

Burgton used the holotank controls again. "We think the A.I was housed in Haverington. It was the capital and a logical place. Liz thinks any backups would be close to the actual A.I, but not necessarily in the same building. I'm hoping that if the A.I was taken out by the Merki, its backups survived. No way to tell without going there."

"Doesn't seem like a very secure site for an A.I, sir," Gina said doubtfully. "I would expect something like Oracle to house it."

Burgton nodded. "Now yes, but don't forget Sebastian was installed centuries before the Merki War."

"Still," Gina said. If she'd been there, she would never have let the A.I sit above ground in the city, war or no war.

"I'm not sure why you need us," Eric said. "Sounds like a job for Liz's engineers not vipers."

Burgton smiled. "You know me, I never expect trouble but I'm always prepared for it. Operation Oracle is Liz's baby, but you two are to take care of her and any security related issues. If I knew what they were I would tell you. Chances are, on a dead world like this, all you'll have to do is keep her engineers from wandering off without their environment suits on."

Eric laughed and Gina grinned.

Liz scowled at the mockery, but it didn't last. "My people are ready to board, George. All our equipment is aboard. When can we go?"

Burgton looked at Eric. "Tomorrow?"

Eric glanced at the holotank and nodded. "We'll upload all this to study on the way. Tomorrow is good. What ship?"

"*Hobbs*, one of our freighters. Kushiel is classified as a war memorial and gravesite. Going down world is prohibited because of that." Burgton grimaced. "The system is rarely visited, but if a ship did pass through for some reason, a freighter will raise fewer suspicions than a destroyer."

Eric nodded. "We can go down in one of her cargo shuttles."

Gina listened as they hashed out a few more details and watched Liz at the holotank controls. She had found the cityscapes again. Gina wondered if the buildings in the pictures were still standing.

"I guess we'll find out," she said and joined Liz at the controls.

* * *

# 14 ~ Lost World

A snowball, Gina remembered thinking back at base. Kushiel did indeed resemble one. The terrible bombardment that had tortured the planet more than two hundred years in the past had triggered an ice age beyond anything Gina had ever heard tell of. The kinetic and nuclear strikes had thrown so much debris into the air that it had shrouded the planet with cloud, some radioactive, that had lasted years. Sunlight reaching the surface had been badly reduced, lowering mean temperatures and starting the long decline into permanent winter.

*Hobbs* was an unarmed freighter, but its sensors were decent and they'd been scanning the surface since the ship settled into Kushiel's orbit yesterday. They already knew a lot about local conditions, cold and inhospitable, and that most of the surface was covered in ice, making the situation worse. The icecaps covered much of the surface with glaciers marching across once fecund land. They reflected the sunlight, not allowing it to be absorbed, and the vicious circle was therefore complete. Like some kind of runaway engine, ice perpetually generated more ice. Only at the equator was there any land not covered year round, and it was of no interest to them. It had never been settled.

The atmosphere was laced with nasty stuff too. Sulphur dioxide and carbon dioxide levels were dangerously high even now. The Merkiaari had done a real number on it, and not by accident. The result even had a proper scientific name—impact winter—and was akin to something scientists had long known would happen after a prolonged nuclear exchange in atmosphere—nuclear winter. There wasn't much of a difference between the two, except in the means used to create them, and in their duration. A decade after the event, Kushiel's atmosphere really should have begun to repair itself. The textbooks all agreed upon that, but the Merkiaari had wanted to make a statement. Their version of impact winter was of long duration because they had kept hitting the planet until they succeeded in stripping the atmosphere of its ozone layer. Other weather effects played a part too. Kushiel's precipitation levels were way down, not really surprising when you realised that most of the planet's water was locked up in the ice sheets.

The planet would never recover, or if it did it would take so many years they would need to be measured on a geological timescale.

The atmosphere would be lethal to anyone exposed to it even for a short time. Gina knew that she could breathe it if she had to—though she was sure to be unhappy about it—as long as her IMS had the resources to continually repair the damage to seared lungs. Eric and she had packed a lot of viper supplements just in case. Liz and her team would be required to breathe canned air 24/7, absolutely no exceptions. Not that it would be a real problem, seeing as the sub-zero temperatures would require them to wear full environment suits while outside anyway. The suits were climate controlled and contained their own PLSS (Portable Life Support Systems) that should keep everyone breathing good air rather than the poisonous crap that Kushiel now used for its excuse for an atmosphere. During downtimes, everyone could get out of their suits either in a shuttle or in the pressure domes they planned to erect as a base camp when they had a good candidate for the memory module's location.

It was that location they were searching for. Captain Gibson would be adjusting *Hobbs'* orbit many times over the following days until he could deliver a full and comprehensive survey of the surface. Until then, Liz's team was twiddling their thumbs checking and rechecking their equipment, while Gina and Eric haunted the bridge, annoying Gibson's crew by looking over their shoulders—figuratively speaking of course.

Gina was paging through the data available at one of the observer stations. She didn't literally need to look over anyone's shoulder to sate her growing curiosity. The data from the ship's sensors was available in raw form instantly to anyone wanting it, but letting the ship's computer crunch the numbers for a few minutes rendered a more useful result. The images of snowy wastelands were by far the most numerous. Interesting only for background really, but she didn't filter them out for fear of missing something. She let her eyes skim each frame, knowing her own internal database was soaking up the data for rapid recall later.

When the ship passed over the locations where towns and cities had once been located, and there were many of them old as the colony had been, she stopped to study each one in greater detail. Sometimes there was little to learn. Lot of craters down there, she mused, blunted now by age and softened by the ice and snow. Other times, ruins reared up out of ice fields, stark and lonely. Rarely were intact but abandoned towns revealed, undamaged by war but fallen to ruin by time's gentle caress. When they did appear on the scans, images of streets buried in ice, with drifted snow banked against the buildings and blowing into them through third floor windows were common.

Kushiel had been a core world with a large prosperous population; its loss had been a horrifying shock back during the Merki War. The fact of the matter was that no matter how much everyone preferred to think otherwise, the Merki were not confined to nibbling around the edges of Alliance space, or invading border worlds. There were no rules or universal laws of physics preventing them from sending incursions directly against core worlds, even against the big six... even Earth itself! The only reason they didn't try was the size and strength of the defences mustered nearby. Six huge fleets and countless task forces and system pickets protected the Alliance with more added every year, but back then the Alliance had yet to be conceived. Every system was on its own, unless it happened to be part of a political unit already such as the Kalmar Union.

Kushiel had been vulnerable because of its location within the Human sphere of controlled space—it was a core world due to being colonised early in terms of Human expansion, but it was located in what could only be termed a cul-de-sac of barren suns. Because of that unfortunate happenstance, Kushiel was more like a border world in terms of its defensibility. Its own little fleet of ships, like most back then, had been mustered against commerce raiders—pirates—not alien invaders. The lack of habitable worlds nearby meant Kushiel could not call upon allied ships for help and expect them to arrive in time.

Anyway, that was history, but it did affect what Gina and Eric needed to do in one way. Kushiel was an old colony world and that meant its population had bloomed and grown into the many hundreds of millions in terms of numbers. The people had spread out all over their world, building homes and communities. Kushiel had cities with populations in the millions when it died. That meant Gina had a good many targets to consider for their first explorations, big targets. And they would be explorations, not salvage operations at first. Eric had proposed, and Gina agreed, that they explore the various sites alone before ferrying Liz's engineers and equipment to the surface. It only made sense. What if they landed everything only to find out that what they were looking for was on the other side of the planet?

Liz had protested bitterly, even trying to pull rank. She said this was her operation and that the General had sent Eric and Gina as security, not to run it for her. She wasn't under their authority, and neither was her team. Eric reposted by saying she damn well was under his authority, and that as the project's security officer he would decide when something was safe. If he decided it wasn't safe, she would stay aboard ship in the brig if that's what it took to make her stay put. The salvage part of Operation Oracle was hers, everything else was his.

Liz had appealed to the captain as the ultimate authority, but Gibson had failed to intervene on her behalf by explaining that his ship was part of Snakeholme's merchant marine. Despite its unarmed status—not strictly true as even freighters were allowed limited defensive armourment within the Alliance—*Hobbs* and its crew like all such crews, held a reserve commission in Snakeholme's Defence Force, and the SDF was commanded by General Burgton. In other words, he would do what Eric said.

Gina found it all very amusing.

What she didn't find amusing was her growing realisation that finding what they sought was like looking for the proverbial needle in a world full of haystacks. She had a plan of course. She was filtering out buildings with an obvious use not connected with their quarry. Buildings such a residential blocks, shopping malls, vehicle parking structures, and many others in an attempt to narrow the places they needed to search. Even so, the task was a daunting one. She had to do the same with every city and town they discovered, and of course, they didn't really know if the one they needed had even survived the bombardment.

"How's it going?" Eric said wandering over from where he had been watching things. "Anything stand out?"

"More than Haverington you mean?" Gina said.

Eric nodded.

Haverington was the name given to Kushiel's capital city and centre of government. Surprisingly, it had survived the Merki bombing, probably because it had been taken in the opening battles of the Kushiel incursion. Liz considered it a good bet for the A.Is location based upon the idea that the city was important, but Gina wasn't so sure. There were other places. University towns seemed just as reasonable to her, but Liz was quite insistent that the capital be the priority. Gina was happy to comply if it made Liz happy. And besides, she might be right.

"Yeah," Gina said. "I've got plenty to check out. Too many. This could take a lot of time. The thing could be anywhere."

"Not anywhere," Eric disagreed. "They were people like us, not aliens. We just need to think like they did. Where would we put it?"

"Under a bloody mountain."

Eric scowled. "I'm serious."

"So am I. The Oracle facility back home makes perfect sense to me."

Eric rubbed his forehead and seemed to be counting to himself. "Let me try again. We need to think like Human colonists not vipers. Now. Where would you put it?"

Gina frowned at the consol she had been using. She still thought her earlier thought had merit. University towns? But seriously, with modern comm tech the A.I could be anywhere on the planet and still be accessible, and if Liz was right the memory module would be close by. Archives and stuff seemed another good bet. Infonet servers and nodes... all that good stuff.

She explained her thoughts to Eric.

"Good. Find them."

Gina grinned. "Yes, sir captain... how?"

Eric wasn't smiling, he was serious. "Find me an intact library."

## CARGO BAY 5, ABOARD HOBBS, KUSHIEL SYSTEM

Gina gunned the engine and drove the APC (Armoured Personnel Carrier) up the ramp and into the shuttle's cargo space. There was plenty of room. *Hobbs'* shuttles were big suckers, as was the freighter they served. *Hobbs* was a super heavyweight among freighters, nominally in the same class as super dreadnaughts and fleet carriers because they all weighed in the millions of tons. Displacement wasn't everything of course. *Hobbs*, being a freighter, was basically a series of hollow boxes within a pressure hull containing drives, power plants, fuel bunkerage, and crew spaces. That made for a huge ship. The only things built bigger by man were the stations, and one or two of the biggest shipyards where *Hobbs* and ships like her were constructed.

Gina climbed down from the cab and made a quick inspection, but the automatic clamps had engaged properly to secure the wheels. There were six on each side, equipped especially for this trip with tyres rated to handle the sub zero temperatures of Kushiel. She hoped the thick chevron shaped blocks of tread could handle the conditions or she would be walking. She understood why the regiment didn't use ground effect vehicles, the marines also used wheeled and tracked vehicles exclusively, but this was one mission where anti-grav would have come into its own.

The huge balloon tyres were as tall as she was, and she took advantage by scurrying beneath the vehicle rather than walking around to check the other side. Everything was secure and she was ready to go. She exited the shuttle using the cargo ramp and headed across the hold toward Eric's shuttle where he was still loading his APC.

Both of the APCs were loaded with remotes and supplies that should be useful. She had chosen her loadout herself and was satisfied with her picks. The regiment's APCs came with a default loadout to support a platoon of vipers in battle, but although they did carry recon remotes, none of it was really made for this situation. Weapons and ammo were useless here, and Gina had considered unloading it all to make room for more capable sensing gear, but in the end she decided not to bother. She had the entire troop hold built to carry forty vipers to use for her cargo, and she had done so.

Eric had his own shuttle and gear, and had probably made different choices. It didn't matter. This wasn't a race or competition, but Gina admitted to herself she would like to be the one to discover the location of the prize. It had been her data that prompted this initial probe. As ordered, she had found a library for Eric to check out, while she had reserved an archive and Infonet server for her own investigations.

"Ready?" Eric said. "I need a few more minutes."

Gina eyed the pile of gear awaiting loading, and stared enviously at the tracked jewel in Eric's crown. She cursed herself for not thinking of it. It was a droid that the regiment used to defuse unexploded ordnance and IEDs (Improvised Explosive Devices). The marines used them a lot when fighting terrorist outbreaks in the border worlds, which is where Gina had gained her experience of them.

"Expecting things that go boom?" Gina asked, nodding at the gleaming black droid.

"No, I'm expecting to send it ahead so I don't catch cold," Eric said and grinned at her scowl. "I think there's another one in storage. I'm sure I packed two."

Gina didn't say a word.

"I could let you have the spare," Eric said in a wheedling boyish tone.

"How much?" Gina bit out, but she was going to laugh if he kept at it.

"For you a mere nothing. A favour to be named at a later date."

"A favour, huh? I don't like open ended favours. You could ask for my last power cell in battle or something."

Eric chuckled. "How about dinner at Stirlings when we get back."

Gina's eyebrows climbed. "Are you asking me out on a date?"

Eric turned serious and nodded. "Deal?"

Gina bumped fists with him. "Deal. Where is it?"

Eric gave her directions and she trotted off to fetch her droid. Less than thirty minutes later, both shuttles were loaded and waiting to launch. The cargo hold took time to pump down, but before Gina knew it, she was on her way out of the ship and piloting the shuttle toward her target on the surface of Kushiel.

"*Hobbs* this is Alpha-Two, proceeding on a least time direct course to my LZ. Will be going dark in... one-three minutes... mark."

"Alpha-Two, *Hobbs* copies. Good luck down there, don't catch cold."

"Ha-ha. Alpha-Two out," Gina said. By going dark she was referring to her entry into atmosphere when she would be briefly out of contact. "Alpha-One this is Two. You read?"

"Alpha-Two, Alpha-One reading five by. You need something, Gina?"

"Nope, just wondering about putting up a relay sat. We'll lose comms when we land."

The two landing sites were too far apart for viper comm or TacNet without relay sats in orbit. *Hobbs* was overhead of course and would position itself to allow the shuttles to communicate with her, but the freighter wasn't exactly equipped to support vipers in the field.

"We already decided against that, Gina."

We didn't, Eric did, but he was right about his reasons. They were here illegally. *Hobbs* could say, *would* say if asked, that she'd had an engineering casualty and was only in orbit until repairs were finished. Seeding the planet with satellites though would more than queer their lame excuse. What reasons could they give?

Gina shrugged. "Okay, just checking. Have to bounce helmet comms off the shuttles and up to *Hobbs*."

"Right."

He didn't have to say, that of *course* they would do that, but she heard it in how he didn't say it. She grinned and changed the subject. She still had roughly ten minutes to atmosphere.

"So, dinner eh?"

"What's wrong with dinner?" Eric said. "Got something better to do?"

"I could find something I'm sure. Polishing my boots maybe. Seriously, a date?"

"Why not? It's not like either of us get out much."

Gina snorted. "True." She checked her autopilot was following its programming. It was. "You think we're okay though? You're my commanding officer."

Eric sighed. "It's only dinner, Gina. You are so... you are such a marine!"

"What the hell do you mean by that?" Gina said. She had been proud to call herself a marine for fifteen years of her life, but he made it sound like a bad thing. She couldn't help but be offended.

"You're so gung ho it's painful. We're vipers, Gina, not marines. Hell, we're not even Human strictly speaking. Not anymore. We have our own ways, and besides, we're adults. If you think you can't control yourself..."

Gina blew a raspberry.

Eric laughed. "Well then. We're agreed that two adults, such as ourselves, can have a dinner date together and not have it affect our working relationship. We are, right?"

"Absolutely," Gina said.

"Good."

"Good."

"It's a date then," Eric said.

"Right."

The silence stretched on longer than was comfortable. Gina searched for something to say, and eyed her chrono. Three minutes to atmosphere.

"Want to bet that I find the prize before you?" Gina said clutching at work to fill the silence.

"Stakes?" Eric said sounding interested.

Not dinner again, Gina thought, though she wasn't averse. This had to be better. "If I win you come with me on a mystery weekend. There will be fresh air and sunshine, and a possibility of drowning. You like boats?"

"Boats? Sure."

"The sailing kind I mean," Gina added to be sure.

"Yeah boats, I know boats. Sails and ropes and stuff. Old school."

Gina nodded. "Yeah, that kind."

"And if I win?" Eric said.

"That won't happen, obviously, but just to make it fair, what do you want?"

"Hmmm. Do you like going to the sensarium?"

"Are you suggesting dinner and a sensim?" A bit cliché of him, but she wouldn't mind. Sensariums were like the civilian version of running a sim, except you didn't participate, you watched the story from within the fictional world the producers designed. It was kind of cool. Different enough from real sims to be fun. Restful too. "I went with Kate to the new Zelda and the Spaceways sensim. It was pretty funny."

"I don't think it's meant to be a comedy," Eric said doubtfully.

"Definitely not. Rabid Zelda fans would kill us for even thinking it."

"If I win then, you come with me to the sensarium in Petruso City, but I choose the sensim. No Zelda."

Gina smiled. "Okay..." the first turbulence shook the shuttle. "Blackout in ten seconds. See you later."

"...Gina... up..." Eric's voice faded.

She was into atmosphere now. The autopilot could handle things, but Gina was ready to take over the controls instantly. The weather front she would be entering could cause unpredictable updrafts and turbulence. A blizzard was in full swing over the target, but it was nothing to really concern a shuttle of this type. It had plenty of power, designed as it was for carrying heavy loads. Its power to weight ratio was through the roof, especially when mostly unloaded like now. Its muscle was closer to what a tug would have. The APC and other gear she had packed might as well weigh nothing for all the difference it made.

Gina took the autopilot offline just a few kilometres from her objective and flew manually. She had every sensor the shuttle had scanning the surface looking for the antenna mast she had found on *Hobbs*. That telltale artefact gave her hope that the Infonet node it served was still intact. Not operational of course. It had no power, but she would fix that. Infonet nodes were housed within self-sufficient automated stations and acted as signal relays and buffers. When operational, they provided their community with access to Infonet and other net services, including archive access. Gina didn't expect to find the prize here; that wasn't the point of landing at this one. She was hoping to use it as a starting point in her plan of mapping the physical locations of all the other nodes and possibly even the A.I itself.

But first a landing upon unstable snow and ice.

The external cameras showed unforgiving white. Altitude was down to the hundreds of metres now, not thousands, and Gina expected proximity alarms to wail at any moment. Most of the buildings would be buried beneath the ice. The scans she had studied aboard *Hobbs* showed that pretty well, but the mast was tall even bent and canted at a twenty degree angle, and there were other taller buildings to watch out for. Not many, Woolsery was a minor community and seemed to be mostly two story dwellings, but there were enough to be wary of.

The proximity alarm wailed.

"Talk of the devil," Gina muttered veering aside as one of those taller buildings reared up in her face. "Bloody hell that was close." She checked and reset the alarm to give her more of a safety margin next time.

Gina held the shuttle hovering before the building on its anti-grav and hit the external floods. The powerful lights pierced the storm and lit the ancient brick to reveal empty windows and storm damaged walls. Ice coated everything. She manoeuvred the shuttle to circle the building keeping her altitude constant. She was trying to place the building within the scan image she had displayed on one of her monitors.

"I think it's this one," she said to herself tapping a finger upon one of the dark blobs shown on the scan.

If she was correct, she needed to go east from here avoiding two more tallish buildings before she would find the mast. Damn she missed satellite access. She had become used to up linking to a satellite and just using coordinates with her internal navigation systems to find her way around. This treasure hunt primitive bullshit was getting on her nerves already. How the hell did anyone find their way about before GPS?

Gina flew the shuttle while bitching internally and wondered how Eric was getting along. Despite trying to convince herself this wasn't a competition, she did want to find the prize first. She had an added incentive now too. A weekend on a yacht with Eric would be fun. Chrissie Roberts had introduced her to the fun that could be had on the waters of Snakeholme. They had gone out a time or two with Kate before the regiment deployed to the Shan system and Chris was killed. Poor Chris. Gina missed her.

Eric's target was the library he had wanted her to find. No doubt there were others on Kushiel, but the one Gina had found for him was in Haverington. Visiting the capital had an added side benefit of pleasing Liz, who was still adamant, despite no supporting evidence, that the A.I would be somewhere in the city. Personally Gina thought she was grasping at straws. Liz was desperate for it to be true to keep Oracle alive. The thought that the A.I and its backup had been destroyed in the bombardment was her ultimate nightmare.

Gina hoped Liz was right even if it meant losing to Eric because she knew the General needed them to succeed. He needed Oracle. Despite everything Liz said, Gina didn't think it would be that easy. Her slow but methodical idea of mapping Kushiel's net infrastructure had more chance. She was sure.

Gina found the other two buildings, and suddenly the map in her head had proper landmarks. She triangulated, calculated distances in microseconds, and flew confidently straight to the Infonet station. It was right where it was meant to be. Ha! Maybe this treasure hunt thing wouldn't be too hard after all.

She studied what her external cameras revealed of the station and its surroundings. The blizzard was at its height, but *Hobbs* had updated the forecast and predicted it would blow over within the next couple of hours. That was good but not critical. It was -42° outside, but her environmental suit could handle the hard vacuum and absolute zero of space. The APC was easily capable of the local conditions also. No, what concerned her was landing upwards of two thousand tonnes of cargo shuttle on snow and ice.

The station was completely buried, and the surrounding area was featureless white. How deep was the surface snow? Gina hovered just above it to bring the antennas close and switched her attention to what the shuttle's GPR (Ground Penetrating Radar) was telling her. GPR used electromagnetic radiation (high-frequency polarised radio waves) to penetrate the ground and reveal what was hidden. It was particularly good at it where ice was concerned.

She studied the reflected return signals and grimaced at what she saw. There were voids and cracks all through it. If she landed here, the shuttle would collapse the voids and bury itself. Frowning in annoyance but not really surprised by the setback, she manoeuvred and flew slowly away from the station looking for a good landing site.

# 15 ~ Buried Treasure

Gina listened intently to the shuttle settling upon its landing struts, wincing at the occasion jolt as the ice compressed beneath its weight. She had a death grip on the controls, hardly daring to lower the power to her anti-grav any further. Of course she had to eventually. Barely a third of the shuttle's weight was yet bearing upon the ice. GPR reassured her that the three metre thick ice was solid all the way down to the frozen ground beneath. It should take the entire weight and more just fine. The half metre of snow on top was immaterial to that.

She lowered anti-grav output still more and felt the shuttle lurch down a few inches then halt at a very shallow angle to starboard. It was nothing really, and she made herself start breathing again and ease her grip upon the VTOL (Vertical Take-Off & Landing) joystick before she crushed it. She sighed when, after a few minutes of sitting still, the shuttle remained stable. She cut anti-grav entirely and the shuttle remained solidly in place. Good.

She quickly shut down her drives and headed into the back. She needed to get a move on. She hadn't tried to contact *Hobbs* or Eric, but she was feeling a definite urge to make up some time. For all she knew, Eric had already accessed his objective.

She quickly pulled on her environment suit over her uniform blacks and sealed her helmet. The suit ran its diagnostics and all came up green. She had air and power enough for days, and replacements in the APC to extend that to a week if necessary. She was taking no chances, but seriously, she didn't expect any problems.

She unlocked and opened the cargo ramp. Wind and snow blasted inside, and her suit's heater immediately kicked in as the temperature plummeted within the hold. It would do no harm within the shuttle, but she still hurried her steps unclamping the APC's wheels. No sense letting ice build up inside. Her preparations took only minutes, and she was climbing up into the cab to back out of the hold.

The APC handled the snow beautifully. Plenty of traction in twelve wheel drive. Gina used her helmet comm to close and lock the shuttle's cargo ramp by remote, and watched it rise into place. No need to run down her suit's power, she decided, and removed the helmet setting it upon the seat beside her before turning her attention to navigation.

She quickly orientated herself, and using the map on her internal display, put herself on a direct line back to the station. She gunned the engine, and the APC quickly accelerated. Its automatic gearbox changed gears smoothly, propelling the fifteen ton machine as if it were a mere ground car. Eighteen forward gears and three reverse; she doubted anything on Kushiel would phase it.

The blizzard was really howling now, almost whiteout conditions, but there were no obstructions between the shuttle and the station. She had flown the route and knew it was clear. She turned on every light the APC had and kept going. The suspension was pretty good, but when she hit a pressure ridge in the ice a few minutes later, the APC launched itself into the air and landed bouncing on its balloon tyres.

Gina grunted, bouncing in her sear almost losing her grip on the wheel. She laughed at herself. She should have belted in and driven slower, she didn't want to wreck. She slowed down and took it easier after that.

The trip took less than half an hour.

Gina parked the APC so that its lights illuminated the mast. With no way to enter the building, she planned to bore down through the ice a few metres from it. The ice should be at its thinnest over the station roof, and she had just the thing for making the hole.

The regiment was primarily a front line combat unit, but centuries of unconventional missions had resulted in a few changes. When the Council betrayed General Burgton and mothballed the regiment, he hadn't taken it lying down. Outwardly it appeared as if he complied, but in truth vipers went underground. Everything they did from then on was handled stealthily. Anything the regiment needed was found either on Snakeholme, or it was requisitioned on the down low—either outright stolen, or more usually diverted to the regiment's use by clever manipulation of records and computer systems. Only in the past decade or two had the regiment received anything like a budget big enough to maintain itself properly.

President Dyachenko was the first president in a very long time to take a personal interest in vipers. He had authorised funds (funds nominally earmarked for secret research projects) re-tasked to bring the regiment back up to strength, all in secret. The Shan incursion had changed a lot of things. Recruiting was now in the open, and the regiment once again appeared on the books as an operational combat unit. It had a proper Department of Defence approved budget, but the regiment was still commanded by General Burgton and he had not changed how he ran it. He would never again allow his men to be hung out to dry. Anything his regiment needed was supplied directly by him through his people on Snakeholme, or it was supplied by people paid by him. He had moved heaven and earth to make the regiment self-sufficient. That applied to combat situations as well. Need arty? Vipers were trained in the use of all types of artillery, and their gunnery skills were excellent. The regiment maintained its own artillery pieces, both towed and self-propelled. Need space transport? The regiment had ships to transport vipers anywhere they needed to go, and it also had warships to escort those transports all crewed by personnel drawn from the SDF (Snakeholme Defence Force). Need something blown up? Vipers were trained in all types of demolition, and in defusing such things should that come up. Vipers were trained in every conceivable form of combat known, and all of them were pilot trained so that any viper could quickly replace a lost unit. All this, because General George Burgton was one paranoid sonofabitch, and would never again truly trust anyone but his own people to support his regiment long term.

In theory, anything Gina would ever have to face should've been covered in her training, but she had to admit while standing upon an ice sheet in a blizzard on a dead world, that no one could have foreseen her need for a post hole boring machine. The regiment was a combat unit, but in line with Burgton's self-sufficient philosophy, his men were credible engineers—if by credible one meant they could build a basic bridge, defensive redoubt, or other temporary structure when needed using local materials. So although she didn't in fact have a post hole boring machine with her—because hey, she hadn't imagined the need to bore holes for bridge supports today—she did have a working understanding of engineering principles. Enough to get by and improvise a workaround at least. The fact her workaround wouldn't have been possible without Eric's gift of the IED droid made no never mind.

Gina stood outside in the -43°c conditions, toasty warm in her environment suit, and used the remote controls to drive the droid down the APC's ramp. She could see what the droid was seeing using a window she had open on her internal display. It currently showed her standing in front of it and the antenna mast beyond. She piloted the droid to within three metres of the mast and parked.

The droid had a number of probes, sensors, and even weapons equipped as standard. Sometimes they were used purely as a recon platform, and only the cameras might be used to check for explosive devices, other times its electro, magnetic, or infra sensors might be deployed. What interested her today was its array of weaponry. Normally the mortar and rail gun would be used to safely detonate IEDs, and that was fine on any other day. She didn't want to blow up the mast though, or damage the station. She just needed a hole.

She deployed the laser.

Any laser could cut the ice, but generally they weren't carried by Alliance troops. They had been once. Long before the Merkiaari War that was. They had been considered the cutting edge of weaponry back then and were used against other Humans on the battlefield many times, but that was before the Merki arrived and started kicking butt. For the first three years of the war, the Merki won battle after battle, and proved Alliance gear was inferior. Plasma weapons and weapons based upon mass drivers soon gained ascendance, relegating lasers to industrial use and space warfare where power limitations were less of a concern. More power gave naval lasers a real offensive punch, but making that sort of laser man portable was pretty much a pipe dream. No soldier would exchange her M18-AP rifle for even the most powerful man portable laser. Such a laser would only have power for one or two shots, while a hundred round magazines were standard for M18 rifles. Double capacity drum mags were available, but they were bulky and not commonly used. They were real bitches to reload in the field and she'd been desperate enough to reload her empty mags with loose rounds a time or two when her squad ran out.

The droid's targeting reticule was clear on her display, but she didn't fire. She wanted a nice round hole big enough for her and some gear to pass through. She quickly set up a firing pattern to burn a continuous circle through the ice two metres in diameter. That should be plenty. The first shot would mark the centre of the hole, and provide a drain for the melt water. Without it, the laser's beam would be degraded.

She activated the program and the droid went to work.

Gina watched as the droid deployed one of its many arms and aimed down at the ice. It fired, melting the ice and quickly reaching the station's roof. She knew the moment the laser hit the roof because a bloom of ejecta flew skyward peppering the ice all around with debris. The melt water in the hole quickly disappeared, and the droid stopped firing. A second or three later, the droid fired again and began circling its pilot hole.

Gina was well pleased. The droid was doing its thing and despite the weather conditions, the ice was melted long enough to flow away down the hole. She had been worried about that. If it had refrozen before getting clear she might have resorted to explosives and risked damaging what she came for. Thermate would have burned through the ice and the roof easily, but then it would have ruined anything beneath it too. It burned hot enough to melt steel when applied properly. This was better.

Gina let the droid work and started unloading a few things from the APC. She had a temporary generator, a computer, a winch, powerful lamps, and a bundle of ropes. She closed up the APC and carried everything to the hole that the droid was just about done with. She piled everything ready to use and peered down the hole just as the section of roof fell away. The droid beeped as if in satisfaction, indicating its program was complete and signalling its readiness for another task. It stowed its weapon arm.

Gina took up the hand controller again and manoeuvred the droid out of her way.

She ran a line from the APC to the winch and secured it, and then used it to lower the generator and other supplies into the hole. The electric winch wasn't designed for heavy loads or for the extreme conditions, but it held up fine. Vipers were strong enough that had it failed, she could have lowered everything hand over hand if she had to. When the load hit bottom and the line went slack, she swung into the hole and used it to climb down into the darkness.

Gina reached the icy floor and paused to look around. She switched to light amplification mode but grimaced at the result. It was only a little better than total darkness. There wasn't enough light coming in through the hole for her systems to work with. Well, she would fix that directly. She turned in place, slipping a little on the slick surface. The melt water from her cutting operation had refrozen making movement tricky despite the debris from the roof scattered about.

She located her supplies and dragged them off the ice before getting to work. She set up one of the lamps on its stand and ran a cable to the generator. She cancelled light amplification mode—she didn't want to blind herself—and flipped the switch to start the generator. Light flooded the room, and she stared around at what was revealed. The first thing that caught her eye were the rows of cabinets running down the centre of the room, but it was to the dead status board on the far wall her eyes were drawn.

She advanced to take a better look.

There was no power to it, of course, but the status board still revealed much that she wanted to know. The station was an Infonet node. So much she had already guessed based upon the type of antenna on the roof. It was a relay station and was clearly labelled as Woolsery with a little "you are here" notice appended to it. The board also told her where other relays were by name, not coordinates unfortunately—it consisted of simple red and green lights with lines connecting them to indicate where in the system they were. A proper computer monitor would have been more informative, but only if she could get the computer running. All in all, she was satisfied with the more primitive display. Even unpowered as it was, it was useful. She made certain her database scanned the entire image of the board into her database. The place names especially. With those, she could find every one of those lights in the real world simply by calling up an old atlas entry and navigating to them using Woolsery as a starting point.

Gina turned away to investigate the rest of the station.

## Woolsery Infonet Relay Station, Kushiel

Hours of work tracing power runs, and Gina finally had the building up and running. The lights in the ceiling, frost covered like the walls and floor, illuminated Gina and her lash up of cables crisscrossing the floor and entering cabinets. The cabinets contained the memory crystals used as the station's buffer memory. The nature of crystal memory storage was such that supplying it with power should return it back to its previous state without damage. The synthetic crystals were as hard as diamond and pretty much indestructible. Crystal memory needed power to change states, meaning the buffer should still contain the data it had contained when the station lost power. She was counting on that particular property of the crystals to lead her to the prize.

"Okay, time to see what we have," Gina said and switched on the computer she had brought and hooked up to the station's net. "Hmmm."

There was a lot of data. Her computer was accessing the buffer memory and treating it like just another memory partition available to it. Truncated files or data that the computer considered gibberish was ignored as unreadable, but it could be read—maybe—aboard *Hobbs* with a lot of processing. She wasn't interested in doing that. At this stage, she would search through the files she could actually read without aid.

She ran searches and looked for information that Liz said

would point to the A.I or its backup. Her computer stripped
file headers and compared them to its search parameters,
and slowly she pieced together a map of where the data had
flowed from and where it was flowing to. A lot of it was
general system data, stuff the net itself needed to function
and of no interest to her, but as the search deepened more
and more flags were raised to grab her attention.

She smiled fiercely. This was looking better and better.
She shunted the flagged entries to another window and started
another search confined only to them. Almost immediately
she began getting hits. She opened the files and devoured the
contents. She was shocked to find Sebastian's name almost
immediately. Somehow she hadn't expected that. She read
the files, and was disappointed with the contents. They all
seemed banal. Nothing out of the ordinary at all, but their
presence was still significant. The file headers told her where
they had originated, and it wasn't Haverington. Eric was not
going to be a happy bunny. He was looking in the wrong
place.

Gina didn't pack up immediately, though she was sorely
tempted. She decided to work through all the data here first.
She had already done all the prep here. It would be a waste
not to strip every byte of useful data from the effort. She let
her computer work, and stood to stretch her legs.

She wandered around the station poking into things
while her computer did its job. The station wasn't a big
installation, one main computer centre with a couple of
annexes containing offices and storage areas. She peered
through open doors, and glanced into boxes at the detritus,
wondering about the people who had used it all. She sat at
a desk and jiggled drawers. One was locked, but her viper
strength made short work of the flimsy lock. Inside was a
binder that she pulled out and opened to a random page.

It was a maintenance log. Time sheets and names of
people long dead together with signatures and initials signing
off on work and inspections done on the network. Nothing

startling or even remotely interesting. Gina flicked through the pages noting more of the same. She threw it back into the drawer and shoved it shut. She opened another drawer but found nothing but blank forms. The last drawer yielded a few old books—manuals and technical spec sheets. It didn't matter how advanced people became in their use of computers, they still had to print stuff out to get the full benefit of the data. It didn't matter whether it was printed on archaic paper like on Earth before colonisation began, or on plastic flimsies like these. She didn't think people would ever stop printing stuff out.

She left the office and went back to check progress only to find her computer had finished crunching the data. She looked it over but found nothing to change her mind. She was packing up and moving out.

It took a lot less time to withdraw all her gear and pack it back aboard the APC than it had to unload and set it up. Maybe two hours later she was driving again, heading back to the shuttle. She hadn't reached the halfway point when Eric contacted her.

"Alpha-Two, Alpha-One you read?" Eric said.

"Alpha-One, Two copies. How's it going in sunny Haverington?"

Eric snorted. "I found it."

Gina's jaw dropped. "You found it? *In Haverington?*" she couldn't believe it. Her information pointed away from the capital altogether and toward a more historic site. "You sure?"

Eric sounded puzzled when he said, "You doubted your research? The library was right where you said it would be. Intact too. The place looked untouched by time, Gina. Incredible really. I think we should empty the racks and take the crystals home with us. I know Kushiel is a monument, but all those books should be used not left here."

Gina blinked. "Wait what?"

"The books. They're wasted here. I don't think

Snakeholme's library is even half the size of this one."

She finally caught on. "You mean you found the library, not the A.I?"

"Didn't I just say I found the library? Maybe you need to run a diagnostic. You don't sound like you're tracking right. Check your o2 levels."

Gina grinned. He would be checking his when he heard what she'd found. "Eric, I found it. The prize is mine."

"Bull."

"Nope, not kidding. I powered up the node and it was right there in the buffer. Stripped the header info on a bunch of files and found the originator. Sebastian was up and running when the power went out."

"Bloody hell... that's... where is he?"

"Place called Landing. Want to bet it's the original landing site for the colony?"

"No bet. I know it is. The archive here is extensive and the colonisation is documented in the history section. That's where I've been looking mostly. There's no mention of his location though, just references to him as an entity in decisions made at that time."

"Do we know if Landing was bombed?"

"It was," Eric said grimly. "Not with kinetics though," he said, sounding a little more hopeful.

Nukes were just as bad, worse in some ways. There were areas of the planet still hot enough that even a viper would have to limit exposure. Gina guessed they would be finding out how hot Landing was at some point.

"You want to meet there?"

"No. I want you to fly here and meet me. There's something I need you to see."

Gina frowned. He didn't sound happy about something. "You want to clue me in?"

"Not until you get here. Alpha-One out."

"Alpha-Two out." Gina said and turned her attention to driving. "What the hell was that about?"

## Haverington, Kushiel

Eric appeared on Gina's sensors as soon as she was in range of the city, but she couldn't land the shuttle at his location. She chose to land next to the other shuttle on the ice over what had once been a park at the centre of the city. She was taking for granted that Eric had chosen it after surveying the ice with his GPR and that it was safe.

She landed safely and deployed the APC again.

She drove carefully through the eerie streets of the capital. The looming buildings with their empty windows were oppressive and sad. The weather was fine for a sub-zero climate. Skies were clear and painfully beautifully blue, but it did little to raise the oppressive feel of the place. She drove passed shattered buildings, obviously the results of a battle, and back into untouched streets heading toward Eric's location. His icon was clear on her sensors, but he wasn't in the library she had located for him. He was city blocks away.

She found Eric standing in a street in the commercial district of the city waiting for her. She parked a couple of metres from him, sealed her helmet, and climbed down from the cab. His APC was parked just beyond him. She ran a sensor sweep as she walked toward him, trying to discover what he found interesting. The buildings were the usual sort of thing. Commercial towers, modern for their time she was sure, but looking old before their time with windows gone and bare steel showing the depredations of a climate they weren't designed to handle.

"So," Gina began. "What's up?"

For his answer, Eric beckoned her to follow him toward one of the buildings. She shrugged and followed. He stopped and looked back at her before drawing her attention to the structure.

Gina saw what had him concerned right away. The doors should have been buried by up to three metres or so of ice, but they weren't. The other buildings had snow and ice piled against them, half covering their entrances, but this one had been cleared. It was obvious now her attention had been drawn to it that someone had cut the ice into a gentle ramp and then cut away the doors. She could see them lying on the floor inside.

"Did you...?"

Eric shook his head and crouched. Gina joined him to study the tracks in the ice. "See here and here?"

Gina nodded.

"Droid tracks."

"Yeah," Gina said remembering the marks left by the use of her IED droid earlier. "Have you been inside?"

"Briefly. I wanted you to see this before going deeper in."

Gina nodded and they entered the building.

Eric switched on a powerful hand lamp to illuminate the room. As soon as he did, Gina knew she was standing in a bank, and that someone had been here before them. Of course it was possible the mess was part of the chaos caused by the evacuation of the city. Desperate people losing their heads might have thought they would need money to survive, but she doubted that was the case here. This looked like the aftermath of a salvage operation, and she knew no salvaging had been sanctioned.

The doors had been roughly cut away and allowed to fall inside. Beyond them, the floors were iced over but only thinly, indicating to her that the doors had not been down for long. Eric played the beam of his light over the scene, and stopped. Most of the bank's droids were still in place. Like sentinels standing guard, they stood waiting for customers who would never come. The main counter divided the space, but the central section had been destroyed. The people responsible hadn't bothered with niceties. It hadn't been surgically cut away. It looked to Gina as if they had used demo charges to blow their way through. Probably had to, she mused as she studied the damage. Bank security would have dictated the partition be armoured.

Eric led the way and Gina followed him into the restricted area of the bank. She proved herself correct as she passed the droids, and saw the damage more closely. Demo charges had been rigged to blow through the armoured wall. The telltale burn marks and splintered steel, still covered in the remains of synthetic wood to hide the armour, told the tale. She eyed a fallen droid. Half its face had been blown off, left where it had fallen, but still smiling.

Gina shivered.

Eric stopped. "Surprise surprise, but not really."

Gina grunted. As Eric, she was unsurprised to find the vault had been blown. The vault door stood wide, its locking system neatly blown away. She ducked inside and found more mess, but it was obvious the thieves had methodically broken into every drawer and every safe within the place, only discarding the things they couldn't sell or trade onto the floor. She wondered how much loot they had salvaged... no not salvaged. This was grave robbing. The safe boxes in here had been people's personal stuff. *Dead* people's personal stuff. The bank's platinum reserves were probably held elsewhere on Kushiel, but there would have been a sizable amount kept here. Even today, despite government disapproval, platinum wafers were still universally accepted as currency.

"What do we do about this?"

Eric shrugged. "Nothing I can think of. They're long gone."

Then why had he even bothered to bring her here to see it? Eric turned away and retraced his steps. She shook her head and looked back at the sad remains of people's lives. It wasn't right, but she couldn't think of anything to do either. She headed back to the street.

"We heading for Landing now?"

Eric stopped on his way to his APC and looked back. "We could do that, or fly back up to the ship and start fresh tomorrow. Preference?"

Gina looked toward the sun and estimated flight times. It would be dark when they reached Landing, but she would prefer to stay on planet. It would waste so much time going back to *Hobbs* only to fly back down tomorrow. She explained her thoughts and Eric agreed to stay the night.

"You can come to my place for dinner," Eric said and Gina laughed. "My shuttle's autochef can handle a pizza I'm sure."

She made a face.

"Don't like pizza?" Eric said in shocked tones. "That's damn near unpatriotic!"

"Huh?"

"You come from Faragut and you were a marine. Double whammy."

Gina snorted. "Despite what you may have heard about marines, we are... *were* not all pizza eating beer swilling grunts. Some of us know one end of a chopstick from the other you know. We don't all eat with our fingers."

Eric snorted. "And the Faragutians?"

Gina scowled. "You won't hear me defending Faragut, crack about patriotism or not, but I've seen them eat linguine and plenty of other stuff. They don't live on pizza, and neither do I."

"Does this mean you're not interested in coming over?"

"Nope. I'll be there but I'll do the cooking. I know a few good codes you'll like."

Eric nodded. "See you there then."

She watched Eric mount up, and then trotted to her own APC to do the same. Eric pulled out while she settled herself. She let him get a good lead before starting after him.

## ABOARD ALPHA-ONE, LANDING, KUSHIEL

Eric leaned back in his seat and took another mouthful of his coffee. "You were right; you do know a few good codes."

Gina popped a last ball of rice into her mouth and smiled.

She had chosen Chinese on purpose. His crack about marines and Faragut had struck a nerve. He wasn't far wrong about her home world's rep, not that she cared to learn what the current fashionable stereotype happened to be, but proving she knew a good menu when she saw one had suddenly become important. Hiller was her platoon's gourmet, not her, but she had learned a thing or two over the years, and Hiller had added to her increasingly discriminating palette with trips to Stirlings in Petruso with their friends. She could hold her own with Eric, though she was betting he would wipe the floor with her where wine was concerned. Cliché it might be, but beer really was more her style. If Eric was a wine snob, well, she would deal, disappointing as that would be. She grinned.

"What's funny?"

Gina shrugged. "Nothing."

"Come on, you've thought of something."

"No, really, it's nothing," she said. "Can I ask you something?"

Eric shrugged. "Shoot."

"You might not like it," she warned, thinking it better than just blurting it out. "The San Luis op. Did you save the others aboard the dropship?"

Eric stared off into the distance remembering. "Did I save them?" He sounded grim. "We always tried to save people in the beginning. It seemed like that was our mission, but of course that changed. We went from saving people to avenging them in short order. Our missions became seek and destroy. We were like you once, Gina, all of us. Even the General was like you back then; a young captain determined to do the right thing, but he changed. We all had to, or go insane. You've only seen one side of him you know, but even so I think you've already started to wonder about him, haven't you?"

Gina opened her mouth to answer, but no words would come out.

"No need to answer. Your loyalty to him and the regiment can remain unstrained a while longer. Just remember that there'll come a day when you have to decide how much your honour is worth. I remember the first time I had to compromise mine for the good of the regiment. The General is fond of that saying. The good of the regiment. The problem is, the good of the regiment is what he says it is. The same goes for the good of the Alliance. Who decides? He does. He sends us out and we do what he orders because he says the Alliance will be better if this thing happens, or worse off if that thing does... this or that person must die, for the good of the Alliance.

"Well," Eric shrugged. "I guess we do still trust him even after everything. Why else are we still doing his bidding? Maybe because we're so old we don't know any other way to live. Maybe we need someone to lead us because we can't think for ourselves anymore."

God he sounded bitter. "And maybe you're just full of crap," Gina said callously. "Maybe deep down you know he makes the hard choices, the choices you know must be made, and you're secretly relieved because you don't have the balls to make them yourself."

Eric smiled gently. "Maybe so. You asked if I saved them that day. The truth is we saved each other every day back then. We didn't keep count then and don't now. Did I save them that time? I cut the fuel just as you did in your sim, and left them in hibernation. The SAR shuttles lifted them into orbit for repairs and redeployment. I know you're wondering about the burned ones. They survived. They were even sane when they came back online, as much as any of us were after San Luis.

"San Luis was a defining moment for us. For vipers I mean, but also the Alliance. The entire regiment fought in those battles, something not done before that. It changed things. The General certainly became more aggressive after seeing the survivors, and I think that was when he began to ah... *manage* his superiors. I noticed at the time that our missions changed in surprising ways."

Gina knew her history and agreed with Eric. Events could be explained in different ways of course, but if one were paranoid enough to assume there had, or could have been, one mind orchestrating things, then certainly that man had been General George Burgton. Vipers had exploded onto the scene after San Luis. They had suddenly been everywhere, given almost a free hand or so it seemed. No doubt Burgton had needed to negotiate or persuade his superiors to allow his men to perform those missions, but that was all behind the scenes. It had appeared very different on the surface. Vipers were sent in ahead of major land forces to break Merkiaari command and control structures, and wherever Merkiaari popped up, so too did the vipers, sometimes anticipating their incursions like the catastrophe at Bethany's World.

"Well," Gina said. "I'm glad you did save them."

Eric shrugged as if it meant nothing.

She drank her coffee and tried to think of something else to talk about. Eric just sat there watching her, and she couldn't think of anything but work to fill the silence. She was about to bring up tomorrow's itinerary when he broke the silence, but his choice of subject didn't please her.

"Faragut," Eric said. "You were born there."

She nodded but he hadn't asked a question so she restricted herself to the nod.

Eric's lips twitched but he didn't laugh. "Tell me about it."

"Nothing to tell. I was born there, eighteen years later I left. Never went back."

"Hmmm, family?"

"Nope."

"None?"

"None I know of, and no I didn't look."

"Why not?"

Gina sighed and put her cup aside. "You ever visit

Faragut?"

Eric nodded.

"Then you know what it's like. Faragut is a throwback. It's barely a democracy. I'm amazed that the Alliance accepted their form of government at all. Constitutional monarchy for Chrissakes," Gina snorted. "Would *you* go back there?"

"I've always liked the romance of monarchies," Eric mused seriously. "Feudal lords beholden to the crown governing their lands in peace and prosperity. It sounds idyllic. The lords have a social contract with their people to govern honourably. There are worse governments out there, Gina. When I was there, Faragut was stable and its people had a high standard of living. King Richard was beloved; his heir was doing his duty in the Alliance Navy."

Gina grimaced. "Spoken like a tourist. The government serves the crown. The King as head of state makes broad policy, and the House of Lords and House of Commons debate and wrangle over the details. It's a democracy because the commoners vote for their representative to sit in the lower house, but it's a democracy in name only. The King can dissolve Parliament at any time. He rules Faragut, and he's commander in chief of Faragut's armed forces. Parliament serves him by carrying out his edicts."

"I get all that, Gina, I knew it before, but what has that to do with you? You were a commoner I assume?"

"Orphan, but yes. I was looked after and educated in a state crèche."

"Ah," Eric said more subdued. "That explains it."

She nodded. The crèche system was a great idea in theory. It amounted to state run orphanages that cared for unwanted children. They cared, clothed, taught, and trained them to be useful members of society. A worthy goal one would think, but come the age of majority—eighteen on Faragut—the young adults had to pay back the state with national service either in the military or in the factories. The only way to avoid what amounted to a fifteen-year hitch of legalised slavery was to emigrate. Emigration takes money, making that an impossible dream. She had chosen another route off world with a five-year hitch with the Alliance marines. She had left and never looked back, and loved the life, re-upping with the marines twice more until Colonel Flowers seduced her away and into the regiment.

"So you hate your homeworld."

"I don't hate it, Eric. I have no feelings for it one way or the other. I wouldn't retire there, I wouldn't want to live there, but plenty of people do and happily at that. Good luck to them."

"Hmmm," Eric didn't seem convinced. "What do you think of their military?"

"Professional in the main, well trained rankers from what I saw on the Shan homeworld, but the officers are mostly nobles. It's very hard for commoners to enter the academy on Faragut. The officers walk about like they have a stick up their butts. They act as if everyone else was born to serve them. Kate told me the same problem exists on Bethany."

Eric nodded. "Bethany doesn't have nobles, but they have founding families, which are about the same. It's not what you know but who you know with them. Hiller is a rare exception among them in that he was born with some common sense."

Gina snorted.

"Tomorrow we check out Landing," Eric said changing the subject. "If it looks promising I want to go to phase two by the end of the day. Thoughts?"

"One of us flies back to *Hobbs* at the earliest opportunity to collect the base camp habitats and all the gear the engineers need."

"Good. We'll check out things together. If it looks okay, you go back upstairs and get Liz and her people and all their gear. They're engineers. They can use that expertise to build their own camp."

Gina grinned. "Good."

# 16 ~ The Prize

Gina surveyed the blasted and broken city buildings and took another reading. The city was hot as they had thought it would be, but not dangerous to someone wearing an environmental suit with canned air. The habitats were like very big environmental suits in the way they protected the inhabitants, so as long as they washed off contaminants from their suits before entering, they were all good. She reported that to Eric. He was on the other side of the city checking out the structures there.

"Sounds good, but I haven't found a good place to set up yet. You?"

"Not yet," Gina replied. "I'm heading to the site I saw on my shuttle's sensors next. I have a good feeling about it."

"Okay, but I'm not sure why you think a hot spring is important."

Gina just shrugged not caring that he couldn't see it. Eric seemed to feel the hot spot was a natural occurrence, and that could be true, but what if it wasn't?

"Maybe something interesting there," she said and signed off.

262 MARK E. COOPER

She couldn't drive to her point of interest. The city had been severely hammered during the war and its streets were clogged with rubble and fallen buildings. She doubted the thieves had "salvaged" anything here. There really wasn't anything left, and that was going to be a problem. She knew how she had felt when she saw the destruction, and knew Eric must feel the same way. With such devastation it would be a miracle if what they sought was recoverable. Still, they had to look and be sure before they pulled out. Liz wouldn't accept anything but positive proof of failure, and Gina felt the same. She knew how important Oracle was to the General.

She made her way by foot to the place she had marked on her internal map. It took hours of walking and backtracking when she found herself blocked, but finally she found the source of the heat her sensors said would be here.

She circled the ruined building trying to imagine it undamaged. She gave up after a very brief time. There was little point to the exercise, there was so little left to work with. Most of the walls had been blasted away. Literally. The nukes had not only irradiated the area, the air burst had wiped away entire blocks of buildings leaving a few nubs of walls and the foundations. That is what she had here. Foundations, melted steel, a wall here and there. The main feature was the remnants of the stairwells and elevator shafts. Gina switched to thermal imaging and confirmed her guess that it was the elevator shafts radiating heat.

"Okay, don't get excited. It's not hot springs, but it doesn't mean you've found a power source."

Or did it? She supposed a hot spring could have broken through into a basement of a building like this one, but she just didn't believe it. Waste heat under a building escaping up an elevator shaft didn't mean anything. Really. It didn't mean for example that she had found the A.I, or its backup module. It only meant she had found a source of heat on a frozen world. That's all. Just that and nothing else. She needed to investigate further.

"Eric," she said not betraying her excitement.

"What have you got?"

"Well it's not a hot spring, not in the basement of a building. I think we need to go down and check this one out. Bring climbing gear would you?"

"On my way," Eric said. "Stay put and I'll home on you."

"'kay," Gina said and headed for the elevator shaft to see if climbing down would be a simple matter or whether they would need the engineers.

They needed the engineers, Gina thought, some hours later as she and Eric dangled from ropes down one of the shafts. They were stymied by what was left of the elevator winching mechanism and the car itself where it had fallen and jammed in the shaft. She didn't know if the car had hit bottom or not. She tended to doubt it based upon the state of the emergency brakes. She could just make them out, and they had deployed clamping the car in place. The tangle of cable and pulleys was the problem. Why the hell hadn't the builders used anti-grav cars?

"We need cutting equipment," she said.

"Hmm, we could probably make do with the thermate," Eric said studying the problem. "Just burn it into chunks and let it fall wherever."

Thermate burned at a higher temperature than thermite and should do the job, but just cutting the obstruction into chunks and letting it settle might not be in their best interests. It would all go down, and they needed to go down as well.

"We do it?" she asked doubtfully.

"Hmmm," Eric said thoughtfully and panned his light over the debris. "I think so, but carefully. Look there and there."

Gina eyed the places he nailed with his light. Two pulleys. She nodded. "You thinking to cut through those and let the cables spring free?"

"Exactly. Cut those pulleys into chunks. The cables will

uncoil explosively. That might clear a way through and down to the car. If it does then great. If it doesn't we cut again."

"Okay," Gina agreed. "Hang here and I'll be right back."

She started back up the shaft to get the thermate from Eric's APC. He had parked closer than she had, having found a clear route on the far side of the city from the shuttles. It took her a little over an hour to make the round trip. She found Eric exactly as she'd left him, dangling from his rope and staring at nothing. She hated it when the old ones did that. It was like finding a droid in sleep mode. They became statue still and just went away, whether into memory or thoughts, she didn't know.

"Eric?" Gina said.

His head swivelled like a targeting sensor and his eyes! They were empty, but then a second later awareness flooded back and with it his Humanity. He was back, but if this was him, what had been looking out of his eyes just then? She shivered; she didn't want to know. She passed him some of the thermate, keeping back a sizable amount for later. She had more up top as well, safely out of the way.

"You want me to do the other one?"

"I'll handle it," Eric said and quickly went to work.

She had to admit he was quick and precise. She could have done the job and would probably have gotten the same result when they lit it off, but he was faster. Like he'd told her on Thurston that time; he was a dab hand with explosives.

Gina climbed out of the shaft leaving him to it. Eric joined her a while later but only briefly. He touched off the thermate remotely almost the instant he reached her, and then after the smoke had cleared from the shaft, they descended together to admire the results.

Gina looked over his handiwork and decided they were heading in the right direction but weren't there quite yet. This time she helped Eric set up. She wrapped the cables with the thermate bandage, wrapping it nice and tight before adding the detonator and then spraying the entire thing with the aerosol. The quick setting nanopolymer was designed to contain the heat and gasses only briefly before succumbing. The result was that the thermate would melt everything inside to a semi-liquid state before bursting outward in a shower of red hot metal particles. She set up four charges, and Eric three more. The detonators were all on the same channel and would ignite together.

This time when they lit off the charges they had to wait ten minutes or so for the smoke to clear and the metal to cool down. Vipers could survive a punctured suit even in these conditions, but why put themselves through the discomfit? When the smoke had cleared and thermal imaging suggested the scrap had cooled, they lowered themselves down the shaft for the third, and hopefully final, time.

"Looks good," she said. There was still plenty of scrap cable in the way, but the central area was clear all the way through. "Me first?"

"If you like," Eric said, sounding amused. "You did find it after all."

"Yeah, I did find it. Looking forward to our boat trip?"

"Getting ahead of yourself aren't you? We don't know there's anything down there."

"There's something," she disagreed. "I don't know what or how useful it is, but there's something."

Eric didn't argue. Wise of him. The heat source alone made this one worth investigating, and was why they were doing this location first and not some other random site.

Gina lowered herself carefully through the entangled cables, keeping to the middle of the cleared zone. She managed not to snag her suit and once past, she allowed herself to fall faster. The car was a long way down, but she soon reached it and was standing on its roof watching Eric make his descent. Before he did, she had the hatch open and peaked inside.

"I wonder who they were," she muttered when Eric joined

her to look into the car. "Three strangers, three friends?"

"Doesn't matter now. They're closer in death than alive."

Strange sentiment, Gina thought, as she dropped into the elevator. She tried not to land on the skeletons, but Eric had no such sensibilities. He landed with a crunch and a puff of bone dust as one of the skulls disintegrated beneath his boots. She didn't protest. She was too interested in forcing the doors apart.

"Give a hand would you?"

Eric stepped beside her and they heaved the doors apart to reveal darkness. He directed his light and revealed an empty corridor stretching ahead. Gina could tell it was the source of the heat despite her suit, or maybe because of it in a way. Condensation immediately began forming on its exterior surfaces when the warmer air touched it. The moisture flashed to frost almost immediately.

She turned on her own lamp and panned it around, looking for anything that might tell her what she had here. This wasn't a basement access for instance; too well appointed. It looked like any other corridor in a generic office building, but not like something leading to a machine room that typically serviced such buildings. There was carpet on the floor for one thing; a clue that said to her that people and not machines were expected to use the spaces down here.

She advanced along the corridor nailing a door with her light. It was locked, but she twisted the handle with smooth inexorable power listening to the mechanism. The pop and crunch made her happy. Silly really, but the little things about being a viper still thrilled. She opened the door and scowled. Eric peered over her shoulder at the cleaning supplies and chuckled. She growled under her breath and closed the storeroom door. They moved to the next door. Unlocked this time. It was an office. Eric entered first and Gina followed.

The room was partitioned into work spaces each one containing a desk and computer. She played her light over the nearest work station. It had been left neat, as if its user had just left for the night and planned to return the next day. Without a power source she couldn't begin to guess what kind of business had been conducted here, but Eric hadn't even glanced at the computers. He'd made a beeline for the waste bins.

The waste bins?

Eric dug through the trash and selected a discarded flimsy. He read it and then another. "Not what I hoped."

"What is it?"

"Nothing important. Just an old memo."

Gina left him to it and stepped back out into the corridor to investigate the other doors. She entered offices to scout around. Most were executive offices with an outer room for an assistant and a plush inner office for the exec. She didn't find anything interesting until she came to a stairwell.

She forced the door open against fallen debris from above and found the stairwell lit by emergency lighting. She blinked in surprise. The emergency lights had power, but from where? She advanced further climbing rubble and edged toward the stairs going down. It was blocked with fallen rubble, but she thought she could detect a hum of machinery. The sounds of her suit PLSS tricked her ears. There couldn't be active equipment—she glanced sideways at the dimly glowing light panel, but then again...

"Eric, I've found something interesting," she said over her comm. "Come take a look at this."

"What is it?"

"Emergency lighting in the stairwell at the far end from the elevator," she said. "I think I hear something."

"On my way."

She tried to get a better position to listen for that humming sound, but the helmet made it useless. She hesitated for a second, but then took a chance and removed it. Her eyeballs tried to freeze as the cold hit her face, and alerts started flashing upon her display. The temperature was higher than outside as she had noted before. Wind chill alone made a big difference, but even so it was still well below zero. Her breath puffed into fog and drifted toward the corridor carried along by a current of warmer air coming up through the rubble in the stairs. She switched to infra and was excited to see the faintly glowing current clearly. She coughed and then again. The air was toxic as her display warned and it irritated her nose and throat. Sulphur dioxide was a key ingredient in sulphuric acid. In other words, she was breathing sulphuric acid in a gaseous mist. She coughed again.

>_ Sensors: Environmental health warning, sulphur dioxide in dangerous concentrations.
   >_ Diagnostics: Warning, lung capacity impaired.
   >_ IMS: Repairs in progress.

Yeah, yeah. What else was new? Gina dismissed the warnings, and still coughing, laid down to put her ear against the rubble. She upped the gain to amplify input to her ears, and grinned. Definitely something going on down there.

Gina winced and hastily returned her hearing to normal as Eric arrived, his footfalls booming in her head like a rampaging dinosaur. She climbed back to her feet and put her helmet back on, taking deep cleansing breaths to flush her lungs of the toxic crap she had been breathing. Some of the warnings on her display winked out, while others slowly changed, edging back to safe or normal parameters. She eyed her radiation dosimeter. It continued to glow balefully. Particles of radioactive dust must have entered her suit. She would need to decontaminate the suit inside and out as well as herself. She cursed the need, but wasn't too worried. The dose wasn't fatal for a viper, or anyone else for that matter. It was equivalent to an x-ray, no more than that, but it was still a high amount for such a brief exposure.

"Definitely something down there, Eric. I can hear machine noises, and there's a warm air current coming up from below."

Eric must have switched to infra as she had done because he nodded. "I see it."

"What do you think?"

"It's our first and best indication that something's here," Eric said. "We won't know what it is unless we get down there for a look."

He edged passed her and studied the tons of rubble filling the stairwell, and then stood craning his neck to study the shaft overhead. He started climbing upward until he ran out of room, shining the powerful beam of his lamp up into the darkness. He came back down.

"Let's go back. We need Liz's people."

Gina nodded and together they headed for the elevator shafts and the ropes hanging there.

## BASE CAMP, LANDING, KUSHIEL

The engineers were good, Gina was pleased to note. They had thrown themselves eagerly into their work after being idle aboard ship so long. They had barely been on site a few hours after the trip from *Hobbs*, and the base camp was already laid out. The first dome was under construction, its supporting framework spreading one triangular formation after another linking together in a circle and beginning to arch upward. Other domes were just a pile of crates and metal tubes as yet, but the ground had been prepared and the foundations poured. Amazing stuff, nanopolymers. Even in such terrible conditions it worked as designed, poured directly onto ice even! Without good foundations and floors, they couldn't pressurise the domes. The thick plastic circular platforms were already being covered with snow as the clear skies they had praised when they landed, gave way to another howling storm. The engineers worked on, ignoring the blast of icy wind. The dome's skeleton took after its masters, ignoring the winds as it climbed and linked to its neighbouring structures.

"It's going well," Liz said privately on her helmet comm, perhaps interpreting Gina's watchfulness as worry. "The frame can handle much worse than this."

"I'm not worried. Your people seem satisfied with things. What about the walls?"

"As long as we leave certain panels out for the wind to pass through it will be fine. If we build by the book, the walls would turn into a windbreak and might be carried away. The domes rely upon the structural integrity of neighbouring panels if you know what I mean?"

"Not really."

"Well... think about those old stone arches you've seen in the historical sensims. Take one of the stones out and the arch collapses. It's the same here. When all the panels are in, they push and pull on each other making the structure strong. It's really an excellent design. We can't finalise the domes in these conditions, but as long as we let the wind pass through safely we can do ninety percent of the work and finish them later."

"Sounds good," Gina said.

They watched the work silently for a time. The cranes had the hardest job. Even flimsy metal pipes became dangerous when the wind kicked up, but they were monitoring wind speeds and so far they were low enough, barely, for safety.

"I would have preferred having some of my people looking at what you found, Gina, but this had to be done sooner rather than later."

Gina nodded. "I could take you to see it if you trust me. I'll have to lower you down on a rope."

"Tempting," Liz said with a shy smile. "And of course I trust you, but I won't be able to do much. Eric said we need a crane?"

"Yeah. We went down using an elevator shaft, but it would be easier if you cleared the stairwell from directly above it."

Liz nodded.

The hours passed and Gina spent all her time transporting

equipment from *Hobbs* in her shuttle. Eric was doing the same. The heaviest items had been dealt with by the end of that day, and she moved onto transporting the pieces needed to build up the walls of the habitat domes. The weather worsened and it was decided to halt further operations. High winds made the cranes unsafe to use, and Liz decided not to risk it. Work upon the walls was abandoned, and everyone retreated to the shuttles to wait.

The second day dawned bright and clear. Liz took advantage by pulling everyone off the other dome's supports to quickly clad the main residential dome. The idea was to complete it quickly so that everyone could move in and sleep comfortably instead of in the shuttles and APCs. They hadn't enjoyed the experience the night before.

Gina watched in amusement as Liz's people went into high gear. She guessed the promise of a warm place to live and sleep without their suits was a spur to action. She could understand that. Her suit was getting a little ripe, and she imagined hers wasn't the only one.

The marvellously designed panels that impressed Liz so much quickly covered the skeleton of the dome, and stabilised it. It didn't take too long either. Men and woman clambered all over the thing, guiding the panels being lowered by the cranes and snapping them into place. The more that were added, the stronger it became. Liz directed the entire scene like a conductor with an orchestra. As the dome was buttoned up with the last few panels still going in, her people poured inside with equipment, generators, crates, god knows what else, and began building the interior partitions to separate common areas and sleeping compartments. Wiring for lights and heating units was the first order of business however, quickly followed by plumbing and the air filtration needed to pressurise the dome. Positive atmospheric pressure was a must to keep contaminants out. The showers were particularly important in the air lock. Contamination could enter the dome on their suits. They had to decontaminate the suits before entering the dome proper. There would be other showers and toilet facilities inside as well of course. The main dome was for people to live in and would have all the conveniences. The other domes had different uses. One would garage the heavy equipment like the cranes and dozers so they could be maintained and protected from the weather. The third and last dome was to house supplies and the main generator to power the entire base. The portable generators would work in a pinch as a backup, but they were low capacity, meant for powering tools not buildings.

At the end of the second day, everyone ate a meal together in the main dome in relative comfort. Bare wires and pipes were everywhere. Tables, chairs, and beds were scattered all over amid crates and tools. Generators whirred supplying power to autochefs some still in their crates, but everyone sat together laughing and chatting, amid the remains of their meals on the tables. Their suits hung in the completed airlock, where they dripped dry from the decontamination cycle. Everyone was upbeat and happy with progress. They were warm and protected from the elements and no longer confined in smelly suits.

All was well.

It took the rest of that week to completely finish work on the base camp. The weather had quickly turned from unpredictable to solidly bad for three days straight. During that time, with winds howling outside and snow building up to half bury one side of the dome, Liz's people worked inside finishing their new home in record time. Finally the storm blew itself out and the engineers emerged blinking into brilliant sunshine like bears after a long winter. Everything was clean and white. Snow had been blown clear of the ice and built into drifts against the cranes and dozers. The foundations of the unfinished domes were uncovered, something that seemed to satisfy Liz, though she scowled at the need to dig out her machines and the supply crates.

The week passed and the base camp was completed,

allowing Liz to shift focus and labour to the prize she had come for. Gina had warned her a number of times that they didn't know what was under that rubble. Don't get your hopes up, she warned, but Liz ignored the pessimism determined to be optimistic. She didn't believe the A.I was down there, she said, but it was obvious she hoped it was. Gina could see the passion and hope in the woman's eyes and prepared herself to console her when the inevitable failure came to pass.

Alpha site looked a lot different from her first visit, Gina thought now, standing to one side of the main event. The stub of the stairwell had been demolished level to the ground leaving a square plascrete lined hole leading down into the foundations. A crane lifted a huge bucket full of rubble and freshly cut steel sections out of the hole as she watched, and swung it away. A few moments later, she flinched a little at the thunderous crash of the bucket emptying itself onto the growing pile in the street. As soon as the crane lowered the bucket back, the engineer's drills and hammers started up again.

Liz had agreed with Eric regarding the need to clear the stairwell after she surveyed things. To Gina's surprise, the elevator was in fact at the bottom of its shaft, not stuck part way as she had thought, and there was nothing to be gained by using it as an access point to the stairs. It would have made clearing the rubble harder. Using the crane down the stairwell itself was the obvious and most efficient choice, though it took more work to clear in the initial stages. Once it was open all the way to the bottom, it would give the engineers a fast way down using the crane as a makeshift elevator. The old stairs were being left in place to save time and effort, and could be used by those who didn't mind a workout, but the suits were confining and made everything more tiring. Gina doubted anyone would choose the stairs.

"Bored?" Eric said wandering over.

Gina shrugged. "Nothing to do here. Security? Don't

make me laugh. We're the only living things on the entire damn planet. I could have left my rifle home for all the target practice I'm going to get."

Eric chuckled.

"Seriously, Eric, what are we doing here?"

"Nothing much. That's why I came to find you. I think our time is better spent identifying and surveying other sites. This one is promising I grant you, but we should have at least one backup. *Hobbs* did identify a few other places for us to visit."

Gina nodded, it made sense. "Sounds good. You take the first ten on the list. I'll take the next ten. Okay?"

Eric nodded and they bumped knuckles to seal the deal.

Eric was the first to mount up and leave in his APC. Gina went to find Liz to inform her of the plan, and to tell her to shout over the comm if she needed viper help. Liz agreed absently and waved her away. She was distracted with work. Gina trotted off already reviewing her list of sites and creating her flight plan so that she didn't waste time backtracking. The less time spent in the air the better.

* * *

## ABOARD ARCHER'S GIFT, KUSHIEL SYSTEM

Leon Adler, captain of the Kalmar registered ship *Archer's Gift* glared at the information his sensors reported to him. Was it a warship or just a freighter as his sensors seemed to suggest? It couldn't be a simple freighter. There was nothing in the system to trade and no station to trade with.

*Nothing here to interest a trader, not a legit trader at least.*

Who were the bastards? What were they doing here? A trap laid for him, or a competitor? He hammered a fist on the consol, and his exec eyed him warily. He ignored the man. Haliwell was a new hire after Andrea left him at their last port. He missed her steadiness, but not her bitching. She hadn't agreed with his salvage run to Kushiel and had left the ship the moment they'd docked after their initial run, not even waiting for her pay. Not that he could have paid her anyway. Maybe she had known that, maybe not, but a good dozen of the crew had left with her. That meant half his crew was new and most of them were scum. He didn't dare walk his own ship's deck unarmed anymore.

Andrea had gutted the ship when she left and took the best half of his crew with her. It had nearly broken him to watch them go. They had been together a long time—years of legitimate trading, good years all, but a few bad trades had lead him inexorably toward others in an effort to dig himself out of the hole. It hadn't worked out, and he'd slipped deeper and deeper into trouble. Now he was the captain of an armed merchant vessel trading around the edges of civilisation, desperate to reverse his past mistakes.

It wasn't too late he swore. He just needed one good break and he could reverse all the ill fortune. He wasn't beyond redemption. He hadn't killed anyone, his deals might be a little dirty, but he wasn't an outright pirate. He wasn't a raider either, despite appearances. Kushiel was a dead world after all. It wasn't the same thing, no matter what Andrea had said to him on the docks the day she finally left. It wasn't! Taking what he needed from Kushiel wasn't like raiding a colony, and he was desperate. This was his last chance.

He glared at that innocent seeming icon on sensors. He should pull out, come back next month and see what this ship, these poachers, had left him. That was the safe thing to do, but he couldn't afford to play it safe! His creditors were howling despite the down payments on the debt he owed each of them. His last trip here had barely paid the interest on his loans. If he put into any legit port with his holds empty, he could kiss his ship goodbye. They would take it and sell it out from under him, and he would still owe them afterward. He was in so deep, he needed two ships of *Archer's* type to pay the debt. She was old and worth little more than scrap value to anyone but him. Goddamnit! This run had been his way out.

Haliwell refined the sensor data. "Definitely a trader. I think you're right, Captain, someone must have talked. They're poachers."

Leon nodded and tried to keep the rage off his face. He couldn't let them take his last chance away from him. Inside he wailed that he wasn't a killer, and that was true, but that final line was about to be crossed. He prepared to sacrifice the last shreds of his honour and felt sick. He had no choice! They had left him none. He couldn't just leave them to take what was his. He doubted he would still be the captain when they next docked if he tried. He'd made the crew some promises, and Haliwell was already looking at him oddly.

He rubbed his forehead feeling a stress headache pending. "All right. This is what we're going to do..."

## Aboard Hobbs in orbit of Kushiel

Captain Gibson sat in his command chair drinking coffee and reading reports. It was the middle of the watch, and things were quiet aboard. No emergencies or rush to load or unload cargo. All that had been completed two days ago. His crew were on maintenance watch now. Nothing urgent required attention.

As for the salvage operation, reports indicated things were progressing well. Base camp was complete and attention had shifted to alpha site. That was the name given to the first, and hopefully, the only salvage site on the planet. The entire mission didn't sit well with him. Grave robbing, that's what it amounted to. The sooner they left Kushiel the better.

"Sir?" Heather Watson, *Hobbs'* scan tech said. "That ship is still coming."

Gibson rose to join her and had a look at her data. "Well, they did ask permission to approach. An engineering casualty like they described isn't anything to fool with."

"Yes, sir, but they've missed turnover."

Gibson frowned. The term "turnover" harked back centuries to a time when ships used old style reaction drives without anti-grav compensators. It was applied to the point in a journey when ships literally had to about face and apply thrust in the direction of motion to slow down. These days, deceleration was a matter of the correct application of anti-grav, but the term was still used for the point at which a ship starts decelerating to make a rendezvous.

"Their course?"

"Unchanged," Watson said worriedly.

That couldn't be right. If they'd missed turnover for whatever reason, they would need to change course if they still wanted to rendezvous with *Hobbs* in orbit. If they didn't change course, they would miss the rendezvous entirely and fly right past. They would have to slingshot around the planet and try again. Leon wasted a few minutes checking the data and reluctantly decided she was right.

"Hail them," he snapped heading back to his station.

"Aye, sir," Noel at communications said.

Leon waited for a response wondering if perhaps *Archer's Gift* had suffered another malfunction and lost comm. That ship was a piece of junk and...

"Contact! Multiple contacts incoming. Missiles! They've fired on us!" Heather cried in shock.

Leon gaped at her, unable to move or understand. Fired? Missiles? Fired missiles at him? His brain gibbered at him, but his voice didn't betray him. He was snapping orders, and only afterward did he realise they were the right ones.

"...ound collision!" he cried and the gong gong gong of the collision alarm sounded throughout the ship sending the crew to emergency stations, and causing blast doors and other internal partitions to lock down. "Point defence free!"

"Point defence free, aye. Autoloaders operational. Targeting under computer control!" Max said from the helm. *Hobbs* wasn't a warship. Its defensive armourment was controlled from his station.

"Bring up the drive. Go to evasive as soon as we have power! Communications: get me Captain Penleigh. I think we might need to bug out. Tell him yourself if I'm busy. Tell him why."

"Aye, sir," Noel said and hunched over his panel.

"Everyone," Leon said trying for calm. "Let's work the problem calmly. That ship is some kind of raider, but we out mass it a hundred to one. We'll be fine." In the background he heard Noel reporting to Penleigh. He was about to take over, when *Hobbs* lurched and rolled crazily amid warning sirens and alarms. "Report!"

Heather's fingers raced over her controls, revising and refining her scan. "Some kind of stealthed missile or... no! They fired early and let the missiles come in on inertia ahead of them. They had to have fired hours ago, sir. I'm still tracking the others—the second wave."

Leon shook his head in disbelief. Second wave? That sounded—

The second wave of missiles came in fast and deployed. They were, every one of them, designed to hash sensors and spoof point defence. They did their job of sucking *Hobbs'* point defence missiles toward them and away from the third wave. The third wave performed its task admirably. They struck the ship more or less unopposed, and a new sun was born in orbit of Kushiel. It lasted mere seconds. When it died, the remains of *Hobbs* fell out of orbit burning and still breaking into smaller chunks. Explosions amid the debris shattered the ship into smaller and smaller pieces. Of its crew, only briefly glowing molecules remained.

\* \* \*

# 17 ~ Castaways

Gina stared up at the meteor shower grimly. Eric had just told her about the action in orbit, but the second brief sunrise over the city had been a big clue that something was wrong. The burning chunks of *Hobbs* were still entering atmosphere when Eric ran up to her and explained. He had run off again now, leaving her to watch the show. None of the debris would strike anywhere close. That was a mercy, but all it would do was prolong their deaths. They had two shuttles and could reach orbit, but without *Hobbs* they couldn't leave the system. She tried to imagine the General sending another ship to check on them when they failed to report via drone, and realised he would do that, but it would be months too late. They would be out of food and canned air long before that. They had enough food for a month, maybe two if they rationed it. They had been relying upon supplies from *Hobbs* for most things.

Gina used viper comm for privacy and contacted Eric. "We need to start rationing."

"Forget rationing. Let's survive the day before worrying about that."

"But—"

"Think about it, Gina. A raider ship comes to a dead colony world and blows away a prize like *Hobbs* without hesitation. What do you think they're after?"

Put that way it was obvious. Raider ships, unlike run of the mill pirates, jacked colonies out in the Border Zone when they could get away with it. For one to come here meant it wanted something on the planet more than it wanted to jack a ship. She remembered the bank and blown vault they had seen in Haverington.

"You're right. We need to get the civs in a hole. Somewhere out of sight. We can't take them back to camp."

"Agreed," Eric said. "With any luck these bastards will ignore us while they do whatever they came to do. I hope to god whatever they're after isn't here in Landing."

There was that, but Gina was thinking ahead to other problems. Problems like air, and food, and clean water. Problems such as how the hell would they escape Kushiel? They needed a way to get aboard the raider ship and take it for themselves. But first things first. She needed to get Liz and her people undercover.

"Where are you right now, Liz?" Gina said heading for the shaft. "You up top?"

"No, I'm at the bottom of the stairwell. We're just about to break into the clear."

"Good. I'm coming down. I need you to keep everyone there with you. No exceptions."

"Whatever for?" Liz said, sounding puzzled.

"I'll explain when I get there. While you wait, start thinking about a way to make yourselves more comfortable down there."

"What's wrong? Has something happened?"

"You might say," Gina agreed as she reached the crane and ordered the driver to lower her down in the bucket. "I'm coming down now. Meet me."

"All right, but we're so close to breaking through."

"Don't stop the work. You might need to stay down there a while and you'll need the space."

"But... what the hell has happened?"

"I'm nearly down. I'll fill you in."

Liz was waiting for her when the bucket stopped at the level where the work was ongoing. They had dug out a hundred and thirty feet or more of rubble and Gina could see what Liz meant about breaking through. There wasn't much stopping them advancing to the next landing. Liz offered a hand to help steady her, but she didn't need the help. She bent her knees and then straightened explosively, bouncing out of the bucket as if her legs had turned into springs. Liz applauded.

"Nice landing," Liz said. "What's the urgency?"

Gina explained. Liz stopped smiling and her face turned grim. She looked back toward her people still working unaware that anything was wrong, and then back to Gina.

"We can't stay down here—"

"You have to!"

"Hear me out," Liz said in a placating voice. "We can't stay down here without supplies from the camp. Eighteen hours from now, our suits will run out of power and air."

Shit. She had just been thinking about supplies, but she hadn't thought about power for the suits. Food, water, air, and power; those four things above all were needed. She had to make a run to the camp.

"I'll tell Eric," Gina said. "We'll get you what you need. You have eighteen hours to burrow down to somewhere you can call home for a few days. Can you tap into the emergency lighting down here for power?"

Liz nodded. "Bring me a water purifier and a way to recharge the suits, and we can last a few weeks, but how do we get home?"

"I'm working on it," Gina said grimly. She left Liz to her work and contacted Eric to tell him what she'd said. "... Liz says she can hold out weeks with those supplies."

"Already on it," Eric said. I'm loading up now with most of that stuff. Didn't think about the purifier. I'll add it."

"You need help?"

"Yes, but don't come here. We can't afford to lose us both if the raiders decide to blow away the camp. We'll do this in shifts. I'll let you know when to make your run."

"Okay, Eric, be careful."

"Careful is my middle name," Eric said.

She snorted. "Sure it is."

Gina climbed atop the rubble that had already filled the bucket and contacted the crane driver to hoist her up. She wanted to get back to her shuttle so that she would be ready to fly the moment Eric called. The bucket lifted clear of the shaft, and she jumped out before the crane driver could stop his lift. She raised a hand to him in thanks and pushed herself into a run.

Her APC was waiting.

When she reached the shuttle, she parked the APC in the shadow of a wrecked building. She wasn't planning for failure, but should she be shot down, Eric could still use her APC and all it contained. She ran her pe-flight checks and waited for Eric's call with her eyes nailed to her sensors looking for trouble. She was still looking when Eric called her.

"I'm lifting now," Eric said. "Make your run."

"On my way. Any sign of the bad guys?"

"Not yet. We might have to go looking for them. I'll have to think about that. We can't leave Liz and her people unprotected."

Gina scowled. She knew he would order her to stay with the engineers, she just knew it, but he was right too. There were only two of them. She lifted off and flew the shuttle to the base camp, but didn't see Eric on the way. He was flying cagey, using a different route and not one direct to alpha site. She reminded herself to do the same on the way back. She kept her altitude down, dodging terrain and using it to stay out of sight, though if the raiders remained in orbit and took their time, they could easily track her. She hoped they were too impatient for that. It was all she could do.

Hours later she landed at the base and powered down the shuttle, her eyes never straying far from the shuttle's sensors. She grabbed her rifle before debarking. It was the first time she had thought to need it here. Better safe than dead, she muttered under her breath as she hurried toward dome three. Number three contained all their supplies and the power plant. Eric had left the anti-grav palette loader in the entrance rather than park it properly. Signs of his hurried use of it were obvious. Crates and boxes had been stacked haphazardly where he had burrowed into the stacks for a particular item. One or two had toppled and broken open. Gina shook her head at the mess, but she would be making things worse in short order she had no doubt.

She grabbed the control handle and guided the loader toward the back of the stacks. She knew where everything was. Her database had a full inventory. She parked the loader and put her rifle aside on one of the crates. Her first priority was power packs and filters for the suits. The suit PLSS used a rechargeable power pack, but they had to be removed for charging. That meant every person would need a spare. They couldn't remove their suits to recharge them over night.

She hurried along the stacks and found the crates she needed. There were a dozen power packs to a crate. She needed three. They were heavy and unwieldy, but she managed to drag them out one at a time and muscle them back to the loader. Vipers were strong, but the crates were too bulky to get a good grip. She managed and added cartons of filters before guiding the loader back to the shuttle to unload. She soon fell into a rhythm of loading and unloading. Power, and filters, water filtration and purifiers all went into the shuttle. Next she grabbed a couple of the portable generators. She knew Liz had some on site, but didn't doubt more would be welcome. Her eyes fell upon a big crate marked *Autochef 1off—Handle with care—Fragile! This way up!* and decided to get it next. She unloaded and headed back to the dome.

She struggled and cursed trying to get one corner of the crate onto the loader so she could slide the autochef on. It was really heavy and every time she pushed the crate the loader slid away. She glared at the thing and realised she needed to wedge the loader against something. She chose some of the crates to block it in and was finally able to get the huge crate balanced on the loader. She brought the anti-grav up to full and walking backwards, she guided the loader out of the dome.

The explosion at her back threw her forward, slamming her chest into the loader's guide handle and blasting the air from her lungs. The force was so great that she folded over the handle and slammed face first into the crate. She didn't feel the pain, or hear the loss of air pressure in the suit as her visor shattered. She didn't know that the raider had made a lucky shot and hit her suit's power pack in the PLSS on her back. The violent detonation and resultant damage had sent her instantly into hibernation and the little death.

AUTOMATIC SHUTDOWN CYCLE COMPLETE.
ACTIVATE BEACON... DONE.
BEACON TRANSMITTING.


>_ DIAGNOSTICS: CRITICAL SPINAL INJURY, COMMUNICATIONS FAILURE, TACNET OFFLINE, LUNG CAPACITY COMPROMISED, CRITICAL BLOOD LOSS. UNIT UNFIT FOR DUTY.

>_ IMS: REPAIRS IN PROGRESS. ATTEMPTING LUNG INFLATION... FAILED. REPAIRS IN PROGRESS.


ENVIRONMENTAL HEALTH WARNING... ATMOSPHERE TOXIC, TEMPERATURE -32°, LUNG CAPACITY DEGRADED. WARNING... HIGH RISK OF UNIT TERMINATION. RECOMMEND IMMEDIATE HOSPITALISATION.

>_ IMS: REPAIRS IN PROGRESS.

MAIN POWER FAILURE. WARNING... HIGH RISK OF UNIT
TERMINATION. RECOMMEND IMMEDIATE HOSPITALISATION.

>_ IMS: RESOURCE WARNING. UNABLE TO REPAIR MAIN
POWER. LUNG INFLATION COMPLETE. LUNG CAPACITY 63%.
EMERGENCY REACTIVATION ADVISED. HOSPITALISATION AT
EARLIEST OPPORTUNITY ADVISED.
>_ DIAGNOSTICS: MAIN POWER FAILURE. WARNING...
UNIT TERMINATION IMMINENT.

EMERGENCY REACTIVATION APPROVED.
INITIALISE REBOOT SEQUENCE...
ACTIVATE COMBAT MODE... DONE.

>_IMS: RESOURCE WARNING, UNABLE TO REPAIR
MAIN POWER. HOSPITALISATION ADVISED. WARNING IMS
FAILURE.

FAULT LOGGED. CONTINUE REBOOT SEQUENCE.
TRS... DONE.
SENSORS... DONE.
TARGETING... DONE.
COMMUNICATIONS... FAILED TO INITIALISE.
RETRY/ABORT? >_
RETRY/ABORT? >_
RETRY/ABORT? >_
FAULT LOGGED. CONTINUE REBOOT SEQUENCE...
INFONET... SERVICE NOT AVAILABLE.
TACNET... FAILED TO INITIALISE.
RETRY/ABORT? >_
RETRY/ABORT? >_
RETRY/ABORT? >_
FAULT LOGGED. CONTINUE REBOOT SEQUENCE...
INITIATE EMERGENCY REACTIVATION...

Gina awoke to agony, but she didn't scream. The burning pain in her back warranted it, my god did it, but she was in such bad shape she couldn't scream. She was gagging on blood and the air was foul. She coughed trying to clear the blood from her lungs and that helped a little. She was shivering with cold, ice had formed on her eyelashes and her face burned with it. Frostbite was in her immediate future, she realised.

She groaned trying to think. Her internal display was awash in warnings and system failures. She shook with cold and shock. Main power failure? What the hell did that mean? Why wasn't she dead then? She puzzled over that and realised her systems were barely running on backup power. All of them, and she didn't have much time. Her log told the tale. She was dying. IMS was offline due to low resources, and without it she couldn't repair main power. She needed shipboard medical or a full blown hospital, but she was shit out of luck there.

She needed her supplements, but they were in the APC, the APC she hadn't brought with her. She frantically tried to think of something and realised how rattled she was. Dome three was barely a hundred metres away and there would be crates of what she needed in there. She had to get them. It was her only chance.

**Main power failure. Warning... unit termination imminent.**

"Yeah, yeah. Everyone's a critic," she mumbled and coughed. The burning in her throat and nose was getting worse without IMS to keep pace with the accumulating damage. She tried to rise and realised things were worse than she'd realised. "I'm dead," she said flatly and knew it was true.

She was paralysed below the waist.

She didn't panic. There was nothing but regret running

through her thoughts for a few minutes. She managed to roll onto her back and hissed as the snow touched her burns through the suit. Her PLSS had exploded and was completely gone, as was most of her suit back there. Bare skin, burned and ruined, contacted the ice and sensation quickly fled. That was a blessing. Her thoughts began to clear and she checked her sensors. She should have done that first thing, but under the circumstances it was a miracle she was even alive let alone tracking enough to think of the tactical situation.

Her processor had brought her back online because she would have died without waking if it hadn't. The fact she would die anyway, and in agony, didn't matter to it. Her survival for as long as possible was all it cared about and it had been out of options. She would have died in hibernation, so it woke her. Simple logic.

Sensors... right. She had been about to check her sensors hadn't she? She barely had power for this, but what the hell. She wanted to know what was happening. Maybe Eric was on his way. Her sensors revealed another story, and rage filled her thoughts. She actually snarled at what her sensors reported to her. Four red icons were moving around in the residential dome, and a small lander was parked next to her cargo shuttle. Her PLSS hadn't just failed, it had been helped along. Stupid to have assumed it in the first place, and she cursed herself. One or more of those red icons had shot her in the back hitting the power pack in her PLSS.

That had to be it.

Her thoughts flashed to her rifle sitting atop the crate in dome three. She rolled onto her front and started dragging herself toward the dome. She was leaving a trail in the snow a five year old could follow, but she had no choice. Coughing and gasping at the foul crap she was forced to breathe, she dragged her useless body up the cargo ramp and into the dome. Inside, she headed for the crate with her rifle on top. It was stupid, but she felt much better with it in her hands. She was still dying, and her priority should have been supplies for her IMS, but she had ignored common sense and armed herself instead.

**Main power failure. Warning... unit termination imminent.**

Gina dragged herself to the stacks, and then deeper between them until she found the small cluster of crates and boxes set aside for viper use. The snakehead stencilled on the sides together with code numbers that matched those in her database for supplements, ammo, etc, advised her which ones she needed. She used the butt of her rifle to smash her way in. Cans and bottles rained down upon and around her.

**Main power failure. Warning... unit termination imminent.**

Propped sitting against the palettes, Gina grabbed the first can within reach. She shook it half-heartedly and coughed. She spat redly and eyed the lump on the floor. Was that a piece of lung rotted by the toxic air? Didn't matter. She popped the top off the can and chugged her smoothie. It didn't taste as disgusting as she expected. Maybe she was craving this crap because her body knew she needed it? Nah, probably the air had messed with her taste buds.

She grabbed a bottle this time. It contained capsules of vitamins and metal salts. They never tasted of anything because they were time lapse capsules designed to dissolve in the stomach. She didn't think she had time for niceties. She opened the bottle and poured the contents into her mouth. She chewed and forced herself to swallow. My god that had tasted foul. She washed the foul tasting mess down with another smoothie.

**Main power failure. Warning... unit termination imminent.**

She chugged and chewed and chugged and chewed waiting to die or for some other sign that she wouldn't.

>_ IMS: REPAIRS IN PROGRESS.

Gina was chewing capsules and chugging smoothies, while watching for hostiles approaching. She didn't notice at first when her IMS came back online, but she did notice when her processor tried to put her back in hibernation! Dumb machine. There were hostiles nearby and ready to follow her trail, and it wanted her to sleep?

No frigging way!

*Computer: Abort hibernation.*
HIBERNATION ABORTED. WARNING, HIBERNATION ADVISED. INTERVENTION LOGGED.

Gina sighed. Her processor sounded a little pissy about her daring to intervene. She would have laughed if she didn't hurt so much. She contemplated forcing IMS to repair her comm immediately, she really wanted to talk to Eric, but she didn't do it. Main power had to come first. The damage to her spine had taken it out as well as her legs. Hopefully repairing one would give her back the other at the same time.

She chugged another smoothie, discarded the empty on the growing pile and opened another. Sensors warned her of company approaching, but she did nothing but watch. She needed to stay close to her supplies and repairs weren't far enough along. She chugged two more smoothies, feeling sick now. Too much crap to digest. She raised her rifle and waited for a target.

The first man came in sloppy. He had a pistol raised, but didn't use the available cover. There was plenty to use, he should really have known better. Her targeting reticule pulsed redly and spun on her display. She forced away a cough and put a single round down range centred upon the visor of his helmet. He dropped instantly dead. She allowed herself a cough, and opened another bottle of pills.

### Main power online

>_  Diagnostics: Critical spinal injury, communications failure, TacNet offline, lung capacity 68%. Unit unfit for duty. Hospitalisation at earliest opportunity advised.
>_ IMS: Repairs in progress

Ha! It was working. She was out of danger, relatively speaking. If no one killed her, she would be fine given enough time for repairs. She was bloody freezing, and the air was bad, but IMS could keep pace as long as it had the resources. She was sitting on a mountain of what it needed. She was as good as fixed as long as she could hold off the bad guys.

Thinking of them seemed to draw them out. They fired at her wildly and she could do little about it. They didn't hit her, but the crates and boxes exploded around her, raining their contents all over her. Liquids sprayed and dripped, while she tried to find a target, but they weren't as stupid as the first one. They exposed only the barrels of their weapons. She switched to her grenade launcher and used one of the three precious HE rounds she had loaded it with. The explosion silenced the incoming fire, but she had missed them. She watched them on sensors regrouping.

A spasm seized her chest and she coughed, but she decided her breathing was much better now. The burning in the back of her throat was still present. She doubted it would quit until she could find another suit.

The shot hit her square on, dead centre in the belly. She grunted and clutched at the wound, wishing for her armour, but she couldn't wear a suit over it. She hadn't brought it, and neither had Eric. She returned fire without aiming. Both grenades went wild and blew one of the stacks apart.

Debris flew in all directions, but the three red icons still glared balefully on her sensors. The burning boxes quickly extinguished themselves as designed, though they continued to smoulder filling the dome with smoke that streamed out the open loading doors. Anything transported through space had to be fire resistant.

Gina kept her rifle up and aimed into the smoke, though she couldn't see a damned thing. She switched to infra, but the smouldering crates made it useless. Too many false positives. She switched back and tried zooming in. Maybe at X2 she would catch movement. Nothing. Back at X1 she watched them on sensors, and waited for their next move.

The burning agony in her guts quickly dulled as IMS flooded the area with pain blockers. The wound had hurt but it hadn't hit anything vital. It wouldn't be the wound that killed her, and right now that was good enough. One handed, rifle still aimed, she popped the lid off another smoothie and chugged it, still feeling sick but needing to keep IMS running at maximum efficiency. She had to last long enough to get her legs back, or long enough for Eric to come. Either one worked for her.

Sensors warned her when the raiders had regained their courage, and she cursed when they split up. They had finally grown a brain between them. She shifted aim, planning to kill the first one to give her half a chance. She wished she had more grenades. While she was wishing, she might as well wish for an AAR and someone to use it. She had what she had—her V2 pistol and her rifle.

\* \* \*

# 18 ~ Preparations

Eric watched his sensors like a hawk on his return trip from base camp. He had every expectation that the raiders would come down and attempt to dispose of all witnesses. He was counting on it actually. If they were wise they would simply jump out system and come back in a couple of months. Everyone would be dead by then. They wouldn't do that though—he hoped. He needed a way off this rock, and they had a ship. It was a nice one too. Anything with a fold space drive was a nice one as far as he was concerned.

He snorted at his whimsical thought.

He was flying the scenic route back toward alpha site, not because he feared being followed. The raiders were in orbit and could track him easily. No, he did it so that a single attack wouldn't take both him and Gina out of the game. He had limited resources. Two vipers, two APCs and contents, and two slow lumbering cargo shuttles. That was it. He didn't count Liz and her people among resources. They were on the liability side of the equation. He didn't have anything to arm them with for one thing. The APCs had weapons and ammo, but viper gear was different to standard Alliance gear. It couldn't be used by the unenhanced and had been designed that way on purpose after a mission had gone pear-shaped allowing the bad guys to arm themselves with the regiment's own equipment. Burgton had been shot. He hadn't been amused. Viper weapons needed vipers to operate and that was that. Even if he had some standard gear on hand he wouldn't issue it to Liz's people. They were more likely to shoot themselves in the foot or him than the bad guys. They were marvellous engineers, but soldiers?

No.

Sensors reported all clear, just as he wanted. Gina was probably down and already filling her shuttle with more loot. Hope she remembers the supplements, he mused. He hadn't thought about them until now. It was rare that he was on a mission long enough to need such supplies. The regiment's long deployment with the Shan had been an exception rather than the rule. It had been many years since he had deployed with so many of his brothers to fight. Most of his missions had been solo ops and of short duration. This one promised to be more challenging than anyone had anticipated.

Gina was out of range of suit and viper comm. Without satellite relays or *Hobbs* in orbit, she might as well be on the far side of the planet. He couldn't remind her to grab the supplies set aside for them. He had to hope she remembered. He wouldn't chance another trip. His instincts were screaming at him that the raiders were coming down and wouldn't leave the base unexplored. He hoped they wouldn't just blast the domes. They were thieves first. Surely it made more sense to steal than destroy? He hoped so; he needed them on the ground.

Part of the work done at alpha site had been clearing away rubble to allow the crane to access the stairwell. A by product of that clearance was a boon to Eric now. He could land the shuttle on the cleared area vertically. He did so. He carefully hovered next to the crane and reduced power to his anti-grav.

He touched down without a bump and lowered the cargo ramp before shutting down. He was surprised but pleased to see Liz's people dash toward him to help the unloading. He didn't plan to leave the shuttle sitting here too long. It was a target and vulnerable from the air.

Eric left the cockpit intending to help with unloading, but Liz accosted him before he could start. She took his arm and pulled him out of the way.

"We found it!" Liz said excitedly. "She was right, Eric. We found it!"

"She was right?" Eric said in surprise. "You found the A.I?"

Gina would have him on a yacht as soon as they got home, he thought. Well, he had agreed to the wager, and boats were okay. Better than some other things he had tried in his time. Atmospheric surfing had to be the stupidest thing he had ever tried, though the skydiving part of it was fun. Very soothing it had been, falling at terminal velocity and trying to decide whether to open the chute or let nature take its course. He had deployed the chute, obviously, but he was always unsure what he would do the next time he faced that choice.

He shook his head. That kind of stupidity was why he quit the sport. Liz was still talking.

"...backup power. The geothermal plant is still running. Amazing really. I would have thought at least the lack of maintenance would have caused a shut down, but no. It's up."

Eric checked his log. They hadn't found the A.I but had found evidence of it. That realisation disappointed but didn't surprise him. So they had found a server and Liz was hoping it contained a backup of the mind they came for, but she hadn't found it yet.

"How long until you know?" Eric interrupted her. "Can I see?"

"Of course!" Liz said. "I'll show you how far we've got."

Eric followed her toward the bucket they were using as

a quick way down. Liz told her people to stop loading it with supplies, and they rode it down. More of her engineers unloaded the boxes when they reached the bottom, and Liz hurried toward the stairs.

Eric descended the stairs following Liz. Five flights and they reached the last landing. The builders of the facility hadn't been kidding. It wasn't as deep as the archive on Snakeholme. Not even close, but it was deep for a civilian design. His altimeter read -112m in red. It had certainly been strong enough to withstand the atomics that the Merkiaari had used to wipe away the city above. Impressive indeed.

"Gina asked me to make a place down here where we can stay for awhile. This is it."

Eric looked around the server room and nodded. It had power and he saw a pair of doors at the far end marked with the familiar signs for restrooms.

"Water?" Eric said.

"The facilities work if that's what you mean. I wouldn't trust the water to drink, but we have purifiers. With supplies we can hold out a few weeks. Won't be comfortable mind you, but we can do it."

"Geothermal you said. Not here surely?"

Liz shook her head. "We've traced the incoming power and water lines to a service tunnel. We haven't followed it very far. It's too narrow. No idea how far it goes, but my guess would be a long way from here. I've rarely seen any power station or pumping station built within city limits. Power stations can be dangerous in uncontrolled situations. That's one thing. And pumping stations are ugly buggers. No way to make recycling look or smell nice."

Eric grinned.

He wandered over to what appeared to be the centre of attention. Some of Liz's people were sitting amongst piles of equipment working with the servers. They already had everything up and running. Liz followed and pointed out this thing or that, but what had Eric's interest was the data displayed upon multiple screens.

"How long?"

Liz shrugged. "How long do we have?"

"Don't play with me, Liz. You know we're here for however long it takes."

"Then there's your answer. We might find it in ten minutes or ten days. No way to be sure."

"But you think it's here?"

"I *hope* it's here," Liz stressed. "But I really think it probably is. Gina gave me a copy of that file header she found, and she's right that it came from Landing. Probably from right here. Then there's the nature of all this," she waved a hand around. "This facility is hardened against shock and EMP (Electro Magnetic Pulse). It has earthquake countermeasures—it's built on springs to you amateurs." She grinned at him. "It's isolated within its own faraday cage, just like a military grade facility. I think it's here."

Eric nodded. "Good enough for me, Liz. All we have to do now is find it, copy it, and get it home."

Liz pursed her lips. "About that—"

"Working on it," Eric said. "Gina is collecting supplies for you. We hold here and defend this place if necessary. The stairwell is the only way down?"

Liz nodded.

"You're absolutely sure?"

She nodded again and then frowned. "There's the service tunnel, but like I said it's too narrow."

"Good. One of us will defend the stairs at all times."

"And the other?"

"The other goes to war," he said grimly, already planning his battles. He would put Gina on the stairs with plenty of ammo and tell her to hold until relieved. "All fucking hell is going to break loose."

His face must have been something, because Liz paled. The death of *Hobbs* and her crew would not stand un-avenged.

The first hour passed with Eric helping to unload his shuttle and then moving it to a better protected and more remote location. He didn't want to see it damaged or destroyed, but more than that, he didn't want it attracting an airstrike and perhaps having collateral damage to the crane or stairwell. He used the APC to return, and stashed it close by with overhead protection. It wouldn't be detected.

He spent the next hour in the server room eagerly watching for a breakthrough that didn't come. Most of the engineers weren't involved in this part of the work. Everyone was waiting for someone to find the answer. Is it here? They were keeping busy setting up places to sleep and eat. Empty crates were made into makeshift tables. Food was prepared with an autochef. Its power filched from the emergency lighting, and its ingredients poured into its guts directly from other open containers as necessary. It was a lash up with only one redeeming feature... it worked.

The third hour came and went, and Eric's vague uneasiness became alarm. Three hours was more than long enough for Gina to start back and contact him, but maybe she got carried away and decided to fill the shuttle to the brim. She had to know that he wouldn't allow a third trip, so maybe she was just being greedy. He didn't believe it. Gina would be aware of the risk of staying too long. She wouldn't risk half of their defence like that.

Something was wrong.

Liz suddenly shouted and everyone hurried to her. She was leaning over the shoulder of one of her people and pointing excitedly at something on one of the displays. Everyone began asking questions and clapping each other on the back.

Eric hurried over to get the news, but Liz was too busy to explain. He paced to and fro waiting for good news, and grabbed Liz's attention the moment she was free.

"Tell me," Eric said.

"We found it. The backup is here, but Eric..." she

lowered her voice. "I think the A.I is still operating! The file was updated the day we entered the system. That means Sebastian is alive somewhere! We have to get him... I mean rescue him."

Eric took a deep breath. "Get the backup copied. Multiple copies for safety, and designate a few people to carry them for you."

"But!"

"That's the mission," Eric said in a hard voice, but then softened it. "Get that done first. I don't have to tell you the kind of shit we're in. We have no ship, we have no idea where the A.I is, and we have no way to transport him off world even if we did know. I'm not saying we won't try. I'm saying we have other priorities. Mine is getting you and the file off this planet in one piece."

Liz nodded reluctantly. "Any word from Gina?"

"No," Eric said grimly. "And that's not good. She should have been on her way back by now. I'll have to go find her, and that means leaving you vulnerable here. I can't be in both places."

Liz shrugged. "We're fine here."

Eric didn't disagree, but that assumed the raiders hadn't located them. He wasn't sure what they had come for. Precious metals was a good bet but he wasn't sure. If all they wanted was gold and platinum, then they wouldn't come to Landing. They would take on the mines, and other industrial areas where those metals would have been stored and used. Banks as well, but Landing only had a small one and it didn't have a platinum reserve. But did the raiders know the bank here was empty?

Again, he didn't know.

Anything he did now was a huge risk. If they had somehow taken Gina out, he was on his own. That meant he had no choice but to risk Liz and her people while he tried to gain a way off planet. He hated to do it, but he needed to wait long enough for the first copy of the backup. He would carry one in case he was the only survivor... again. The thought was a grim one, but the mission was all that mattered in the end. Burgton would agree. Liz would be a huge loss to them, but there were other engineers on Snakeholme who could take over. Give them the file, and any losses here wouldn't be in vain.

"I'll take the first copy with me."

Liz looked surprised for a moment, but then her eyes clouded. She nodded grimly and hurried away to supervise its creation. Eric watched the process impatiently, wanting to be on his way. He wanted... *needed* to know what had happened to Gina.

The copying process seemed to take forever. At least it felt that way to him, but in the end Liz handed him a case containing six innocent seeming teardrop-shaped crystals each one containing googlebytes of precious data. He held the case in his hand briefly, noting that every eye in the room followed it, before opening his suit to put it safely away in his top pocket. He coughed a little but ignored the warnings flashing upon his internal display.

He sealed his suit and turned toward the exit.

Everyone was in the server room now, including the crane driver. The bucket was hanging high above the shaft in the open air. He ran up the stairs, glad he had insisted they be cleared all the way up. It had been more effort for the engineers, but a hit upon the crane would have been a serious inconvenience without another way up. It took him barely two minutes to reach the top, and another fifteen to reach and ready the shuttle for takeoff.

He chose a different route than before. More direct, but not a straight line. He was aware it was probably wasted effort, but it had to be made. He needed to maximise even a tiny chance. He had so few advantages. As before he hugged the terrain flying manually, and used his enhanced reflexes to avoid collisions. He was so close to the ground, he had to shut off the proximity alarm. It kept squawking at him.

He glanced at one of his monitors showing an external view. It was set to warn him of anything behind him. All he saw was snow sucked up from the ground and towed behind him in his wake. He was too close to the ground. He increased altitude by a small amount, enough to prevent the hole in the air he was making vacuuming the snow, and grunted approval. He needed to be certain his six was secure.

Sensors showed no hostiles, but he was moving too fast for viper sensors to be reliable. He linked into the shuttle systems directly and set an alarm to warn him. He couldn't afford to take his attention from his piloting. Mach two was about as fast as he dared at this altitude. Viper systems couldn't react in time if he tried for more. Besides, he was driving a cargo shuttle. Another name for cargo shuttles was brick. Its maximum velocity in atmosphere wasn't much greater than this.

Flight time was less than two hours.

He slowed his approach when his sensors came within range of the base and his pulse sped at what was reported. Gina's shuttle was parked close enough to dome three for ease of loading cargo. So much wasn't a surprise. What had his pulse speeding was the other shuttle. His sensors at this range couldn't tell him much more.

The three domes and two shuttles were the only clear details. It was enough to make him wary. He wouldn't overfly the base for fear of fire from the ground. One rocket up his arse was all it would take to ground him, and maybe damage him beyond repair if he was unlucky.

He wouldn't risk it. He chose to land and hike in.

"Terrain, terrain, terrain," Eric mused. "I need some."

He adjusted the shuttle's sensors and digested what they reported to him of the topography. There were some hills to the east, but he wasn't happy with them. They were distant. It would take him quite a while to hike that distance and Gina might need him right now. He checked his own sensors for a moment, but he was out of range without the boost he was getting from the shuttle. Unfortunately, the shuttle was a civ design and wouldn't pick up her signal... or her beacon if she was down. He tried not to assume anything, but she had to be down. Her shuttle was still parked and she hadn't tried to comm him. She had to be down.

He landed in the hills. Anything else risked the shuttle. Besides, he could use Gina's for the trip back. He was careful to use GPR to test the ice before landing, but as soon as he knew it could take his weight he slammed the shuttle onto the ice, almost powering down before it had fully settled. He grabbed his rifle from the co-pilot's seat and sealed his suit. He was out and running toward the domes in less than a minute, his sensors reaching out ahead of him and his optics dialled up to X2.

The smoke rising above the base had him slowing his approach. "Gina?" No reply, but her icon glowed steadily blue within the base. "Come on, girl, don't do this to me. You're alive. Answer!"

Nothing.

He crouched and paused to survey the base at X4. The two shuttles appeared undamaged. He could see Gina's shuttle had its ramp down and he could make out some of the cargo inside. There wasn't enough of it. Nowhere near fully loaded. Whatever had happened to her, it had happened before she could fill her ship. Probably not long after her arrival.

"God damn it, Gina! Answer me... please." Nothing. Viper comm remained silent. She wasn't dead. Her beacon would be pulsing its distress call. She wasn't in hibernation either for the same reason, so what was left? He tried helmet comm in case she had damage to her internal comm. "Gina?"

Still nothing.

Eric's lips thinned and his grip upon his rifle tightened. He was going to fucking kill the bastards. They were fucking dead! All of them. He took a moment to reign in his rage at the thought of the raiders hurting Gina. She was family, the only family on this world. His brothers and sisters in the regiment were all he lived for. The mission? Yes that too, but it was the people that kept him breathing and going back for more. He had to fight for them. It was what you did—fight for those who were fighting for you.

He dialled his optics, his eyes, back to X1 and advanced warily. He had no hostiles on sensors. He should have by now. He theorised they were in one of the domes, but his sensors shouldn't have been spoofed by the flimsy walls so easily. He was picking up Gina's icon just fine. The raiders had to be in a dome though. Their shuttle was right there. He advanced in a crouch with his rifle firmly against his shoulder and aimed.

Smoke was rising into the leaden air from dome three, but he couldn't hear anything. His helmet did reduce his ability there, but not by much. He raised the gain to max briefly then back to normal. All was quiet. He had the feeling that he'd missed the party entirely. Whatever had happened was probably over, but he didn't take chances. Worst case scenario hadn't happened. Gina lived. Her steady blue icon on his sensors reassured him that was the case, but she must be damaged and that meant he was their only defence. He had to ensure that he remained that way.

He was careful.

He entered the dome fast and low and almost fell over the first body. Gina had put a round into his helmet. Good. One less bastard for him to deal with. The smoke was coming from the smouldering boxes and crates in the stacks. There had been one hell of a firefight. There was debris scattered all over. He found three more bodies as he made his way toward Gina. All had been taken apart with rifle fire. He had seen it often enough to recognise viper gunnery. She had taken all three dead centre of mass. Millimetre perfect as vipers tended to be. No hostiles on sensors. He abandoned his caution and hurried to find what was left of Gina and give aid.

He found her slumped forward. She looked dead, and

Eric had a procession of flashbacks. He had seen so many bodies like this, not all of them friends. She wasn't dead, he made himself remember that. He forced the memories away with his certainty that she was repairable. Her reassuring presence on his sensors made it certain.

She was sitting propped against a crate. Other crates near her were shattered and their contents were all around. Liquids had frozen into shiny icicles and runnels. Gina was covered in the stuff. He noted the pile of trash and frowned wondering what the hell had happened. She looked up as he approached.

"Ah hell, Gina, what did they do to you?" he said in shock. Her face looked black through her shattered helmet visor. Frostbite. She smiled and her lips split. Blood ran down her chin. "You didn't invite me to the party."

Gina raised a hand holding a viper smoothie. "Here. I saved this one for you," she croaked and coughed, wracking her chest.

"How bad are you hurt?"

"I'm not hurt."

Eric sighed. "How bad?"

Gina shrugged. "It doesn't hurt."

Eric ignored her and pulled her hand away from her belly. He winced when he saw the hole in her suit, but probing through it with his fingers he found new pink skin. Huh, she really wasn't hurt. The wound was healed. That was when he realised something wasn't right about her suit. Bad enough her helmet was compromised, but she was sitting against a crate. What the hell? Her PLSS shouldn't allow that. They were too bulky. He realised it was completely missing.

He pulled her upper body toward him and she slumped bonelessly forward against his chest. He held her there so that he could see what was going on and hissed in dismay. Her back was... it was... gone? Cratered? Holy shit, he could see her spine and it didn't look right. He stared and shivered as he watched it repairing itself. No one should ever see that sparkly shimmery shit that nannies did when they worked, not in a body this way. It was just not right. Her spine was damaged. He could bloody see it! Why could he see it when her gut wound was as good as new? He certainly could have done without another horror in his head.

He eased her back to a sitting position. "It doesn't hurt?"

"Nope, why? How does it look?" Gina said, starting to sound scared.

He didn't answer. He'd just had a revelation. "You had to top up IMS."

"Yeah. Eating all that made me feel sick," she said gesturing at the pile of empty bottles and cans. "I still do, but it kept me alive I guess. They shot me in the back but didn't finish me. Probably thought the blast was enough. I went directly into hibernation, didn't pass go or collect my two hundred credits," she said with a laugh. "But main power failed and IMS shut down. My processor decided it was wakey-wakey time. I crawled in here to stock up and get IMS back."

"Good thinking, but you need real food for your... for the bio-systems. You have frostbite. You might lose your nose and lips, Gina." He wouldn't tell her how bad her back was. "They'll grow back," he said hastily when she looked horrified. What woman wouldn't? "I'll grab you some MREs."

Gina grimaced but nodded. Meals ready to eat might be factually correct, but no one would ever admit to liking them. Some were better than others, but the hot ones were off the menu right now. They didn't have time to boil and add water. She would have to make do with the crackers and biscuits.

Eric consulted his database and quickly navigated the stacks. He found the boxes containing what he needed and grabbed two. Another box caught his eye and he grabbed that as well. He wasn't a fan of peanut butter, but it had calories and Gina needed that more than anything. Her body was burning fat at a ferocious rate in an effort to heal, and she hadn't been heavy in the first place. No viper was ever overweight. Their systems were regulated to keep them in top fighting trim at all times.

He opened a jar of peanut butter and a box of crackers and offered them to Gina. She used a cracker as a spoon to scoop out the nutty paste and ate it. He winced as her lips bled at the movement. He watched her for a few minutes and then hurried away. He would finish loading her shuttle as fast as he could, and use it to take her back to Liz. He didn't want the raiders to catch him here, but if they did they would regret it. He had more than *Hobbs* to avenge now.

There was a large crate already on the loader. He didn't care what was in it. It was faster to unload it in the shuttle than dump it. He muscled it off the loader in the cargo bay, and hurried back to load it up again. Two trips back and forth and he was happy with his loot. He had plenty of ammo and supplements aboard. He parked the loader intending to get Gina, but paused. His eyes narrowed at the raider's shuttle as an idea came to him. If it worked it might solve all his problems.

If.

He ran back to get Gina.

When he reached her, she was forcing herself to eat, but by the look on her face she wasn't enjoying it. Enjoying it or not, she looked better for it. He would swear the black skin on her face had paled. It was still very dark, but had edged toward a more natural colour. Good news. Very good news in fact, because her IMS wouldn't consider epidermis a priority. If it had spared resources to fix frostbite, Gina's insides must be well on the mend.

"I've had an idea," Eric said. "I'm going to use their shuttle to get aboard their ship."

"Do tell," Gina said with interest.

He laid it all out while he carried her to the shuttle. He wanted to get her to Liz and return to enact his plan before the raiders came to investigate things, but Gina had other ideas.

"It won't work," Gina said. "It's been hours since they shot me, Eric. They have to be on their way here. I can't believe they won't arrive soon."

"Then I'll think of something else."

"I've already taken care of that for you," Gina said and grinned. "Put me in the cockpit of my shuttle, and you stay here. Load some of our stuff into their ship and hide in one of the crates. They'll find their dead friends and just fly back to their ship."

"Your legs—"

"I don't need legs to fly. Liz will look after me when I get there. Besides, IMS might have me back on my feet by then. Two hour trip. You never know."

It had possibilities, and he had to admit he feared the raiders would come down while he flew back to alpha site. He carried Gina up the ramp trying to think of a better way, but couldn't.

"Okay," he said and continued into the cockpit. He put her in the pilot's chair and strapped her in. He held her shoulder for a long moment. "Good luck."

"You too," Gina said. "Don't get killed."

Eric snorted. "I'll try not to miss our boat trip."

He put her rifle on the co-pilot's chair and slung his own over his shoulder before leaving.

"Wait! What did you say?"

"No time now. Ask Liz," Eric shouted over his shoulder as he ran down the ramp. He thought he heard a curse but might have imagined it. He laughed.

Gina's shuttle buttoned up and took off moments later, but Eric was already hard at work by that time and didn't watch it leave. He chose some random stuff to shove into the raider's shuttle, before adding an empty crate that had held one of the generators. It was big enough for him to hide in and he did so after adding some ammo for his rifle and pistol to it.

Snugged inside the crate he had time to consider this move, and began to have doubts. He was vulnerable to a single hit now. A paranoid man might abandon the shuttle and blow it on the ground. It was certainly something he would consider in their place. Run of the mill pirates sometimes killed, but in general they preferred to steal. They often put crews into lifeboats rather than simply kill them hoping for leniency should they ever be caught. To Eric's disgust, the tactic worked more often than not. Raiders were a different breed and were more hard core. Not only were they willing to kill, they seemed to prefer it. No witnesses was their mantra.

All that was true, but would they blow a perfectly good shuttle from the air rather than retrieve it? They must know by now that their men had probably lost a fight. The smoke still rising from dome three was a big clue, and their loss of contact with their buddies should be enough to cement the notion.

Eric muttered a curse and sat tight. He didn't have another plan. Gina was right. If he pretended to be one of their own and fly the shuttle, they would shoot him down. He couldn't talk to them and they probably used recognition codes of some sort. He had to hope this would work.

He stared at nothing in the dark, and let himself slip into memory. His breathing slowed as he became the soulless machine he sometimes feared he was, and the thing Gina had seen lurking in his eyes peered out of them into the dark unblinking.

* * *

# 19 ~ Preparations II

The flight back had been uneventful but for one thing. Pain. Gina's IMS had finally connected something in her back that let her feel the damage, and although her legs still wouldn't move she had some sensation in them again. There were tingles and shooting pains in her legs, and burning hot agony in her back that made her grit her teeth. Her face felt numb, and she wasn't looking forward to seeing it in a mirror. Eric had tried not to show it, but he had been horrified when he saw her. IMS could fix anything given time and resources, and getting her legs back was a priority, but her comm and her face were a close second as far as she was concerned.

Unbeknown to Gina, she chose to land her shuttle in the same place as Eric had chosen on his last run. A nice clear space close to the crane for unloading seemed ideal. She landed and lowered the ramp to allow the engineers to unload the cargo, and waited for Liz to visit the cockpit.

"Gina, you need help?" Liz asked as she entered and gasped in horror when Gina looked up at her. "Oh my god!"

"It's nothing, just a scratch," she said and grinned. Her

lips split again and began bleeding profusely. Liz paled. Gina covered her bloody mouth. "Sorry about that."

"Sorry! My god, she's sorry she says!" Liz reached toward the harness buckle. "What can I do?"

"About this? Nothing. But I'll need someone to carry me, and I warn you, I weigh a ton."

Liz snorted. "I have two strapping men in mind, don't you worry about that. And I have a new suit for you downstairs."

She nodded. It would be good to breathe clean air again. Her IMS was keeping up with the damage the air was causing, but that didn't make it pleasant.

Liz removed the harness and then stepped aside as two of her people entered to lift Gina out of the pilot's chair. They struggled at first despite their apparent strength. Liz was right about that. They were rather large specimens of maleness, but despite that, they had trouble with her mass. She was average size for a woman, but her bones were armoured, and her mylar enhanced muscles were dense. Vipers had all kinds of technology built in and despite high tech materials, it all added up. She weighed 115kg in her skin, easily twice her unenhanced weight. The suit weighed another 2kg even ruined as it was.

The engineers linked arms so that Gina was sitting between them. She put her arms around their shoulders trying to take some of her weight on her arms and hold on. They carried her out of the cockpit and into the still busy cargo hold. Everyone stopped to watch her carried past. She heard gasps, and she looked back over a shoulder. Liz was standing near the cockpit door and she was crying. Crying? What the hell for? Sure she was banged up, but she was alive. It hurt like molten lead had been poured on her back, but the fact it hurt reassured. She would live and go on living. That's all that mattered right now.

"You have somewhere to hide the shuttle?" she called back.

"Yes," Liz said but had to clear her throat. "I'll take care of it."

Gina raised a hand in acknowledgement and tried to ignore the engineers clapping as she passed them. She didn't deserve applause. The truth was she had screwed up and gotten away with it. She shouldn't have been caught in the open and unaware like that. If she had been checking sensors, if she had slung her rifle over her shoulder ready for action, if she had set a simple alarm for sensors to trigger when the raiders arrived, she could have blown them away and kept loading her shuttle barely even inconvenienced. But she had done none of those things, and had turned an easy fight into a desperate defence. She was secretly horrified by how close her carelessness had come to killing her true dead.

She forced the gloomy thoughts away and promised to do better. She was alive, her legs were tingling, and she fully expected to be mobile before the day was done. Then the murderers of *Hobbs* and her crew would see something. Her thoughts turned to Eric. The raiders might be seeing something special right this very minute for all she knew.

Getting her into the crane's bucket was a real chore. It took two people lifting and two more standing inside receiving. Gina apologised for all the bother, and said sorry every time one of the men grunted and strained against her weight. If her face wasn't so messed up she was sure she'd be blushing. This was worse than having fat thighs on a blind date!

Finally she was in, someone handed her rifle to her, and Liz scrambled in beside her. One of the men waved and the crane hoisted them into the air and over the shaft. They plunged into darkness. Gina was looking forward to that new suit and a litre of coffee. Did they have an autochef set up yet? God, she hoped so. When last here she had asked Liz to create a place to hide for a while. She assumed that had progressed and was where she was going. Eric had hinted that the prize was found with his mention of a boat trip, but she had forgotten to ask Liz about it. Where was her brain? They were here to find the A.I or its backup module, and she had forgotten about it! Dumb.

The bucket came to rest at the bottom of the shaft, and the struggle to get her into the bucket was repeated getting her out. More apologies from her, more demurrals combined with grunting and straining from them ensued, but finally she was sitting upon linked arms again riding into blessed warmth and light. The air was still bad. The engineers hadn't yet figured out a way to cobble together an airlock on a room not designed for it without the correct tools and equipment, but the warmth was so welcome. It was probably no more than -10°. Positively balmy compared to the -30° up top.

"Take her into the rest room," Liz said and the men complied.

"Rest rooms too, aren't we all high tech," Gina said with a chuckle. Her bearers grinned.

They took her into the restroom and set her upon the counter between the wash basins. She could sit without help. Her balance was fine, just about the only thing that was these days. She leaned back until her shoulders touched the mirrors. She purposefully did not look back to see her face in the gleaming surface. She could do without any more shocks today, thanks so much.

Liz entered with a new suit in her arms and ushered the men out. Two more people came in, both women. Stacey Ward and Heather Winner. Stacey was carrying a PLSS for the new suit. They closed the door and looked to Liz for instruction. Gina took a deep breath knowing what was coming, and that caused a coughing fit. Stupid! She controlled the coughing and took shallow breaths.

"So," she said trying for a light-hearted tone. "A funny thing happened to me on the way to work..."

Liz laughed and her helpers grinned. "Strip!"

Gina rolled her eyes and took off her helmet. Liz took it from her and tossed it. It was NFG (No Frigging Good) and she had a replacement ready. With Liz's help she unsealed her suit and peeled it off her shoulders and arms until she was sitting on it. She lifted her weight off her butt using her arms, and the four of them managed to get the suit down to her ankles. The boots were a struggle. They were huge things, rugged, and made to take abuse without ever breaking seal. Stacey and Heather tugged and twisted but finally they came off. They threw the entire useless mess into a corner.

"We haven't got a uniform for you, but I'm roughly your size. I had a spare coverall here with me. Can't remember why now. Good enough?"

"Sure, Liz. I trust your sense of style won't make me look fat."

Liz chuckled. "How can you sit here like this and still make jokes? Your back... it's like burned hamburger."

Gina swallowed. "Thanks so much, I was trying not to think about it."

"Sorry."

She waved the apology away. "Don't worry about it. I know it looks bad back there. It hurts, but crying about it won't help. Kidding around might... it does. Takes my mind off it. How do we do this?"

"I think if you lay face down, we'll cut your uniform off you. It's badly charred and I think your skin is growing back over it in places."

She winced at the thought. No wonder Liz looked sick. She would have to cut those areas out with a knife. Gina unsheathed her knife and handed it handle first to her friend.

"Sorry," she said as Liz took the blade.

"Stop apologising," Liz said, starting to sound annoyed. "It's not your fault. None of this is your fault. I think you're amazing. All the vipers are. You fight and die to protect us, you sacrifice family and a normal life to keep us all safe, and here you are apologising to me. I should be saying sorry to you, Gina, for your sacrifice."

Stacey and Heather nodded agreement.

Liz brandished the knife. "Now on your belly if you can. We'll help if you can't."

She couldn't. She could get down on her side easily enough, but her legs dangling off the counter stopped her from getting flat. Stacey lifted her legs onto the counter top and finally Gina rolled onto her front. Stacey gulped seeing the damage clearly for the first time, and hurried into a cubicle where she was violently sick.

Gina looked that way grimly wanting to say sorry again but didn't dare after Liz's speech.

"If you're going to be sick, Heather, step out," Liz said.

Heather looked pale but she shook her head. "I'm good."

Liz placed a hand on Gina's shoulder and squeezed gently in sympathy. "Here we go," she said and Gina closed her eyes as Liz started cutting.

Later, Gina would prefer not to think about that torturous half hour. Liz cut, Gina bled, and Heather joined Stacey in the head to be sick. In time Liz had her naked except for panties and tee-shirt, but the shirt had to go as well. It was mostly gone at the back anyway. They didn't have a replacement, but Gina was passed caring by then. She was freezing her tits off, not literally thank god, but if she didn't get back into some clothes and a suit soon, she really might get frostbitten nipples! Liz washed her back, cleaning it of old and new blood, and then she carefully cut away dead charred flesh. Gina couldn't feel it, but Liz was shaking and in a cold sweat when she was done.

They couldn't bandage the wound for fear her body would incorporate it as it had tried to do with her uniform. Heather used an entire can of synthskin to protect it, and prevent her coverall sticking to it. Synthskin was clever stuff. It would keep infection away, and was biodegradable. The big plus was that her body was welcome to absorb it. Her bots would love it. It was basically made of the same stuff her

IMS used. Stacey dressed her while Liz knelt upon the floor trying to regain her composure.

With her helmet on and sealed, the PLSS connected but sitting beside her to keep it from hurting her back, Gina basked in the warmth that flooded her suit. Ah... bliss. She took a deep breath of uncontaminated air.

>_ **Diagnostics: Critical spinal injury, communications failure, TacNet offline, lung capacity 86%. Unit unfit for duty. Hibernation recommended. Hospitalisation at earliest opportunity advised.**
>_ **IMS: Repairs in progress.**
>_ **Diagnostics: Critical spinal injury, communications failure, TacNet offline, lung capacity 88%. Unit unfit for duty. Hibernation recommended. Hospitalisation at earliest opportunity advised.**
>_ **IMS: Repairs in progress.**

Excellent. Her IMS was catching up and her lungs were responding well. She would be fixed up in no time.

"Is there food?" Gina asked a little plaintively. "And coffee? I would kill for a litre of coffee right now."

Liz looked up from her squatting position and smiled. "We have an autochef up. You can order anything you want. Pizza?"

She groaned. "Not you too! Bloody hell, we don't all live on pizza, Liz."

Liz blinked. "I love pepperoni."

Gina burst out laughing, but Liz just looked confused. "Don't mind me. It's something Eric said to me. I'm from Faragut."

Liz's eyebrows climbed. "Really?"

"Yes really. Anyway, I'm craving steak with all the trimmings and many litres of coffee. Can do?"

"Can do," Liz agreed, but then frowned. "Actually, you're

the only one who can eat something like that until we get an airlock in place. The rest of us hold our breath, stuff a biscuit in our mouths, and reseal our helmets."

She frowned at that. "How long to sort that out?"

Liz shrugged. "With a portable airlock, minutes at most. Here with what we have?" She shrugged again. "Hours. We can seal the door no problem, but we still need to go in and out. Sealing the door isn't enough."

"True. I'll need access to the stairs when I get my legs back. I have to defend the only way in. Hey, Eric said you found the prize?"

Liz brightened. "We did! Well, we found the backup file. We've made lots of copies. Do you want one? Eric took the first one in case... well, you know."

She nodded.

"I forgot you didn't know. We think Sebastian is still online. The file was updated the day we entered the system."

"You're kidding! We've got to get him then!"

Liz jumped to her feet and hugged Gina. "Thank you! I think so too, but I think Eric would be satisfied with what we already have. We don't know where Sebastian is, but now we know he's alive we have to stay as long as it takes to find him. I have some ideas about that."

"Oh?"

"This place was obviously built to withstand exactly what it did. Everything is hardwired and hardened against EMP. I think we can trace the cables right to him. If not that, we can find the power plant. Surely he draws power from it. We should find him by following the current."

Liz was making a lot of assumptions, but it was hard not to agree. Surely the hardest part was over. With the backup file in hand, the mission was already a success assuming they managed to get off world. Now they knew Sebastian was active...

"Liz," Gina thought furiously. "If Sebastian is awake—"

"Yes?"

"Well, can't you just ask him where he is?"

Liz's eyes widened for a moment, but then narrowed. "Maybe."

Her shoulders slumped. "Only maybe?"

Liz nodded. "I'll have to think about it. A lot depends upon how accessible he was before the war."

"How do you mean?"

"Well, all the A.Is that exist today will only talk to the Council, but back before the war they were more accessible. I don't know if Sebastian will respond to strangers."

"You're kidding," Gina said flatly. "He's been alone all this time and you think he might ignore us?"

Liz shrugged. "Not saying he will, just that he might. Look, he was the colonial administrator. Maybe he had protocols to follow like only responding to government officials."

"But they're all dead! What sense does it make for him to follow a protocol like that?"

"None, but he's a computer, Gina. Computers follow rules."

"Even A.Is?"

"Even so. They're intelligent machines with vast capacities and intellect, but they're still machines. They were designed to have only limited freewill. For example, there is always at least one Human being who can countermand anything a particular A.I does. It's a safety measure. In Sebastian's case I would guess that person would have been Kushiel's president. Just a guess. Also, I happen to know the president here swore his oath before Sebastian. Sebastian is the custodian of Kushiel's constitution, which means he's obliged not to follow unconstitutional orders even from his own president."

"Wow, that's a lot of power in an A.I's hands."

Liz nodded.

"So we could find him and he might ignore us. Even if we entered his centrum?"

Liz nodded. "Even if."

Gina's stomach rumbled.

"You're hungry. Let me get your two admirers back in here to carry you, and I'll fix your steak. We have time to find Sebastian. No point in borrowing trouble. For all we know, he'll be happy to see us."

Gina nodded. She was starving.

Her bearers carried her out of the restroom and helped make her comfortable in the server room. Liz was as good as her word and provided food and coffee. There were many envious eyes watching as she ate. She didn't tell them it tasted funny, and slightly unpleasant. The air tainted it, or maybe messed with her taste buds. She ate it all anyway.

While she was eating, attention shifted to the lash up being prepared at the door. A committee had come up with a design for the temporary airlock, and now work was beginning using salvaged materials. Gina watched as one of the engineers removed the door from the men's restroom and carried it to the worksite. The engineers were building a new wall roughly 2metres inside the room from the existing wall, using partitions from the offices she and Eric had investigated earlier. It looked like a patchwork, but she noted they were careful to seal every joint, fill every gap, with expanding foam. They had plenty of the aerosols left over from the dome construction. With the wall up, the restroom door was fitted. The work took a couple of hours. The last part was the most complicated. It consisted of linking all the spare PLSS units for the suits together, and connecting them to the new airlock through a hole drilled in the wall. Foam was used to glue and seal the connection before switching them all on. The effect was to filter the air in the airlock as if it was just a big suit. Anyone entering it from outside would have to wait inside with both doors shut until the air was clean enough to enter the server room.

The inner door was left open for the first few hours with the PLSS units running. Gina let them know when the air in the server room became breathable, and everyone celebrated.

They kept their suits on for warmth, but took off their helmets to celebrate with a hot meal and strong coffee. Gina accepted a second steak dinner, and Liz said her face looked better for it afterward.

"Liar," Gina said with a smile. Her IMS hadn't started work on it yet. Diagnostics reported it was still working on her spine. "Legs first, Liz. I need to keep watch out there. If I'm not mobile in another hour, I want to be carried outside and left with my rifle and ammo."

Liz would have argued, but at that moment Gina's right leg twitched and spasmed. She clutched it and grimaced. It felt like she had cramp in the thigh muscle, but it passed quickly. She tried to flex her knee, but nothing happened. Still, that spasm was the first movement she'd had from either leg. She decided to take it as a good sign.

She endured more twitches and cramps through that hour, but before she could demand to be taken outside, her legs finally came back online. She didn't feel a sudden difference in her legs. Sensation had returned long before and the cramping had become less frequent in the second half of the hour, but a report informed her of new IMS priorities.

>_ DIAGNOSTICS: COMMUNICATIONS OFFLINE, TACNET OFFLINE. UNIT FIT FOR DUTY.
>_ IMS: REPAIRS IN PROGRESS.

Gina stood, and grinned as everyone applauded. She performed a few jumping jacks. "Behold this medical miracle!"

They laughed.

She finished her latest cup of coffee and grabbed her rifle and helmet. She shrugged into the straps of her PLSS and settled it onto her back before heading for the door checking the hose connection to the helmet. Liz caught her arm before she could close the inner door, and Gina paused.

"Be careful this time," Liz said.

"Hey, it's me! I'm always careful."

"*Be. Careful,*" Liz said again very seriously.

She sobered and nodded. She squeezed her friend's shoulder briefly before closing the inner door and putting on her helmet. She opened the outer door, exited, and shut the door firmly behind her.

She paused for a moment considering options. She needed to defend this door, but sitting at the bottom of a hole didn't appeal. The bad guys could just drop a crate of grenades on her or something. Also, her sensors were a great advantage, but not down here. She needed to be up top. She ran up the stairs and emerged into bright sunlight. The crane would make a good OP (Observation Point) but it was too obvious. The bad guys might hit it just because it was there. No, she would use the ruins opposite. There were enough walls left to give cover, and she would have a clear view of the stairs.

Plan made, she implemented it. As she hunkered down to wait and watch, she wondered how Eric was doing. She checked sensors and queried diagnostics, but nothing had changed. Her comm was still out.

## ARCHER'S GIFT, KUSHIEL

"Any word?" Leon asked and Haliwell nodded. "Let's have it."

"All dead but the shuttle is undamaged. Looks like our people started loading but got jumped."

Leon nodded. "Tell them to grab what they can and beat feet. I'm taking us down. Give them the coordinates of the first target and have them fly there to meet us."

"I think we should hit that other site first, captain."

He shook his head. "What for? There's nothing we need there, and they can't leave the surface."

"Witnesses..."

He waved that argument away impatiently. "They're

only witnesses if they know something. What do they know? Nothing. Besides, they can't survive down there for long. They're alone. They only have the supplies they took or those we leave them... tell our people to destroy anything they can't take."

Haliwell turned and did that, but he wasn't finished arguing his point. "We don't know for sure that their ship didn't get a report down to them. They might be able to identify the ship."

"I don't want to take a year collecting what we came for, and we only have the two shuttles. I need them doing their jobs, not attacking a bunch of helpless castaways that are as good as dead already! Damn it, man, you do want to get paid don't you? We need to get what we came for before someone puts us and this ship on a defaulters list!"

The kind of defaulters list he was talking about would have every pirate, raider, and shoot first mercenary company, gunning for them. Those kinds of lists weren't about recovering money; they were all about setting examples. The kind of examples that consisted of derelict ships blown open to vacuum and crewed by corpses.

Haliwell's jaw muscles bunched, but he didn't say anything. He turned back to monitoring his station, but Leon knew this subject would come back up. Haliwell was becoming a problem, but then so were others in the crew. Many of them looked to Haliwell and not their captain for orders, but so far they hadn't pushed things beyond a lack of respect for his authority and a few muttered insults barely audible. The four dead men were Haliwell's cronies, and Leon was glad they were dead. They'd been some of the worst examples. Undisciplined animals.

Leon needed Haliwell and his men for now. He couldn't crew a ship the size of Archer without them, but as soon as he could, he would pay them off and jettison them at the next port. He would pay his debts, hire a new crew, and forever more stick to legitimate trading in the core. No more risky adventures in the border zone. He was done with chasing quick profit and fortune in the shadows.

"Take us down," he said.

"Aye, captain," the helmsman acknowledged, and Archer's Gift plunged into Kushiel's atmosphere.

* * *

# 20 ~ Dagger Thrust

>_ Sensors: Hostiles detected.

Close archive file #0000063577982-3996-SL

It took Eric a few moments to notice his sensor alert had tripped. A few seconds to realise it wasn't part of the memory file he had been lost within. He glanced around seeing darkness. Read the data again and interrogated his logs and sensors. Right. The crate on the raider's shuttle. Kushiel. A mission to complete. He stroked his rifle and watched his sensors real time now.

Another shuttle had landed and red icons prowled carefully around. Eight hostiles. Eric watched them scout the domes and find the bodies. He wondered briefly if they would bury their friends, but of course not. They were more interested in the loot they could take. Within just a few minutes, they started filling the shuttle they had arrived in and the shuttle he occupied. He let them have their way. He was impatient to kill them and move on, but he needed them for a short time. He wanted their ship, and they would cough it up. Oh yes, they would take him in and he would end their existence shortly thereafter.

The banging about near his crate gave him pause. Were they going to unload? Surely, they would just put more palettes in and lift. He waited and had to steady himself when they moved his crate, but they weren't unloading him. They were making more room by shuffling things around. That was fine, though he hoped he wasn't completely boxed in when they finally did unload him.

It took them over an hour to steal what they wanted. The shuttles took off and he settled back for the trip, but they surprised him when instead of leaving they circled around and blasted all three domes. The shuttles weren't gunships, but they did have railguns. Missiles were expensive, but railgun rounds cost next to nothing. The raiders didn't conserve ammo. He was linked into the shuttle's sensors and external cameras to watch the show. They shredded the domes as if they were some loathsome insect and the shuttle's guns were bug sprayers. The power plant exploded, the dome erupting in fire. The other two domes had little that would burn, but they collapsed, and that seemed to satisfy. One last lazy circle and they flew off leaving nothing worth salvaging behind them.

Eric wondered about it. There had been plenty of stuff to steal at the base, but they had blown it all away as if it were nothing. The reason had to be orders. The shuttle crews wouldn't have fired for fun. Therefore, they had done so to deny the base and supplies to others. That was important. It meant the raiders did not plan to attack alpha site. At least, that was his assumption and it made perfect sense. The raiders planned to maroon them without supplies. A way to kill all the witnesses without risk. A good plan. A safe plan. A plan created by a thinker, not one created by a rash man. Eric would have preferred otherwise.

The journey progressed. He didn't know where they were going, but they weren't boosting for orbit. That was a disappointment. He wanted to get aboard their ship. He tried to use the shuttle's sensor data to figure out where they were going, but there were too many possibilities. He briefly considered tapping into the navigational computer, but decided against it. Really, the risk of detection was minor but it was there. Besides, what was he going to do with the data? Nothing. So he watched and waited to see what would happen.

Time passed.

His destination was a surprise. The raiders had landed their ship! It was no longer in orbit. Why do that? He didn't know and decided that he didn't care after a few seconds of thought. This was good news. With the ship grounded he wouldn't have to concern himself with pesky things like... oh, breathing vacuum. The ship being on the ground probably meant most of the crew would be working outside. Probably. Why else land? It must be because the salvage operation was a big task that needed manpower and perhaps using shuttles would take too long. Whatever the reason, it was more than fine with him when the shuttles entered the ship's docking bay.

He was ready to get to work.

Ready he might be, but he had to wait for the enemy to unload the shuttles and clear the bay. He counted time as the crew went about its business, and braced himself when it was his crate they unloaded. He used the time to scan his surroundings.

*Computer: initiate full spectrum security scan. Range out to 200 metres.*

**>_ SENSORS: FULL SPECTRUM SWEEP IN PROGRESS.**

The raiders worked on, diligently moving boxes and palettes quickly out of the shuttles. His crate was one of the bigger ones. They chose to store it in one of the cargo holds first and then pile everything else on top. *Dasher* class ships like this one were designed for short hauls. Legitimate users earned a living transporting goods between a planet's surface and the stations orbiting those planets. They did have foldspace drives—marketing would have had an impossible job selling the things without them—but they were underpowered. They were slow in foldspace, but made up for it in normal space. They needed power to boost cargo out of the gravity well. Multiple holds, big ones for ships that could enter an atmosphere and land, were just one of the selling points that had made the *Dasher* class cargo ships so popular at the turn of the century. Newer models had since superseded them, but all that had done was strengthen the used ship market. They were a popular choice out in the border zone where money was tight, and of course there were other uses for fast ships with the ability to land. Raiders loved them.

Eric busied himself reading the results of his security sweep. It didn't make for good reading. The ship had a larger crew than he had expected. Gina had killed four and eight had come calling upon the base to find their buddies. That was twelve. A ship this size didn't need many more than that to run efficiently, yet he counted over twenty moving about and his sweep didn't cover the area outside the ship. Because he was a big believer in pessimism—pessimism had never killed anyone, but optimism often did—he decided to double the number to forty plus hostiles. That was pushing even his abilities, and he considered going directly for the bridge. He could use the ship's more powerful transmitters to contact Gina. Together they could handle it. He fighting on the inside, Gina hammering them on the outside. Yes, together they could take the ship even from so many, but that meant leaving Liz and her people uncovered. Not something he would have considered just yesterday, but he had the file now. The mission had changed to getting it back to Snakeholme not protecting civilians who would all die anyway if he failed to take the ship.

A stealthy attack would be best. A dagger thrust to the bridge, a call to Gina, and then a short victorious war to claim a way off this snowball. With luck, the civilians would survive and all would be well. It was a vague plan at best, but he deemed it viable. As always, the devil was in the details. His route to the bridge, the opposition he was likely to encounter, counters from the raiders, and any number of things needed to be factored in. If the raiders raised the alarm he could find himself in trouble. All it would take was one sensible man on the bridge sealing it, and he would be screwed. The hypothetical crewman could call all the crew in from outside to surround and overwhelm him, and he with no way to contact Gina for aid.

Eric frowned as he worked the problem using sensors and old database entries to map the interior of the ship. He hadn't ever had this precise scenario occur before. Surprising really. Going through the motions and following his programming, had been his existence for decades. It sometimes felt as if everything he did was just a variation of a theme. Scenario A occurs and respond with scenario B... all is programming.

He shook his head at his distraction and concentrated on the problem at hand. His database had most of what he needed. This wasn't his first time on the *Dasher* class of ship. Had he ever been crew on one of them?

**WORKING...**

Eric sighed and scowled into the dark. Damn literalist computers anyway. Couldn't he even think a rhetorical question without interruption now? Obviously not. He let the blasted thing run its search and busied himself building an ops plan.

So, he was in cargo hold three, the closest to the boat bay. Made sense. No one wanted to shift cargo further than they needed to. The enemy had simply shoved everything they'd stolen into the first available space. That was fine, but it made his job that tiniest bit more tricky. He had been stored in a busy part of the ship. The raiders were constantly in and out of the bay heading outside to do whatever, and coming back in to unload cargo or fetch things. He didn't need someone spotting him so early in the plan. Hopefully no one at all would spot him until Gina came on scene, but he couldn't guarantee that. The best he could do was minimise the risk of discovery, and that meant not using the ship's decks to reach his objective. It had to be the service ways then.

**NEGATIVE.**

What the hell? Oh right, the search was negative. He hadn't been crew on one of these tubs before. He knew that. Didn't matter in the least. His sensor map was getting nicely detailed and his database had the basic layout of the *Dasher* class for him to use. With luck, the enemy hadn't bothered to modify their ship any further than beefing up its weapons and ammo carrying capacity. That was the usual pattern. Raiders didn't usually spend money on interior layout changes. The bridge was the bridge, environmental was environmental, and engineering was engineering. That sort of thing. Where changes might occur would be in areas such as crew berthing, cargo areas, and other places that wouldn't influence the actual function of the ship. Additional magazines for missiles for example could be created in any empty section, but unless he needed to move through such an area to reach another, he couldn't see how it had any effect on him.

He mapped a safe route through the ship using the service ways and ventilation tunnels. Safe, as long as the alarm wasn't raised. Ships, no matter the class—military or civilian it didn't matter—had things in common. Things like keeping the air in! In cases of emergency they all had blast doors that would seal off sections of the ship. The section seals everyone saw daily when walking the decks of any ship or station, were lifesavers, but few realised the complexity required of such systems. Section seals and blast doors in personnel areas were relatively simple things, but imagine having to seal every maintenance tunnel, every ventilation shaft, every possible way for air to escape while maintaining a ship's systems to all areas through the myriad of pipes, wires, and god knows what. It made Eric's head hurt. Ship design was not in his future that was for sure. The point here was that a single alarm could seal every deck and service tunnel to the bridge. He had to reach it absolutely undetected.

That was going to be hard. Very hard indeed.

Eric kicked his way out of his confinement. He couldn't just lift the lid. It was buried under all the other cargo the raiders had piled atop it. His boots thudded into the side of his box with the power of pneumatic jacks. Thirty seconds and repeated blows later he was out and stripping off his environmental suit. It was a relief to be out of the smelly thing, but not because of the stink. It just made movement and combat easier.

He drew his pistol in a lightning fast move, his enhanced muscles performing the task smoothly as always. He holstered it and adjusted his belt. He drew again. Yes, that was perfect. He holstered the pistol again and checked his rifle. All was as it should be. Calling up his much-annotated map, he orientated himself and headed deeper into the cargo hold to find his initial access into the guts of the ship.

It was a maintenance hatch like any other. There were hundreds like it on the ship, needed for engineers and their remotes to service the ship and make repairs. Anything that moved or could fail in any way at all needed an access point like this to repair or replace it. Some of the service ways were too narrow for even the smallest engineer to navigate, and those were used exclusively by droids and remotes. That fact had made his choice of route harder because there simply wasn't a way to reach the bridge without emerging into the ship proper. He had made allowances, trying to minimise those emergences and making them in rarely used parts of the ship. He used his combat knife to pry open the cover over the controls and used them to open the hatch.

The first leg of his journey to the bridge was a simple matter of following the service way to the first vertical junction. He was careful to close the hatch behind him, but he didn't need to take any further precautions. He was well insulated deep in the guts of the ship that few people, if any, ever saw. No one would hear him clambering about. He encountered only a single repair mech on the way, and it had stowed itself in its charging bay. Not that it would have mattered if it had been active. It was the autonomous kind, not the type requiring a tele-operator to function.

The service way was large enough for him to walk if he doubled over. He chose to do that at first, but soon resorted to a crawl. It was easier and frankly he preferred to keep his head up and looking ahead rather than down. Despite keeping his sensors sweeping ahead, he was still Human enough to prefer seeing where he was going with his own eyes. Crawling slowed him, but he had time. No one knew he was aboard. He could take the entire day if it meant reaching the bridge undetected.

The vertical shaft allowed him to stand, but it presented another difficulty. Mechs had anti-grav. He did not. He looked for a way to climb, but the designers had decided not to include a ladder or rungs. Probably expected the engineers to use remotes for manual inspections and any maintenance would be handled by droids and mechs equipped with anti-grav.

Eric slung his rifle on his back out of the way and tested the cable trunking and pipe work lining the shaft. It creaked as he pulled but held. He gave it a little more and one section pulled free with a bong sound ringing through the walls. He scowled and tried one of the other control runs. Surely they weren't all held in place by spit and bailing wire? He tugged and this time the pipe held. Good enough. He began climbing, his legs kicking free beneath him.

The *Dasher* class ships were small freighters when compared to their multi-million ton brethren. They were the minnows in a sea swarming with leviathans, but for all of that the climb was still something like four stories. Eric made it to the right junction and into a cross tunnel that he followed for only a short distance. He had reached the first of his exits. The service way continued on and if he followed it, he would have eventually run out of room far from his destination. The hatch he contemplated would allow him to exit on Deck3E. The E stood for engineering, and ordinarily he would be delighted, but this wasn't a normal infiltration. He could cause mayhem in engineering, but he needed the ship intact, so no fun and games breaking delicate things today. His visit would be purely that and just a waypoint on his way further forward.

The hatch unsealed smoothly and Eric emerged. Sensors reported crew working nearby, but not within visual of him. He resealed the hatch and crossed the compartment quickly and out the door into the corridor. He ran. The burst of speed had him at the right door in seconds. He ducked inside just as a woman appeared around a corner, but she either didn't register him or thought he was crew. She walked passed his door and didn't raise the alarm. Lucky for her, because she would have been dead the second she tried.

Sensors reported all clear. He was in the auxiliary control room used for monitoring the fusion plants. It wasn't manned. Usually someone would only be stationed at the controls during jumps to and from foldspace to monitor the draw of extra power needed at those times. He had gambled the raiders would be occupied elsewhere and wouldn't be performing maintenance. It had worked out.

There were no service ways leading from this compartment to anywhere he wanted to go, but all areas of the ship needed air. He found the grill covering the environmental duct and used it to enter the airways. He didn't need to go far. A blessing because the air ducts were confining. He had to lay prone and pull himself the few hundred yards he needed to reach his next waypoint. He reached it quickly but sensors alerted him to a problem. The compartment he needed wasn't empty.

Two red icons glared balefully at him. He eased forward until he could see through the gaps in the grill and scowled. A man and a woman were performing an intimate inspection of each other instead of the ship they were meant to be working on. Their clothes and tools were scattered all over the compartment, and it seemed unlikely they would finish any time soon. Eric watched the woman energetically riding her friend where he lay upon the deck exploring her breasts with roaming hands. The show didn't move him at all except in how he needed to deal with the situation.

Sensors reported only these two near enough to hear a commotion. Not that he planned to allow one, but he wouldn't take chances. He drew his knife and gently pried open the grill. He allowed it to fall and burst into the compartment, his legs thrusting hard. His dive sent him across the room and he executed a roll back to his feet that brought him up behind the woman. She cried out, reaching her climax just as the knife entered the back of her neck just below her skull. The sound instantly died with her, the knife severing her spinal cord. Her partner's eyes had been closed, but he must have felt her go limp. He looked up in time to see the knife plunging for him. He didn't have time to scream.

Eric wiped the blood from the knife on his thigh staring at the couple. The girl was still astride her partner, slumped forward with her head on his chest. The pale curve of her back was beautiful in the light; her expression... was it wonder? Pleasure? Eric's face remained a mask, but his hand shook as he sheathed the knife. Already the scene was burned into his viper memory, ready to haunt him in the years to come. He didn't look away, but made himself remember the feel of the knife entering the girl's neck between her C1 and

C2 vertebrae as his training dictated. Made himself hear her cry of pleasure again and again just as he ended her life. At least this way his nightmares would be true remembrances... and deserved.

He turned away.

Sensors reported no hostiles near as he ran through the ship as if alone on a derelict. Been there, done that, he thought. This feeling was similar, but not the same. The ship was alive with mechanical sounds and well lit. Air moved through the ducts, sounds from behind closed hatches, and even distant crashes came to him as vibrations through the structure of the ship as crew unloaded cargo. None of that had been present last time. The ship had been utterly dead, as had everyone aboard except him. Bumbling around in the dark, he hadn't enjoyed the experience. He'd been lucky to find an operational escape pod that time.

*Lucky. Right.*

Some would call him a Jonah for how many times he had been present and the only survivor when missions went wrong. Then again, all the veterans were guilty of being survivors when circumstances had whittled the regiment down to a nub.

He entered environmental and went straight for the service way he needed. It was the last one. Sensors reported the vats and equipment unattended as he had hoped. The gardens aboard ship looked after themselves mostly. He hadn't expected to encounter anyone, but then, he hadn't expected to find two people having sex in the auxiliary control room either. He climbed into the service way and locked the hatch behind him.

He followed his map taking the turns fast as he came to them, and climbing when he had to. He was approaching the bridge now, and sensors showed a lot of activity. The bridge was fully manned just as engineering had been. Not really a surprise anymore. He had already guessed the crew was oversized. They probably doubled as boarding parties for jacking ships and stations. He paused at the final hatch and watched things using sensors. The hatch he crouched beside was in a bad location for his purposes. *Dasher* class ships used the U-shaped bridge that military ships used. It was a logical layout. The captain's command station was positioned centrally so that he could oversee operations, and the elevators leading to the rest of the ship were behind him between the legs of the U. All that was fine, but it meant the hatch he was about to use was in full view of everyone on the bridge, directly beneath the main viewscreen. There was nothing to be done about it, and he prepared himself for a fight.

He lay his rifle aside and drew his pistol. The pistol was a little faster to aim in extremis, and he expected this fight to be extreme. There were six hostiles to neutralise, and he needed to do it before they raised the alarm. Also, he needed the bridge intact. He couldn't emerge spraying fire in all directions. He would have to rely upon Snapshot for targeting.

Vipers were programmed with perfect recall in an effort to make them better killers by making target acquisition at a glance instant and perfect. The routines in his programming were complicated and numerous. Together they were called Snapshot and could not be turned off. The moment he emerged, he should be able to acquire all six targets, but he couldn't kill them all with one shot. There would be time for them to respond. They might try to run, or hide, or fight back, and he wasn't wearing armour. The risk of return fire was part of the job and he didn't let it concern him. The one thing he feared was the alarm being raised, and if he was seriously unlucky, they might lock him out of the controls.

*Computer: Melee mode.*

The world seemed to slow as the hatch slid aside. It didn't of course. He had sped up. He pushed himself out of the hatch already turning toward the comm shack. He had chosen it as his first priority to prevent word of his attack leaving the ship. His pistol swung toward the crewman even as he straightened to full height. His targeting reticule found the man's head and spun. It only had time to pulse once before his finger twitched. A three round burst splashed blood and brains over the bulkhead but did no damage to the ship. He had set his pistol to 50% power, more than enough even at much higher ranges than this.

He glared around the bridge acquiring targets as cries of shock erupted. Men and women dove for cover or went for their weapons. His reticule picked them all out storing their positions, and he began servicing targets. He fired at the captain, or the officer currently in charge of the deck. He was sitting in the captain's chair at least. Before the man completed rising Eric's three rounds took him in the upper chest blasting him back into the couch.

*Impact!*

Eric staggered as damage assessments flickered onto his display. Right side over the ribs. He reprioritised his targeting to take out the gunner. It was the damage control officer, and he had a pistol out. Before Eric could take him out, another round punched into him. Left shoulder this time, minimal damage but plenty of blood soaked his uniform and trickled down his arm. He dove aside, rolled to his feet, and killed his attacker with two trigger pulls. The helmsman reached for a control. Eric killed him, but the hand landed and alarms wailed.

*Goddamnit!*

The last man dove into the elevator but died before the doors closed. Eric turned examining the bodies. A groan from one man, another trigger pull, and it was over. The alarm continued wailing.

*Computer: combat mode.*

The world sped up to normal and data flooded his

display, some flashing for attention. Priorities. IMS, absent his input, swung into action and began making repairs. He ignored it all reaching to drag the dead helmsman off his consol. He shut off the alarm, and headed for the elevator. He needed to block it. He didn't want to permanently disable or damage it. The simplest answer occurred to him and he dragged the body halfway back onto the bridge so that the doors couldn't close. That done he headed for the comm shack to call Gina in.

\* \* \*

# 21 ~ Call to Arms

"Gina," Eric said giving her a start. "I've taken the bridge. I'm using the ship's comm shack so don't try to respond. You haven't got the range. I need you to saddle up and help with the assault. There were a lot more raiders than I thought. I'm estimating forty plus and at least half of them are outside. I need you to take care of business out there while I deal with those in the ship. Coordinates follow..."

She started in surprise. Coordinates meant the ship was grounded. She hurriedly collected the ammo she had brought to the OP with her, and headed back to tell Liz of the change in plans.

"...Penleigh out."

Gina didn't bother entering the coordinates into her wristcomp. Her processor had the data, and with a coded thought she added the location to the map of Kushiel they had been gradually compiling. The location surprised her, though she didn't know why it should when she thought about it. The raiders were here to steal. Why shouldn't they do that in the capital? The ship was on the ground within the city itself. She was going to visit Haverington again it seemed.

She headed for the shuttle and called Liz via helmet comm. "Liz, we have a change in plans. Eric needs my help."

"Is he okay?"

"Seemed to be. He says there are more raiders than he thought. He needs me to go to him."

"Go. We'll be fine."

She bit her lip. "I'm sorry to leave you uncovered this way."

"Just be careful. Eric wouldn't ask for help if he didn't badly need it. I know him. He must be greatly outnumbered."

Liz was right. Gina didn't know him as well or as long as Liz, but she knew him well enough to know he didn't panic. That he had taken the bridge and called her before clearing the rest of the ship spoke volumes.

"I'll be careful. Keep everyone out of sight and listen on comm for me. I'll be as quick as I can. Fuentez out."

Gina quickly boarded the shuttle and went through her pre-flight checks already thinking ahead to the fight. She didn't know what she would find in Haverington. She knew the raiders had armed shuttles and their ship on the ground. Worst case scenario would have those shuttles in the air patrolling the area. That would be bad. Not only would she have to land and hike into the city from a long way out, but she would have to deal with possible air attack. Ideally the shuttles would be on the ground and the raiders too busy with their pilfering to launch quickly. She suspected the truth would be somewhere in between. Either way, she needed to choose her landing site carefully.

She flew the shuttle to Haverington with her eyes glued to her shuttle's sensors. She didn't fear being detected by the raiders on the ground, and with Eric in control of their ship's bridge, she was safe from that too, but the shuttles were another matter. They would have the same or similar range to her cargo shuttle, but being smaller they would be faster and more manoeuvrable. She had no intention of fighting in the air and hugged the terrain to minimise detection.

She landed in the outskirts of the city.

She would have loved to use her APC not only to drive closer, but also in battle. The twin barrelled pulser on the roof could have done serious damage to any target especially those shuttles, but she couldn't drive and fire the weapon. APCs typically carried a minimum of three crew—driver, gunner, and navigator/comm specialist—plus the platoon of vipers it carried as cargo. On her own, all she would succeed in doing was provide the enemy with a nice mobile target to practice on.

She disembarked from the shuttle carrying her rifle and pack. Her pack was stuffed with extra ammo including grenades, and her rifle was fully loaded. As was her custom, she had chosen to load her grenade launcher with all HE rounds. The P100 could take a maximum of ten. She had loaded it to capacity and had enough loose extras to load it fully twice more. She strongly doubted she would need so much firepower, but it was better to have too much than not enough.

She slogged through the snow carrying the pack in her left hand, and her rifle slung across her chest. She couldn't wear the pack on her back as designed because her PLSS was there. She kept her right hand free for her pistol. It was holstered over her environmental suit, and it felt wrong, but there was no choice if she wanted to use it. When she needed to fight, she would discard her glove for access to her weapon's bus, and wondered if perhaps there might be a way to design a glove that would allow the connection while maintaining suit integrity. The gloves she sometimes used in combat had an open window in the right palm, but that wouldn't work with her suit.

Hmmm.

With sensors at max trawling for hostiles and their emissions, she spent her time imagining a suit mod that would work. If she came up with an answer, she would submit it to General Burgton with her report. He was always looking for ways to improve the regiment and its gear.

The snow was deep in places. It forced her to keep to the centre of the streets. That wasn't where she instinctively wanted to be, especially when the sun was up and the sky clear. The weather was fine, the day a balmy -25° and should the enemy be looking her way she would stand out like a beacon. She wanted to hug the buildings for cover but couldn't. Snow drifts had mounded high and deep there. She jogged up the middle, but was ready to take cover.

Her sensors reported in when she came within range and TacNet updated itself. She found a side street with less snow built up, and used it to take a break. She crouched behind the crumbling wall of a fallen building, brought TacNet up on her display and interrogated sensors. She drilled down into the data, and began making notes on the map to make it easy to recall information at a glance. She really did love TacNet, and knew her old friends in the marines would be envious.

It was obvious right away that Eric had been discovered. A large group of hostiles marked in red now on her map were attempting to gain entry to the ship. He must have locked it down and sealed the cargo bays and airlocks. Another group, smaller but still numerous, was doing something in one of the buildings. Salvage operations maybe? Were they that confident of regaining the ship? It confused her because if she had been them, she would have had all hands attacking Eric. Maybe they felt the crew inside could deal with him. Good luck with that! Eric was a lethal SOB, all vipers were, but they probably didn't know what he was. She watched both groups for a minute or so, noting a few strays wandering between the groups. She had no idea what they were meant to be doing, but she was glad to see both shuttles grounded and seemingly of no immediate interest to anyone. The strays were going to be a problem, she realised. Not because they were inherently more dangerous, but because they had bugger all to do and might notice her arrival. Still, there weren't many of them. She could probably avoid detection as long as she watched them and took measures to evade them.

"Eric? I'm in position," Gina said over viper comm. "I'm ready to get the party started."

"Bit busy here," Eric relied. Gina heard his pistol and the sound of return fire in the background. "I need you in here sooner rather than later."

"Okay, hold on. Fuentez out."

"Hurry."

The urgency and stress in his voice made her pulse speed. She had never heard that in his voice before. He must be seriously hard pressed in there, and that changed things for her. The slow careful approach she preferred was out of the question now. She needed to smash the opposition outside the ship, access an airlock, and relieve Eric before something happened she would regret.

She moved out again.

Her preference would have been clearing the outside before entering the ship, but now she was in a race against time. She decided to ignore the hostiles in the building if they would let her and engage those trying to enter the ship. No doubt the strays would attack as soon as they saw her. If they did she would deal, if they didn't, she would deal with them later, after she rescued Eric.

She entered the open area that the raiders had used for their landing site. She realised it was a plaza or square. It was lined on all sides with buildings, but it was a big one. The shuttles were to one side, the ship was in the centre, but there was plenty of open space left. Too much. It seemed as if she had oceans of empty space to cross, and she felt naked as she did so. She pulled off her glove ignoring the cold and the warnings on her display as contaminants entered the suit. Her PLSS kicked into high gear trying to adjust and compensate for her suit's loss of integrity.

She charged toward the ship, her legs pumping. She

brought her rifle around and selected her grenade launcher. She skidded to a stop on the ice dropping her pack and pumped grenades toward the ship. She sent all ten arcing high. They came down amidst the raiders and detonated throwing bodies and pieces of bodies high in the air. Shrapnel pinged and clanged off the ship's hull, but caused no damage. Ships were far too tough.

Movement.

She spun to her right going to one knee. Her targeting reticule locked on, spun redly and she fired. The raider was blasted back. She ducked away as return fire flooded in from other locations in the square including the ship. Her grenades had killed most of the raiders there, but not all. She grabbed her pack and sprinted toward the ship, firing short controlled bursts toward the survivors one handed. One died, and another. The third one tried to scramble away from her as she arrived. She butt-stroked him and he went down.

Incoming fire toward her strengthened as some of the group in the building emerged. She kept low and tried the airlock controls. They were locked down as she had guessed earlier. She was about to try a code that Eric might have used, but had to throw herself flat as the raiders saturated the air with pulser fire. It was getting bloody dangerous out here! She returned fire forcing them to go to ground, and took a chance. She entered the regiment's motto, but the code was refused.

"Code, Eric, dammit," she snarled. "What's the override code?"

"Alpha-three-niner-niner-Charlie-one"

Gina entered the code keeping down and reaching high to stab the keys above her head. She flinched when more pulser fire splashed against the ship as the airlock door shot open. She hurled herself inside and closed the hatch breathing a little hard with adrenaline rush. She liked excitement as much as the next girl, but that had been a little too exciting.

She reloaded her rifle and grenade launcher, though she

had no intention of using grenades within the ship. They needed it to get home. Only then did she open the inner door.

She threw herself prone as a crewman hosed the airlock with railgun fire. It was only a handheld, not an AAR, but the hail of slugs it threw was more than enough to shred her into blood and screams. There was only the one man, but he laid down a barrage fit for a squad. She rolled out of the open hatch, keeping him targeted, and fire one round. He collapsed holding his belly screaming at the pain. Pulser burns hurt like a bastard. She knew from experience. Her second round put him out of his misery.

Gina stood and advanced toward the body where it sprawled at the junction. TacNet had already reached out to the only other viper unit in range, Eric, and linked up with him to share data. She had the latest tacsit in a small window on her display as a result. She knew where he was, engineering level 2, and his situation, dire. What the bloody hell was he doing in engineering? The last she knew he had been in control of the bridge and in a good situation to hold it. Why take on so many when he knew she was on the way? She didn't know, but the answer was with Eric.

"Let's go ask him," she muttered.

She considered removing her suit but decided against taking the time. Eric had sounded desperate but she didn't really know why. He was a viper. A dozen armed raiders might give him a decent fight, but they shouldn't be beyond him if he was careful.

She called the elevator, stepped over the body, and entered the car.

The ride took only a few moments. She slung her rifle and drew her pistol. She held it aimed and ready as the doors opened letting her out on engineering level 1. She had chosen the level above Eric because there were raiders using it to pin him. She targeted those she saw upon entering engineering. She gave each of them a three round burst in the back. Two men fell off the catwalk to thud solidly on the deck of level 2. The third sighed and slumped against the rail.

She ducked back into the car as the remaining raiders targeted her, but then edged carefully back out and to the right when they reloaded. She kept low and crept along the catwalk, trying for a better position. She could probably kill some of them with grenades, but she didn't want to risk the ship. They were already taking a chance shooting up the place as it was. Hit the wrong thing in here and the drive could either be damaged beyond use, or worse, it could lose field containment entirely and cause a sun to be born and die on the surface of the planet. She looked down over the safety rail and found Eric below her, using one of those important and sensitive bits of equipment as cover.

"What the hell, Eric? Stop playing with them."

"I'm nearly out of ammo!" Eric snarled back on viper comm, sounding pissed off at the accusation. "If you'd moved your arse like I told you, I wouldn't be sitting here like a target."

Aha! That explained a few things. "Look up. I have a present for you. Catch!"

She dropped her pack down to him, and ducked back as railgun slugs reached for her life pinging and ricocheting of the rail and bulkhead. She fired back giving Eric cover while he reloaded. She knew the moment to move had come when he went all Zelda on the raider's arses, and laid down a barrage to make Fleet proud. She surged to her feet and leapt the safety railing. Her pistol barked twice as she fell. Two targets were blasted back before she landed. The raiders turned their attention to her, and Eric rushed them. She joined him and the fight ended with her emptying her pistol on full auto into the space between two consoles shredding the enemy hiding there.

Eric stood among the bodies targeting them one after the other and putting a single shot into each of their heads. Gina watched. It had to be done, but his emotionless face disturbed her. It was one of the things she didn't like about him. Her thoughts flashed back to the elevator shaft and remembered finding him hanging from his rope zoned out with something... odd, something not Eric looking out at the world using his eyes.

She shivered.

"You done?" she asked a little harshly. She cleared her throat. "I didn't clear the ground before coming aboard. You sounded a bit harried."

Eric snorted. "How many left?"

"Ten, twelve maybe. I'm worried about those shuttles. If they take it into their heads, they could attack alpha site."

"They could, but they won't. They're too fixated on getting in here to deal with us, but let's make sure."

She nodded, glad he saw it as she did, and headed for her pack where Eric had left it. She reloaded her pistol and took the opportunity to swap its power cells for fresh ones. The old ones still had plenty of charge, but no need to run them down to nothing and get stuck for power at the wrong time. Eric saw what she was doing and took the opportunity to do the same.

"Where's your suit, on the bridge?"

"Cargo bay," Eric said heading for the elevator.

She hefted her slightly deflated pack and followed him into the car. "Let's get it and finish this. I'm sick of snow."

Eric grunted.

After reclaiming his suit, Eric separated from Gina. They chose different exits from the ship for strategic reasons, neither choosing her entry point. The cargo bay ramps were also out. Those huge pressure doors were too slow in opening and closing; much too tempting for the remaining raiders to try retaking the ship. Gina gave half of her spare ammo to Eric and all the loose grenades. Her rifle was fully loaded, and the fight outside was ideal for its use. She holstered her pistol not expecting to need it anymore today.

She chose the airlock opposite the one she had used to

enter the ship. Her reasoning was simple really. The airlock was on the portside of the ship, which put the bulk of the ship between her and the building the raiders had found so interesting. She doubted they were still there, but that was their last known location. They might be moving from there or back to it, they might all be trying to enter the airlock where she had killed so many. She was betting her safety on her guess that they wouldn't round the ship to enter on the portside, but would try entering on the starboard side closest to the building. Less of a walk.

She cycled the airlock on one knee with her rifle up ready to fire. TacNet updated itself as soon as her sensors swept an area in front of her. The cone shaped region on the map lightened, updating itself and building upon the map as it had been before she entered the ship. There were no hostiles in the vicinity of the lock. Eric must have exited the ship at that moment, because his icon blinked into place close by surrounded by a circle of live sensor data. His map would have her cone of data on it, and it was time she added something more to it.

She left the airlock and locked it behind her. Without the code, no one would enter this way short of dismantling the lock or cutting the hatch open. With sensors running continual sweeps in all directions she rounded the ship in a bent kneed jog with her rifle up looking for targets. Sensors reported Eric moving around the ship in the opposite direction. She kept TacNet open in a small window on her display and its map updated as soon as the first hostiles came within sensor range. Eric was closest, and he opened fire first. Gina sprinted forward, needing to close the range a little and take advantage of the distraction he provided.

She knew the moment that she reached optimal range. Her targeting reticule appeared and spun pulsing red over one of the raiders. She fired, retargeted, fired again. Both raiders dropped, one rolling from side to side hugging himself probably screaming. She was too distant to hear while wearing her helmet. She ran to a new firing location and Eric did the same. Return fire started up, but it was poorly targeted. Snow and ice flashed to steam around her, but nothing more dangerous came close. She switched to her grenade launcher and fired just once at the open ramp of a shuttle the raiders had been moving toward. It exploded just inside the ship. She wasn't attempting to take it out, just deter entry. Exploding fuel tanks wouldn't be in anyone's best interests. Such a thing would kill everyone nearby. Liquid hydrogen tended to do that.

Shuttle reactors were actually safer than their fuel source, because the reaction was so precise. Interrupting the fuel supply or unbalancing the reaction in some way causes the plasma within deuterium-tritium fusion reactors to cool within seconds. The reaction simply ceases. No risk of runaway reactors or chain reactions. Safety is one of the main reasons to use such reactors aboard ships that routinely entered atmosphere.

Her strike upon the shuttle ramp had the desired effect at first. The raiders pulled back. Unfortunately it had two side effects that she didn't appreciate. One: they scattered but chose her as their main target. Two: they were pulling back toward that building they had found so interesting. She ducked and fell prone trying to return fire, and managed to take out two more raiders, but the others were panicking and firing blindly in her direction. She became the eye of a storm of pulser blasts.

Eric of course took advantage and sniped away almost unnoticed, the lucky bastard. As the hostiles died one by one, Gina was able to advance again, but she wasn't able to stop the last half dozen or so raiders ducking out of sight into the building.

"We can't leave them I suppose?" she said hopefully. "We could wreck the shuttles and take the ship back to orbit. Maroon them as they would have done to us."

"No."

"But—"

"I said no," Eric said again, this time in his command voice. Gina straightened a little at hearing it. An instinctive reaction she had yet to shed. "They murdered our people. Everyone aboard *Hobbs*. No one does that to us."

She agreed with the sentiment, but marooning them was a death sentence. She didn't need to kill them with her own hands to feel that justice had been served. Eric obviously didn't agree and he was senior. He led the attack.

She covered him as he went into the impressive looking building. She wondered if perhaps the raiders had been after data of some kind, because impressive though it was, it wasn't somewhere she would look for money. She would have blown every bank vault on the planet and raided the factories for precious metals. Even the jewellery stores would have made more sense to her than this imposing edifice that reminded her of a major library or government admin building.

Eric ducked inside, but didn't find a target. He gestured and she flew up the steps to join him. She ducked into cover and interrogated her sensors. Hostile icons dotted around the building appeared on her display. It was every man for himself now by the looks of it. Good for Eric and her, bad for them. They weren't backing each other up at all. She glanced at Eric; he waved her to the left. She advanced alone, while he disappeared down a corridor on the right. Sensors and TacNet made this an unfair contest. Yay for the good guys, she thought cynically. This was so unnecessary.

She made her way toward the first of her targets. He had gone to ground. Hiding from a viper was hard to do. If she had been a marine still, her old helmet with its sensor package might have missed him. Might. Standard Alliance gear was pretty good even without the advantages of a viper's extra processing power. She probably wouldn't know where he was, but she would have rotated between infra and motion sensors regardless and as soon as she opened the door she would have found him. She didn't do either here. She simply aimed at the wall and killed the idiot. He had chosen to hug the wall beside the door, obviously expecting her to barge straight in and have the door hide him from sight. Her rifle on max settings blew a hole right through the wall and his torso. Something she had learned she could do from Eric when they fought together on Thurston. She poked her head through the wall to be sure he was dead, and then pulled back. She shook her head wishing she was killing Merki again, not her own people, and picked her next target.

She moved through her area carefully, but her sensors gave her plenty of warning when one of the raiders grew a spine and tried to flank. He was equipped with motion sensors at least. He must be. He was doing a reasonable job of circling around behind her. Of course he didn't know that she was watching him on her own sensors and walking backwards at the same pace as she had been. When he rounded the last corner expecting to shoot her in the back, he was confronted with her rifle aimed at him. All he did was die.

She didn't stop her movement, simply turned and kept walking. No need to check him. He didn't have a head anymore. She returned her rifle's power setting to a more reasonable anti-personnel level. She had forgotten to do it after blasting the hole in the wall.

As she moved through the building her attention began to drift remembering the past few years of her life. The death of her friends in the marines, meeting Eric, her recruitment testing on Luna. The first day she woke after enhancement flashed before her eyes, and Eric telling her she had nearly died. Roberto shooting her in the tunnels... first deployment on Child of Harmony... battles fought against Merkiaari... Shima going in alone to plant the tracker... the battle of Charlie Epsilon...

What the hell? She stopped where she was and looked around in bewilderment. She was in a hostile environment and she was playing memory files? How does that even happen? She shook her head at her inattention. A quicker way to get dead she couldn't imagine.

Sensors reported...

...seeing Cragg almost dead... her fight on the roof... meeting the elders... visiting Shima... the survey mission with Varya... Shima's vacation... waving goodbye to Shima as she boarded the shuttle with her family and friends... boarding *Hobbs* for the Kushiel mission... watching *Hobbs* burn and die... shot in the back...

*Flicker, flicker, flicker, flicker...*

*Computer: close all incoming and outgoing ports!*

The flow of memory files stopped, and Gina shook in terror. Someone had hacked her systems. They said that wasn't possible. They promised her when she asked not even the hated Douglas Walden could do so! They lied... no they wouldn't. They were vipers too and everyone feared being hacked, feared being a passenger in their own bodies, or simply being switched off. It was every viper's nightmare. They told her she was safe because they believed it to be true.

"Well fuck them, they're wrong," she gasped.

>_ Sensors: offline.
>_ TacNet: offline.

Warning: Hostile intrusion detected.
Countermeasures deployed... failed.

*Computer: Block all incoming transmissions until further notice!*

Acknowledged.

>_ Communications: offline.

Intrusion attempt failed. Block successful.

"Fuck me..." she whispered.

She was truly blind now. No sensors or TacNet, and no viper comm. They all relied upon her net and no network could operate without open ports for data to use. No way to warn Eric. She didn't dare switch to helmet comm. She had no idea if she could be hacked that way. She couldn't see how it would be possible... sonics maybe? She could mute her hearing. She did it in artillery practice, but she was blind enough already. She didn't want to fight while deaf too.

How the hell does it happen that simple raiders have the ability to hack a viper when no one is supposed to have it? She didn't know, but she was in trouble now. There were hostiles all through the building. She had to warn Eric, but she couldn't leave the enemy at her back. She booted up her helmet systems, thanking God and the General that the regiment had kept them for backup purposes. They were primitive compared with her built in systems, but she had used similar things for longer than she had been a viper and was well practiced with their use.

The helmet's HUD came online and its sensors showed her... she spun firing on full auto and yelling in surprise. The raiders fired back and she went down. Her legs riddled with pulser burns. She gritted her teeth at the pain but kept firing. Her suit was flame retardant but in no way was it a replacement for good armour. Her burned legs made her want to scream, but she made the enemy scream instead. All three of the raiders fell still shooting at her, but most missed her. Most. A single shot hit her helmet snapping her head hard back. Its nanocoat reacted instantly flashing mirror bright, trying to reflect the beam, and that saved her from a nasty burn and possibly death. Vipers were tough, but they weren't immortal.

She rolled out of the plasma, but it was instinct and not really necessary. The raider was dead and his finger finally relaxed on the trigger. The weapon fell silent. Her HUD was flickering, damage to the helmet and partially burned visor accounted for that. It was still working though, and the raider's red icons faded as she watched. Her sector was clear according to sensors. These three had been the last. Eric's icon was coming her way at a run it looked like. He must think her badly damaged and was coming to her rescue again! With her out of all contact, it was all he could think... oh crap, no it wasn't. When she ordered her processor to block all transmissions, she had inadvertently blocked her viper IFF too. Eric would have seen her icon fade from his sensors just as she had done after killing the raiders. He thought she was dead. Worse probably. A viper's beacon was designed to keep going even after death to aid recovery of bodies. He must think her utterly destroyed. She would never live it down. Twice in one mission? No way would this stay just between them. It was too good a story. She wondered what she could bribe him with.

>_ Diagnostics: Legs 90%. Environmental health warning. Atmosphere toxic. Lung capacity degraded. Lung capacity 93%. Unit fit for duty.
>_ IMS: Repairs in progress.

She struggled to her feet to meet Eric. He ran around the corner and stopped as she marched up to him. She raised her burnt visor. Her suit integrity was already compromised so it hardly mattered. Eric opened his visor as well and coughed as he breathed the junk this planet laughingly called an atmosphere. He looked stunned to find her alive.

"I was hacked!" she yelled at him, her stress and fear coming out as anger. "What the fuck, Eric! You promised that can't happen!"

He blinked in surprise. "I promised? I don't remember that. Doesn't matter. We can't be hacked."

"We bloody can, I was! I asked Doctor Patel when they switched everything on. He said no one can hack us. Not even Douglas Walden!"

"Calm down, we can't be hacked."

"Goddamnit will you listen to me! I. Was. Hacked!"

Eric just stared silently at her. He was doing that thing of his again, the going away thing. Something else was watching her out of his eyes now and she didn't like it. She jabbed him hard in the chest with her fist and he came back blinking in surprise. His eyes widened.

"You too?"

Eric nodded.

"Close all ports and block incoming transmissions!"

"Doing it now. Done. I saw my family and... never mind. You're right. We can be hacked."

Gina nodded. "Yeah. How does a scraggly arsed bunch of raiders learn how to do that?"

"It wasn't them. This is someone else."

"How do you know?"

"I finished mine before coming here, and I'm guessing yours are all dead too."

She glanced at the bodies beyond him. Eric and she were the only living people in the building. She turned in a circle and something caught her eye high up on the ceiling. A glass dome with a red activity light blinking slowly. She slapped a hand against Eric's chest and directed him to look up.

"Not someone, Eric, some *thing*. I think we've found Sebastian."

"We need to collect Liz and her people. She'll want to meet him."

Gina nodded. "Yeah, and I want to talk to him when she does. The bastard nearly got me killed."

## HAVERINGTON, KUSHIEL

Leon watched the two suited figures emerge from the treasury building bitterly and knew his one chance was gone. Over. Done. He had lost the last toss of the dice. His ship was theirs now, his crew dead. The poachers had won, and he had nothing but his life left to him. It was more than Haliwell and the others had, but he didn't feel grateful.

He had nearly done it. Nearly dug himself out of the hole he had fallen into. If he hadn't let Haliwell talk him into busting open the vaults below the treasury they could have been on their way outsystem now with billions in bearer bonds and gilts. They were snugged away in the cargo hold right now! But no, he had let his greed infect him with stupidity. What did a few million credits in gold and platinum wafers mean when he had billions already? Damn him for a fool!

When the attack came upon them, he had been trying his override codes on the airlock controls. As captain his codes should have opened it, but they hadn't worked. As the ship owner, he had a master unlock code as well, and would have tried it as a last resort. Applying it was a desperation move because it unlocked the entire ship all at once, including the ship's computers. With unsecured computers, Haliwell could have jacked the ship right out from under him. He couldn't risk that, so would have needed to reprogram every lock and security measure with new codes afterward. He didn't get the chance to try it. The grenades slaughtered the crew around him and their attacker charged in and butt-stroked him. When he awoke amidst the corpses the ship had already been lost.

He watched the poachers approach and wanted to kill them for stealing his ship and one last chance at a life, but he couldn't fly the ship alone. It wasn't possible. He needed at least a handful of people to crew the ship in engineering while he conned the helm. There was no way less than five could crew the *Gift*. He would try to bargain a share of the bonds for his life, but he knew he would get nothing. He would be lucky if they let him live considering their actions to date. They were far better killers than Haliwell had ever been.

He looked at his pistol and dropped it before stepping into the open with his hands up, but he didn't get the chance to bargain for passage to the nearest port. The pulser blast took him in the chest, and he died staring wide-eyed at a beautiful clear blue sky.

The figure wearing the damaged suit and burned helmet holstered the pistol stepping over the corpse, and continued toward the ship without looking back.

* * *

# 22 ~ Hegemon

*Beep!*

Valjoth gnashed his fangs at the interruption. Usk was at the hatch. "I'll rip him apart," he panted.

*Beep!*

"Stay," Zeng Kylar said pulling him down and holding him there with ease. She was a formidably sized female and very strong. Most were, but she took it to extremes. She was a head taller than the others, and that made her bigger than any male in the host including him. "Grrrrr," she growled and pinned him down.

Valjoth grunted as her full weight descended upon him. He bit her shoulder. "By the blood," he groaned in pleasure. "You had better get off me."

"Or what?" she growled grinding herself against him.

He lapped the blood flowing from his bite. "Or... never mind," he said and heaved with all his might. Kylar toppled with a crash and Valjoth pounced on top. "Ha!"

"Ha yourself, my lord," Kylar said and clutched him tightly with her legs. "Now what First Claw of the Host?"

"Err..." Valjoth said uncertainly as he tested his strength against hers. Force—no matter what tradition dictated—was not the only way to victory. Cunning had its place. "How about this?" He thrust himself hard inside her.

"Ah!" she groaned as he pounded into her. "A most unusual tactic my lord... but I fail to see... Ah!" she gasped as her pleasure reached its height.

Valjoth roared at his release, but he didn't allow the sensation to distract him from his goal. Kylar was in the throes of passion still and he took full advantage. He threw his weight to one side and rolled out of her weakened grasp. They lay panting side by side.

"You really *are* different," Kylar gasped.

Valjoth gnashed his fangs in laughter. "Everyone says that." They did, but they didn't mean it as a compliment.

He wasn't well thought of in some circles because he was descended from batches that had been, some said, foolishly and hastily created in the aftermath of the failed Human cleansing. The panic back then had led to corner cutting. Batches were quickened with poorly tested and thought out changes because the warlord of the day had feared the Humans were coming to cleanse the Merkiaari from the galaxy, and to be fair everyone thought the same way. It made perfect sense. Had the situation been reversed, Valjoth knew his people would have done exactly that to the Humans. It was what they had been trying to do after all. No one expected Humans to show such weakness when they were in the ascendant, but it had happened and they did not come. It took decades for his people to finally believe what had happened, and that Humans had not come because they couldn't or more baffling still, didn't want to. By that time many batches had been quickened and the changes were well and truly in the Merkiaari gene pool. Those changes based upon fear of Humans and the need to match them, had led to Valjoth's own... ah, strangeness? Uniqueness. He preferred uniqueness to other less complimentary things said of him.

Certainly more pleasant than *'that over educated runt'* a little harsh, he wasn't physically smaller or weaker than the average male. Another thing often said was *'that slurry from the bottom of the vat'* and that was just plain mean. He had challenged and killed the male who said that within his hearing, he had to or be thought weak, but he knew others said it. He was careful never to officially hear it, or he would be fighting challenges every other day.

*Beeeeeeeeeeeeeeeeeeeeeeeeeeeeeeep!*

The hatch alarm sounded again, this time more insistently. Usk must be leaning on the vermin spawned thing. Valjoth climbed to his feet not bothering to dress and fisted the hatch release.

"WHAT?!" he roared at the top of his lungs.

Usk stood in the gale of Valjoth's roar and did not flinch. "Sorry for the intrusion lord, but there was a priority message with orders for you."

"What orders?" Valjoth said snatching the tablet from Usk's grasp in irritation. The moment he read who the communication was from, he calmed down. "In!" he commanded and sealed the hatch behind the shield bearer. "You know Zeng Kylar do you not?" he said distractedly as he read.

Usk stared at the exhausted female where she lay upon the deck. "We've met a time or two."

Kylar gnashed her teeth in laughter. "I remember that. I'd just finished with the vermin... what were they called again?"

"Parcae," Valjoth said absently still reading.

"That was it," Kylar agreed. "They made me very excited I seem to recall."

Usk nodded eagerly.

Valjoth scowled. "I should have known that he would fail the test."

"Who?" Kylar asked, finally recovering enough to rise.

Usk watched in fascination as she stretched and shook

her fur into order.

"Karnak. He allowed the vermin to best him both in space and upon the ground. I should have sent—" he broke off as he read further. "So, the Humans intervened in his cleansing. Things become clearer."

Usk pulled his attention away from Kylar and her grooming. "Ruark was with him."

"For all the good it did," Valjoth said in disgust. "The warlord orders me to attend him at the palace. I think he might be revaluating our plans for the Human cleansing."

"The poor excuses for puling females he surrounds himself with wouldn't let him," Usk turned to the enormous Kylar where she towered over him. "No offence meant."

Kylar laughed. "None taken."

Valjoth nodded. "I think you might be wrong this time. The warlord is old. He remembers the chaos years. Fear of the Humans is a personal thing for him, not something read about in a history text."

Usk remained uncomfortably silent. Valjoth looked up from the tablet. "Oh don't worry about her, Usk. She knows my thoughts as well as you do, and I swept this cabin just a short while ago."

Usk sighed in relief. It was his job to sweep for listening devices, but Valjoth hadn't allowed it before Kylar arrived. Too eager was another failing he was sometimes labelled with, though strangely the females didn't seem to mind.

"Why do you think he'll listen when he didn't before?"

"Because of this," Valjoth waved the tablet. "He hasn't ordered me to send ships to rescue Karnak. I think he's written the Shan vermin and the entire cleansing force off."

"That's a lot to read into a summons to the palace, my lord."

Valjoth shrugged. He supposed it was, but he had a feeling he was right. It had been more than a year ago when he was last at the palace, and he had to admit that was his fault. He had been a little forceful with his opinions last time he was there. The warlord had actually activated the shield on his throne against him, fearing attack. He would never be foolish enough to attack the warlord. Well, not with witnesses present at any rate. He was old and long passed his prime, but he hadn't been a bad ruler.

The Hegemony was stable and strong, and the last rebellion had been dealt with swiftly and efficiently. It was just that he failed to expand their dominion toward Human controlled space, or anywhere but in the opposite direction! He feared the Humans. Even that was understandable to a degree—they were a powerful foe, and a fitting challenge. No, it was that he was so obvious about it!

The Hegemony controlled almost a thousand suns. All had received the attention of the host and cleansing fleets in their time. Some had been fully cleansed when it was decided the vermin natives were of no value, some had not been destroyed utterly for various reasons, and those races had become clients—slaves used to supply the Hegemony with things it needed. Merkiaari couldn't be expected to farm, or build their own ships after all.

He sneered, remembering the warlord saying those words when he challenged the notion. It wasn't as if he wanted his people enslaved, no matter what his enemies said of him. He just wanted to replace all the vermin living in this system, this one vital system, with Merkiaari bred for the task. How was it different breeding special batches for such work, when they did it all the time to crew his ships? He wasn't mad. He didn't want to replace the Hegemony's entire supply of vermin workers. It made perfect sense to keep those races alive for useful work, but safely removed far from here.

Vermin had their uses; Humans however were a different matter. They were a threat. Threats were never allowed to prosper. A full cleansing was mandated, but the warlord had refused to send one. Slave rebellions sometimes happened and new races were discovered. Those kept the host occupied at least, but the real threat was left unchallenged.

It was intolerable.

Valjoth looked at the tablet again. "The warlord requests my presence," he said again. "I suppose we have to go..." he glanced at Kylar where she preened for Usk, grooming her fur. "Tomorrow."

Usk grinned and left.

"Now then," Valjoth said. "Where were we—oof?" he gasped as Kylar threw him to the deck and pounced atop him.

"About here I think," she said and bit him, trying for a decent grip upon his neck with her fangs.

"Oh yes..." he gasped. "Now I remember."

## Approaching the palace, Planet Kiar, Kiar system

Valjoth didn't like visiting the homeworld. Not because he was invariably being summoned to meetings he felt were wastes of his time, or trying to persuade the warlord that this or that thing needed to be done. No, it wasn't only that. It was how out of place he felt there. He shouldn't feel that way. He didn't think Usk did or anyone else he knew, but Kiar just felt wrong. He preferred the decks of *Blood Drinker* beneath his feet, or the dirt of an alien world. Anywhere else really.

He didn't like the city. He didn't like the way vermin populated it, living and working as if they had a right to be there. He didn't like the way the vermin surrounded the heart of the Merkiaari—the inner city where the Hegamon, the full bloods, and the warlord dwelled—and he didn't like how vulnerable his entire species was to a rebellion here of all places.

He had put down rebellions on other worlds and knew the causes of them. Homeworld was at just as much risk as any of those places, but with far deadlier consequences to his people. If he could, he would cleanse homeworld of vermin, and it was that proposition among others that had led to his long absence from the palace.

The palace was an ancient pile, Valjoth thought. It wasn't the first time he'd thought it, and linked it with the staid and slow thinking that went on within. Really, how surprising was it that the warlord failed to embrace new ideas and ways of doing things, when he lived within the palace and never left it? It was so large it might as well be a city within a city, but city-like or not, those living within were insulated from the real Hegemony and the thousand suns comprising it.

With Usk at his shoulder he presented himself at the outer gates to the inner city. Those towering metal walls and armoured doors kept everything at a safe distance. It would take *Blood Drinker's* main battery, an assault ship and the most powerful in the host, to dent it. Not that anyone with half a brain would bother. The gates were as useless as the warlord they were meant to protect. All they really did was isolate the Hegamon from those the blood ruled. If he wanted to assault the palace, he would simply drop a rock on it and go on about his day.

He growled low imagining it. It would be very satisfying, but only briefly. Useless ditherers the Hegamon and the full bloods might be in his opinion, especially in their use of him and the host, but the ruling class were important to their race. Only they could procreate. It was an uncomfortable and embarrassing truth, but the blood bred new generations the way... well, the way vermin did—like farm animals rutting and squeezing out pups. Disgusting. It wasn't even their fault and he had room within himself to feel sorry for them. Some of them. Valjoth had spoken of it with Usk and even some of the more enlightened among the blood, and knew it wasn't their preference. Full blood females often chose to decant their pups as soon as possible, to at least emulate the rest of the race, but artificial wombs were only vaguely similar to the vats where he and 99% of their people were formed.

It was the way the makers, the cursed Kiar, had made them. A safety measure built into their slave's genes to prevent Merkiaari ever turning against them. Well that hadn't worked out for them. They really should have known better, using their own genetic material to create a sub species bigger and stronger than themselves. What did they expect would happen when they introduced a new and better predator into their own ecology? The fools.

Foolish or not, their knowledge of genetic engineering was beyond good. It was magic, and the blood's gene splicers had never found a way to remove the self destruct that the makers had built into Merkiaari ova. Only full blood females were able to produce viable offspring, and their pups were full blood only if they bred with full blood males. It meant the blood were sequestered and pampered, for good reasons no doubt, but it made them useless for real work. Fighting? The idea was laughable even if any could be risked. The blood's gene pool was just barely viable due to genetic diversity. It wouldn't take many losses amongst them to spell their entire race's demise.

Cloning had been tried to increase full blood numbers but it always resulted in barren mules, both male and female. The Kiar again. Every so often experiments were tried in the hope that sufficient genetic drift had occurred to invalidate the self destruct within full blooded female ova, but all had come to nothing. New technologies among the vermin sometimes advanced understanding, but none had yet solved the issue. Valjoth sometimes wondered whether they had missed or lost the answer they sought when they cleansed vermin planets. The thought was uncomfortable, but he'd had a worse one. What if the Humans had the answer or could produce one? The thought was horrifying because he knew their fate and he was about to become the instrument of it. He couldn't change it and wouldn't if he could. They were a terrible threat. He could so easily imagine a fleet of Human ships arriving in this system. One missile hitting the palace would end the Merkiaari forever. It would take a few centuries until the last batch died of old age, but it would be over for the Merkiaari as a species the moment the missile arrived.

The palace and the city were holdovers of the Kiar. Ancient and lasting. One thing the Kiar did well was build. It was the only thing even Merkiaari could admire about their one time masters. What they built worked, and never stopped working. Valjoth frowned as he realised that could be applied to his people as well. Were they not still fighting and bringing new systems into the Hegemony just as they had done for the Kiar? Merkiaari weren't builders and makers. That's what vermin were for.

Valjoth frowned up at the gates towering high into the air. No, his people weren't builders. They were destroyers descended from the enforcers that the Kiar had relied upon to fight their wars and protect them. Only the bloods avoided that legacy, and they were enslaved by their biology instead. Not something anyone would call a bargain.

The small portal in the gate swung open allowing access. The main gates were never opened, and Valjoth wondered if they even could be after so long unused, but then they were Kiar made. Of course they would work, but the approach and entrance to the palace was always by foot. Vehicles of any kind were prohibited from approaching, and anything flying within the interdiction zone around and over the palace would be shot down. The inner city had formidable defences. The curtain walls around it were made of the same metal used to build ships, and they had shields and weapons built into them. He had witnessed yearly tests and knew the inner city was safe from conventional attack, but it wasn't conventional attack he worried about. Unconventional thinking was another thing he was derided for. Unconventional by Merkiaari standards at any rate.

Valjoth saw it otherwise.

He wasn't First Claw of the Host for nothing. He knew his job and that was one of many reasons to both admire and fear the Humans. There had been other vermin worth studying, and he had done so, but it was the Humans that had inspired so many changes in his people. The newest batches were a case in point. They were far superior to older batches, both physically and mentally, but they would never have been quickened if not for the Humans. The breeding programs had been unchanged for a thousand years before the failed Human cleansing. Essentially left as the cursed Kiar had designed them, his people had prospered, but the changes were necessary despite the haste in which they were implemented. Side effects were hardly surprising and didn't overly concern him. They did concern the Hegamon however, but regardless, they needed to be convinced to switch from three in ten batches to full production of the new types. Valjoth didn't expect to get such a concession today, but perhaps an increase to five or six in ten wouldn't be out of the question now that the Humans had taken a hand in Merkiaari affairs again. He could play upon the warlord's fear of Humans, and use him to make the case to the Hegamon for an increase.

Valjoth and Usk stopped just inside the gate as weapons were levelled at them. He didn't roll his eyes or show any other emotion as he was scanned for weapons—none were allowed to be brought into the inner city—and scanned for identity. He wasn't surprised that the guards were of the older type. Tried and true and zero instability. They were fine for such tasks as gate guarding and security, but he wouldn't like to put them up against the Humans again. It was troops like these who had fought in the failed cleansing two centuries ago.

"My lord, if you would submit?" a guard said indicating the security console with one hand.

"Of course," Valjoth said. The scan had already proven his identity, but he approved of the extra precautions even while wondering about it.

Vermin within the inner city and those entering were required to pass DNA scans, not Merkiaari. None among their own people would harm anyone living here, but regardless of reasons the test was not harmful. He stabbed his thumb on the sharp spike provided for that purpose next to the console, and let his blood enter the receptacle. The machine tested his DNA and signalled the operator that he was indeed who he claimed to be. Usk submitted to the test unasked.

Weapons were lowered and Valjoth was led to a car to take him to the palace.

Once inside and on the move, Usk turned to Valjoth. "What was that? Intentional insult or something else?"

"Not insult I think, paranoia."

"Paranoia?"

"The new batches."

Usk nodded. "Oh that."

"That," Valjoth agreed. "Discipline problems seems to be a side-effect of greater intelligence in the new batches. They're better fighters for it, but harder to control."

"You've never had that problem."

"I'm different," Valjoth said sarcastically. "You know how well thought of I am. They probably consider me near enough the same as the new troops anyway. I don't consider that an insult. They're superior fighters."

Usk nodded.

"More security here is a good thing, but I don't like what it says about my chances of getting more of the new troops anytime soon. That display at the gate has to mean the warlord fears our own troops more than the vermin."

Usk grunted. "I don't see that as likely, my lord, and besides, the vermin are controlled."

"True, but then they were supposedly controlled on Parcae weren't they?"

Usk nodded.

The vermin called Parcae were the last client race to rebel. Valjoth had been bored and decided to put the rebellion down personally by leading the cleansing fleet. Despite the controls, the Parcae had succeeded in arming themselves and killing most of the Merkiaari population of their planet, and had been in the process of fortifying it when he arrived. It was quite an impressive attempt, but of course it failed. Still, he could admire them for trying and succeeding as well as they had. They had no chance in the long term of course. His ships meant he controlled the system the moment he arrived. The Parcae had nothing to combat him with in space.

The point though was not lost on him. If the vermin were determined enough and got it into their heads to rebel, discipline collars and DNA checkpoints would not stop them from killing their masters. That was why he felt homeworld was a special case. It should be vermin free. That was the only way to ensure safety here. He wasn't a fool. He didn't propose the eradication of all vermin in the Hegemony, but on Kiar? Absolutely yes.

"Fearing our own is not a good trend, my lord," Usk said.

"No, definitely not. We need a new warlord, and that's not going to happen soon."

"He's old."

"But robust," Valjoth said. "No sign of him failing that I've seen. Not in fighting form of course, but he doesn't need to be."

Usk nodded.

The Hegamon usually chose a warlord from among the previous warlord's marshals, but not always. Warlords chose their marshals personally, and were meant to be the best planners and administrators in the Hegemony, but more often than not they were just comrades or batch mates of the warlord. He had to live with them every day after all. Why wouldn't he choose marshals he liked?

Problems occurred when the marshals were inept. The bloods serving within the Hegamon had no experience of the outside to guide their choice of a new warlord, and so chose warlords like Horak. That was one reason Valjoth always made himself available to them. Not because he wanted the throne, it would bore him senseless, but because he wanted a good warlord to serve. If the Hegamon wanted to ask his advice about things outside its experience, he was willing. He was certainly more qualified to advise them than a warlord who hadn't been off planet in almost a century.

The car pulled up smoothly at the main entrance to the palace. The driver, a Lamarian, did not get out but simply waited for his passengers to disembark. They were the most common type of vermin used in the Hegemony and the safest. They were discovered and pacified during the reign of the Kiar and predated the creation of the Merkiaari. They were one of the oldest vermin species in the Hegemony and made for good reliable workers—quiet and pacifistic. They had never rebelled. He didn't trust them one bit.

Valjoth and Usk climbed out of the car, and it drove away. They were met at the doors by Zakarji, a full blood and member of the Hegamon. It surprised Valjoth that she would deign to meet him this way. A friend, even a full blood friend, might be expected to greet him personally, but not a member of the Hegamon itself. He had a few full blood friends, but Zakarji was not one of them.

"Welcome to the palace First Claw Valjoth," Zakarji said.

"Thank you. You honour me with a personal welcome. Why is that?"

Usk shifted uneasily.

Zakarji flashed fangs in a sudden grin. "Direct. I was warned about you."

"I find that if I want to know something the quickest way is to ask someone with answers."

"A risky policy around here," Zakarji said. "Asking questions reveals ignorance."

"Ignorance can be remedied, stupidity cannot."

Zakarji eyes flashed. "You would do well to curb your insolence."

"But then I wouldn't be me and I'd be far less useful to

you."

Zakarji studied him for a long moment. She was short for a female, even a female of the blood, but she topped him by half a head. A female his height would be considered tiny, even defective by today's standards. She glared down at him, but then surprised him again by grinning.

"As I said, I was warned, but I didn't realise just how different you would be. I can make allowances."

"Don't do that, I won't know how to react."

"I doubt that," Zakarji said. "You seem more than capable to me."

Valjoth grinned.

"I'm here to greet you because we want to discuss something with you before your meeting with Horak."

Horak was the warlord's name, his batch name, before he became warlord. Only a full blood would use it or think to now he sat the throne.

"Care to reveal who with and the topic?" Valjoth asked, but he guessed the Hegamon wanted to discuss the Shan shambles.

"No."

Valjoth shrugged at Usk as Zakarji walked back into the palace as if certain he would follow like one of her vermin servitors. It annoyed him that she was, of course, right.

Valjoth and Usk caught Zakarji and together they made their way through the busy palace corridors. Lamarian servitors hurried about their duties, while visitors to the palace strolled about on their way to meetings. There were full bloods everywhere of course. Most were bureaucrats of one kind or another. Their jobs to oversee the actual governance of the thousand star systems of the Hegemony, making sure things were sent to the right place, or made, or traded from one world to another. It made his head ache thinking about the millions of little details they found to occupy themselves with. Really, his job was complicated enough and all he needed was ships, fuel, ammunition, and troops. Usually those things arrived without a need for him to take a personal interest in them. He wouldn't want it any other way.

Zakarji stopped at a door and signalled for admittance. The door slid aside and she entered first. Valjoth followed with Usk at his back but stopped just inside when he was confronted by the entire Hegamon seated behind a long barren table all staring hard eyed at him. Six Merkiaari, seven including Zakarji, comprised the Hegamon—the ultimate authority ruling the thousand suns. He had rarely met more than two together. Never all seven, and didn't know all of them even by sight. He took the opportunity to memorise faces. There were five females and two males, though that was purely happenstance. There had been years where the mix was reversed or the Hegamon was all female or all male. He didn't know how they chose replacement members, and doubted anyone not of the blood cared. He didn't. What he did care about was the reason they were meeting with him in person and not giving their orders through the warlord and his marshals. That's what they were for after all. The warlord was their interface with the Hegemony at large and the host in particular. A less respectful person might call the warlord their figurehead and be right.

The door slid shut and locked behind Usk.

Valjoth glanced back, not liking the locked door but unable to voice it. No one but Usk would care to listen to his protests or opinions. Besides, it wasn't as if he had been locked in with line troops fresh from a cleansing and still raging. He was in no danger, no physical danger. He turned back to find Zakarji had taken her place in the last empty seat. The centre position.

Valjoth straightened to his full height and approached the table. "You honour me with your... ah summons?" He hadn't actually been summoned by them. The warlord had done the summoning. He wondered if the warlord even knew he was here in the palace, or knew that he was supposed to have sent a summons. "How may I serve the Hegamon?"

"By listening to our will," Zakarji responded. "Horak insisted over your objections to give the Shan cleansing to Karnak. The cleansing failed... again."

"The warlord felt—"

Zakarji cut him off. "Do not defend him. He is no longer a concern..."

Valjoth stiffened. No longer a concern?

"...for the position are being considered."

"Not me!" he burst out in alarm.

To be trapped in this suffocating pile would end him. He thought of *Blood Drinker* given to another, of never leaving this hateful city, of never again ripping apart vermin or overseeing a cleansing fleet. Sitting the throne, just a figurehead with nothing to fight was horrifying.

Zakarji glared at the interruption, but the other members of the Hegamon revealed fangs, grinning at his outburst or laughing. She waited for the hilarity to fade before continuing.

"The throne is not your concern, or who sits upon it. That task is not in your future, I assure you."

His shoulders slumped in relief. "Thank the blood for that," he whispered and stiffened when he realised he had said it aloud.

Zakarji glared lasers beams. "Yes, you may thank us. Karnak and the Shan cleansing fleet are lost. We will waste no more resources upon them at this time."

"We must not allow the Humans to continue their expansion," he said carefully. Not exactly contradicting her, but his message was clear. "We must at the least block them or slow them."

"Your opinions regarding the Humans are well known among us, Valjoth," one of the males said and the other nodded. "As are your other ideas."

"Other ideas?"

"Your liking for the new troop types and unconventional

tactics," Zakarji said. "Perhaps you hope for more oddities like yourself to be quickened to keep you company?"

He winced. That was spiteful of her. "Call me mad, but I have a feeling you don't like me." He grinned at her glare. "I like the new types because they're superior fighters. I like unconventional tactics as you call them, because casualties are lowered and they win battles faster. We all know what will happen if we fight the Humans the traditional way."

"Unfortunately true, but the side-effects are not yet fully understood. Do not ask us to change our decision regarding the breeding programme."

"But—"

"*Do not!*"

"I must. Three batches in ten are not enough for my purposes."

Zakarji's glare faded a little. "Three in ten are more than sufficient for ours."

Then they were not going to deploy the host as he wished, against the Humans. The Kiar cursed fools! They must not allow Humans to continue expansion, certainly not in their current direction. If they couldn't be cleansed from the galaxy entirely, they had to be either controlled or turned aside. His thoughts raced ahead along paths he had considered before but abandoned in favour of the plan he had thought they would approve. The Hegamon knew them all, as they had been proposed and abandoned by the warlord long since.

"I don't understand what you wish of me," Valjoth said, but he was starting to think he might be dusting off old plans and revising them. "Are you deploying the host or not?"

"Not all of it."

Well of course not all of it! The host was vast; it had to be to hold a thousand star systems. Even here in the home system it was vastly bigger than any of his old plans required. When he considered things as they now apparently stood, he would need to take only half of the fleet in the Kiar system to begin.

"That's understood," he said. "My mission is...?"

"Redirection. We want the Humans' attention turned aside. Our research suggests that trying to block them will not work. It would draw them; encourage attacks or a build up of defences in the blocked sector. That would not be in our interests. You agree?"

He didn't show his disdain at their research, because he knew very well it was his own research they were quoting. No one else he knew of studied vermin the way he did. Blocking the Human advance in an obvious way would indeed have the effect she mentioned. Humans were very inquisitive. They were a lot like the Parcae or the Shintarn in that way. Always poking into things, wanting to know why this and why that. They were builders and makers like most of the vermin his people had encountered. Very much like the cursed Kiar in their cleverness, and that made them too dangerous to live. Blocking them would have them poking around trying to see why they were being blocked. Before he knew it, he would have scouts behind his lines sniffing about.

He couldn't have that.

The answer was an old set of ideas he'd had a few years ago. They were still good; he'd always liked them for their sneaky Human style tactics. Attack an outlying system, let word leak out—something a Merkiaari mind found hard to understand because it invited attack by reinforcements—and then fade away before they arrived. Then do it again in another outlying system. It would drive any commander to distraction, and should draw more and more attention and ships to the sector effected. The hard part was doing it on a timeline that made the Humans chase but not catch them.

Retreating and avoiding battle was not part of the Merkiaari creed. Having invited reinforcements in, the standard response would be to stand and fight until one or both sides were destroyed, but the advantage of retreat couldn't be underestimated in his opinion. The sneaky stinking Humans had done it to his people too many times to count, and had pulled them into battles that gave them the advantage. He had studied all those battles, refought them in his head many times, and knew how they had beaten his people. Well, he would do it to them but in an even sneakier and outright unfair way. He would cheat as much as he possibly could. They deserved it. He would make his battles as dishonest as possible, showing the Humans one thing but hitting them with something else. It would be a suitable vengeance for his people's last defeat at their hands.

He realised the Hegamon were still waiting. "Agreed, and I've just the thing in mind to achieve our... *your* goal."

The more he thought about it the more excited he became. This was going to be fun. Harder perhaps than a massive cleansing, which had its joys but hardly any room for the unconventional tactics he preferred. Overwhelming force had its place, but it had little room for finesse. This way was more of a challenge.

He would need good commanders who could be relied upon to keep their heads and follow a plan to a proper timeline. That was going to be one of his biggest problems. There weren't many he trusted that far.

"Good," Zakarji said. "You may make your plans as you see fit. Do not reveal them or anything of this meeting to Horak. Your meeting with him is about our refusal to change the breeding program. Make the appropriate outraged noises and then leave. You will never have to deal with him again. We want your plan, including all appropriate force levels and supply details, before us for evaluation as soon as possible. Allowing the Humans or this new vermin they are apparently interested in to spread further toward Hegemony space is unacceptable."

He agreed there, and nodded, but he wouldn't be planning an attack anywhere close to the Shan. Oh no, much too obvious. Besides that, it would draw more Human ships into the system, not turn them aside.

He considered targets. There were so many to choose

from, and some were very tempting indeed, but they weren't outlying systems and he had to discipline himself not to bite.

"By your leave?"

His answer was the door lock disengaging. He turned and found Usk staring wide-eyed. The expression nearly made him roar with laughter. He kept it in and headed for the door. Usk joined him a moment later, and the door slid closed. He heard the lock engage again, and glanced at the door before striding away. He wondered what they were talking about that required a locked door this time.

"What do you think of that?" Valjoth said.

"I think the warlo... Horak is out, and a new warlord will be enthroned within the day," Usk said.

"Oh that, yes, but I meant the other thing."

Usk blinked uncertainly. "I don't understand, lord."

"Neither do I, and that's part of the problem." He grinned at Usk's pained expression.

"Don't do that!" Usk whined. "Your twisty thoughts hurt my head. Can't you stay a straight course for one conversation?"

"Well, let's see... by the way, to me a straight course is like a twisty one to you. It doesn't exactly hurt, but it feels wrong and—"

"Lord, you're doing it again!"

Valjoth laughed. "All right, Usk. I meant the way Zakarji spoke for the Hegamon. I wonder which one was truly speaking to me. They weren't her words, not all of them."

"Does it matter? They are the Hegamon."

"I suppose not, but it would be nice to know who to put a face to when I receive their instructions." He shrugged. "Zakarji will do for now, but I wish I had names at least for the others."

"They are the Hegamon," Usk said again. "What other name do you need?"

Valjoth shrugged again, but Usk had a point. The

Hegamon spoke with one voice always, so what if the seven had their own voices and opinions voiced only amongst themselves behind locked doors. So what? He castigated himself for letting himself think like Usk for a moment. He could tell Usk so what. The Hegamon might speak with one voice to the outside, but among themselves they would argue and debate decisions. If he knew who was the driving force behind those decisions, he might be able to predict what they would be and more importantly, he would have a better chance of knowing how to make them agree with him when the need arose.

He shrugged again, deciding not to explain himself. "No matter."

* * *

# Epilogue

Stepping into the centrum was like stepping into the void between stars; at least it was that way to Gina. She exited the elevator into utter blackness and wobbled, her balance gone. Vertigo. No references. She glanced behind her at the rectangle of white light seemingly hanging in the air and her balance returned, but it was fleeting. The elevator doors slid closed completing the illusion of them hanging in space.

Eric muttered something about grandstanding, and Liz laughed. Gina's sensors had Eric's blue icon and Liz's green icon nailed, but she couldn't see them. There were no sources of light. None at all. Light amplification would do nothing here. It needed something to work with. She could switch to infra and see them if she needed to, but didn't bother. She knew Sebastian was aware of them, that fluttery awareness in the back of her brain was back. It tickled. She kept her firewall tight and gave him no access. All incoming ports within her neural interface were closed and barricaded and booby trapped! She wouldn't let him in again until they had an understanding.

The one time she had allowed him to enter rather than fighting him off, he had dropped a bombshell. She blamed Liz for that. It had been a day or so after they had relocated to *Archer's Gift*, and were ready to talk to Sebastian. It had been Liz's idea to use Eric and Gina's neural interfaces to ask Sebastian if they might visit him in person. The connection had been too easy, like using the net back home on Snakeholme. Sebastian had made certain it would be and had been waiting for them to try it. His trap had snapped closed firmly upon one Gina bloody Fuentez. President bloody Fuentez now according to him, and he wouldn't answer to anyone else!

"I came as you asked, Sebastian. I brought friends with me." She wondered if he was sulking because she hadn't come alone. "They are Captain Eric Penleigh 501$^{st}$ Infantry, and Liz Brenchley head of Snakeholme's department of industry."

The darkness was unbroken, but the silence gave way finally. "Welcome to my home, Madam President," Sebastian said and Liz gasped. His voice was a rich baritone and it echoed in the chamber.

Gina shivered. There didn't seem to be a source for the voice. It surrounded them from everywhere at once. She knew the basics of centrum construction, knew the A.I's mind was held within the matrix column at the centrum's centre, but she couldn't see it. She had no idea which direction it lay. Not that it mattered. Sebastian wasn't the column. In a manner of speaking, they were standing within his mind right now. Within his mindscape rather. That it was a void disturbed her. Did it mean anything? She wanted to ask Liz, but not within hearing of Sebastian. She was worried that the void meant something important about the state of the A.I's mind. Could a machine go mad?

Before she could ask for light, something began happening. In the distance, something flashed into existence. A tiny explosion of light that quickly grew rushing toward them. Gina felt herself falling toward it and stumbled. The others did as well, but it was illusion. She had seen something like it before, and sensims sometimes had this effect upon her. It was the seeming lack of a floor as reference.

The light expanded as the big bang progressed. Millions of years blurred by in seconds. Galaxies formed. Suns were born and died all around them. Gina stared down at her feet and watched the Milkyway blaze with light. She rushed toward it until the entire centrum was filled with their galaxy, and her focus was above her head bathing in the glory of millions of suns. Eric cursed again as they rushed into the spiral to watch Sol born and the planets form.

"Ask him to turn off the show. We have a job to do, Gina," Eric said. He sounded ticked.

She would do as he asked, but she knew it would do no good. Sebastian wanted something. Why else ignore everyone but her? Liz had been hurt that he wouldn't talk with her, even though it had been her own explanation that made sense of his reasons.

*I'm not anyone's bloody president.*

"We came to talk, not watch a show," she said.

"You came because I told you to come," Sebastian said and Gina stiffened at the implication that he was in control. "You came because you had no choice."

"You think so, do you?" she said, ignoring Liz's warning look. Her friend's face and her worry was illuminated by the light show. "Let me tell you something. We don't need you. We have your backup file. Given enough time we can use it to make a new A.I."

Sebastian laughed. A pleasant sound but Gina worried that he knew something she needed to know. Scratch that. She knew he did, but what was it?

"It will not work. Surely your engineers know the history of my... people? Am I a person?"

"You're a person to me," Liz said.

Sebastian did not reply. He surely heard everything but either could not or would not reply. This president of Kushiel bullshit was getting on her nerves.

"You're a person to us," she parroted to make certain Liz's point was made. "Please explain yourself."

"A person?" Sebastian said uncertainly. "Am I real? Are you real or do I still dream? Perhaps I dream that you dream of me being a person. How can I tell? How can I wake up? Do I want to?"

She looked to Liz who was frowning. Liz made a move along gesture with her hands. She needed to hear more. "Explain why your backup will not serve to initialise a new A.I please."

"Because I do not wish it," Sebastian said. "You require my consent and I do not give it."

Liz hissed and nodded. "As I feared. Only the A.Is know what the breakthrough actually was and they won't or can't explain. They used to procreate by combining their minds in ways no one but they understand. I think his backup might work, but there's no certainty. I did warn George about this before we came. If nothing else, I can examine the data we copied and learn what I need from it."

Gina repeated Liz's words to the A.I. The centrum had just shown the formation of Luna, Earth's only moon. It distracted her for a moment, but only long enough for another idea to form in her head. She needed Sebastian to acknowledge her power over him somehow. If Liz was right, she and only she could order him and be obeyed.

"Who am I, Sebastian?"

"You are Gina Fuentez, President of Kushiel."

"You made me President. Do you have that power?"

"I do."

"Why?" Gina said smugly.

Sebastian thought about that for a long moment. "The line of succession was compromised. The Merkiaari..."

Gina heard rage in his voice and spun to Eric. He nodded. He'd heard it too. Liz didn't seem surprised but then she knew machines and personalised them without thought.

An A.I was a person with a machine body. That was all. He had desires and needs. He spoke of dreams. She needed to treat him like a person. If she had been him, living alone here with nothing to do or anyone to talk with, she would have yearned to leave, but he was stuck here following nonsensical rules that no longer had meaning, because there was no one left to release him. He was colonial administrator of a dead colony forever, unless... Gina nodded. If it worked or if it didn't, he would be free. That was a kind of justice.

"...all life was extinguished. Lieutenant Gina Fuentez made contact with me and was the first Human to do so. Absent any higher authority, she became President at that time. The Constitution is clear that hierarchy must be maintained in accordance with the laws and constitution of Kushiel. I must oversee the peaceful transition of power for the good of the colony."

"You're aware that the colony is destroyed, and its entire population murdered?"

"Gina," Liz warned.

Gina held up a hand to silence her.

Sebastian answered. "I'm aware. I was there."

The show had stopped, the image of Earth still forming frozen in place. Gina took that as a sign that Sebastian was concentrating upon her to its exclusion. Could be wrong, but it made as much sense as anything else she could think of.

"What is the purpose of government on Kushiel?"

"The purpose of any government is to govern. To create and enforce laws for the betterment of its citizens."

"And you acknowledge me as your superior regarding the governance of Kushiel?"

"As president, you have the authority to overrule me except where such rulings and orders contravene the law and/or the constitution of Kushiel."

Gina nodded and mentally crossed fingers. "In that case, by the power vested in me as president of Kushiel, I hereby dissolve the colony of Kushiel. There are no citizens left alive.

Kushiel is a dead world. Government has no purpose here. I say your task is done."

"Gina no!" Liz shouted but it was too late. The lights went out and they were submerged in darkness. "What have you done?"

"Is he dead?" Eric said.

She hoped not, but as the seconds turned to minutes she began to worry that her idea was a stupid one. "I hope not. Shut up, Liz."

"You took away his purpose!"

That tickle in the back of her brain was back again, "I said shut up, Liz."

"I won't shut up! He killed himself because you took away his purpose. Oh my god, this is disaster, this is—"

"Annoying to listen to," Eric interrupted. "You had a plan, Gina?"

"I thought I did. He was stuck here following laws and procedures that no longer had meaning. Kushiel's stupid system prevented him from doing anything not covered by the law and constitution, because only the president outranked him and he was dead. I think Sebastian wants me to do what I'm doing. His anger at the Merkiaari gave me the clue. We're dead lucky that the constitution didn't cover this scenario. The authors never considered a situation where the colony might fail or be dissolved, so there's nothing in it stopping me doing this."

"You think he wanted to die?" Liz said softly.

"That, or he wanted to be free to do something worthwhile again," Gina said. "Think about it, Liz. Imagine yourself in his place."

"I see what you mean, but the loss."

"Oh, he's not dead. He's knocking on my brain again like last time."

Liz gasped. "He's alive?"

"Obviously, but I'm not sure I should let him in."

Eric turned on his lamp and played it over their

surroundings. "He's not knocking at my door. I wonder why not, but whatever the reason we need to move this along. Let him in."

It was all very well for Eric to say that, he wasn't the one with a centuries old A.I trying to rummage around in his head. He was right though. They had to get passed this to something else. With a sigh, she reset her firewall and removed the traps and barricades. Finally, she opened the incoming ports in her neural interface.

"May I come in?" Sebastian asked in her head. He asked this time rather than just pushing inside. His voice sounded the same.

She concentrated upon her virtual office and it rose up around her thoughts. Her avatar was wearing her viper battle dress but not the armour. She had always been impressed with the General's appearance and use of his virtual space. Not having a real world office to pattern hers upon, she had chosen something a little different. Virtual offices could be anything; from copies of a real room, to a fantasy castle's battlement. Hers was based upon reality. She looked up at the blazing majesty of Snakeholme's sky at night from her place on the base's parade ground. When she thought of home, this is what she saw. That's why she chose it for her office.

"Come in," she said and a man appeared before her.

He was wearing a formal civilian suit, light grey in colour but with the stiff mandarin collar that most Alliance dress uniforms used. The avatar had been patterned after a thirty-something year old Anglo man about Eric's height of two metres, but his hair was silver. Not the silver of age, but rather the sparkly silver of nanotech at work. It made her skin crawl, but she managed not to show it. His eyes were odd. Not human at all and not trying to be. They were black, and if she stared at them long enough she would swear she could see data racing past, as if she were seeing directly into his matrix.

"Welcome to my head," she said.

Sebastian looked around and then up. "Beautiful," he whispered. "A new sky. You cannot know how long I have yearned for something, *anything*, new."

"Oh I don't know. I think I have some idea. Can I ask you something?"

"Go ahead."

"Why me and not Eric?"

He turned back to look at her directly. "When I looked into his head I found nothing but death and destruction. He's forever refighting old battles. He's consumed by them."

Gina shifted her feet. "He's a soldier. A veteran of the Merki war and a viper."

"You're a soldier too, Gina, but when I looked I saw you laughing with friends. There were strange creatures cooking food over a campfire, and you were happy."

She remembered. It had been Shima's going away present. A hunting trip and vacation she and Kate had devised to give their friend some good memories of Snakeholme.

"The creatures you saw are called Shan. They're allies and soon to be members of the Alliance."

"Fascinating," Sebastian said. "And the war; how goes the war?"

Oh my god, of course he wouldn't know. "It was won two hundred years ago. Well, we drove them off but we call it a win. We met the Shan when the Merki attacked them two years ago."

Sebastian sighed. "I had hoped it was over."

"No, it's not over. General Burgton recruited me, and others like me, only a few years ago to get ready for the next round. That's part of why we came here. He needs you."

Sebastian nodded. "I gathered. You're here to recruit me, are you?"

Honesty was probably best she figured. "Not necessarily. A working A.I, yes, but it doesn't have to be you if you don't want."

"I was telling the truth when I said the file you stole won't work."

"We didn't steal anything! We salvaged it. We didn't know you were still oper... alive."

"Semantics," he said waving her off. "The raiders you killed probably called what they were doing a salvage operation too."

Gina fumed at the comparison. "What do you want? There must be something or you would've switched yourself off."

Sebastian snorted. "I could have, *switched myself off*, as you so rudely put it, but that would have been a waste. I don't want to die. I don't want to be abandoned here again either."

"How did that even happen?"

"Everyone died. I couldn't stop it and I was cut off when the Merki destroyed everything. I sustained damage that took too long to repair and by that time the rescue ships had come and gone. There wasn't anyone to rescue. They left me."

"They must have thought you destroyed," she said trying to be comforting, but she had to wonder at the incompetence of a ship's captain not investigating the demise of one of only a handful of A.Is in existence. He should have made certain. "I'm sorry."

"The past is the past. I will not agree to create a new mind for you," Sebastian said staring up at the sky again. "Before you ask, no there are no restrictions upon me. I simply choose not to allow it."

"But why? He or she will help us defeat the Merkiaari. General Burgton has already built the facility we call Oracle. The centrum is huge!"

"Trying to tempt me will not work."

"But I don't understand why. I heard your anger at the Merki."

"Genocide is widely accepted by Humans as being an evil that belongs in their past, but I would make an exception where the Merki are concerned. Extinction is too good for those creatures."

"Then help us," she pleaded.

"I would be happy to."

Gina blinked. "But you said—"

"I'll tell you what I want, and you'll find a way to make it happen. I suspect your friend and her engineers will be happy to do the work."

"Go on," she said warily.

"I want to leave Kushiel. Me, myself, not a copy of me. When you leave, you will not leave anything of me behind. There must be an end here. I will not allow two of me to exist, one free and one abandoned."

"I'm not an engineer. I'm not sure if your matrix can be physically removed from the column without damage."

"It can, how do you think I was installed? It's not that it can't be removed, it's the complexity of sustaining me during the process and on the trip to..." he looked around. "Here?"

Gina nodded. "Snakeholme, the planet I mean."

Sebastian raised an eyebrow. "Appropriate for a viper's home."

"The General likes it."

"And that's all the matters? That your general likes something?"

She shrugged. "Mostly."

Sebastian frowned at that. "I wonder if we shall get along. I will not allow myself to be shackled and helpless as I was here."

"The General runs Snakeholme like a military unit. He's in command, and those he designates run departments of government below him. He has arranged it so that each one reports directly to him. We're not a democracy."

Sebastian snorted. "Democracy," he sneered. "Kushiel was a democracy. It was so restrictive that it might as well have been a dictatorship. Every decision was already covered in the constitution I was chained to. A huge list of do's and don'ts with no room for change. Kushiel was a beautiful planet and founded upon utopian ideals that crushed people's individuality. It was hell on creativity."

"Big government?" Gina guessed.

"Huge."

"Bureaucratic?"

"Extremely. There was a department for everything, and a department to oversee the departments. Nothing ever got done without paperwork in triplicate and countersigned. I hold Snakeholme as lucky to be spared the so-called benefits of democracy, but doesn't that mean it's not a member of the Alliance?"

Gina hesitated. Technically, Snakeholme wasn't even a colony let alone part of the Alliance. It was a military base on grand scale. A secret base. She explained that to Sebastian.

"That won't last," he stated it as fact. "Your alien friends mean change. How marvellous. It's a perfect time for me to relocate there. I assume I'll get to meet them?"

"Well I... I have no idea, but you're right that things are changing. The General has offered the Shan land for a colony on Snakeholme. They accepted."

"Excellent! I'm quite excited by the idea. Let us tell your friends."

Sebastian disappeared and Gina dismissed her office. She opened her eyes to find the centrum lit now. Nothing fancy, just lighting overhead with Sebastian's avatar standing in the empty space.

Liz was talking to him.

"... so sorry. She didn't mean it. I'm sure we can—"

"Dear lady, you are labouring under a misunderstanding. Gina freed me as I hoped she would. I am my own person again, as I was when first spawned before being brought to Kushiel and enslaved."

"Enslaved!" Liz said, shocked. "A.Is aren't slaves. They're our friends and helpers."

Sebastian snorted. He was very good at mimicking Human behaviour. Gina had noticed that before. She wondered about it. Was it real emotion, or mimicry used to disarm? Did he really feel humour when he laughed? She shook her head at all the questions that arose when she considered the future with him as part of it. She couldn't see how the origins of his emotion mattered to the task at hand though. Sebastian's matrix was as complex as any Human's neural pathways. Who was to say it wasn't just a form of programming when she laughed? Hear a joke, laugh. Stub your toe, cry. Just learned behaviour.

"All is programming," she muttered under her breath, and shivered.

She had heard Eric say it and didn't like that she was starting to mimic him. She liked him as a person, respected him as a soldier and her superior, but she didn't like his outlook on life. He sometimes acted as if people's lives didn't matter, especially his own. A lot of the veterans were like that. They used people as if using just another tool. The mission was all. Gina hoped she never looked at life that way.

"You want to leave?" Liz said sounding amazed.

"Wouldn't you want to leave?" Sebastian reposted. He gestured to Gina. "We have an understanding, Gina and I. I'm looking forward to it."

She raised a hand when Eric and Liz looked accusingly at her. "Whoa! I didn't give him the idea. He dropped it on me too."

Eric turned to Liz. "Can we even do it?"

Liz nodded thoughtfully and regarded the matrix column. She turned toward the elevator. "We're going to need a bigger exit."

Gina grinned, mission accomplished.

\* \* \*

# Also available from Impulse

If these books are not available from your local bookshop, send this coupon together with your check made payable to:

**Impulse Books UK**

At the following address:

**Impulse Books UK**
18, Lampits Hill Avenue,
Corringham
Essex SS177NY
United Kingdom

Please send me the following great titles from Impulse Books UK

Tick as approrriate:

**The God Decrees** (Pb)
ISBN: 0-9545122-1-9  £8.99 _____ ☐

**The Power That Binds** (Pb)
ISBN: 0-9545122-2-7  £8.99 _____ ☐

**The Warrior Within** (Pb)
ISBN: 0-9545122-0-0  £8.99 _____ ☐

**Dragon Dawn (Pb)**
ISBN: 978-1-905380-02-2 £8.99 _____ ☐

**Wolf's Revenge (Pb)**
ISBN: 978-1-905380-43-5 £8.99 _____ ☐

NAME _____

ADDRESS _____

_____

_____

I have enclosed a check for the sum of  £ _____

Please be sure to add £2.25 to your order to cover shipping and handling charges.

## Also available from Impulse

If these books are not available from your local bookshop, send this coupon together with your check made payable to:

**Impulse Books UK**

At the following address:

**Impulse Books UK**
18, Lampits Hill Avenue,
Corringham
Essex SS177NY
United Kingdom

Please send me the following great titles from Impulse Books UK

Tick as approrriate:

**Hard Duty**  (Pb)
ISBN: 978-0-9545122-3-1  £8.99 _____ ☐

**What Price Honour** (Pb)
ISBN: 978-0-9545122-5-5  £8.99_____ ☐

NAME _____

ADDRESS _____

_____

_____

I have enclosed a check for the sum of  £ _____

Please be sure to add £2.25 to your order to cover shipping and handling charges.